P9-CRA-359

❧ Circle of Shadows ❧

CAMDEN COUNTY LIBRARY
203 LAUREL ROAD
VOORHEES, NJ 08043

0500000609901 9

HADDON

m Rob
Robertson, Imogen, 1973-
Circle of shadows

JUN 1 2 2013

ALSO BY IMOGEN ROBERTSON

Instruments of Darkness

Anatomy of Murder

Island of Bones

CIRCLE

of

SHADOWS

IMOGEN ROBERTSON

PAMELA DORMAN BOOKS
VIKING

VIKING
Published by the Penguin Group
Penguin Group (USA) Inc., 375 Hudson Street, New York, New York 10014, USA

USA | Canada | UK | Ireland | Australia | New Zealand | India | South Africa | China

Penguin Books Ltd, Registered Offices: 80 Strand, London WC2R 0RL, England
For more information about the Penguin Group visit penguin.com

A Pamela Dorman Book / Viking

Copyright © Imogen Robertson, 2012
All rights reserved. No part of this book may be reproduced, scanned, or distributed in any printed or electronic form without permission. Please do not participate in or encourage piracy of copyrighted materials in violation of the author's rights. Purchase only authorized editions.

Originally published in Great Britain by Headline Book Publishing

Map illustration by David Smith

ISBN 978-0-670-02628-9

Printed in the United States of America
10 9 8 7 6 4 3 2 1

Book design by Carla Bolte

This is a work of fiction. Names, characters, places, and incidents either are the product of the author's imagination or are used fictitiously, and any resemblance to actual persons, living or dead, businesses, companies, events, or locales is entirely coincidental.

M Rob

For Charles and Adam

ACKNOWLEDGMENTS

Huge thanks as always to my friends and family for their support. Much needed, much appreciated. Also to my editor Flora Rees and everyone at Pamel Dorman Books in the United States, and my agent Annette Green for all their help and advice.

Thank you too to the staff of the library at the German Historical Institute in Bloomsbury, the Freemasons' Hall in Covent Garden and, as always, the British Library. To Andrew again for his advice on the esoteric, and particular thanks to Michael and Maria Start at the House of Automata, for their hospitality and kindness, and for showing us their wonderful collection. I also want to thank whoever handed in my wallet to the police station in Karlsruhe in September 2010. A lot. Iestyn Davies and his recordings remain an inspiration for all that is best in Manzerotti. And again, all my thanks to Ned who fell in love with Germany, promised me a cage of singing birds, and is very tolerant of me leaving Seals of Solomon lying about the place. I'm very lucky to have him.

Points of Interest in

Circle of Shadows

The Duchy of Maulberg,
Holy Roman Empire of the German Nation

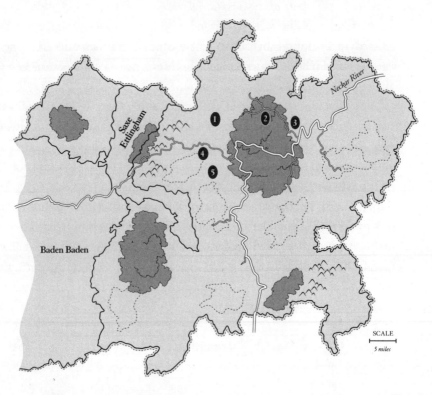

Key

1 : Ulrichsberg

2 : Castle Grenzhow

3 : Leuchtenstadt

4 : Mittelbach

5 : Oberbach

Independent Territory

PROLOGUE

17 July 1782, Ulrichsberg, Duchy of Maulberg,
Holy Roman Empire of the German Nation

The room is dark, lit by only a single candle on the surface of a rough wooden table. The air is perfumed, like church, and heavy with the heat of the day now gone. On one side of the table sits a woman, hardly more than a girl, in a dark blue dress. A gold cross glints at her throat. Her hair, black as pitch and combed to a sleek shine, frames her face and hangs loose over her shoulders. Her face is white and thin. She looks up and smiles.

"Are we prepared?"

Opposite her, seated in a line like children at their lessons, are four other young people. Two men, two women. They do not look as brightly confident as she. Their shoulders are hunched, their eyes wide. To judge by their clothes, they work for a living. The cloth that covers them is of good quality, but earthy in its tones. No silk. No jewelry to throw the light around. The candle flutters suddenly and one of the women jumps, startled by the movement in the still air, but she feels the girl's eyes on her and nods bravely. The girl places her hands flat on the table and the four others copy her. Their fingers creep toward each other till they touch lightly, little finger to little finger, thumb to thumb till the outstretched hands form a circle around the base of the candle, the fronds of their fingers reaching toward the light. The shadows leap and play around them, weaving back and forth as if driven by something more than the flame, running toward them and away like waves. The girl in blue breathes deeply and tosses her dark hair from her face. She begins to speak.

"Sagar, Adona, Egolo, Catan, by our Lord and God, by His holy angels, by the Light of the World, I ask you to come to us. Show what is hidden, tell the truths concealed, open the tomb, pull back the terrible veil of night, and let the dead speak . . ." Her voice begins in a singsong, then sinks to a low, guttural command. It no longer sounds entirely human. Her eyes are half-closed. One of the women opposite begins to tremble and the light flickers again. The strange floral scent in the air has grown stronger. The girl in blue lifts her head and the table starts shaking violently then settles, suddenly. The girl's companions are as white as she now. The older woman has started to recite the Lord's Prayer very quietly.

"The spirits are with us." The girl's eyes are blank, but she tilts her head slightly. "Who is it that comes?" She looks as if she is trying to hear something far off. "A lady, noble . . . she is tall, young. Were you taken from this world in childbirth, madam?" The youngest of the men flinches, and the girl in blue sees it. "She looks so sad." Her companions glance about them, furtively searching the rising and falling shadows, but afraid of what they might see. "What is your name, madam? Sarah?" No, she shakes her head. "Anne?" The young man, barely more than a boy, wets his lips and stares at the girl intently. The girl in blue frowns. "Anna . . ."

The boy opens his mouth. "Antonia, madam? Is it Antonia?"

The girl in blue nods. "Antonia. Antonia sends greetings to her most faithful servant, and friend." The boy flushes, his eyes fill with tears. "Antonia is come to hear news of those she left behind. She fears for them, their grief. Her concern draws her out of the darkness of death to speak to us." The boy is crying now, but he keeps his hands where they are and nods his head.

"Is her son with her?" he asks.

"He plays by her side."

"Praise be."

The girl in blue is silent, listening. From the copse outside an owl calls, its rising voice like a lost question. The woman opposite shudders and continues with her prayers.

"We hear you, madam. She says you have helped her before, and she asks your assistance again. Will you help her?"

"With all my heart, and tell her . . . tell her I'm sorry."

The girl in blue smiles so kindly, all her companions feel a little of their guilt, their worry roll off their shoulders and into the shadows.

"She knows, and she thanks you."

PART I

I

District officer Benedict von Krall lowered his weight onto the stool with a grunt and lit his pipe, all the while watching the young Englishman sitting on the other side of the table. The man was leaning his head against the wall and staring blankly in front of him. The oil lamp sputtered and settled. He gave no sign of having heard Krall enter the room, but he seemed calm enough. Krall jerked his head and heard a shuffle as the guard retreated into the shadows apace. The ties at the neck of the Englishman's shirt were loose, showing the hollows around his throat and collarbone. Krall thought of a portrait he had seen once at the palace of a young man, similarly perfect in looks. The high cheekbones, large eyes, full mouth—a strange mix of the innocent and the sensuous. Here, tucked under the Town Hall of Oberbach with its rough plaster walls and earth floors, they could, like that youth caught on canvas, be from any age, any time. The lamp between them sputtered again and the darkness crossed the young man's face like the wing of a crow, and away. The Englishman was twenty-five—twenty-six, perhaps. His smooth forehead was smeared with blood.

"Why did you kill her, Mr. Clode?"

No answer.

English felt like a forgotten taste on Krall's tongue. The words were rusty with lack of use, but there they were, as soon as he called on them. For a moment he thought he caught the stink of the Thames at Black Wharf. He sniffed sharply and looked down. The Englishman's hands lay on the table in front of him, his bandaged wrists uppermost with dark blooms showing, the wounds declaring themselves, as if he were offering them up, asking for some explanation, but then his face was turned away. Not a request for enlightenment then. More an appeal. *See what you have made me do.* The palms of his hands looked very white. Not the hands of a workingman.

Krall had had thick dark hair once, had it when he spent his years in London, learning trade, learning the language till for a while it was as familiar as his mother tongue. That was long ago, before war and worry turned his hair gray and cut deep lines into his forehead, around his eyes and mouth. Then, during his ten years as district officer in Oberbach, he'd heard enough stories to turn his gray hair white. Women who'd smothered their bastard children; men who had taken a life over a game of cards, or lashed out at a friend to find a moment later that hell had chosen them in that second and they were damned. Nothing quite like this though. He blew the smoke out of his nose, feeling old.

"Tell me what happened," he said more sharply. The floor and walls seemed to muffle his voice, steal it away from the air, so Krall brought his fist down hard on the wooden table, making the timbers dance.

It startled the younger man. He blinked and looked around the cellar as if seeing it for the first time. The cellar smelled of damp earth and woodsmoke. The air here still belonged to winter, as if the town were keeping some of the cold as a souvenir of the season passed.

The Englishman was still dressed in Carnival costume, in the checkered blue and yellow motley of the Fool. He seemed to notice this as Krall watched him, and rubbed the cotton with his fingers. His wooden mask lay on the table between them with its wide carved grin, a nose long and hooked like a beak.

"There was a party."

Krall blew out another lungful of smoke. "Yes, there was a party. It is *Festennacht*, Carnival."

The young man had a slight smile on his lips. He began to sing under his breath. *"Girl, come to my side, pretty as milk and blood."*

Krall crossed his arms over his body. The singing scraped his nerves. He thought of the woman in white stretched out across the floor of the haberdasher's back room. Her bloodshot eyes, open and amazed. The slice across the wrist. The pool of blood shed by the Englishman before Colonel Padfield had beaten down the locked door and rescued him. The open razor, slicked with it.

"The woman," he said loudly, trying to drown out the tune. "Did you smother her? Did you smother her and then try to kill yourself?" The young man was still mouthing the words of the folk tune. Krall leaned forward. "Listen to me!"

The young man flinched away. The song stopped.

"There was blood," he said, and lifted his arms and wrapped them around his head as if fending off a beating. "A man . . ."

"What man?"

"Masked! He said he would help me. I did not feel . . . Things were wrong. I was frightened . . ." He suddenly gasped and his eyes widened. For a moment it seemed to Krall there was some sense there. "Where is my wife?" Suddenly the young man had thrown himself across the table and grabbed at the lapels of Krall's coat. Krall heard a movement behind him and lifted his hand, telling the guard to keep back. The Englishman's blue eyes were glittering, feverish, an inch from Krall's own. "Where is my wife?" There was a strange tang to his scent. Something floral.

"Mrs. Clode is safe," Krall said quietly. "Release me. Release me before the guard knocks you senseless."

The intelligence behind the young man's eyes seemed to fade. He looked at his fingers and gradually uncurled them, retreated to his stool. Krall exhaled slowly. "The lady dressed in white, Mr. Clode. You knew her, did you not? You met at court, in Ulrichsberg. Lady Martesen. You were found with her body. Did you smother her?"

"There were fires everywhere."

"Torches. For the Fool's Parade. Listen, Mr. Clode. The lady in white."

The prisoner looked up and met Krall's gaze. Again, the district officer sensed a struggle for understanding, for reason. The man's lips began to move again. "What is it?" Krall asked.

"Water . . . water . . ."

"You want water?" Krall twisted in his chair to nod to the guard. The Englishman grasped at his throat.

"I am drowning."

"No, Mr. Clode." The Englishman stumbled upright, but at once his legs gave way. He spat onto the floor and hauled himself into a corner, retching and gasping. Krall watched him, frowning deeply, but making no movement. He had seen men drunk, he had seen them mad with grief or rage. He had not seen this. Had the horror of the killing simply snapped the prisoner's mind? The man's breathing evened out. He looked up at Krall from his corner. "Wake me. Please. I am dreaming. Wake me."

The room became silent. Outside, Krall could hear singing—drunks banishing winter with schnapps and country songs of growth and fertility.

"Why did you cut her wrist before you sliced your own?"

The young man held his hands at the sides of his head and began to rock back and forth. There was something unnerving about the movement, its insistent repetition. There was no sense in this. Krall sighed and stuck his pipe into the hanging pockets of his coat.

"I cannot wake you, you are not dreaming." Krall stood up. "Mr. Daniel Clode, in the name of the Duke of Maulberg I am arresting you for the murder of Her Grace Agatha Aralia Maria Martesen, Countess of Fraken-Lichtenberg." He turned to the guard behind him. "Get him out of that damn costume and wash his face."

The same evening, Leuchtenstadt, Maulberg

"I do apologize for keeping you waiting, brothers!" There was a scraping of chairs as two men in dark coats got to their feet. Herr Professor Dunktal closed the door behind him, pulled a signet ring from his pocket, then placed it on the third finger of his right hand. Turning back to his companions, he held it out. They bowed over his hand and kissed it with reverence. It was a small chamber, little more than a closet, so the three men found each other uncommonly close.

"The arrangements are all in place?" Herr Dunktal asked as he rubbed his hands together and blew on them. It was a cold night. He seemed cheerful though. His red, round cheeks were lifted with a broad smile. He was perhaps some ten years older than his companions, nearer to his fortieth year than his thirtieth, but his large eyes and smooth forehead, and those red apple cheeks that looked as if they'd been stolen from a peasant woman gave him a youthful appearance. He would have been handsome were it not for his thin, long nose. Some of his students in the university law faculty revered him. The rest called him "The Beak."

The two young men sharing this closet were of those that thought him a visionary. One of them brought his heels together and lifted his head. His chin was rather weak. "Yes, sir. The supplicant is in the second studio, working on his answers. The room is secure."

Dunktal nodded. "His work so far?"

The second man handed him a sheaf of papers. Dunktal remained standing and read a few paragraphs at random. "'What would your response be if asked by a senior member of the organization to perform an immoral act?' And he answers: 'No senior member of the organization would ask me to perform an immoral act. If it appeared immoral it would only be because I did not comprehend the reasoning. I should perform every act without hesitation, trusting in the superior knowledge and enlightenment of my seniors.'" He smiled. "Very good. Is he sincere in this, Nickolaus?"

The man who had handed him the papers nodded. "Yes, sir. He is quite devoted." He hesitated. "But sir, nevertheless, are you sure it is correct to award him the next rank? He is still young, impulsive. More heart than head. I fear he might say more than he should if entrusted with our more . . .'"

Dunktal patted him on the shoulder, then moved past him to open the door into the second studio. It was a larger room, almost entirely empty but for a writing desk and table at which sat a youth, blond and slight, with inks, papers, and pen in front of him, and hanging on the wall above his desk an image of an owl, its talons holding open a book. He had heard Dunktal enter and ceased to write, but according to his instructions, did not turn around. Dunktal allowed himself another small smile and withdrew again, continuing his conversation as if there had been no interruption.

"It is not in our hands, brothers. Our superiors see this young man as quite a prize. He is rich. His father has become intimate with the duke. You have done well, Nickolaus, to bring him so far, so quickly." He placed a fatherly hand on the young man's shoulder and squeezed. "It has been noted. I was told to tell you. It has been noted."

It was clear Nickolaus still had his doubts. Dunktal watched. It was another opportunity to see if the habits of secrecy and obedience so carefully trained into these men still held.

"For the greater good, and by your command, sir."

They held. "Quite right, my brother. We grow stronger every day."

Four hours later the rooms were swept clean, the papers removed, and the picture of the owl taken down. The place looked innocent once more. Nickolaus and his friend led the young man between them from the place. There was a shadow among the shadows on the opposite side of the street but they did not see it. When they had passed, the dark shifted and a rather nondescript youth with a snub nose emerged from the side street. It was a cold night to spend so long watching a locked door, but it had been worth it. He drove his hands into his pockets, hunched his shoulders, and followed.

Herr Benedict von Krall drew the cold air into his lungs. In the last ten years his duties as district officer had rarely taken him to the palace of his sovereign, the Duke of Maulberg. He feared they would now. He visited once a year, as a rule, to report on the people under his jurisdiction. Sometimes, when violence was done it had been necessary to submit a supplementary report, and a recommendation to the Privy Council of sentence. In such a way the seasons had passed. His daughters were married, and would have made their mother proud, had she lived. The rivals in the empire continued to growl and push, busy old Prussia weighing down on them from above, Austria attempting to embrace them from below, but for the last twenty years at least they had not shed each other's blood. The people had grown used to peace. With his encouragement and that of the mayor of Oberbach, his little town had started to do rather well in the linen trade. They had built a new town hall and begun to grow fat. But now this. Members of the court always attended the Shrove Tuesday Carnival in Oberbach. It made a change from their usual entertainments at the palace. Operas. Masked Balls. Krall spat on the hard ground. They had never set about murdering each other before on his patch. Perhaps he could bundle the hurt of it and carry it back to the court, and so defend his town from the shame and scandal.

Krall considered. A victim much respected at court, a killer who was English and a guest at the palace, yet in its way it seemed simple enough. An attempt at seduction, fueled by the bacchanalia of Carnival, which turned to violence then an attempt at suicide. Where did the Englishman get the razor from? It was one sold by Kupfel's in Karlstrasse back in Ulrichsberg. Pearl handle. Perhaps his new wife had bought it for him—but why would he bring it to Carnival? Krall growled softly to himself. It was as if he had a little demon locked in his own mind, always asking these wheedling questions. And why, the little demon continued, did Lady Martesen show no bruising? No clothing torn? Krall came out into the backyard of the Town Hall, then moved slowly along the path toward the main square, where he found His Excellency, Chancellor Swann, waiting for him.

"This is a bad business, Krall," Swann said at once. "It was a pity Colonel Padfield found Mr. Clode before he bled to death."

"Perhaps, Your Excellency." He realized the chancellor was looking at him sideways, eyebrows raised, and cursed his questioning demon. "He's in a strange state. Like a simpleton. Mad. Unless his mind clears, we may need to lock him away for good. We cannot behead an imbecile—even an English one."

"Shock, I'd imagine. Guilt." The chancellor's words came from his mouth spiked and white-hot.

"Perhaps. He says a masked man led him to the room. That he felt dizzy."

"Not terribly convincing," the chancellor said, turning away again.

The moon was young, a fat sickle, but there were still torches guttering here and there along the main thoroughfare, giving light to the street and casting monstrous shadows up the walls. Chancellor Swann was a shadow himself, dressed, as always, in black. It was not surprising the people suspected him of being a Jesuit. Marshal of the Court, President of the Court of the Exchequer and of the Court of Chancery and the Consistorial Court, the thin dry voice in the duke's ear.

Only a few hours ago Krall had watched the Fool's Parade from the balcony of the town hall. At its head a figure on stilts, all in black, had led a man on a leash dressed in a peasant's mockery of royal finery complete with a huge straw wig. The man had danced in and out of the crowd, yapping at the girls and throwing showers of colored confetti over their heads, then clutching at the collar around his throat when he was yanked back at intervals to the side of the stilt walker. He thought the duke would probably have laughed at the spectacle, but that Swann himself would not have been amused.

He had got here damn quick. Krall calculated. His first message would have taken at least an hour to reach Ulrichsberg, even if the rider rode hard. He imagined the messenger, dirty with the road, being shown into Swann's study, handing over Krall's message among all those gilt flourishes and polished floors. Swann must have been on the road back to Oberbach in minutes. Yet, as always, he exhibited this icy control. Krall thought of what the chancellor was managing as the wedding of their sovereign approached. Paper mountains of procedure, a squeezing of the last ducats out of the Maulberg Treasury. A series of feasts and celebrations, royal hunts, balls, and contracts the length of the good Bible itself. There would be a hundred visiting dignitaries coming to peer at Maulberg and her sovereign, assessing her strengths and weaknesses. And now this, a much-valued member of the court, murdered by an Englishman. Perhaps it was no surprise after all that he had ridden hard.

"Lady Martesen was a friend of mine." The statement surprised Krall. He had never thought of Swann as a man to have friends. "Her loss is . . . grievous."

The chancellor was watching the last of the Feast of Fools revelers stumble and weave along the road, singing as they went. Their costumes were half-undone and most had thrust their masks up off their faces or trailed them from their befuddled fingers. Witches and demons with their thick red papier-mâché tongues hanging out, and strange birdmen, still flocking together and singing some inventive obscenity in surprisingly neat harmony. They shed feathers from their backs as they slapped one another across the shoulders.

"No witnesses, Herr District Officer?"

Krall shook his head. "Nothing." He paused. "The room was fastened from the inside, though the key was not in the lock but on the floor nearby. Nobody saw this man Mr. Clode says led him to the room, though no one saw him cross alone either. Not for certain."

Krall found the chancellor looking at him, his eyes narrowed. "There must have been fifty men in that type of motley tonight, Your Excellency," he added.

"Have you anything *useful* to tell me, Krall?"

He cleared his throat. "When the parade was done, Colonel Padfield and his wife went to the council chambers with Mr. and Mrs. Clode for the Mayor's Ball. According to Colonel Padfield, Mr. Clode appeared drunk. The colonel took him outside to avoid a scene and went to fetch water. When he returned, Mr. Clode was missing. Some half hour later, during the search, he heard sounds from the haberdasher's shop and broke down the door."

"Why did the colonel think to look there?"

"His party had hired the back room of the shop to change into their costumes." Swann nodded and waved a hand. Krall continued. "No one can swear to seeing Lady Martesen after the parade. It seems she never entered the rooms where the ball was held."

A long silence.

"Do you know, Krall, that Mr. Daniel Clode is closely connected with the Earl of Sussex?"

"I did not."

"Lord Sussex holds a number of bonds issued by the Maulberg Treasury that are due to be renewed or paid off before midsummer."

Krall frowned. The duke's love of opera and show was expensive, and he knew the state owed money to half of Europe. Murder was murder, but how righteous could Maulberg afford to be? Could an English earl render them bankrupt?

"Awkward."

"Indeed. We were to start negotiations this week. A British citizen, a well-connected British citizen—we must hope his mind will clear and then he will offer a full confession. We cannot execute him with less. And to torture him might be politically unwise."

"The Duke outlawed torture three years ago."

"He sometimes speaks regretfully of that but, as I say, we cannot do it in any case, even if the ban were repealed. The English would paint us as barbarians, and then they would immediately present the bonds to the Treasury. If that were to happen before the duke's wedding . . . Make your inquiries carefully, Herr District Officer."

"What do you wish doing with him, Your Excellency?"

"Castle Grenzhow, I think."

Krall turned to go, but something was pulling and twitching in the back of his mind, making him pause. Sussex. Krall read the English papers every month. It kept his knowledge of that language turning in his mind even if he seldom spoke it, and reminded him of the years he had spent in London in his youth. The unruly people, their outspoken press, the way they went charging out from their cold little island and swaggered about the world. He remembered now reading of the scandal of the Earl of Sussex. A young boy, Jonathan Adams, the heir to that great estate, and his older sister Susan, rescued from danger by a woman and a recluse with a taste for anatomy. The papers had told and retold the story for weeks, and each new element of the story made it grow ever more unlikely until the point came when it was so unbelievable, it could only have been true.

"Is Mr. Clode acquainted with Mrs. Westerman and Mr. Crowther then, Chancellor?" he asked. "Do you think it likely Sussex will ask them to come and plead his case?"

"I cannot imagine anything will be able to keep them away." Swann stroked one thin eyebrow with the leather forefinger of his glove. "Mrs. Clode, who was enjoying her first few months of married life in travel until you arrested her husband for murder, is the younger sister of Harriet Westerman."

Krall digested the news in silence, and his mind filled with the image of wheels churning up the roads across Europe. How long would it take a woman, determined and rich, to reach them?

"Be thorough," Swann continued, "and take a room at court. We will be seeing a great deal of each other over the weeks to come."

"Your Excellency," Krall said and bowed, bringing his heels together.

Swann raised his hand and, as if he had conjured it out of nowhere, one of the neat fast vehicles the court officials used to travel about Maulberg emerged from the darkness of the street opposite. So polished was it, a deep black, that it seemed to catch the torchlight and hold it. All this show. A court built on paper, bills, bonds, promissory notes, contracts of marriage. The Palace of Ulrichsberg was a splendid lie. The modest Town Hall of Oberbach a more solid structure.

Krall watched as Swann climbed in and the coachman drove his horses into a swift trot, then he crossed the square to the haberdasher's shop. He nodded to the guards and went inside, closing the door behind him. Lady Martesen was waiting for him, her eyes open, her arms outstretched, her long white dress washing around her like moonlight. Her fingers seemed to be pointing to the pool of the Englishman's blood as it soaked into the wooden floor.

2

15 March 1784, Caveley, Hartswood, Sussex, England

Harriet Westerman was in the garden with her four-year-old daughter the morning the news came. They were hand in hand, examining the flower-beds for the first signs of snowdrops, some promise that the vicious grip of the winter was loosening. The soil still looked stunned with cold, but the air was warming. Anne was singing her mother nursery rhymes, and when Harriet glanced toward the house she could see the shadows of her son and his tutor at study in the library. She was aware of her good fortune. On her desk in the salon there were letters waiting for her and her accounts books. She knew she would be able to read both with pleasure.

Then came the crunch and rattle of hooves on the gravel driveway. They came at a fast trot, and Harriet turned from her daughter. She saw a liveried messenger, straight in the saddle, his coat splashed high with the dreck of the road. He had been traveling fast. The laugh died in Harriet's throat. She remembered the moment the news arrived of her late husband's injury at sea, and seemed to be caught in that moment again. Anne tugged on her fingers but Harriet did not move. A minute passed, then she heard the kitchen door open and Mrs. Heathcote, her housekeeper, emerged from the walled garden behind the house and began to jog across the lawn toward her, the letter in her hand. Don't come so fast, Harriet found herself thinking. Give me a moment more of not knowing.

"Mama! You are hurting my fingers!"

She released her and looked down. Her daughter had Rachel's coloring, her hair the color of old brass rather than Harriet's fierce copper. "Sorry, darling," she said quietly, then put her hand out to take the letter from her housekeeper. Mrs. Heathcote bent down to gather up the child.

"Come, my lovely. Cook wants your help and Mama has a letter to read."

"Let her read it later—why is it a *now* letter? I haven't finished singing."

Mrs. Heathcote bundled the little girl into the kitchen, then returned to hover around the garden door. She heard Harriet cry out, and saw her sit suddenly on the cold ground as if her legs had given way.

Mrs. Heathcote marched back into the house.

"William! Get to Mr. Graves. Tell him bad news come to Caveley. Mr. Heathcote, if you could go deliver the same to Mr. Crowther. Your hat's on the hook, man. Quick, quick. Dido, a word to Mr. Quince, if you please."

"What on earth is happening, Mrs. Heathcote?" the cook asked, floury and blinking. Little Anne sat on the floor at her feet, oblivious to everything when there was cake mixture to be cleaned out from the bowl.

"No notion, Mrs. Brooks. But if Mrs. Westerman's taken like that, it's something serious, that's all I know. Now if you'll excuse me, I'll tend to my mistress."

After the trials, scandals, and losses of the previous years, Harriet Westerman had been trying to live quietly. There would come a time when her children would need to be launched on the world, but she thought before then to have some peace, to let people forget her. In Keswick the previous summer she had shot and killed a man. She was satisfied she had been justified, but she had seen that yank against the trigger as some finale to her adventures in blood. Scandal had flared, and slowly fallen away. She had decided to concentrate her mind on domestic concerns.

Her friend Mr. Owen Graves had married Miss Verity Chase in November of 1783, and had removed her from London to Thornleigh Hall in Sussex, the home of his ward, the Earl of Sussex. Lord Sussex was now ten years old, his sister thirteen, their uncle almost eight. This strange group of aristocratic orphans the new Mrs. Graves had taken to herself, and they loved her for it. Marriage had lessened Owen's burdens and made him happy.

Miss Rachel Trench, Harriet's younger sister, married Daniel Clode in early December, and soon afterward the newlyweds had left Hartswood for some months abroad. Rachel and Daniel Clode had intended to spend most of the year on the Continent. Neither had yet enjoyed the opportunity to travel, but it was not in their nature to do so only for pleasure. Daniel Clode was Graves's right hand in the administration of the estates of the Earl of

Sussex, and Lord Sussex's financial interests spread beyond the borders of Great Britain and onto the Continent like ivy, even while he skated on the frozen lake behind his ancestral home and played soldiers with Harriet's son, Stephen. Clode justified his trip with the thought that he could establish some sort of contact with Lord Sussex's debtors and partners on his way, and so the path they intended to take across Europe was paved with money and interest. It should have made for a smooth passage.

Once these celebrations were complete, the winter had proved a rather lonely time for Harriet. Her friends at Thornleigh Hall called often, but she saw little of Mr. Gabriel Crowther. He always had been reclusive and was quite rich enough to never leave his house. She told herself it was winter, and therefore his preferred season for his anatomical studies. The cold meant he could work without the smell of corruption crawling through the house, upsetting the servants. She also told herself that the bullet wound he had received in his shoulder in the summer was still troubling him, making the short ride to her house uncomfortable. Then she would read, in one of the newspapers her housekeeper had failed to hide, the continuing speculations about their adventures in the Lake Country, consider how much she had learned about Crowther's family, his childhood, and wonder as she stared out over her frost-covered lawns if he was avoiding her company, whether seeing her reminded him of the gothic horrors of his history. He was already over fifty when they first met and had grown comfortable in his isolation from society. She asked herself if he was trying to become what he had been before they met in 1780, a closeted eccentric cut off from human society, working his knives by candlelight and content only in the company of the dead. Yet during their time in the Lakes they had met his nephew, Felix. Crowther was making the boy, his heir, a generous allowance and heard regularly from him. He had also taken into his care Felix's wife and child. Harriet herself was godmother to the infant. He could not retreat entirely from the world now. Harriet would sigh and return to the estate papers on her desk.

Her household still recognized Crowther as part of the larger family of Caveley however. It was never questioned that on seeing Harriet in distress, they would send for Mr. Crowther at once. Their faith was justified. Whatever Crowther's involvement with his work or reluctance to stir from his house, he was in the Long Salon at Caveley within half an hour of the messenger stirring the gravel on the driveway. He had been afraid on seeing her servant's pale face and ridden at a pace that would have impressed even in a far younger man, but as he rode he did not speculate, only concentrated on the speed he could draw from his horse. Mrs. Heathcote had the door open for him before he had dismounted. He handed her his hat and, following her nod, walked into the Long Salon unannounced. Harriet was seated on the settee, her back straight. She was not ill, it seemed. He felt his relief, took the letter she held out toward him, and retreated to one of the armchairs. It was only then he became aware that his heart was thudding at a startling rate and a blossom of pain opened out through his shoulder. He put his fingertips to his forehead and tried to read.

At first he could hardly make it out, an hysterical outpouring of fear, an assertion of Daniel's innocence, a sudden conviction that the terrible misunderstanding would be speedily cleared up. He would have struggled to make any sense of it at all, but there was another, longer letter attached from a Colonel Padfield. The colonel appeared to be an Englishman, employed in Maulberg and resident there some two years. This letter was a great deal clearer, but in its way more worrying. It gave a short account of the facts of the case against Clode, the seriousness of the situation, and a simple statement that Mr. and Mrs. Clode were in need of support from their friends in England. Crowther only had time to read it twice, carefully, before Mr. and Mrs. Graves arrived from Thornleigh Hall and he put it into their hands. Mrs. Heathcote served coffee, and he noticed that her eyes were red. Stephen could be heard in the hallway demanding information, and his tutor sharply insisting he return to his lessons. At last Verity Graves spoke.

"You will go, Owen, at once, of course."

Graves nodded. "Thank you, my dear. Though I hate to leave you with so much business to conduct."

"Mrs. Service already has the hall running like clockwork," his wife answered briskly. "I shall ask my father and mother to make a long visit while you are away. You trust Papa to advise me?"

"No one better than Mr. Chase."

"His poor parents!" Verity turned to her hostess. "Harriet, would you like me to carry this news to Pulborough?"

Harriet started. "Oh, yes! His father and mother . . . I had forgotten. Thank you, Verity."

"I shall tell them Graves leaves at once, and . . . ?"

"I shall come with you, Graves," Harriet said, then looked at Crowther. "Gabriel?" He only nodded. "Thank you." He watched her as she covered her mouth with the back of her hand, staring at the carpet, her eyes slightly wide. He wished they were alone, then he could tell her to stop trying to think of everything at once. He did not find the company of Mr. and Mrs. Graves overly trying, which in the general scheme of humanity made them part of a particular and privileged group, but he could not speak to Harriet as frankly as he would wish in front of them. "Should I go and see them too?" Harriet said. "Clode's parents?"

Verity put out her hand and took Harriet's. "I shall take the news to them. They will be relieved and grateful you are all going to his aid and will not want you to waste time calling on them. Leave this to me, Harriet." Crowther thought, not for the first time, that Graves had chosen very well.

The company parted and returned to their households to share the news, or what parts of it they felt they must, and make their preparations for an uncertain journey. Crowther's housekeeper received her instructions calmly and began her work. He retreated to his study, a generously sized space that had served as the dining room of the house when it had more sociable occupants, and wondered what he could save from the work he was now forced to abandon. There was no time to take the steps necessary to preserve the samples he had been studying, and it would be difficult to replace them. Still, it could not be helped. Mrs. Westerman had asked him to go, and go he would.

He unwound the soft leather roll that held his knives to check all was in place, then opened the walnut case that held his bone saw, forceps, tweezers, and hammers. The instruments were German-made, commissioned and bought while he was a student in Wittenberg some thirty years before. It had been the first place he had fled to after the execution of his elder brother. He had abandoned his title, sold his estate, and under the name of Gabriel Crowther had turned his interest in anatomy into his occupation; his knowledge into expertise. He fitted the magnifying glass into its velvet bed. It was ridiculous to carry them. The body of this Lady Martesen was buried already, and by the time he and his companions could reach Maulberg the flesh would have putrefied, but he intended to take them with him anyway. They were, like his cane, his signifiers. His markers and talismans. In all likelihood he was leaving his home for no good reason at all, but it never occurred to him not to go. If Mrs. Westerman was riding off into any sort of danger he would always follow while he had the strength.

It dawned on him, slowly, that while he had been packing away his effects the street door had opened and closed a number of times. Indeed, it sounded as if the door had just closed again now. He looked into the hall.

"Hannah?"

His housekeeper turned toward him. She had a large wicker basket over her arm.

"The news has spread, sir. Just about every soul in the village has come to the door with something to ease the journey. Wool blankets from the drapers . . . enough dried meats to feed you all half a year." Crowther frowned and Hannah smiled at him. "Mr. and Mrs. Clode are well liked, sir, and it is more convenient to leave things in this house rather than take them to Caveley or Thornleigh Hall."

"They do have food on the Continent."

"Not any that our butcher thinks healthy for an Englishman."

"Of course." He was about to turn back into his study when he hesitated. "I do not know how long I shall be gone, Hannah."

She nodded. "Of course, sir. But do not concern yourself. We shall manage quite well."

"If you find yourself in any need, you may apply to Thornleigh Hall."

"I know, Mr. Crowther. Your friends there will take good care of us for your sake."

He said no more, but withdrew to his study and his papers.

3

16 March 1784, Caveley

Crowther's luggage and the offerings of the village were carried to Caveley just after dawn. He followed them some hours later. The front of Mrs. Westerman's house was all activity. The party was to travel in two coaches. One for Graves, Crowther, and Mrs. Westerman, the other for their luggage and Mrs. Westerman's maid, Dido. It seemed to Crowther that as they were traveling without the usual large entourage of servants, they could have managed with only one coach. He said as much to Graves, who was observing the activity with an expression of wonder.

"Michaels insists, Mr. Crowther," Graves said. Crowther only now noticed the landlord of the Bear and Crown, who was directing the placing of the baggage and checking that the leather straps around the bandboxes were properly tightened. "He says it's better to travel with two lightly packed, otherwise we shall spend a month up to our axles in mud, this time of year."

Harriet had emerged from the house, and having cast her eye over the arrangements and decided not to intervene, joined the gentlemen. "Michaels has volunteered to be our guide, Crowther, and will not be persuaded to remain at home," she said. "He has the same distrust of the postillions and innkeepers of Germany as the butcher seems to have of the meat."

"He is fond of your sister," Graves said.

"Yes, everyone is. Our bulging supplies are testament to that. Graves, my children will be with Verity at Thornleigh Hall before nightfall, all packed up and Anne's nurse and Mr. Quince with them."

"They are very welcome."

Harriet's voice became low. "Stephen is very angry with me. He feels he should be allowed to accompany us."

"I have spent half the night denying the appeals of Susan and Jonathan,"

Graves replied wearily. "They claim that as Clode once saved them, it is their right to come with us to save him. Little Eustache wishes to go because he fears being left behind. They are with Stephen in your old nursery now, talking bitterly and plotting to pursue us."

"If you will allow me, I shall have a word with the young people," Crowther said.

Graves and Harriet looked at him with a mixture of surprise and faint hope.

At the point the cavalcade was ready to make for the coast, the children presented themselves for their farewells. They were affectionate, and though distressed at the separation, they no longer seemed angry. Stephen simply whispered to his mother that she must be very careful. He did so with the seriousness only a ten year old with large blue eyes can manage. She promised him she would, rather wonderingly. She watched from the carriage window until the house was out of sight, before wiping her eyes and asking, bewildered, "Crowther, what on earth did you say to them?"

He leaned back into his corner of the carriage. "I explained that before they could hope to be of any practical help to us on occasions such as these, they must learn to shoot a pistol accurately, improve their riding, their French, and their geography. I also suggested wrestling. They aim to spend the time we are absent in continual practice."

Graves made a slight choking sound, and Harriet shook her head. Crowther folded his long fingers over the top of his cane, and closed his eyes.

From *The Gazetteer of Europe for the Informed Traveler*, 1782

The Duchy of Maulberg

Situation: lying in the southwest between Bavaria, Wirtemburg, and Saxe Ettlingham.

Extent: some 1,500 square miles, supporting some 100,000 souls. Mostly forest and agricultural land.

Raised to Duchy: 1495.

Ruler: Ludwig Christoph II born 1745, succeeded to title 1756.

Exports: wine, linen, paper.

Principal rivers: Neckar, Enz.

Principal cities: Ulrichsberg (capital) founded 1713 on building of ducal palace; Leuctenstadt, seat of University of Maulberg founded 1512.

Some remarks:

Some commentators have said that if every county in England, and some of the larger parishes, had their own king, then we might learn to understand the situation that pertains in the Holy Roman Empire of the German Nation. Maulberg is a fine example of this sort of government. The duke is, to all intents and purposes, an absolute ruler in his territory, but his lands are punctured by other tiny sovereign states and he owes a polite allegiance to the emperor. He has, however, his own troops, his own government and to an extent his own laws, and should always be treated with the deference due to a monarch.

Maulberg and its people suffered greatly during the Seven Years' War as the armies of their great neighbors Austria and Prussia marched over their lands. However, we are glad to report that the situation seems to have improved of late. Much of the duchy appears to be productively farmed once more and its population grows.

The Palace of Ulrichsberg deserves qualified admiration. It is modeled on Versailles and certainly gives an impression of great splendor. The palace is also famous due to the quality of musicians and artists of all sorts the current ruler continually attracts to him. The other buildings in the city are also most elegant. An Englishman passing through this city must, however, ask himself how a state only a little larger than Wiltshire can afford a court so splendid.

As with all parts of Germany and Austria, we advise travelers to be very careful in matters of rank and recommend they seek guidance from their hosts in all questions of forms of address at all levels in society. French is generally used among people of quality, and almost exclusively in court except when dealing with servants. The peasants speak only their local version of the German tongue. Unsurprising then, that even these little states seem divided into classes of people staring at each other with a profound degree of mutual incomprehension.

PART II

4

2 May 1784, outskirts of Ulrichsberg, capital of Maulberg

Harriet felt the jolt of the carriage and the papers she was reading slid from her hand. She bit her lip to silence a curse and closed her eyes briefly. When she opened them again Crowther was holding the fallen sheets toward her. She took them with a nod, and both returned to their reading. She could hear Michaels on the roof of the carriage haranguing the driver. Graves was sitting opposite her, occasionally lifting his neck and making the vertebrae crack. She fought to focus her attention once more on the documents in her hand.

The journey had been a foul one. The sulfurous and heavy summer of 1783 had given way to a winter more severe than anyone living in England could remember. Now the ice cracked, and across Europe the rivers swelled and beat at their banks. The crossing of the Channel had left Crowther gray with fatigue and even Mrs. Westerman took no pleasure in being at sea again. Then the roads that led them from the coast of Denmark through Prussia down toward the forests and hills of the south were treacly with mud and full of these sudden dips and lurches. Still, such was the determination with which they pressed forward, it had become clear the party would reach the Palace of Ulrichsberg only a little after Easter.

With the ringing of the bells for that festival, the weather began to improve. The rivers calmed themselves, retreated to their usual boundaries, and looked innocent once more. The roads started to dry and the sun to show itself, and in showing itself revealed to the occupants of the carriage a world gradually greening with a late spring. The fresh leaves of the beech and ash fluttered open, the oak shook up its greenery, and the verges were cheerful with wildflowers. Even the air smelled more hopeful. But the traveling chaise still carried winter in it. The faces of its occupants were drawn and weary, as if the sunlight could not reach them. There was some advantage in the rigors they faced, however, since these had left them too tired to be afraid of what awaited them in Maulberg.

They had crossed the border early in the morning of May 2. Great packets of letters and documents, bundled and sealed, were handed to them and they were asked to retire to the parlor of the customshouse as their luggage was politely searched. Harriet tore at the strings while the gentlemen watched.

"Clode is alive," she said at once. "The investigation into the death of Lady Martesen continues." She heard Graves exhale. The fear that Clode might have been condemned and executed before they had even crossed into Europe had been with her every hour since they left England, but she had never given it voice. Only on hearing the air escape from Graves's lungs did she realize that he had feared the same thing—that they had ridden so hard to collect a body and a widow. "He is being held at Castle Grenzhow."

There was a rap at the door and a gentleman in a magnificent uniform of green and gold entered. He introduced himself as Major Auwerk of the Duke of Maulberg's Turkish hussars, and in fluent French welcomed them to Maulberg.

"I have sent on my best rider to inform the court of your arrival," he said with a bow. "My company shall ride with you into Ulrichsberg. Apartments have been set aside for you at the palace."

Harriet had often complained of the inadequacy of her education, but her father had taken advantage of the fact that one of his parishioners had been born in Paris to insist that both his daughters learn the language; now they spoke excellent French. Nevertheless her steady fear, then her sudden relief, silted up her tongue.

"Our thanks, Major," she said. "My sister?"

The major smiled. "Is also in residence and in good health to the best of my knowledge." He glanced out of the window. "It seems the formalities are completed. Your man and maid have been watching our officials like hawks."

He bowed again and offered Harriet his arm back to the waiting carriage.

The packets were found to contain copies of every document Krall's investigations had produced in the previous weeks. Rachel's note that accompanied them was short; warm words wishing for their speedy arrival. They were the first words of Rachel's Harriet had seen since the messenger had delivered her wild and confused letter. Harriet read the note very carefully and a number of times before handing it to Crowther then attacking the seals on the official documents.

The district officer, Herr von Krall, had signed and stamped each one. It seemed he had been very thorough, and as a further courtesy, the papers had been translated into English for the convenience of the accused and his friends. There were descriptions of Oberbach, a map of its principal buildings, detailed testimony from the friends and companions of Lady Martesen and from Rachel herself. There was an account of the examination of Lady Martesen's body and a careful description of the room in which she was found. The language was legal, dry, the accumulating detail horrific to Harriet. After weeks of knowing nothing, she felt her mind constrict as if it now wished to avoid knowing too much.

They divided the papers between them and the beauties of Maulberg were ignored. The cultivation of the land went unnoticed, the ruins of ancient towers along the Neckar glowered in vain, the cheerful faces of the peasantry received no friendly glances from the finely dressed inhabitants of the coach. It rattled on. They read.

"This is very strange."

Harriet heard Crowther speak and looked up. Her head ached. She was trying to absorb the names on the papers in front of her. Each person mentioned seemed to have a string of titles that must have reduced the scribe to tears.

"You are reading the account of the examination of the body, Crowther?"

"I am. Have you the document that details the initial discovery of Lady Martesen?"

She looked through the papers on her lap. The air was still cold enough for her to need her gloves and they made her fingers awkward.

"No, all I have here are accounts of her activities in the weeks preceding her murder. Card parties and salons. Her pleasure at being chosen as a lady-in-waiting to the new duchess when she arrives. It seems she all but lived at court."

"I wonder if it made her rich," Graves said, and Harriet looked up at him, eyebrows raised. "Many of these small German courts are terribly corrupt, Mrs. Westerman. Large sums of money are given in exchange for honors or lucrative positions, often via the women of the court."

"It says here her estate and jewels are left to her cousin, the Countess Judith Dieth, but does not say what the amount is. You are well-informed, Graves," Harriet said.

Graves gave a rather lopsided grin. "I have had to become so. The financial interests of my ward extend into too many of these statelets. I have the document you want, Crowther," he added, juggling papers.

"Would you tell me what it says?" Crowther asked.

"It is the District Officer von Krall's own account," Graves said, running his finger down the page while Crowther set aside his own papers. The spring sunlight gleamed hopefully on the silver head of his cane and was ignored. "He says the back parlor and bedroom of the haberdasher's in Oberbach had been hired by Colonel Padfield to allow his party to change into their Carnival costumes on their arrival in the town. Oberbach is some eight miles from the town of Ulrichsberg where all our principals reside in or near the court. Rachel and Daniel had been given the honor of rooms at the palace. I should think so too, the amount their Treasury owes to Thornleigh. Well, at some point after the main parade in Oberbach was done, the better people went to dance in the town hall's council chambers. It seems Daniel appeared drunk." Harriet shook her head. In the four years she had known him, she had never seen Daniel the worse for drink. "I know, Mrs. Westerman. I do not believe it either, but he seems to have been behaving oddly," Graves continued. "Now Colonel Padfield took him outside, and went to fetch water for him. When he returned, Daniel was gone. Padfield searched the immediate area and found no sign. Returned to Rachel and his wife to tell them what had passed, then went to look again with a couple of his friends." Graves glanced up at his two companions. Harriet turned away as if to admire the view, but saw nothing. "It is just as Padfield wrote in his letter to you. He thought to go back to the room where they had prepared for the party, and found the door locked—but he says he heard a noise within. There was no response to his calls, so he and another man broke down the door. Lady Martesen was lying dead in the center of the room. There follow details of her costume . . . Her eyes were bloodshot and there was a deep wound to her left wrist." He cleared his throat. "Daniel was crouched in the corner of the room, bleeding heavily from wounds to his own wrists. He seemed to have no idea where he was or what he was about. Good God, to see it set down like this . . ."

Harriet had folded her arms tightly around herself. "Anything more?"

"There was a cutthroat razor between his feet."

"Anything further about the body, Graves, other than the costume?" Crowther asked from his corner.

"No—wait. Krall reports very little blood around her body. He says other than the cut on her wrist and the bloodshot eyes, she appeared unharmed, her clothing not disarranged or torn. No bruises. God, they must think . . ." He controlled himself. "There was some damp about her clothes. One moment—a carafe of water was broken on the floor. And there was a pinkish foam around her lips and mouth."

Crowther sat forward. "A pinkish foam? Those are the words?"

"Yes. Is that significant?"

Harriet thought of the girl laid out across the floor, hardly marked, her wounded hand trailing behind her, but her eyes open. Unmistakably dead.

"The cut on her wrist," she said, before Crowther could reply to Graves's question. "Crowther, does the account of the body say how deep it was?"

"It severed the artery," he replied, without referring to the report.

"Surely a wound like that would have bled profusely? And it would have taken some minutes before she even fainted away. If she had struggled or fought after it was sliced, there should have been blood spattered everywhere, and all around her." She noticed that Graves had put his head in his hands.

"If it were administered while she was alive, then yes," Crowther said. "If she had been killed, and the wound made afterward, it would only leak a little." He examined the papers in his hand once more. "That is the conclusion they seem to have reached. No bruises to show she was throttled. Hyoid bone intact. They suggest she was smothered."

"Is that possible? To smother someone and leave no bruises?" Harriet frowned, concentrating.

"Yes," Crowther said simply.

"She did not defend herself at all?"

"If so, it left no mark on her or on Daniel."

"Of course Daniel had no mark on him," Graves said. "He didn't kill that woman."

"He was deranged when they found him, Graves," Crowther said. "And he is a strong man; he could have smothered her quite easily."

"I did not know you had come all this way to help put his head in a noose."

"He has killed before."

"In defense of my wards, in a fair fight! Good God, Crowther, if you were a younger man, I would call you out."

"Do not let my age hinder you, Graves."

"Gentlemen!" Harriet said. "Peace, please. Graves, you know perfectly well Crowther believes Clode to be a victim of some evil here, just as Lady Martesen was. And Crowther, please, have some humanity. What of the wounds on Clode's wrists?"

Crowther shook his head. "Nothing to suggest they were *not* self-inflicted, other than the fact they make no mention of hesitation marks."

"How could he have been in such a state that he would let someone slice his wrists! Even if he were dead drunk." Harriet bit her lip. "And do not say that perhaps he *did* do it himself or Graves will fly at you again." Crowther preserved a diplomatic silence. Harriet's fingers rapped against her dress. "You said there was something strange here."

"Clode spoke about dreaming of water, did he not, in his first meeting with Krall?"

Graves breathed deeply and calmly replied, "Yes, he dreamed he was drowning. Then dreamed this devil creature was slicing his wrists. They do not believe him. They think he was driven suddenly mad by guilt and somehow magicked a razor into the air and slit his own wrists. They think this devil is his conscience."

Crowther said softly, "A pinkish foam around the mouth is indicative of death by drowning."

"Drowning?" Harriet said. "In a locked room?"

"Colonel Padfield said in his letter that the key was not in the lock when he broke down the door. If a door does not fit well in its frame, it is easy enough to lock it from the outside, then slide the key back in under the bottom edge. I experimented with the door to the dining room in Caveley while you were bullying your maid, Mrs. Westerman."

"There is a terrible draft in that room. I wondered why Mrs. Heathcote was looking at you so severely."

There was a rustling from Graves. "Mr. Crowther, is this foam conclusive proof of drowning?"

Harriet watched Gabriel as he replied, and began to see how much the journey had tired him. There was a grayness in his skin. She had not realized how much she had asked of him. "No, not conclusive. There are a couple of other telling phrases in Krall's description of the autopsy, his comments on the appearance of the lungs, and so on. I think it was not his own drowning Daniel dreamed of, but hers."

"But how?" Harriet exclaimed.

"I do not know," Crowther said slowly. "It is possible to drown in a gutter, of course."

"I saw some who died like that, during the riots in eighty," Graves said. "But she would have been soaked to the skin, or at least her hair would have been wet if she had been held in even a basin of water."

Harriet straightened the papers on her lap and struggled to think clearly. "Suppose she were placed in the chair, her head tilted back, water poured down her throat in that position?"

"Possible," Crowther said, "but she would have resisted. Her hair and clothes would be soaked as she tried to avoid inhaling the water. She would have exerted herself against the necessary restraints . . . It is in our nature to fight death. She would have to have been unconscious, but there is no mention of a head wound, no smell of alcohol or sign of opiates here. Yet, the foam, the shape of the lungs . . . The report does not realize it tells us she died by inhaling water, but I believe it does."

"Dear God, what a foul death," Harriet said, and they were all silent for a while, until Graves cleared his throat.

"But what could have caused this strange confusion in Clode? He sounds as if he was seeing visions."

"That I cannot say," Crowther replied. "He must have been drugged in some way, but the effects are not like anything with which I am familiar." Harriet watched him out of the corner of her eye. She suspected from the manner in which he held himself that his shoulder was paining him, but knew better than to inquire.

"Still. At least we have made a beginning," she said determinedly. "Where did this razor come from? If we can demonstrate that she drowned, who would believe that a man, as stumbling and confused as they testify Daniel was, could manage such a thing? They cannot hang him with us asking these questions."

"They would probably behead him," Crowther said. His shoulder was definitely troubling him.

"They will do neither, Mrs. Westerman," Graves said. "We have money, we have reputation, and we have the support of King George. We will not lose him."

The horses slowed to a walk and the company arrived at Ulrichsberg just as the church bells were ringing midday.

5

A century of chalk dust rather than incense, the silted spirits of many years of intense intellectual strain rather than devoted prayer, but the old lecture hall did have the atmosphere of a cathedral, that reverential attention of the congregation listening while a single voice unfolded mysteries in Latin—though these mysteries were mathematical rather than metaphysical. It was usually silent, so when someone yawned very loudly then returned to gnawing the last flesh off his apple core, the sound echoed out like someone singing bawdy ballads at Communion. The professor's chalk ceased to move across the board. He abandoned Monsieur Clairaut's explanation of the motion of the apsis to turn slowly toward the auditorium of students.

It was quickly obvious who the offender was. The significant glances of his more cowardly pupils guided the professor's gaze toward the center of the room where a youth sat—no, not sat, lolled—core in hand and staring up at the plain, whitewashed ceiling above him. The professor stared his famous Medusa-like stare until the boy, apparently aware that the low drone of his voice had ceased, turned toward him and grinned. He spoke in German, like a shopkeeper.

"Sorry, Professor, do carry on. I think you were still on the second order effects, weren't you?" The youth yawned again, and the professor found himself on the receiving end of what could only be described as an encouraging wink.

The boy who delivered it could not be more than twenty. His light brown hair was unpowdered and the eyes somewhere between gray and blue. It was not a very handsome face; the nose was snub and its expression was rather foolish, or rather innocent to the point of foolishness. He looked—the professor's mind rummaged through its clutter of equations and Latin maxims for the right word—fresh.

The silence in the room that followed this remark deepened as forty young men of good family and high expectations drew in their breath and waited for the explosion.

"I would hate to think I am boring you, Mr. . . . ?"

"Pegel, Herr Professor, Jacob Pegel at your service." He waved the remnants of his breakfast. "No, not boring me exactly, but this is all quite basic stuff, isn't it? Good old Clairaut." He looked about him at the white, awestruck faces of his fellow students, the same foolish grin on his face.

The professor had been at pains to impress upon his students, in awful tones that made them tremble as if they found themselves at the gates of hell, that only the occasional mathematical genius among them might hope to come to a true understanding of the three-body problem. The rest must be left to wail in the limbo of mathematical ignorance. He had had them in the palm of his wrinkled hand, terrified and obedient, and now this boy appeared, blowing raspberries at him. This new boy. The professor recognized the name only too well. The head of the university had had a quiet word with him about letting this snub-nosed little whelp attend his lectures. He had no title, no apparent wealth, but still the dean had asked that the doors of the old lecture theater be opened to him, and eventually, after a series of deep sighs and shakings of his head, the herr professor had agreed that this boy would be allowed to attend his lectures without the usual qualifications and stipulations. It had obviously been a mistake.

The tension of hearing the great learning of Clairaut spoken of in such a way was too much for one young man in the back row. He giggled, then attempted to disappear behind his companions while simultaneously stuffing his handkerchief into his mouth.

The professor smiled, a thin evil smile. Those who had feared an explosion of his temper now almost wished for it. "Perhaps," he said, "Herr Pegel, you would like to continue the lecture, in that case. Do educate us poor provincial half-wits."

Forty pairs of eyes swung back to Pegel. He must apologize now, surely, then the great rage of the professor would tear forth in rush and thunder and fall upon him like the waters of the Red Sea closing over Pharaoh's troops.

"Righty-ho then!" Pegel said cheerfully, swinging himself upright and trotting down the stairs. "But you shouldn't be so hard on yourself, really. I know this sort of thing was all the go thirty-odd years ago." He sprang up onto the dais and put his hand out for the chalk. The professor, beginning to suspect he had not woken up this morning after all, handed it over.

Pegel stood back from the board a moment, then picking up a duster wiped the slate clean. The gasp this time was audible. He paused again, then, whistling, began to write, occasionally interrupting himself to tap his chalk and bark an explanation of his terms. In five minutes the board was filled once more. Pegel made a final underlining and stepped back. "And here we are! Spherical harmonics, you see? Track that little beggar through and there's your explanation of the great inequality of Jupiter and Saturn."

He turned to his audience. Thirty-nine pairs of eyes stared back at him over thirty-nine open mouths, but in the front row one youth was scribbling furiously, glancing up to the board and back down. "That's a good lad," Pegel said softly to himself.

If the professor heard him, he gave no sign. He was staring at the board and murmuring under his breath, "It can't be that simple. No, surely not, you'd have to . . . then . . ."

Pegel clapped his hands together to knock the chalk dust off them. "Lord, there's the hour up already. Off you go, chaps." Looking as if they had been collectively stunned, the students began to file out silently from the room. Pegel watched them go affably enough, but as the scribbler of the front row passed him, his face was briefly lit by a slower, more genuine smile. He heard the clatter of conversation in the hall, then turned back to the professor.

"Sorry about that! Good, solid work you've been doing here. Just it's nice to put on a show when you're new in town. Sure you understand, Herr Professor." He clapped him on the shoulder, causing a haze of ancient chalk to lift from his gown. Pegel's eyes watered and he coughed.

The professor did not seem to notice. His eyes were still tracking back and forth across the calculations on the board.

Pegel picked up the duster again. "Shall I rub this all off for you then, sir? Leave it nice and clean for your next group?" The professor's thin hand clamped suddenly around Pegel's wrist.

"Do. Not. Touch. It."

"All right, governor." Pegel was released and started to shake the blood back into his fingers, stepping back a pace as he did.

"Righty-ho then, as you like, Herr Professor! Any points you want clearing up I shall be knocking about the university for a few weeks, I suppose."

The professor spun toward him. His eyes really were red. "Tonight. Come tonight."

Pegel began to back away slowly. "Sorry, not possible. Busy. Very busy. Can't work all the time. Tomorrow, or the day after maybe. But soon, certainly soon. Promise."

The professor hissed and turned back to the equation, leaving Pegel to escape with a skipping step into the corridor. He was not surprised to find the blond scribbler waiting for him. He put his hand out to Pegel and blushed.

"My name is Florian zu Frenzel—Lord, actually. I wanted to ask—"

Pegel took the hand offered him and put his free arm around Florian's shoulders.

"Course you must, Your Holy Graceness. But I've got a question too. Where does a fellow get a drink round here?"

Frenzel stuttered a little. "I w-would be very glad if you w-would be my guest at—"

"Then be glad!" Jacob interrupted, giving his shoulder a squeeze. "Lead on, and tell me where we're going only when we get there. I love to be surprised."

Pegel had taken rooms in Leuchtenstadt on February 3, and in the three months since then had grown very fond of the little town, its medieval buildings all tumbling down in cheerful disorder to the river. The university held its classes in halls and buildings scattered all around the town, which meant the roadways were constantly filled with young men making their way from lecture to lecture, spending their money in the taverns or their youth bent over their books depending on their abilities, rank, and proclivities. The professors stalked the streets like little kings, nodding each to each and scowling at the young men. Pegel watched, listened, heard, and followed. He mapped the streets in his mind till he could make his way through them blindfolded. He handed out pennies to children, flirted with housemaids, and made a lot of notes in a pocketbook that never left his side. He had a healthy supply of gold sewn into the lining of his coat, but lived frugally. When the proper time came and his plans were laid he presented himself to the head of the university and handed him a letter. The head of the university read the letter and went rather pale. The boy in front of him was so unremarkable. The letter was remarkable and deeply upsetting. It mentioned his mistress, his gaming debts, and some rather unfortunate remarks he had made about two of his senior colleagues. The head of the university offered Mr. Pegel whatever assistance he required. Pegel took the letter back and asked to be admitted to the higher maths lectures, then reassured the head of the university that he would not return. Pegel left, whistling.

Pegel's first talent was mathematics. It came to him as naturally as speech and before he was eight years old he had leaped ahead of his parish schoolmaster. The schoolmaster, rather amazed, handed the child book after book, but when he realized Jacob had managed to teach himself passable French and better Latin to read further, he acknowledged that he could do no more and appealed to the bishop. Pegel was removed to the bishop's palace at ten and fed sweetmeats and the contents of the bishop's library. It was just after his fourteenth birthday that the old empress paid the bishop a visit and Pegel's life became rather more interesting. She carried back the little prodigy to Vienna, and there Pegel began work breaking codes to read a great deal of European diplomatic correspondence. When he was eighteen he met a man who suggested he might prefer a line of work less confined to a desk. Life got a lot more interesting again. He had developed several other talents in the last few years, but numbers were still his closest friends. Some said God was an architect, but Pegel had seen too many misshaped beings in the world to believe that. No, for Pegel, God was a mathematician. Numbers worked. It had been a delight then to learn, within a week of following him home with his two older friends, that Florian was regarded as gifted in that science and was a slightly shy, lonely young man among the duellists and drinkers who made up the greater part of the student body. He was perfect. Pegel went, for the first and only time, to class. Then, on Florian's arm, to the tavern.

6

The clouds parted to let the sun smile on the long frontage of the Palace of Ulrichsberg. The butter-colored walls glowed and the windows flashed even as the sky behind it remained dark slate and stormy. The vast curving wings of the palace that faced the city were like the wings of an eagle. In front of its high central portico, a company of soldiers in blue and gold were performing the complicated choreography of the changing of the guard, dwarfed by the architecture they protected. The steel on their pikes glimmered, as did the polish on their high boots. Their commander's sharp, barked instructions echoed off the walls.

Between the palace and the road lay an extensive, open formal garden of sculpted hedgerows and a series of fountains, each sending great plumes of water into the air. There were perhaps a dozen men at work here, clearing any leaf or weed that dared to litter the lawns, all dwarfed by the ranks of clipped yew trees that extended from each side of the garden. Some looked up as the jangle of the hussars' spurs reached them to watch the oil-black horses and their straight-backed riders pass by, then turn north along Eugene Strasse, leading the carriages they accompanied toward the rear of the palace. None of the gardeners recognized the coat of arms on the carriage doors.

District Officer von Krall, seated on a bench in the market square on the other side of the road, did recognize it. The crest of the Earl of Sussex. So they had arrived. He tapped out his pipe and stuck it into his pocket, then rubbed at his forehead with his gnarled fingers. After nearly two months of laborious work, Krall had found himself awaiting the arrival of Mrs. Westerman and Mr. Crowther a confused and frustrated man. Mr. Clode still had only a fragmentary memory of the Carnival. He was no longer the rather deranged creature that Krall had first encountered, however. He had spent almost the entirety of his first two days of confinement asleep, then woken weak, but with his senses restored. Krall crossed his ankles and glowered at the cobbles, thinking of the young man in the tower like something out of a fairy story. Clode could recall preparing for the parade with perfect clarity, but sometime after his party had joined the crowd he seemed to have lost his mind. He admitted to Krall, haltingly, that he had started to see not men and women in costumes, but actual demons and gods. Spirits that whispered to him. One memory that seemed horribly clear was the look of disgust and shame on his young wife's face when he tried to dance with her at the ball. Then there was this man in the black mask who promised to look after him. Of his time in the room with Lady Martesen he seemed to recall nothing but his own fear, his dream of drowning and pain.

Krall realized he was hungry. He got to his feet and began to stamp away from the castle toward a little tavern he knew where he could get a good beer and simple cooking. Dining so often from the court kitchen was playing merry devils with his digestion. He looked at the higher ranks of the old nobility with a new respect, having tasted the riches on which they subsisted. Clode never claimed he was innocent. He left that to his pretty wife. All he said was he had no memory of doing harm to Lady Martesen. That he had no memory of his first meeting with Krall either. Krall hesitated on the tavern steps. He had to admit he liked Daniel Clode. He seemed an honest man, and a brave one. He had a haunted look, but Krall was reasonably sure it was not fear of the ax that disturbed his rest and hampered his recovery, but those odd visions of Festennacht. Krall could give a full account of the movements, histories, and passions of all the principals, but as to the facts of Carnival night he could only say that Lady Martesen should not be dead, though she was, and though Clode was the only man who, it seemed, could have killed her, Krall had doubts about his guilt. Well, it was all written down. Let these clever friends of Mr. Clode's worry at the problems now. He pushed the door to the tavern open and welcomed the sour yeasty smell of the beer, and the sharp tang of liver coming off the grill. He breathed deeply and found a place among the tables.

The carriage turned down a road on the far side of the garden, and after a significant journey down the east flank of the palace, the horsemen preceded them under a great arch into one of the interior courtyards. The hussars wheeled about and exited at once, all flashing braid and polished stirrups. The carriage halted, and Harriet peered out of the window.

A gentleman was there to meet them, dressed magnificently in pink satin and with a small squadron of liveried footmen behind him. Two stepped forward and with the formalized movements of ballet dancers, they let down the steps of the coach, and, as Harriet emerged, one, without looking at her, offered her his arm to help her descend. The footman's wig was such a startling white she had to fight the impulse to reach out and touch it.

The cobbles looked as if they had only just been laid, so clean and neat they were. The man in pink satin introduced himself in slightly affected French as the court harbinger and requested the honor of showing them to their apartments. Harriet replied in as flowery a manner as she knew how. She glanced backward at Michaels as the gentlemen took their turn at exchanging civilities. He winked at her and climbed down from the box, his leather bag over his shoulder. Her maid emerged from the other carriage and shot a look of such concentrated suspicion at one of the footmen, he blinked. Monsieur Clemme waved his hand and the liveried footmen swarmed over the luggage like scarlet ants attacking the picnic meats. Harriet realized she was being addressed by the magnificent Monsieur Clemme once more.

"Mrs. Clode is waiting for you in your rooms, madam." He bowed and offered his arm.

The servants of such a palace as Ulrichsberg naturally prided themselves on not being overly impressed by the rank and fame of visitors to the court. Monarchs, lords, and luminaries of the world of music and art passed through Ulrichsberg continually, but they watched the arrival of the Englishwoman and her companions with interest. A little knot of some of the more senior servants in the east wing had found it convenient to pause in their labors and watch as the carriage was unloaded and the gentry led away.

Mr. Kinkel, head footman in the east wing, the cook to the servants' hall, and the housekeeper observed while their more junior fellows bustled around with baggage and bandboxes in the swept yard. Mr. Crowther, he that was some lord or other in his own country but liked to pretend otherwise, was easy to identify. Thin as a rake with a long nose—and, Mr. Kinkel suspected, a habit of looking down it. The younger man they thought perhaps a prince of some sort. Handsome youth, still some years short of thirty and awkward as a newborn calf. He stumbled on the cobbles as Monsieur Clemme led them off. The maid remained rooted to the spot, obviously intending to keep her eye on the luggage. The likeness between Mrs. Westerman and her pretty sister young Mrs. Clode was easy to spot.

"That poor little cabbage, marry a man and find him a murderer!" Cook observed, preserving her reputation for great kindness to the unfortunate. "Lovely frock Mrs. Westerman has on though. Green is such a blessing for redheads. Isn't it true her husband was murdered himself?"

"Unlucky in love, that's true enough. Covered in tragic blood, the pair of them." The housekeeper sighed. She was the romantic.

Mr. Kinkel's attention was distracted by the sight of a large muscular-looking man having a word with one of the underfootmen, then approaching his little group with a leather bag over his shoulder. He walked with rather more swagger than Kinkel thought appropriate to those in service. He wore no livery. Kinkel had seen the valets and secretaries of kings cross the yard before him, but this great bearded fellow looked like none of those. Certainly not a valet in that coat, and his hands looked too broad and meaty to wield a pen.

As he came closer to them, Kinkel leaned toward the two women at his side and muttered to them. "The English have brought their tame bear with them. It is true what they say, an English person will not be separated from their pets!" The ladies tittered. He was their satirist. The man stopped in front of them and to their collective shock spoke to them in their own dialect.

"They've brought a friend with big fists and big ears, brother." With his free hand he slapped the pocket of his coat and made it jingle promisingly. "Now my preference is to sleep warm on my own bedroll and eat as the servants eat. Can you accommodate me?"

Kinkel shut his hanging jaw and managed a bow. "Naturally, whatever sir wishes. I am Mr. Kinkel."

"Don't 'sir' me. I am Michaels. As long as my friends are looked after, I'm a lamb and a generous friend. If they are spoken of without respect, then I am like to get a little riled. Do we understand each other?"

Mr. Kinkel hesitated, then put out his hand. Michaels took it and grinned. His teeth looked very white and sharp. Was he a fox or bear? Mr. Kinkel could not decide. "Can I ask how you come to speak our language so well, Mr. Michaels?"

"Mother was born on the border here, and wont to express herself very free in her native tongue. So I came to see my party traveled fast and safe. Now can I trouble you for a billet and hot water? The roads are nothing but dust and I can hardly breathe for the muck on me."

Kinkel considered. He thought of himself as a clever man and pondered the problem at hand with a certain confidence. Service at the palace often threw up interesting problems of this nature. This Michaels was too large a creature, and his money clattered too nicely for Kinkel to think it appropriate to put him to sleep among the servants, but at the same time he could not see a man who wanted to sleep on his own bedroll wishing to stay in the luxurious surroundings of the guest suites. After a moment's thought he smiled. "I think I have an idea where you might be comfortable, Mr. Michaels, if you don't mind being a little bit out of the way."

"Out of the way is fine with me, Mr. Kinkel." With a significant glance at his companions, Kinkel put his hand on Michaels's sleeve and guided him out of the courtyard.

By the time the sausage, bread, and potatoes had been disposed of and their leavings carried away by a sweet-faced daughter of the house, Florian zu Frenzel was well on his way to being drunk. Jacob Pegel was giving a good impression of being so.

The tavern was popular with the middle-ranking students. The beer was strong and cheap, the food not bad at all, and it was clean enough for a man brought up in respectable comfort to feel at his ease. In other places a man might risk his wealth among a crowd of men who liked to gamble as deep as their courage would let them. In other dark corners, especially those nearest the river on the edge of the old town, he might risk his health with one of the whores who sashayed to and fro for business, or lose his pocketbook to the thieves and slutmasters who watched the drunken young gentlemen like wolves seeking out the injured deer in the herd.

To be fair Pegel had never seen Florian in that corner of town and found he liked him for it. A serious devotion to cards or women might have made him easy to blackmail, but Pegel suspected the more earnest and serious the young man was, the closer he might lead him to his goal. Pegel suspected he would only get what was required from an idealist.

The beer had loosened their tongues, then smeared the talk from mathematics to the personal. Pegel began laying down his lies to build a friendship on like a mason settling his first cornerstone. There were ways to dance into intimacy with a boy such as Florian, like a mountain goat, but he needed to establish a solid base first.

"There are some good men in Weimar," he said. "Good thinkers. I thought there was a chance of a place there, but no! Some squid who can barely add up got the job."

"Why?"

"His father was a baron, of course. He had the name, he had the grease . . ." He rubbed his fingers together. "So, it's 'Sorry, Mr. Pegel, maybe next year.' Bah! Perhaps I should go to England. They take a man there for his brains, not some bit of paper that proves no man in his family has done a day's work in generations."

"My father is a count."

"I'll try not to hold it against you, but honestly, don't you ever feel this . . . this rage against the system we live in? Good men ground down, the arrogance of the nobility while better men starve. Ah, forgive me. The beer is heating me up."

Florian put a hand on Pegel's sleeve. "You are not alone." Then in a lower tone, "You are not alone, brother."

Pegel had his pocket watch in his hand. There were no numbers on it, but a compass, set square, radiant eye. He flicked it shut and thrust it into his pocket now it had done its work. He had bought it from a man in Strasbourg who had offered him some interesting stories of Leuchtenstadt for the chance to rant about his own misfortunes. Now Florian had seen it and assumed Pegel was a member of a masonic lodge. He had also confessed, by calling Pegel "brother," that he was one himself. Easy. Pegel began to build. "I don't know. There are good men in the fraternity, but in the lodge in Weimar they seemed more interested in legends of Templars and alchemy than in the truth of universal brotherhood. I am afraid I held out hopes . . ." He turned away slightly and touched the corner of his eye as if wiping away a manly tear. He almost felt it. Germany had lost a fine actor when Pegel was trained as a code breaker. When Jacob looked back, Florian's eyes were sparkling in sympathy. God, it was too easy.

"Do not give up hope! Some have taken a false path, a path of vanity and mysticism. But. There. Are. Others."

Pegel began to worry that the boy was drunker than he had thought. The afternoon would not go as planned if he could not walk.

"Air!" He stood up and was dismayed to find the room swayed a little. "Come along, Your Graciness. I want you to show me this town. I have been here a day already and have hardly seen a thing."

Florian looked up at him and gave a slightly fuddled nod, then lifted his hand to summon the girl.

After five minutes' walk Florian and Pegel reached the embankment and rested against the stone wall, looking back the way they had come. The lapping tiles on the roofs on the half-timbered houses ran in wavelets up the hill toward the castle and cathedral, washing up the high, steeply pitched roofs. The slates were small and tightly packed enough to look like dragon scales. Neither spoke. Pegel glanced at his new friend out of the corner of his eye. He still seemed a little bleary, but he was awake.

"Is that man staring at us, Mr. Pegel?"

Jacob glanced in the direction Florian nodded. A tall man in a slightly old-fashioned brown frock coat and dark breeches was standing at the east entrance to the little square. His wig was rather yellow. He seemed to notice that he was observed and crossed toward them before making a bow that both young men, a little unsteadily, returned.

"May I inquire," he said in the voice of an educated man, "if I have the pleasure of addressing His Grace Lord Florian zu Frenzel?"

Florian nodded. "I am he. May I have the honor of learning who it is that inquires?" he said, slurring only very slightly.

The man was perhaps in his late thirties or early forties and had a vigorous air to him. Solid. A gentleman with a modest estate, perhaps. "My name I cannot give you, Your Grace. I am come to Leuchtenstadt to give you a message. One which I hope you will carry to your friends. We do not want you here. Any of you. We do not like your ideas or your leaders. Disband and return to your proper studies." Florian seemed able to do nothing but look amazed. The man reached into his pocket and pulled from it a folded sheet of paper that he held out to Florian with another bow. Florian took it from him automatically. "This is a warning, Your Grace. Heed it or worse will follow." With that the man turned and walked away from them.

Pegel plucked the page from Florian's hand and opened it out. It was a drawing of a cross with a rose at its center.

"What on earth was that about? Fellow must be a bit simple. Do you know him?" He glanced up when Florian did not reply. He looked pale. Pegel looked down at the paper again and frowned. "Still, not that much of a warning, is it? A picture?" A shadow fell across him and he looked up again to see a man twice the size of the last with the red face of a drinker and the blossomed nose of a fighter towering over him. The giant spoke. "That be more of the signature, gentlemen. This is the warning."

He grabbed Florian by the collar with his right hand and slapped him across the face with his left. The boy's head was twisted sharply sideways and the giant dropped him to the ground, drew back his boot, and kicked Florian hard in the stomach. Florian groaned and curled into a ball and the man drew back his foot again. Pegel lowered his head and charged him, catching him while he still had one foot lifted and making him stagger away from his victim. Pegel lifted his fists and stared up into the man's glowing face. Behind him he heard a retching noise as Florian tried to lift himself up. The giant let his arms hang at his side and lifted one eyebrow. Pegel clenched his fists more tightly and gave a tiny nod. The blow came from his left and he felt himself flying through the air. A starburst of pain spread over his face and he found himself suddenly on his knees. The giant hesitated a moment. Someone emerged from a shopfront on the side of the square and yelled something Pegel could not quite hear through the thumping of blood in his head. The giant looked about him, then set off down the side street at a lumbering run. Trying desperately not to faint, Pegel stumbled over to Florian. The shopkeeper who had shouted took a step or two toward them, looking a little uncertain. Jacob got his arm under Florian's and hauled him to his feet. His right cheek was raw and red and it seemed he could not stand straight.

"Let's get out of here," Pegel hissed, watching the shopkeeper, "before that man calls the beadles. My rooms are near here. We can recover there. Can you walk?" Florian managed to nod. "Come on then."

7

Monsieur Clemme had the sense to do no more than open the door and then depart murmuring something about seeing to the disposal of their belongings. Harriet stepped into the large parlor in time to see her sister stand, but before she could form any impression of Rachel's looks, the latter had thrown herself into her sister's arms and buried her face in her neck.

"Oh Harry, you came! Thank God!" She stepped back and offered her hands to Crowther and then Graves. "Crowther, Graves—how glad I am to have you here."

Her composure deserted her entirely and she burst into tears. The gentlemen examined the furnishings of the room, a great deal of gilding, while Harriet put her arm around her sister's shoulders and gave her a handkerchief. She leaned her cheek against her hair, which was silk smooth. Rachel had been only fourteen years old when their father had died. Harriet had walked into the salon of the parsonage, and after four years of sailing with her husband around the world it had seemed small, and her own clothes and demeanor too grand for the modest little room. Then Rachel had hesitated, only for a moment, before running to embrace her sister, and Harriet had thought, Lord, another person to look after. It was months before she discovered that her modest, quiet little sister had been her father's housekeeper and nurse, that Rachel's trials might not have been as dramatic, bloody, or adventurous as Harriet's but she had faced them alone and withstood them bravely.

The room in which she now held her sister could not have been a greater contrast to the modest parsonage. The walls were a frenzy of plaster figures picked out in gold against pale green paneling, and the furniture itself, all gilt flourishes and elaborate curves, seemed to disapprove of them. The parsonage had smelled of mown grass, of the Norfolk summer; this room tasted of hothouse lilies. It seemed to Harriet that even the carved marble Graces holding up the mantelpiece were staring at them.

After a few moments Rachel managed to say, damply, "My apologies, but I have so wished to have you here. However did you manage it? When Colonel Padfield told me you were arriving today, I did not think it possible."

Harriet guided Rachel to a chair in a convenient grouping by the fireplace and the gentlemen took their seats opposite the sisters. "Michaels, Mrs. Clode!" Graves said, smiling. "We would have been another fortnight on the road at least, were it not for him. He knows the lingo and he knows when to press and when not. But that's all that needs to be said of our journey."

"Michaels here too? Lord, what trouble we have given you all."

Graves leaned forward and took Rachel's hand with the easy intimacy of long friendship. "What of you, my dear? How are you and poor Daniel managing? Verity, Mrs. Service, and the children send all their love."

"Their letters outpaced you, just. I had my first words from home only two days ago. Verity said the kindest, wisest things and poor Susan sounded quite distraught." She smiled very slightly and freed her hand to wipe her eyes again. It was known that Lady Susan had fallen madly in love with Daniel Clode at the age of nine while he helped save the lives of herself and her younger brother the earl, and was still, while also loving Rachel sincerely, not quite free of the attachment. "I am as well as you might expect. The district officer, Krall, has been fair, and Colonel and Mrs. Padfield have been quite kind. The colonel is an Englishman employed by the duke. His wife is a German lady he met here; she accompanies me whenever I am allowed to visit Daniel in Castle Grenzhow and waits in the carriage for me. But none of them knows us! They all think Daniel did this terrible thing. They all but confess they think it would have been better if he had died in that horrid little room! Lord, I am so glad you are come! You know he didn't do it, don't you?"

Harriet held her to her side. "Of course he didn't, darling. We have been reading all the papers since this morning." She held her away from her for a second. Her sister's green eyes seemed rather large in her face, and her skin had a gray tinge to it. "You have grown thin, my love."

"I am well, Harry. Only promise me you can make them set Daniel free again and I shall be better."

"We have enough to save him, even in those papers, I think, thanks to Crowther. But who would do this? Who would frame Daniel for the killing in such a way? And attempt to murder him?"

She saw a wild hope light in Rachel's eyes. "There *was* a man! You think so? We have been trying to believe, I have been trying to think, some terrible accident. But who could we have offended so? We are strangers here..."

"And how is Daniel?" Graves frowned as he asked the question. The letters that had met them on their way had been from Rachel alone. They reported her husband's health as good and his mind clear, only he seemed unable to remember any more than snatches of the night of the festival parade. No word written by his own hand, however, was found in the packets.

Rachel leaned into Harriet's shoulder and Harriet bent to kiss the top of her head.

"Oh Graves, I cannot say. Not well. He says he has bad dreams. The wounds on his wrists are healing cleanly, but he lost a lot of blood—it left him weak and confused for days. He spends hours staring out at the forest from that horrible place and trying to recall." She shook her head. "I have told him a thousand times I think him incapable of doing harm to that woman, but he tortures himself. He could never have harmed her, could he?"

"Of course not. It is unthinkable," Harriet said firmly.

Rachel peered out from under her honeyish curls toward Crowther. "Mr. Crowther?"

He gave a thin smile. "Mrs. Clode, from all I know of your husband, and all I have read of the matter, I think it highly unlikely."

Harriet felt her sister's body soften slightly against her. "Thank you for coming here, Crowther," she said.

"Daniel is as innocent as I am," Graves said in the same determined tone Harriet had used, "but I suppose we must find who the guilty party is indeed before we can convince him. The man has far too much imagination for a lawyer."

Harriet almost laughed and tightened her grip around Rachel's shoulder.

"We shall certainly do our best. Rachel, has Herr von Krall no other suspects in the case? Has anyone discovered how poor Daniel came to be in such a confused state?"

Rachel straightened up. "No, it is all in the reports I sent along to you."

"Uncomfortable to have any scandal in court when all eyes are turned in this direction for the duke's wedding," Crowther said. "No wonder then they would like to believe it to be the work of a deranged foreigner."

"Crowther, for goodness sake!" Harriet glared across at him, and he gave a slight shrug.

"My apologies, Mrs. Clode."

"I am not offended, Harry. Crowther must say what he likes, he always does after all and he is quite right. But Herr von Krall . . . he has doubts about Daniel's guilt, I think. If it weren't for him, the way he stops sometimes and frowns, I am afraid I could have almost started believing it myself."

She was looking down as she finished, so did not see the look of shock that passed over Graves's face. Harriet could not help noticing the corner of Crowther's mouth twitch, however. He is proud of her, Harriet thought, for having the courage to doubt her husband.

"Rachel?" she said out loud. "My dear, I am sorry. We are interrogating you within moments of our arrival."

Rachel managed to smile. "No, Harry. I am sorry to be so weak. I want—all I want is to tell you all I can, but my head is spinning."

"Darling, are you quite well?" A suspicion began to form in Harriet's mind.

Rachel held onto Harriet's hand very tightly. "Oh Harry, hardly anyone will speak to me, and even those who do only pity me. I have eaten almost every meal alone."

"You have been in prison too, child," Crowther said, as she wiped her eyes.

"Lord, I would do anything to stop crying! Do not indulge me, Crowther. It is a comfortable prison. And my sufferings are *nothing* to my husband's." She said the word firmly, almost as a declaration. "And I have made some friends. There is a pair of brothers I wish you to meet. Mrs. Padfield introduced me to them. They, like us, are not members of the nobility here, and have helped me a great deal in learning how to behave, who to petition for Daniel. They have a workshop in the palace grounds."

Harriet glanced at her sister, then her companions. "Perhaps you could take me to see them now, Rachel? I am sure Graves and Crowther will understand if we have a little time to ourselves, and the fresh air will do you good."

Rachel nodded. "But you have only just arrived . . . I would not wish to seem ungrateful."

Crowther half-closed his eyes. "I have spent the better part of the last two months in a carriage with your sister and Mr. Graves. The greatest kindness you could do me at this moment is to allow me an hour or two alone."

Rachel grinned and Harriet caught Crowther's gaze. She knew he would be pleased with himself when he could hide his thoughtfulness with rudeness. His blue eyes glimmered.

"Of course, Mrs. Clode," Graves said with his usual smile. "I shall find a slightly less travel-worn coat and then go and present our credentials to Chancellor Swann. Crowther, I shall not make you come with me."

"Thank you, Graves."

Graves sighed. "Is Swann as dry as his correspondence? Lord, no doubt now they have one of my closest friends locked away they find the time has come to renegotiate those bonds. Very well, let us wash the dirt from us and try to give the proper impression of importance." He leaned forward and patted Rachel's hand again. "Do not fret, my dear. Mrs. Westerman and Mr. Crowther will return your husband to you."

8

Pegel's room was in an attic in the oldest quarter of the medieval city. As the stairs were uneven and narrow, and he had to fetch his own water and fuel, the rates were low for the space he had. He could have used some of the gold in the lining of his coat and bought the whole building, but the money was not his and the man who had given it to him would expect him to account for his spending. In any case his new home suited him. The attic ran the whole length of the building and the south end gable was dominated by a large window that overlooked the small market square of the quarter. The few sticks of furniture provided seemed to make it look more cavernous, it was impossible to heat and if he wanted to avoid freezing as he sat at his desk in the window, he had to carry his fire with him in a brass coal-carrier such as maids cradled to church to keep their mistresses' feet warm. But it was secure. No one could approach without the complaints of the stairs giving notice, and no one had any business to hover outside his door. Also, for all the chill, he liked the view. It made him feel like some wise bird watching the comings and goings below. A king, or a magician able to watch the people move about on their paths like little walking toys.

He dropped Florian onto the couch a little heavily—getting him up the stairs had been uncomfortable—rolled his shoulders and crouched down to get a fire going in the grate. When he was satisfied that the flames were alive and felt a little heat crawling off the coals, he turned his back on them to study his guest. Florian had his chin tucked into his chest and his arms wrapped about him. "Your Grace? Does it pain you much? Perhaps we should get you to a sawbones."

He looked up sharply at that. "No, no, it's sore is all. I'd rather stay here. And you may call me Florian, if you wish." He tried to smile and winced a little.

Pegel remained seated on the floor by the fire, but extended his hand.

"Jacob." He nodded to the decanter of wine and glasses by the couch. "Can you move enough to pour us a glass then, Florian?"

The young man blushed slightly as his Christian name was spoken as if he were not used to hearing it out loud, but reached over and filled the glasses. Pegel took the glass offered him with his right hand and with his left pushed his hair back, revealing the redness on his jaw. He heard Florian gasp and was glad that the giant had not pulled his punches.

"I am so sorry you got hurt, Jacob. And thank you for coming to my assistance."

Pegel sniffed. "Can't leave a fellow on the ground like that. Not sure what morals I have, but I know that isn't right."

"I think you are a good man, Jacob."

He yawned and studied the ancient bowing beams above them. "Don't know. I just do as I do and leave good and evil to the priests. It's why I like numbers. No good and evil there, but there's still wonder. Here I am, mind of man, that's all, and now I can explain how the planets move. That I like."

Florian was frowning. It seemed a strange expression on that rather child-like face. "But you must seek something more than that, Pegel. You are a member of the Brotherhood, are you not? Your watch is marked with symbols. You mentioned a lodge in Weimar. You are a Freemason, I know it."

"I . . . I try to be," Pegel said, turning away slightly so he could stare soulfully into the fire while still displaying the reddening on the side of his face. "My uncle introduced me to his lodge and for a while I thought there was some . . . higher purpose worth serving. But, I don't know, Florian, mostly I've just found it useful as a way to meet people as I travel about. That stuff in the lecture hall today—it's the work of a man called Laplace I met in one of the Paris lodges."

It was a lie, of course. The work *was* Laplace's but Pegel had no uncle and had never been introduced at any Lodge. He knew enough about Freemasonry to fake his way along with a green boy like Florian though, just as he knew the right air of wistful longing to assume when talking about the higher dreams of men.

He felt a touch on his sleeve and found Florian had reached forward to place a hand on him. His face was terribly earnest. "Oh, but there is! There *is* a purpose, a great purpose." He withdrew his hand, and it seemed to Pegel that the room suddenly became a little colder. "You must have been wondering why that man attacked me; you have been terribly good by not asking."

Pegel gave a little attention to the fire. "Not my concern, Florian. Don't want to intrude."

The young voice became firm. "It would give me great pleasure to talk on these matters. Before I do though, I must ask you, Jacob Pegel, to swear to keep secret what I reveal to you, by everything you hold dear. I don't want to sound like an idiot, but it is terribly important."

"I'll swear if you like." Pegel smiled. "Don't worry, Florian. I know how to keep a secret."

9

The sisters left the palace and entered the gardens that lay to the north of the house. Harriet looked over her shoulder. This side of the building was painted pink and white. Huge windows glittered down over them. Directly behind the palace was an artificial lake, large enough to boat on, with another central fountain. Beyond it reared an artificial waterfall and it was guarded by a series of marble heroes and Graces. The high hedgerows behind the statuary were cut into doorways.

Harriet still thought Rachel's color high and her eyes overbright, so at first she simply told all the news she could think of from Hartswood, then the news of their friends elsewhere.

"So Crowther's nephew has a son?" Rachel asked. "How was Sophia's confinement?"

"Sophia seems to have managed very well once she was able to find an accoucheur that Crowther did not think a fool. She is comfortably established in Bath, though I suspect she finds it a little lonely. Did you receive my letter about the almshouses I plan to have built in the village?"

"Yes, while we were in Berlin. We were pleased to hear that you had . . ." Her sentence trailed away.

"Found some occupation other than the investigation of murder?" Harriet said a trifle dryly. "Well, you cannot blame me for involving myself on this occasion."

Rachel blushed. "I know how it must seem to you, given I have been so opposed to you and Crowther helping others, then to be in so much need of you myself. Perhaps there is some justice in it."

Harriet came to a halt and turned her sister toward her.

"Rachel, never say that. There is no justice in this." She felt herself watched suddenly and looked about. There were a number of other finely dressed ladies and gentlemen in the garden wandering alone or in small groups. She felt their casual glances touch her and lowered her voice. "You do not think I have come here to crow over you? You cannot."

"No, Harry, of course not, but I have said such things to you in the past. You would have the right." Then Rachel seemed to become aware of the looks of the strangers around the lake. "This place! They have nothing to do but study each other. Come, this way."

She led Harriet through one of the arches in the hedge and Harriet found herself in a small garden room: it contained a number of flowerbeds and stone benches, the pathways between them mosaicked with chips of red porphyry and quartz. Rachel, it seemed, was not disposed to linger, but led her through another arch into another such miniature garden, this one with the center-piece of an ornamental birdbath, where one of Titan's handmaidens eternally poured water from a conch for the palace sparrows to wash.

"Rachel, if you leave me now, I shall be lost forever."

Her sister tilted her head to press her cheek briefly against Harriet's shoulder. "I have spent the last forty days wandering through here."

"Like Christ in the wilderness?"

"My feelings have been hardly Christlike, and this is an unusual wilderness. Wait until you see the place I am taking you to."

"The air is doing you good. You sound more like yourself. Now tell me frankly, do you think you are with child?"

"I knew you would realize at once. I was horribly sick this morning, so I suspect so."

"You must take care of yourself, Rachel. And we must get you home to Caveley."

"But Caveley is not my home anymore. I know that's not what you meant exactly, Harry, and just hearing you say it, part of me is sad that Caveley isn't home anymore, but it's not, not now I am married." She lifted her hands as if to examine the wedding ring on her finger, then dropped them again. "Have I mentioned that I am terribly, terribly glad that you are here?"

"You have."

While Harriet was in the gardens with her sister and Graves was making the acquaintance of Chancellor Swann, Crowther found himself at leisure to arrange his room to his liking and read those documents provided by the district officer that he had not yet been at liberty to peruse. His respect for Mr. von Krall continued to grow. In England he had found, to his cost, that justice was administrated in an arbitrary manner by unimpressive men. What they could not understand made them angry, so they cast about for a solution, and when they had fixed on one, rigorously ignored any contrary evidence presented to them, locking their fleshy jaws remorselessly around the first explanation available.

Things seemed different here. No matter how convinced the authorities were of Daniel's guilt, no shortcuts had been taken. No half measures pursued. Pages and pages of transcript had been collected, every word spoken by Daniel, by the haberdasher, by anyone who had conversation with Lady Martesen that evening, or with Daniel. It seemed the lady had become detached from her party a little earlier than Daniel. She had not been seen at the ball at all, though no one had thought at that point to be concerned. Crowther put another page down, not convinced he was learning anything very material to the case in hand, but with a growing sense of admiration for Krall and for Maulberg. When he heard a knock at his door, he half-expected to see the district officer, but instead there was hovering in the doorway a gentleman of about his own age dressed in the splendid green and gold of the soldiers who had accompanied them from the border. Though this gentleman had a great deal more braid about him.

They made their bows. "Forgive the disturbance," the military man said in English. He was a vigorous-looking specimen, and showed no sign Crowther could see of the usual dissipation that seemed to come to military men. His skin was clear and his eye sharp. "I am Colonel Padfield, and you are Mr. Crowther, of course."

The man had a trace of a West Country burr lingering on his tongue. "I am glad to meet you, Colonel Padfield. Mrs. Clode has told us of your kindness. I am afraid she and Mrs. Westerman are in the gardens at the moment."

"No matter. I shall have the pleasure of making Mrs. Westerman's acquaintance this evening, but I was wondering if I might have a moment of your time."

Crowther nodded and gestured to the chair by the fire, but Colonel Padfield preferred to stand.

"Ticklish times," he said, after a considerable pause.

"Are they?" Crowther said, and put his fingertips together.

"Indeed they are, Mr. Crowther. You know the duke's bride is to arrive here in four days' time. There are any number of court entertainments planned. Dinners. Concerts. Hunts. Maulberg wishes to make you welcome, of course..."

"But perhaps Maulberg wishes we would not make ourselves too obvious?"

"You have it," Colonel Padfield said with a cautious smile.

Crowther rather liked the colonel's face. It was as weathered as a sailor's with the bright eyes of a man used to looking far into the distance. He looked, in spite of the braid, more like a prosperous farmer than a functionary of the court.

"May I ask, Colonel, how you came to be in Maulberg? And in the employ of the duke?"

Colonel Padfield rapped his fingers on the mantelpiece. "I stand out a little among all this magnificence, don't I?" Crowther found the steady brown eyes were examining him carefully. Then the man seemed to reach some decision and nodded to himself. "I was in the Fifth Regiment of Foot. Fought in America. My family spent their last penny to get me my Colors, but once the fighting was done, I found England had little use for my skills. I was recruited in London to drill the duke's troops—been here near two years now."

Crowther wondered if he had offended the man. "I hope you forgive my curiosity, Colonel."

Padfield shook his head. "Nothing to forgive, Mr. Crowther. Only it seems to me that here, no one asks a question or answers it without calculation, some hidden reasons of their own. I have grown suspicious of my own shadow."

"Your military concerns mean you spend a lot of time at court?"

"They shouldn't, but the duke has taken a liking to me, it seems, so I have been forced to turn courtier. However, I have no complaint. He rewards his friends handsomely and I was lucky enough to marry a clever woman. She keeps an eye on the politics for me."

His face softened as he spoke of his wife. Crowther looked away and tugged at his cuff.

"And as I seem to be interrogating you, Colonel, may I ask your opinion of the case of Mr. Clode? Rachel tells us there is a distressing lack of other suspects."

Padfield straightened. It was lucky for him that his back was so broad; so much braid on a smaller man would have made him ridiculous.

"I like Mr. and Mrs. Clode, but I am certain some madness took him at the Carnival and that he killed Lady Martesen. I hope you may throw up enough smoke and dust to confuse the authorities and steal him away back to England, but be careful. Lady Martesen was a favorite here, and no one will thank you for helping her killer to escape justice." The evenness of his tone made the verdict all the more damning. "You will be presented to the duke this evening and are invited to sup with the company. But after that . . . You have been provided with your own private dining room."

"We may have to ask some uncomfortable questions."

"Then, Mr. Crowther, you may have to face some uncomfortable answers. If you require anything, you may send for me."

He bowed and left Crowther to his papers and his thoughts.

Harriet came to a sudden halt and looked around her. "Good Lord," she said. She was apparently standing in the main square of a village. Or rather it seemed to be the drawing of a village square such as one might find in a child's storybook. A well stood in the center, complete with its own pitched slate roof. Elaborate wooden carvings of fruits and vines supported it. Four double-storied houses stood, neat sentinels at the compass points, facing the well. There was something wrong about them, something, for all their solidity, that looked false. Their half-timbering was too exact, their paint too neat, and the signs that hung from them rather too extravagant in their metalwork curls. The balconies on each house were elaborately carved and lined with flower baskets. Harriet realized with a start that she was looking at a very expensive version of rural simplicity. She turned around. The square was surrounded by a mature copse through which she had just walked with Rachel. It hid the buildings from the palace, and the palace from the buildings. It was certainly impressive, but there hung over it the strange air of falseness such as a dream takes on just before a sleeper wakes.

"The duke developed a great passion for the rural some years ago," Rachel said, watching her sister's confusion. "The courtiers would dress in peasant costumes and play skittles while the duke poured beer. Then he learned that the Prince of Condé had created a larger village complete with a working mill on his estate, and this lost its appeal. He started work on his theater to the west and these houses became workshops for some of the artists he keeps at the court."

"They do not appear to be neglected."

"He treats the artists he persuades here very well. And pays them large retainers just to live here. There is a portrait artist living there." She pointed to the north. "And in the east cottage lives a man called Julius, famous for his fine metalwork."

Harriet shook her head. "How are we ever to make sense of such a place?"

Rachel hung her head. "Harry, I know I have said terrible things in the past about your actions . . ."

"Rachel, we've spoken about this."

"We have, but I must say this, so do listen. You have a talent, Harry, for asking the right questions. And you read people the way Jocasta Bligh reads those cards of hers."

"I am so often wrong," Harriet said quietly.

"And so often right. Please do not lose your nerve now, Harry. Don't be blinded by all this glitter and show. They are still people under the powder and lace."

The sound of a door opening came from their right and to her great surprise Harriet saw Michaels appear in his shirtsleeves with his jacket over his arm.

"Thought I heard yabbering out here."

Harriet grinned, and Rachel dropped her sister's arm and ran toward him.

"Oh, Michaels!" She stood on her tiptoes to kiss his cheek. "I heard you had come!"

He blushed and patted her shoulder. "There, Mrs. Rachel. Wanted to get them to you safe."

Harriet stepped forward. "Thank goodness. I thought they had stolen you away. You have found a bed here?"

"I came to a friendly understanding with the head footman." He turned to Rachel again. "You're not eating enough, girlie. I like your friends though, my neighbors."

"They are kind, aren't they?" She raised her voice. "Mr. Al-Said? Mr. Sami? I have brought my sister to you as promised!"

The door of the southern building was opened and a man also in shirt sleeves emerged and approached them with his hands outstretched. "Mrs. Clode! I am so happy you are come. If you did not visit us, we would think ourselves lost in the wilds."

"Harriet, this is Mr. Adnan Al-Said. Mr. Al-Said, this is my sister, Mrs. Westerman."

Harriet curtsied and the gentleman bowed, still smiling. He had the same dark complexion as the duke's Turkish hussars, though none of their bristling mustaches. He moved easily and there were laughter lines around his large dark eyes. Harriet guessed he was around forty, but there was something very youthful in his manner. He looked like the sort of man who found his life interesting.

"I am delighted to meet you, Mrs. Westerman."

"You speak excellent English, Mr. Al-Said," she said.

"But of course, I learned much of my trade in London in the workshop of James Cox. My brother and I have worked all over the Continent in the last ten years. A man such as myself must be a linguist to sell to the limited number who can afford what we offer."

The name of Cox sounded vaguely familiar to Harriet, something she had read in a newspaper. "What is your trade, sir? Rachel has refused to tell me anything on our way here, other than how helpful you have been to her."

Al-Said smiled with genuine delight. "Come in and drink some tea with my brother and me, Mrs. Westerman, and you shall see all. We are makers of automata. Come. Take some relief from your worries and see our work."

"I would be delighted. Michaels?"

He shook his head, smiling. "I've already seen the wonders. I aim to wash and sleep. You know where I am if you have need of me." He turned to Rachel again. "I am glad to see you, Mrs. Clode. We will get you and your fella out of here safe if I have to tear down their castle with my bare hands."

Pegel and Florian had been debating for some hours. They agreed, repeatedly and with frequent examples, that society was viciously unfair and it was obscene that so much wealth should be enjoyed by the privileged when others went hungry. There followed an hour on Rousseau and his *Discourse on Inequality*. Pegel wondered how often young men had debated such matters in attic rooms, heated up by wine and the flourishes of their own rhetoric.

"You are lucky," Florian said, leaning forward, then twitching as his side ached. "It is much better to have been born poor. You are an honest man. My birth, the fortune I am to inherit, makes it so much harder to be honest."

Pegel almost choked on his wine. "Give it to me then! You have a try at being poor. There have been times I haven't had the blunt to feed myself. Nothing makes a man dishonest quicker than that."

"I did not mean to offend."

"You can either hand over your wealth, or promise not to say such stupid things. Choice is yours."

Florian smiled a little reluctantly. "I shan't hand it over just yet, Jacob. I mean to make use of it."

"I'd make use of it," Pegel said, drawing up his knees. "Steak every day and my own horse. No more hired nags. He can have steak every day too." He pressed his cheek onto his knees, feeling the rough texture of the material. "That might not be good for him. He can have his hay on a silver platter instead. He shall be very beautiful and I shall call him Philippe."

"No, I shall use it for the greater good. There are ways, Jacob. Things can change."

"No, they can't."

"But listen—"

Pegel suddenly jumped to his feet. "I cannot listen anymore without some food and more wine." He put his hand out. "Give me a thaler and watch the fire."

Frenzel rolled his eyes, but handed over the coin quickly enough. Pegel swung on his coat on his way to the door.

"Jacob?"

"What is it? A minute more and I die of thirst. Or starve."

He turned back. Florian seemed very slight curled up on the settee. He glanced at Pegel then back at his glass. "Do you think those men might have followed us here?"

"No." Pegel paused. "Tell you what. Key's on the table beside you. Lock yourself in while I'm gone. When I come back I'll knock three then two then one—all right, Florian?"

Frenzel swallowed and nodded and Pegel slammed the door shut behind him and headed down his rickety staircase whistling.

The two gentlemen were waiting opposite the bottom of the stairs. He walked west twenty yards and turned down a side street then waited for them to catch him up.

"Ooh, sir!" the giant said. "Your poor jaw. I'm ever so sorry—I didn't want to hit you so hard."

"Not at all, Titus," Pegel said, pulling out a purse. "Absolutely splendid job. Nothing that needs a surgeon and yet looks as dramatic as you please. Could *not* be happier!" He counted out five thick and heavy-looking coins, then paused and added a sixth and handed them to the giant.

"Ooh, now there's handsome," he said with glee as he closed his great paw around them. Pegel turned to the man in the wig and coat.

"Now you! You! What a triumph! Come here at once." Pegel clasped the man by the shoulders and kissed him firmly on each cheek. The man blushed.

"Really, merest trifle. You think I convinced the lad? Truly?"

"Convinced him? You scared the hell out of him. Brilliant performance! You must, *must* use this money to get to Berlin." He counted out the five coins, again apparently had a slight struggle with himself and added a sixth. "You are wasted, absolutely wasted in country fairs. No, not Berlin. They don't deserve you. There's a fellow called Schiller doing lovely work in

Mannheim. Excellent chap. Tell him you are sent with a recommendation from Jacob Pegel and you'll get the audience you deserve."

"Herr Friedrich Schiller? *The* Schiller? You mean it, Mr. Pegel?"

"But of course! Leave tonight, gentlemen—destiny calls!" The men grinned at each other. "Now would you be so kind as to do me one small favor before you go?"

When Pegel gave the coded knock at the door to his room he found Frenzel so pale that the growing bruises around his eye stood out like a sunset.

"Florian, you're white as a ghost. What is it?"

"I saw them," he said, dragging Pegel in and slamming the door behind him.

"Who, those men?"

"Yes, of course—from your window. You were gone so long, I looked out to see if I could catch sight of you."

Pegel held out the steaming plates he carried in front of him by way of explanation. "Mother Brown makes a splendid cutlet. You have to wait a bit this time of day."

"Never mind that. They were there in the square looking around them as if they knew we had come this far, then did not know where to find us exactly. Then you came out from the shop."

"Did they spot me?" Pegel said quickly, glancing toward the door.

"No! It was the luckiest thing, they were looking at the other side of the square as you came past. You went within an inch of them!"

"Are they still there?" Pegel said, putting down his tray and making for the window. Frenzel grabbed hold of his coat.

"Don't look! Jacob, I hate to have you think me a coward, but might I stay here tonight, just while I think what to do? There are people who should be warned."

Pegel put his hand on the young count's shoulder. "Naturally, my friend. You are welcome here. But don't you think you might see your way clear to giving a fellow a bit of a hint as to what is going on? You say you will, then it's all philosophy till my head is aching."

Frenzel turned away from him slightly. "Yes, of course. I must. I have . . . I have exposed you to some danger; it is your right to know something of this."

Pegel settled himself on the floor again. "Can we eat first?"

For the first time since the messenger had arrived at Caveley, Harriet could think of nothing but what was in front of her eyes. The tiger turned its head warily toward her, blinked, then continued to pad across the worktop until Adnan picked it up, pressed a brass pin on its side and it became still. Harriet sat with her elbows on the workbench and her chin in her hand. Entranced.

"I'd swear it was alive! It looked into my eyes. Mr. Al-Said, you are a miracle worker."

Adnan laughed and reached upward to unhook a cage from the ceiling that held two brilliantly colored, frozen birds each about the size of Harriet's thumb. "No, Mrs. Westerman, a craftsman. I learned how to make watches in Constantinople, but when the first automaton was given to the sultan by the French ambassador, I fell in love. Why have something simply tell you the hour when you can make it do all this." Harriet put out a hand and touched the sleeping tiger. Al-Said watched her. "The paws are weighted, madam. A simple trick when you know it, which gives the illusion of natural movement."

He touched something on the base of the cage and the birds began to pipe to each other, their beaks opening in time with their song and their wings flapping. Suddenly one sprang from one side of the cage to the other and Harriet laughed.

"Oh, I must have one like that for my children! They would adore it."

"They are not toys, Mrs. Westerman," he said, somewhat serious.

"Of course not, Mr. Al-Said. I have no doubt that they will treat it with the proper respect." Adnan gave a slight nod. "Were you acquainted with Lady Martesen, sir?"

He touched the base of the cage and the birds were still again. "I am not certain how to answer you, madam. The courtiers are not sure how to treat my brother and I. They like to have us here—we, as well as what we create, are ornaments to be boasted of—yet we work, and with our hands. So they flatter us and pay us well, but you will not see us at the supper table in the palace. And even if I were a prince, how many men have you met of my complexion in the palaces of Europe?"

"I have not visited many of them, Mr. Al-Said. Yet Rachel tells me you have been of great assistance to her."

"It is interesting what one hears by pretending not to listen. Lady Martesen was a clever woman, and one of several at court who thought of more than their own amusement. The duke asked us to make one of these cages of singing birds for her, and she visited us on several occasions while it was being made to discuss the design and decide on the plumage of the birds. She came often with Countess Dieth, once with Glucke, I think, and another time with Swann."

"Who is Glucke?" Harriet asked. "I have not heard his name before."

Adnan's face darkened and he bent over the cage, leaving Sami to answer in a stage whisper. He was far younger than his brother, not more than twenty-five, and so quick and light in his movements it would be as easy to think him ten years younger again.

"Herr von Glucke is a scholar and member of the duke's Privy Council, but he made the mistake of asking Adnan to create a few mechanical mice . . ."

Harriet was confused.

"For his cats!" Adnan said, with bitter emphasis. "Some respectable children *might* be allowed to handle our creations, but playthings for animals! They say he is a wise man, and a good one, but I cannot see it."

"So did Chancellor Swann come to discuss the plumage of the singing birds?" Rachel asked.

Adnan smiled briefly, as if amused by his own anger. "He did not contribute to the conversation. But I believe he was a friend of Lady Martesen; one saw them together from time to time."

"Did they have . . . some understanding?" Harriet thought she saw Adnan's cheeks blush dark pink.

"I do not think so." He placed the cage on the worktop once more, and glanced at Rachel. "You have not told your sister then, the little details that could not be written down?"

She shook her head. "She has only just arrived, and all I know, I know only from you, Mr. Al-Said."

"I dislike gossip, Mrs. Westerman," he said, "but none of us can work blindly. Lady Martesen had an understanding with the duke. Or rather she did, until such time as his betrothal was announced."

"Oh Lord," Harriet said softly. "That rather complicates matters, does it not?"

Rachel said quickly, "She was rather poor, Harriet. And the duke was generous to his . . . friends. Some years ago he was the protector of Lady Martesen's cousin, Countess Dieth. He bought her an estate when their liaison came to an end."

"Then, as I understand it, Countess Dieth thrust her cousin into the sovereign's bed," Sami said cheerfully. His elder brother looked at him severely and he dropped his gaze. Harriet held up her hand.

"Please, gentlemen, I would be most grateful if you speak openly."

Adnan cleared his throat. "So you see, it is unlikely that Chancellor Swann would ever begin an . . . understanding with Lady Martesen during the time they were visiting me here. There was no betrothal then. Lady Martesen was still the acknowledged favorite. It would be a dangerous alliance, would it not? The duke has a fearsome temper when roused, and his good opinion once lost is difficult to regain. One hears stories of those who have suffered greatly on having disappointed him. I imagine Swann and Lady Martesen were discussing politics."

"The competing marriages perhaps," Sami said with a shrug. Harriet looked toward the younger brother as he perched on the bench swinging his legs. "Some in the court—Swann included, I think—did not regard the duke's choice as the best."

Rachel was examining some of the half-painted faces that lined the walls. "You see, Harry? Mr. Al-Said knows everything. When I wanted to be sure that Daniel would be allowed books and writing materials, Mr. Al-Said told me to talk to Count Frenzel or Herr Zeller. Frenzel because he is never seen with Countess Dieth or Swann, Zeller because as a librarian of the court he understands the comfort of reading."

"I see," Harriet said. "So Mr. Al-Said, who do *you* think murdered Lady Martesen, and why?"

He shrugged. "The other reason I love my automata, Mrs. Westerman, is they do exactly what they were designed and made to do, and nothing more. People I find interesting to watch because they are the opposite. But I can only tell you what I see. I offer no conclusions."

"You sound like Crowther," Harriet said dryly.

"In such a place as this there are many alliances made and broken from day to day. Passions run high and whoever has the ear of the duke has great power. Secrets and signs are passed back and forth."

He did not look at her as he spoke, and Harriet realized that perhaps he too thought Clode a murderer, and herself and her sister deluded. She began to understand how lonely the past weeks must have been. Harriet thought of the papers from Krall. The people who knew Lady Martesen best: had they been asked the right questions? She put her chin in her hand, and looked around her.

The ground floor of the fake cottage was taken up with a light and airy workshop. At its center were two workbenches set into an L-shape. On one, small metal instruments and knives predominated; on the other, paints and brushes. The walls were stacked with papier-mâché faces, curled lengths of metal, brass cones, strange limbs, sharp crops of pointed files, and pinned to the wall from time to time, pencil drawings and watercolors, designs of cogs and levers. To Harriet's right stood a deep stack of leather notebooks, and to her left where Rachel sat with a glass of tea in her hand and a cautious smile on her lips, a tiny lathe drawn by a bow. From the ceiling hung bunches of keys and garlands of clean brass disks. The place smelled of paint and metal.

The younger Mr. Al-Said slipped down from his perch.

"Our little friend is ready, if Mrs. Westerman would like to see him."

Crowther had almost finished his pile of papers when there was the sound of a knock on the door. Again he half-expected to see Krall, and again he was disappointed. It was Graves, his cheeks flushed.

"Crowther! Where is Mrs. Westerman?"

"Still visiting these acquaintances of Mrs. Clode and touring the gardens. I understand that they are quite extensive."

"We must find her at once."

"Do you require her assistance to negotiate with Chancellor Swann?"

Graves looked angry and Crowther put down his pen. "I am sorry, Graves. What has happened?"

"Manzerotti."

"What of him?"

"He is here."

"Damn. How long has he been here?" Crowther said, reaching for his coat. "How could Rachel not tell us?"

"She cannot have known," Graves said, almost dancing with impatience. "He arrived only this morning, with a troupe of French dancers to swell the crowd of performers here for the wedding celebrations. It is a great coup for the duke to have such a star perform at his court. Swann mentioned it in passing at the end of our discussion. Said he understood we were acquainted with Manzerotti and that the monster sent his regards. Well, he did not phrase it quite like that . . ."

"Did he see your reaction?"

"I think not—he was bent over his papers again. Crowther, what will she do if she meets him?"

Crowther found himself transported back to the room in Highgate where James had died, saw Harriet's face as she bent over her husband, his hand clasped between her own and his blood pooling around her dress. She had loved her husband very much. "I should imagine she'll try very hard to kill him," he said, and took up his hat.

Krall decided he had given the English travelers enough time to settle into their luxurious cages and, his pipe still clamped between his teeth, was making his way through the rear courtyard to pay his respects when he saw two gentlemen, strangers to him, walking swiftly out into the gardens.

"Kinkel?" The head footman turned from the underling he was berating and approached, his shiny black shoes tapping out a quick tripping rhythm over the flagstones under the colonnade.

"Herr District Officer?"

Krall pointed with his pipe at the disappearing strangers.

"Milords Crowther and Graves, sir," Kinkel said. "Perhaps they go to meet Mrs. Clode and her sister. The ladies left to tour the gardens some little time ago."

Krall decided it might be better to put off introducing himself for a while. To pursue the two men would necessitate walking so fast he might disturb his digestion. The two men, both tall, angular beings, disappeared from sight and Krall sniffed and looked about him, patting his belly. The courtyard was lively. Footmen went back and forth with large trunks held between them, and another carriage, emptied of its dignitaries, was being led back out under the arch toward the stables. Krall thought it spoke well of Kinkel's organizational talents that he was able to watch this with apparent calm.

"Any other notable arrivals today, Herr Kinkel?"

The footman clasped his hands behind his back. "The Princess Theresa Anna, the Duke of Mecklenburg, a troupe of French dancers, and Manzerotti himself." Herr Kinkel allowed himself a small sigh. "Herr District Officer, I could almost wish myself a valet again if it meant the chance of dressing Manzerotti. The most beautiful clothes, such taste, and on such a handsome man. His looks are as remarkable as his talent."

Krall looked sideways at Kinkel from under his heavy brows, but it seemed the latter was too lost in admiration to note it. "We're more likely to clap a fiddler who knows a good dance tune than these opera types in Oberbach," he grunted. "Anyway, this Manzerotti ain't quite a man, is he?"

Kinkel smiled. "The best castrato singer in Europe here among us. I understand the duke is delighted."

Deep in Krall's mind another bell rang, softly; another page of English newsprint swam before his inner eye.

"Wasn't he in London when those folk were murdered at the opera house? Weren't our English guests caught up in that in some way?"

Kinkel nodded. "Yes, indeed! I believe Mrs. Westerman was at the theater the night Mademoiselle Marin was murdered on stage. It was just before her husband was killed by some French spy. Manzerotti was the toast of the season there." He stared off into the air again. "They must be acquainted. How delightful it will be, for them to meet again."

Krall sucked on his pipe. "Delightful indeed."

"Remarkable!" Harriet said softly as the cover was removed.

Adnan nodded. "I have been fortunate in the sons of my mother, Mrs. Westerman. Sami is an artist. The sculpting of the models and the painting of the features I leave all to him. I find my enthusiasm confined to giving these creatures of ours the power of movement and communication."

Harriet looked skeptical. "Did I hear you right, sir? Communication? Have you trapped some spirit in the statue?"

"No, madam, there is no—how can I put it?—ghost in this machine. But let me show you." Harriet was aware in the background of Sami almost dancing with delight and whispering to Rachel. She was profoundly glad these brothers had been here to offer her sister some refuge, some relief. Sami reminded her of her son when he had some powerful secret to share, and the thought of him both tugged on her sore heart and made her smile.

They were grouped around the figure of a young boy seated at a wooden desk and dressed like the child of a prosperous family. He would have been perhaps four years old, if living. His head was a natural confusion of blond curls and his eyes were bright blue and glimmering glass. The coloring of his face was very beautiful. Harriet expected that if she touched his cheek it would be warm. In his right hand he held a quill pen. He looked with steady contemplation at the piece of parchment in front of him. Adnan pressed some switch on the underside of the mahogany table and then moved to one side where he could observe both the automaton and Harriet's reaction.

After a momentary pause, the boy's head lifted and, blinking his eyes, he nodded at Harriet, then dipped his quill in the inkpot at his side and put his pen to the paper. His chest rose and fell and he tilted his head to one side as he began to write, then to the other. After a moment he seemed to shift the paper a little to his left and he continued, his chin now tucked into his lace cravat. There was the faintest sound of whirr and click in the air, but the illusion was remarkable. Half of Harriet's mind told her she was seeing a clever copy of life, but watching it move, breathe and concentrate, half of her protested that this was a living being. The effect was distinctly unsettling.

"This is a masterpiece," she whispered, almost expecting the child to complain of the interruption.

"We have only excelled it once," Adnan said, watching his creation with affectionate pride, "with a walking automaton—and I think we were both a little in love with her before she left us." A minute or two passed, and the little boy looked up again and moved his arm away from the page with a nod. Harriet could hear the smile in Al-Said's voice as he said, "Do examine the paper, madam."

Harriet approached the desk warily, half-expecting the child to drop the pretense and start laughing at her, and peered down at the paper before the inert little scholar.

Good afternoon, Mrs. Westerman, it read, *and welcome to my home.*

"You are both magicians, I can barely comprehend it! Are there many machines that write like this?"

"Some. We have made several that draw also. It is a matter only of examining the movements of the hand as it performs the action we wish, forward and back, right and left, then translating it onto our little brass disks."

"You make it sound easy," Harriet said wonderingly, and touched the paper face of the child with a fingertip.

"Not easy no, but in some way simple."

Sami approached the mechanism and picked up the sheet to cover it. "Adnan is too modest," he said. He ruffled the model's hair affectionately, and just as he dropped the sheet over it there came the sound of a male voice calling outside. "Oh, perhaps that is Julius," he said, and headed for the door with long strides.

"My apologies, Mrs. Westerman," Al-Said said, watching him go. "Our neighbor is a metalworker called Julius. He and Sami are good friends."

The words were only just out of his mouth when Sami returned and handed a folded sheet of paper to Harriet. "It was a message for you, Mrs. Westerman, from the palace."

Harriet took it from him and broke the seal. She felt the smile fall from her lips and her skin whiten. She thrust the note into her pocket. "I am afraid I must go at once. I hope to see you both again, gentlemen."

"Harriet, what is it?" Rachel asked. "Is Daniel well?"

"It is nothing to do with Daniel, dear. If you would stay here and finish your tea, then perhaps the gentlemen may escort you back to the palace."

"Don't be foolish, Harry. I am coming with you."

"Stay here." She said it so sharply, Rachel almost shrank away. Without trusting herself to speak further, and with only a nod to the astonished brothers, Harriet hurriedly left the house and started out along the northward path from the village.

The directions she had received were very clear. Harriet found the Temple of Apollo at the far end of the formal gardens, at the summit of an artificial hill that gave it views back across the expanse of water, hedges, and flower gardens to the pink face of the palace itself. It was a smallish, circular-domed building, the roof supported by Doric columns. Below them was a wall covered in frescoes of the Muses. She mounted the steps and found herself in its stone interior. A marble bench curved around the low wall, and taking his ease on it, a lazy smile on his lips and surrounded by various gods apparently offering him lyres and laurel wreaths, was Manzerotti. He was as beautiful as ever. She hesitated.

"Mrs. Westerman," he said, his voice light and high as a dove cooing to its mate, and nodded to his right. On the bench, just out of his reach was an open walnut case with a pair of traveling pistols in it. She did not speak but took a seat next to it and removed one of the guns. It was a beautiful object—walnut grip, full silver mount. It was cold and smooth in her hand. Heavy without being cumbersome, it felt full of its purpose. She glanced up at its owner. It was like him to own something so perfect, so lovingly made, and so deadly.

"Are we to fight a duel?" she said at last. Her voice broke in her throat; it sounded harsh and ugly in her ears.

He shook his head and looked out across the view away from the palace and toward the great forests of Maulberg swelling and falling over the hills.

"I would not challenge you, madam. There are the guns. Do with them what you will."

In her mind, during the three years since she had seen him in triumph on the stage of His Majesty's Theater, she had tried to make him ugly. She felt his sins should show in his face: this spymaster, for whoever would pay him, this monster without principle or ideal who had sown destruction then fled England, protected by her government. They had made use of him in the past too, and his work meant they were willing to let him leave trailing glory and fame, adored and mourned by the public while others who had done less than he were hung as traitors. Harriet remembered that before she had first laid eyes on Manzerotti, she had been told that a woman had gone mad with love for him and thrown herself under his coach. She had thought the story ridiculous, then having seen him and heard him sing, she had believed it. The years had made no mark on him. He was still an ideal model of a human. And with a casual command from his rosebud mouth, he had ordered the murder of her husband.

She lifted the powder flask from its niche among the velvet and unscrewed the lid, noticing that the motif of leaves and flowers from the metalwork on the gun was repeated around the shoulder of the flask. It was full. There was enough powder there to kill Manzerotti a dozen times over.

Crowther and Graves hurried along the path without any clear idea of where they were going.

"Why is he here?" Graves hissed. "We should never have agreed to keep silent!"

"It was an order from the king, Graves. Even if it was framed as a request." Crowther could move with surprising speed when he wished. Graves jogged along at his side. Crowther continued. "Manzerotti, I am sure, is here on his usual business. The marriage of a sovereign duke, a murder. The foreign powers will be interested in Maulberg at the moment. No doubt Manzerotti is working for Catherine, or Frederick of Prussia. Both, possibly. There is Mrs. Clode . . . I cannot see Mrs. Westerman."

Rachel had just emerged from one of the side paths, accompanied by a dark-complexioned man. Crowther did not take any trouble with formalities. "Where is she?"

Rachel looked between them. "She received a note and left at once. I thought she would be meeting you, Crowther."

"Manzerotti is here," Graves said, and Rachel covered her mouth with her hand. "Do you have any notion where she went?"

Rachel shook her head. Al-Said frowned. "I think I saw her take the path toward the Temple of Apollo."

"Manzerotti absolutely," Crowther said through gritted teeth. "Can you take us there, sir? As quickly as possible, please."

Al-Said hesitated, then nodded. "This way."

"I am sorry your husband was killed, Mrs. Westerman." Manzerotti still had the trick of making every phrase he spoke sound like a snatch of music in his lightly accented English. He crossed his legs and the black silk whispered. He seemed quite calm.

"Murdered. On your order." She rolled one of the lead bullets around the center of her palm.

"All wars have casualties. Your husband sank many ships, drowned many men, and was called a hero."

Harriet made a sound of disgust in her throat.

Manzerotti continued as if he had not heard her. "I regret his death now. It proved unnecessary, given my identity was already discovered, but we were not to know that then." Harriet picked up the gun again and examined the mechanism. "But then I was not the only person to order a murder, was I, Mrs. Westerman?"

She paused. "I do not know what you mean, Manzerotti."

He watched her carefully, examining her face as if he were about to draw it.

"I think the authorities would have preferred my friend Johannes delivered to them alive, yet he was given over to an angry mob. Mr. Crowther is hardly the creature to do such a thing unprompted. His blood, for the most part, runs too cold." Harriet felt herself flinch, felt it seen. "No, Mrs. Westerman, I believe it was *you* who ordered Johannes's death. Asked Crowther to perform that act of revenge on your behalf from your husband's bedside. Johannes had been my companion since childhood, you know."

Harriet tried to concentrate on the pistol, heavy in her hand, and tapped powder into the muzzle. Her hand had begun to shake a little. "He was your knife man. Did you keep a tally of the murders he did for you?"

Manzerotti nodded, his eyebrows slightly lifted as if considering what she said. "I am sure you thought the murder justified. Though I have never murdered for revenge. And that is what it was, my dear, revenge." She dropped the ball into the barrel and rammed home the charge with all her strength. "And you have killed since, I understand, with your own hand. Some evildoer in Keswick, was it not? The same man who shot Mr. Crowther?"

"I was defending my son."

"I applauded you then, as I do now, but tell me, do you think that business would have been tidied away so neatly, just as the removal of Johannes was forgiven so completely, were you not thought of as useful? I suspect England holds you in reserve."

"Your point, Manzerotti?"

"My individual talents have made me of help to many governments and many individuals; my sins have likewise been occasionally overlooked. I can be useful too, Mrs. Westerman. I might even be of help to you. What do you know of this place? These people?"

Harriet pointed the pistol at Manzerotti's chest; she could feel the pulse of blood in her brain. "We are not the same, Manzerotti."

He licked his lips. "No, my dear, I do not think we are. In fact, I seem to be betting my life on it. I only say we can be of use to each other. Now either you must shoot me, or we must come to some sort of accommodation. The world is too small to prevent us from bumping into each other from time to time."

"Why are you here? Why have you come to Maulberg?" Her mouth was dry, each word came painfully from her lips.

His eyes glittered. "One step at a time. This I shall tell you, Mrs. Westerman: I do not come for you, or Mr. Clode."

Her finger tightened on the trigger. She felt the grief of every day since James had died wash over her in a black tide, seemed to live again that moment she had watched him die, felt him torn away from her, leaving this creeping dark at her core. She closed her eyes as it fell over her, then opened them again. Manzerotti was still watching her with that close attention, but there was something in his eyes more human than she had ever seen before, some reflection of her grief. The wave retreated, she became aware of the sound of the wind breathing through the trees. He spoke again, softly, kindly.

"Where is Mr. Clode's mask, Mrs. Westerman? Ask District Officer Krall that, and he will know what to do." He tilted his head to one side. "The moment has come, my dear. You must shoot me or set that pistol down. Know only that in my mind, we are even in blood."

Harriet felt a tremor run through her arm, then she laid the gun down in its case. She felt as if the life had drained from her body and left her suddenly powerless; all she could do was listen to the leaves shivering on the branches, the distant trill and burst of the song thrush.

Manzerotti, however, seemed suddenly renewed. He slid along the bench like a child, spun the gun case toward him and as he spoke began to disassemble the charge. "Excellent, my dear. If you would just give me a moment to render this safe . . . it would be too bathetic if I blew my own leg off carrying it down the hill again." In the middle distance, Harriet could hear her sister calling her. "Ah, the cavalry approach," he added.

"Why?"

"Why what, dear lady?"

"Why must we meet?"

He blew loose powder from the muzzle and settled the gun back into its velvet seat, then flicked the box closed and snapped the catches. He did not reply until he was looking at her again. His eyes were dancing, his exhilaration obvious. "You are by far the most interesting woman in Europe, Mrs. Westerman. I am one of the most interesting men. It could not be avoided."

He stood and tucked the box under his arm. Harriet felt a hundred years older than she had when she arrived in Maulberg, but there was a sort of peace there too, rolling over her like sea fog.

"The mask?" she asked, passing her hand over her forehead.

"They all ate the same and drank the same. Mr. Clode saw visions. If he did not eat or drink the substances that gave him those visions, it might well have come through the skin. There are drugs that can be administered in such a fashion. The mask would be the best method."

She nodded and he turned to leave her. "We are not even in blood," she said in a dull voice. "We never can be." He did not turn back toward her.

"Opinions differ." He reached the top of the stairs just as Graves was running up them with Crowther at his heels. Harriet lowered her head and stared at her hands lying idle in her lap. "Mr. Graves, Mr. Crowther. Delighted to see you again. You aimed to be my saviors? How touching. It has proved unnecessary. In any case, I doubt you could have done much for me; she is far too good a shot."

Graves stood aside and Manzerotti skipped lightly down the steps, bowing briefly to Rachel as he went.

They gathered around her carefully, leaving Mr. Al-Said waiting nervously at the bottom of the steps.

Their nearness, the looks of tender concern felt suddenly oppressive. She stood up swiftly and turned away from them, looking back toward the palace. The network of garden rooms was quite plain from here, branching out from the central lawns in a regular honeycomb. She let her hand lie on the balustrade, feeling its chill against her skin. "I could not kill him," she said at last. "I had a gun pointed at his chest and I could not, though I wanted to very much." No one spoke, but Rachel joined her and placed her gloved hand over Harriet's bare fingers. Harriet closed her eyes for a moment and drew in her breath. "Did you see how beautiful he still is?"

"He makes me believe in devils, Harry."

She turned back to face Crowther, who was still pale with worry. She thought of the losses and tragedies he had endured and tried to smile at him. He only offered his arm. She took it, and for the briefest of moments rested her forehead on his shoulder. Then they walked down the steps together and Harriet paused by Mr. Al-Said. She drew a sharp metal sliver from her glove. "I do apologize, sir. I seem to have picked up one of your files as I left the workshop. Very absentminded of me."

Adnan took it from her and bowed.

Krall looked at his watch. It seemed there would no longer be an opportunity to meet the English today. The timetable at court was strictly observed. The party would need to change into court dress to be presented to Ludwig Christoph and that was a fussy business. Krall would not dine with them. He had the liberty to demand what he wanted from the kitchen at his convenience and for now he would rather stare at the plaster cherubs cavorting over his ceiling than anything else. Time enough to meet the English tomorrow.

Since the murder of Lady Martesen, Krall had been in the habit of spending two or three nights in the palace every week to consult with Chancellor Swann and place before him the latest sheafs of reports and interviews. He would have preferred his own home, his own fireside and books, but he accepted the necessity of spending more time among the elaborate flourishes of Ulrichsberg with his usual stoicism. The manner of Lady Martesen's death itched at him. A smothering was possible, but unlikely, the more he thought of it. The professor from the University of Leuchtenstadt who had performed the examination of the body was an elderly gentleman, more comfortable with the teachings of ancient Rome than anything discovered in the current century. He agreed it was a little strange there was not more blood, and *supposed* the lack of other signs of violence was unusual. He suggested that perhaps Miss Martesen had been transfixed with fear. Krall had thought the suggestion ridiculous. It was likely he showed it. He mentioned the pink foam around the woman's mouth before her body was cleaned. The professor thought it without significance. Krall suggested examining the internal organs for any sign of poison; the professor recoiled. Krall was adamant, however, and the professor summoned his assistant. That young man was at least efficient with his knife, but so in awe of his master Krall had difficulty getting any opinion from him. At last the young man whispered that there was no sign of damage that would suggest any poison he knew. He pointed out one or two features he thought out of the ordinary. Krall growled and spent some hours describing the corpse in as much detail as he could manage on paper in hopes the remarkable Mr. Crowther might supply some answer to the riddle.

There was a knock at the door, and with his gruff consent a footman entered. As always, Krall marveled at how clean the servants kept themselves. It was as if they were scrubbed on the hour. This one he knew a little. Wimpf. A good young lad who had polished his riding boots to such a shine, Krall had sworn at first they were not his. Krall suddenly realized his boots were not that clean anymore and resting on the bed. He swung them off rather guiltily. The boy grinned. Krall knew his family, had known them for years. Strange to think this shiny boy had sprung from that farm, neat as it was. He had a look of his mother about him. Hair so fair his eyebrows and lashes seemed white, and he had her trick of turning away a bit to hide a smile. Though he had the cleft chin of his father.

"What's afoot, Christian?"

The footman held out a note, and Krall took it with a look of great suspicion.

"From Mrs. Westerman, sir. With her compliments."

He harrumphed then read through the note twice. "Looks like I need to ride back to Oberbach tonight, my boy. If anyone needs me, I'll be back before the duke wakes in the morning."

The footman bowed and retreated, and Krall read the note once more. Interesting.

Harriet sat in front of the mirror while her maid arranged her hair. She studied her own face and wondered if it had changed in the course of the day. It was true that she had asked Crowther to make sure the assassin who killed her husband would die. She remembered the weight of the gun as she had it aimed at Manzerotti's chest and wondered why she had not pulled the trigger. It was not, she admitted to herself, wondering what grief she would cause to her family. It was not even for her children, and it was a lie to say, as she had said, that she simply could not. She could have done it; no hysterical passion prevented her from squeezing the trigger, no sudden regard for the sanctity of life. At first she wondered if she had simply chosen not to be the sort of person who shoots another in cold blood. Manzerotti was clever to provide the gun. If she had had the opportunity to stab him with Al-Said's file at that first moment of meeting, she might have done it, but the gun, while being a more reliable method of execution, was also slower. She had been forced to hear him speak, and had discovered in those moments that she did not loathe Manzerotti as much as she had thought. It was not his talent, the beauty of his voice, nor of his person. No, suddenly it seemed to her that hating Manzerotti was like hating storms and high-gusting squalls that cracked the masts and cast a ship about with no care for the souls it contained. And in his utter lack of compunction, in his undoubted brilliance, he was like them, in his way, magnificent.

"Dear God, what have I become?" she said to the mirror.

"Madam?" the maid said, confused, not quite understanding.

"Nothing, Dido. Fetch me my pearls." The girl padded over to the press and returned with Harriet's jewel case. She unlocked it with the key from her pocket, took out the necklace and matching eardrops, and placed them in Harriet's hands. They had been a wedding present from James, and an extravagant one it had seemed in those times before his luck and skill as a naval commander had made them rich.

There was a tap at the door and Rachel slipped into the room like a shadow. She was still wearing her day dress and Harriet remembered what she had said about avoiding dining with the court. "You look very fine, Harry."

"All Dido's work," her sister replied and caught the maid's smile in the mirror.

"Harry, do you think, if you are not too tired, I might sit with you a while by ourselves after supper?"

"Of course, my dear."

Rachel smiled briefly and retreated as quickly and quietly as she had come. Harriet frowned at her reflection.

Dido began the work of fixing yet more pearls into Harriet's hair and sighed.

"What is it, Dido?"

"Well, ma'am, I have no aim to marry myself, but it seems to me, judging from my sisters and cousins, the first months of marriage are hard enough without your husband being locked away for murder."

Harriet smoothed down her sleeves. "I can hardly remember, it seems such an age since I was a bride. Will you make sure she eats something this evening, Dido?"

"That I will, ma'am." She stepped back. "There, Mrs. Westerman. You are ready."

11

Harriet, Graves, and Crowther were gathered in the Garden Salon to meet another officer of the court whose particular business it was to introduce strangers to the nobility in general and to the duke in particular. This gentleman must be occupied indeed, for it was already a quarter after the hour that they had been asked to meet him. Harriet, as was her habit, paced back and forth, the wide silk skirts of her court dress running after her over the polished boards, while Crowther watched her. Graves, bewigged and in a splendidly embroidered coat he obviously hated, was sprawled in an armchair, admiring the view of the lawns, and entertaining them, in a glum tone of voice, with a list of some of the titles and sinecures available at the palace. Harriet suspected he was trying to stop her thinking about Manzerotti and was grateful to be distracted.

"There is an admiral here! An admiral for four pleasure boats kept on the Neckar! We now wait for the palace marshal, and there is a man maintained in Paris at great expense whose sole, *sole* duty is to write a monthly report on the fashions."

Crowther examined his fingernails. "You know, Graves, it is not my disposition to praise luxury, but Maulberg is not England. There are many noblemen with titles that will fill pages who dine on soup at home in order to wear silk at court. Status is important here. Do remember to call every man you meet Your Honor, and every woman My Lady, or Gracious Madam. To use a simpler form of address might make you an enemy for life." Graves sighed. "And stop picking at your lace, Graves! It was a great deal worse when I lived here twenty years ago. Incorrect seatings at dinner could cause a storm of pamphlets and a number of legal cases."

"Did it not send you quite mad?" Graves said.

"Graves, Crowther would never have come into company. He will have spent his days and nights in study. I can only imagine he read about the pamphlets in the newspaper."

"Mrs. Westerman is quite right," Crowther admitted. "I did dine with my professors from time to time, but they did not have the rank to indulge in such flummery, and I did not have the inclination."

Graves abandoned his attack on his lace cuffs. "Still I am curious to see His Serene Highness Ludwig Christoph, Duke of Maulberg. He must cut quite a figure if he is not dwarfed by the magnificence of his surroundings." Then he added, "Mrs. Westerman, are you really resolved to stay here with Manzerotti in residence?"

She stopped walking. "I am not happy to be here at all, Graves. But I can bear him."

"He is a fascinating man," Crowther said.

"He is a monster," Graves said, plucking at his lace again.

Harriet straightened her back. The weight of her gown felt as if it would drag her to her knees.

"Graves, you have seen enough of the anatomical curiosities Crowther has collected to know there is no contradiction between his monstrosity and Crowther's fascination."

The door opened, and a rather wizened-looking gentleman made his slow way toward them with the aid of a pair of ebony canes. He introduced himself, though Harriet got a little lost in the list of titles. He produced a watch, enameled with the arms of Maulberg, and tapped it unhappily.

"I must take you in almost immediately! Well, we must do what we can in the minutes that are left to us. Though," he squeezed his eyes almost shut, "I would normally insist on an hour at least. We have our ways in Maulberg, and we expect them to be honored. Forgive my lateness. The new duchess means we have many strangers in court, and they must be accommodated and introduced in the proper fashion. Now a few words on the correct form for meeting the duke and how to address His Highness . . ."

The twenty minutes that followed were the longest in Harriet's life.

As Harriet entered the ballroom on Graves's arm, with Crowther a pace behind them, she caught her breath. The long hall was lit by a series of magnificent crystal chandeliers, great fountains of light. Above them the ceiling curved, its height amplified by trompe l'oeil that made the walls into the walls of temples, reaching up in romantic pediments and balconies into a false sky of pinks and reds full of angels. The polished floors glistened. The English party found themselves surrounded with men and women in the full costume of the Ulrichsberg court. Every variety of blue and gold was worn, skirts of huge width and flounces, hair piled high and padded, white faces, rouged and painted, in the French fashion, pursed lips. Gold lace, jewels at every neck and waist. It was an assault on the senses that left Harriet's throat rather dry. There was, she was happy to see, no sign of Manzerotti in the crowd.

It seemed there was a conscious effort among the thirty or forty ladies and gentlemen present to ignore them, though Harriet felt any number of eyes drift over them and away. They were prepared for this reception; until they were presented to the duke himself they did not quite exist in the room, so it was only right their presence should be unacknowledged. In some ways it was preferable to the occasions when Harriet had entered some gathering and found the conversation come to a halt. The air was heavy with florid scents. A way seemed to clear in front of them. The gentlemen and ladies drifted aside, a lazy embroidered and powdered parting of the waves, or like fantastically patterned theater drapes opening to reveal the stage at the far end of the room.

It was an impressive setting. A pair of pink marble columns reached from a raised dais to a small palisaded balcony. Under it, a plumed canopy, with red and gold drapery, flowed down to frame a slight, elegant gentleman in his late thirties sitting cross-legged in a gilt armchair. There was a woman seated on a stool beside him. Her hair was dressed very high and crowned with ostrich feathers, and her sleeves so flounced they almost obscured the diamonds at her wrist. She was a handsome woman, her slender figure much like Harriet's own, and though she was certainly not in the first flush of youth, her features were so finely sculpted one could still call her beautiful. Harriet felt the woman's assessing gaze on her and lowered her eyes.

The duke continued to pet his dog as they walked toward him. The officer of introduction indicated they should wait some paces from him and himself scuttled up on his sticks like a spider to the duke's side and whispered in his ear. The duke glanced up and smiled. Harriet at once swept as deep a curtsey as she could manage and held the pose. Crowther and Graves slid into similarly respectful bows. Eventually she heard the command to rise.

The duke stood and approached, swaying a little from side to side as if hearing some invisible music and with the spaniel in his arms. His heels clicked on the floor. "Mrs. Westerman, a delight to meet you."

Harriet kept her eyes lowered. The duke's shoes were patterned with seed pearls on scarlet velvet. "An honor, Your Highness."

He laughed. The sound was musical but not entirely pleasant. "I see dear Carlton has been instructing you well. You may look at me now, dear, and talk to me just like a real person, as the formalities are dealt with."

She did. His Serene Highness Ludwig Christoph, Duke of Maulberg, was a rather mild-looking man with large hazel eyes and thin lips. His skin was very white with powder. Harriet had expected him to resemble an English squire for some reason, but Ludwig Christoph would have looked like a delicate bloom next to a hunting, drinking, and dining Englishman, yet there was great confidence in his bearing. His fingers, clasped around the panting flanks of his spaniel, working into its soft fur, were long and thin. She could imagine them exerting great pressure when they wished.

"So you wish to release my prisoner, you and your Mr. Crowther?" He turned to Crowther. "Is it true what they tell me, that you are in fact a baron, yet refuse to make use of the title and go about with a common name?"

"It is, sire."

"Well, we can see straight away that you are no German!" The ladies and gentlemen around the room laughed.

"We are convinced of Mr. Clode's innocence, sire," Harriet said softly, "and hope to convince you too."

The duke tilted his head. "Do you now, Mrs. Westerman? I suppose you would not have come so far or so fast with any other intention. Some opinions, such as those of my friend Countess Dieth, are against you." He nodded slightly in the direction of the woman on the dais, then continued, "Mr. Clode's loss of memory seems a little convenient, does it not?"

"Convenient to the true murderer also," Harriet replied.

The duke looked amused. "Your reputation as an interesting sort of person is justified, I see. You are welcome to Maulberg, madam." The eyes hardened. "But remember, Lady Martesen was our friend. Whoever killed her will suffer for it, whosoever that might be." He raised his voice slightly. "We wish it to be known that Mrs. Westerman and her party are to be given every assistance. Their requests are our requests. Their questions, our questions."

There was a whispering shush as the company bowed or curtseyed and their silks slid over the tessellated hardwood floors. The duke leaned toward Harriet. "There, I think that went rather well."

Another meal cleared away, another pair of wine bottles empty on the floor. Pegel was silent and stared into the fire for a long while before he spoke.

"Secret societies, Florian? The Freemasons are one thing—good works and fellowship—but you seem to be talking about something else."

Florian was bent over his glass. "Suppose, Jacob, just suppose there was a group of men and women—enlightened, ready to lead the rest, with faithful followers across Europe. Things could change. We could build a new world. A fairer world."

Pegel shook his head slowly. "Such things cannot be. A rational society, built on learning not mysticism such as you describe..."

"They can! Ready to free the people! Ready in time to sweep away privileges of birth, the tyranny of property, the black night of religious superstition..."

Pegel lifted his hands. "Florian! Enough! It cannot exist. It would be a handful of powerless dreamers. No one in any position of power would join such an organization."

"There are intelligent men in positions of power. Idealists! The correctness of these arguments cannot be disputed. They can see the truth." The twisting light from the fire fell on the injured side of his face. He still looked perfect in the imperfect light, warmed by his own enthusiasms. "The leaders will guide, lead, educate. They will create a better world for us all. What better cause can a man serve?"

Jacob was almost shouting. "I know there could be no better cause! No greater glory in devoting oneself to such ends. But no such society could ever exist. Never. It is impossible."

Florian leaned toward him, his face glowing like a mystic's. "Oh, Jacob. It already does."

Pegel gasped and opened his eyes wide. Internally he sighed, thinking, Of course it does, you little fool. You are the Minervals, and I am come here to blow you all to kingdom come.

Manzerotti made his appearance as they went in to supper and was immediately surrounded by a number of admirers. As Harriet was guided to her place she heard his laugh and felt a lurch of anger. For a moment she wished she had shot him; she glanced in his direction and found he was looking straight at her. She felt her cheeks redden as if she had spoken her wish out loud. Harriet found herself seated a good distance from Manzerotti, between Colonel Padfield and a gentleman of the court named Frenzel. Krall was nowhere to be seen. Frenzel greeted her in an affable manner and easy French, but saying he was certain she would enjoy conversing in her own tongue, left her to Colonel Padfield. Having thanked the latter for his kindness to her sister, Harriet would have been content to talk about the floods that were at last retreating across the Holy Roman Empire rather than continue to think on recent horrors, but Colonel Padfield seemed distracted. He was constantly glancing toward a handsome young woman on the opposite side of the table who seemed to be chatting happily to a young man in uniform at her side.

"Who is that lady, Colonel?" Harriet said at last.

He started and blushed a little. "My wife, Mrs. Westerman."

"I should be glad to know her. Rachel tells me she has been very kind to her."

"She *is* kind," said the Colonel with sudden emphasis. "And I should have been lost without her here. Madam, do you think we should judge people because of where they come from, because they might have kept some secrets from us?"

Harriet thought of some of the people whom she had met in the last years who had concealed their origins, lied to keep a place in the world. She weighed her words very carefully. "I think we should be very slow to judge others, Colonel. I once knew a lady who was brought up very harshly, and if her history were generally known it would have caused great scandal. I thought her an excellent woman and was proud to know her." She noticed Mrs. Padfield glance toward them as she spoke, then quickly back to her companion. "I was shocked when this lady told me her history. But also touched that she trusted me with her confidence."

The Colonel let out a long sigh. "I am glad you have come to Maulberg, Mrs. Westerman." He lifted his head and his glass toward his wife and Harriet saw the look returned. The lady's thin shoulders seemed to relax a fraction before she returned her attention to her neighbor.

"Madam Westerman, I have been wondering what conversation to offer you." Harriet realized the gentleman on her other side was speaking to her. "Usually one asks visitors to the court of their impressions of Maulberg . . ." He had exactly the right sort of amused but sorry smile on his face as he spoke. "But I dare not ask that of you." She smiled at him in turn. He was perhaps some ten years older than herself, nearer fifty than forty, his coloring pale and his eyes framed with a network of thin lines.

"Do you dine at court often, Count?" she asked.

"Oh, an excellent notion, I shall talk about myself. Yes, since I took a position with the duke, before last year hardly at all. I have an estate which I hold *unmittelbar* an hour's ride away. I return there often." He saw her confusion. "*Unmittelbar*. My estate lies entirely *within* Maulberg, but I am not subject to the duke. In my more limited territory I have the same power as he does."

"I confess I find the complexities of the country confusing."

"As Mr. Voltaire said, the Holy Roman Empire is neither Holy, Roman, nor an empire. We are a family, but like most families more often at war with each other than with outsiders. But we find you equally difficult to understand. Your people seem to think they are all kings, the judges lords, and the king himself your servant."

"Our people value their freedom."

"They abuse it. A glance at your newspapers tell us that." He tutted a little.

"No, matters are a great deal better organized on the Continent. Of course, we have our little philosophers who like to rail against the established order, but they will not triumph. Here and in France the people know their place. It is better so."

Harriet began to find his smile less pleasing than she had at first thought, then noticed that a young gentleman on the opposite side of the table had been listening intently. It was the major who had ridden with them from the border. He wore a similar uniform to that of Colonel Padfield and rapped his fingers on the table as he spoke.

"Indeed? And when we have crushed the will out of the people, and squeezed out every thaler from their pockets, who will pay for your toys then, Frenzel?"

He shrugged and waved his fork. "They do breed, Major Auwerk."

Harriet believed the major was about to say something else, but she noticed him glance along the table toward a much older man; thin and bent, she thought he looked a little like Crowther might have become, had she not dragged him into the sunlight. He was looking very steadily at Major Auwerk, and though his expression seemed neutral, the younger man only bit his lip and summoned his glass from the footman behind him.

Harriet turned to the plate in front of her. It was silver-gilt, with the arms of Maulberg emblazoned on it. She saw the shadow of her face reflected there among the fragments of rich food and wondered again how she could possibly come to an understanding of those people. She felt, heavily, that Rachel's trust in her was misplaced.

Pegel had not been able to get any more details of the secret society. Instead, Florian instructed him on the glories of Rousseau till Pegel felt like throwing himself into the fire. It was deep in the night when Florian finally let himself lie down on the couch, but if the drink hadn't exhausted him, his own rhetoric had. He was snoring lightly even before Pegel had thrown a blanket over him. Pegel himself had no intention of sleeping. It only took a moment to go through Frenzel's satchel and he now sat cross-legged on the floor and considered. Three volumes lay on the boards in front of him, and in front of each was a sheet of paper with a crease to show it had been folded once and placed into the book. On each was a nonsense stream of letters, grouped into little islands of five. There was also a small medallion with an owl embossed on one side. With its claws it held open a book with *PMCV* stamped across the pages.

With a sigh Pegel got to his feet. The bag, with its less interesting content returned to it, and the medallion slid once more into its lining, he placed by Frenzel's head. The books and codes he took to the desk by the window and lit a candle. Having sniffed and shaken each sheet, and held it up to the light, he set about making his copies, carefully noting the titles of each book and the page where the note was hidden. The copies made, the books and their contents were returned to the satchel.

Frenzel still snored, and Jacob smiled at him, then reached down and smoothed one lock of blond hair away from his face. A very promising beginning, and now dawn had become day.

PART III

12

Harriet woke early. It seemed to take her a strangely long time to remember where she was and why. Then the impressions of the previous day rushed over her and she lay back down in her bed with a groan.

Her maid arrived to help her dress.

"You are being looked after, Dido?" Harriet asked as the little maid smoothed her petticoats down.

"Yes, bless you, ma'am," she said. "We have a little trouble understanding each other, but they are helpful enough and everything is to hand. Couple of them have enough English to chat." She paused to pull Harriet's laces tight at her back. "Everyone speaks nicely of Mrs. Clode. Seems they've taken quite a liking to her below stairs, as far as I can tell."

Harriet felt Dido's quick fingers at the ties. "Have you ever left England before, Dido?"

"Never, ma'am. Though I am glad to have had the chance now! William is so full of stories of the time he served with your husband. Now I shall have some stories of my own." She pursed her lips and went to gather Harriet's riding dress in her arms. The heavy green fabric dwarfed her. "Now, I understand this will do nicely during the day." Harriet allowed herself to be pinned and smoothed into the folds. It was more comfortable than court dress, at any rate. "They are a superstitious lot though."

"Indeed?"

"Yes, full of all sorts of ghost stories. If I believed half of it, I swear I wouldn't sleep at night. Not enough work to do, I believe. Can you imagine Mrs. Heathcote's face if she found me and Cook trying to talk to spirits and paying our wages to folks who claimed powers in that way? Lord, they'd hear the shrieks in Thornleigh Hall." Harriet grinned. "There, ma'am. If you will just tidy your hair a little while I fetch your coffee, you will do us credit."

———————

Florian groaned and Pegel saw his arms stretching from his perch by the window.

"What is the time?"

Pegel glanced out at the clock in the market square. "Something after ten. Are you hungry? Shall we eat?"

Florian pulled himself into a sitting position and ran his fingers through his hair. "No, no. I have . . . I have business I must attend to. How is your jaw?"

"Stiff, but it still works. What of your ribs?"

Florian got to his feet and pressed his hand gingerly to his side. "Sore, but I am whole, I think. Will you attend lectures today?"

Pegel shook his head. "No, my head is too swollen with your talk to deal with the professor. I will work here."

Florian buttoned his waistcoat, wincing, then picked up his coat. "Will you be here this afternoon? I still have questions about your formula, if I may call on you?" There was a slight, awkward formality in his tone.

"Just as you wish. I shall probably be here. Throw a rock at the window, if you want to save yourself the climb. If I'm here, I shall hear it and call down to you."

"Very well." Florian picked up his satchel and fitted it over his shoulder. "Jacob . . . ?"

"Hmm?" Pegel said, already apparently engrossed by the papers on his desk.

"Thank you."

Pegel raised his hand in a lazy farewell, and Florian left the room. Jacob heard his steps disappearing down the stairs, then went to the side of his window and looked out. Florian emerged into the square, hesitated, and then headed north.

"Home rather than the lecture hall, hey?" Pegel said to himself, then grabbed up his coat and tripped off in pursuit.

It was not that Pegel went in disguise, but rather he had the talent to assume a shape in the air that seemed to take up no room in it. He waited in the shadows opposite Florian's lodgings, a straw in his mouth and his hands in his pockets, and no one paid any mind to him. He might have been one of the paintings on the town hall watching the people move around him and no one ever looking up and across. Florian's rooms were in a far nicer corner of Leuchtenstadt than Pegel's. But then Florian was nobility, and though he might not seem to like the system of nobility, he took the money, it seemed, and spent it. It was almost half an hour before the door opened again and a young woman stepped out into the road. She wore the neat linen and slightly harried expression of a maid asked to abandon her duties when she had not time enough as it was to complete them. She looked up and down the street. Still with his straw and his slouch, Pegel emerged from the shadows and joined the stream of people passing, just glancing up as he got close to her.

"You there!"

He paused and touched the brim of his hat. "All right there, miss? Cold again, ain't it?"

"Can you read?"

"My name and numbers."

She put a folded note into his hand. "Now this is to go to Mr. Wilhelm Gray, he's a lawyer at the university. You're to take it to him and wait for a reply. Bring it straight back and there'll be a fair reward for it."

Pegel considered telling her he'd do it for a kiss. But she'd start looking at him then whether she'd pay the price or no. Better to resist the temptation to make conversation for now. Wilhelm Gray, was it? He'd seen him around. A wizened-faced old bird who had a fondness for folding lavender into his worn cloak and a liking for his more fresh-faced young students. Pegel touched his hat and pocketed the note. It was time to summon his irregular little army of urchins. If this went the way he thought it might, he'd need extra feet and extra hands to track the little rabbits home. As soon as he turned the corner he pulled the note out of his pocket and looked at it more closely. Sealed. Well, Florian was not a complete fool.

13

Krall returned to the palace, cold from his early ride but content, and made his way at once to Chancellor Swann with Clode's Carnival mask wrapped in linen in his hands. He found the chancellor with the duke and a mass of papers. There was a harpsichord in the room, and as was his custom, the duke was signing his papers to its accompaniment. In the other corner of the room the Countess Dieth sat at a small table, amusing herself, it seemed, playing games of Patience. Krall made his bow and readied himself to wait until business was concluded, but the duke had seen the package in his hands and, it appeared, wanted distraction.

"What do you have there, Krall?" It was a point of pride among his people that their duke spoke the local dialect as fluently as they. He used it now.

"Mr. Clode's Carnival mask, sire," he replied.

The duke put down his pen and beckoned Krall over. Krall approached, and as he unwrapped the mask explained the theory that it had been used to drug Mr. Clode in some way, as suggested in Mrs. Westerman's note.

The duke smiled broadly. "Fascinating! How do you propose to test the theory?"

"I thought to ask for a volunteer from among the servants, and observe the results, sire."

The duke sat back in his chair. "Oh, what an excellent idea! I should like to see that. May we try it at once?"

The music stopped and Krall glanced toward the musician. Turning from the keyboard was an extremely handsome man Krall did not recognize.

"With your permission, sire," the man said in precise German.

"What is it, Manzerotti?"

"If the mask were drugged, its effects may have weakened over time. It might be better to experiment on a child. I think I know where one might be found at this time."

The duke crossed his legs. "Thank you, Manzerotti. Fetch it at once. Countess Dieth? Would you be so kind as to gather our English friends? It was Mrs. Westerman's suggestion, after all. She should see it tried."

The lady stood up. "It is nonsense. You should have executed that monstrous Englishman a month ago."

"Now, now, my dear," the duke said very softly. "Indulge me."

From the moment they were introduced, Harriet realized Krall was cut of a very different cloth from the other people she had met at court so far. He looked, Harriet realized, a little like Michaels, though he was clean shaven. His face was deeply lined, a granite escarpment weathered and harried by the elements, and his coat was far more workaday than any others worn at court. She could hardly imagine him moving among them. He was a charcoal sketch among the heavy oils around him. She found she was being studied in her turn, though with a friendly eye.

The Countess Dieth had hardly shared a word with them on their walk through the mirrored and shining corridors of the palace. She had simply told them to come with her. Rachel had shaken her head, saying she needed to rest, but Graves, Crowther, and Harriet had followed in her silken wake, though Harriet saw signs of irritation on both their faces. Chancellor Swann was standing by the desk when they entered and bowed politely to them. Countess Dieth immediately retook her seat at the card table and turned away from them all.

The duke sat on a small daybed and indicated the area of carpet in front of the marble fireplace with a jeweled hand. He had his spaniel on his lap again. "If you would just stand there . . . excellent. Now we shall all have a perfect view. Continue, Krall."

Krall bowed a little awkwardly, as if the movement did not come naturally to him. The duke began to feed his dog sweetmeats from between his own lips. Harriet looked around her. After the great hall, this room seemed almost domestic. Classical drapery, but it had some lightness to it. If Harriet had chosen to fill the ceiling of the Long Salon in Caveley with putti and fill the walls with oil paintings, it might look something like this.

"By your leave, sire." Krall pushed open a door just behind him, and from the antechamber beyond entered a young woman, fashionably if not richly dressed, who led by the hand a little girl of some seven or eight years of age.

"Perfect," the duke said. The countess looked up briefly from her cards, shuddered, and turned away. Krall led the little girl into the middle of the room then turned to a side table and picked up a small bundle. He folded back the material and Harriet saw the fixed open grin of the Carnival mask for the first time. She started forward, but felt Crowther's hand on her arm.

"But Crowther—a child!" she whispered.

He shook his head.

Krall spoke; his French was not as fluent as his English—he sounded awkward, like a bad actor. "Sire, this young lady is Elizabeta, daughter to one of Monsieur Rapinat's dancers in the corps de ballet."

The duke peered at the child for a moment. "Probably the fruit of Mr. Rapinat's loins. Continue."

The duke's French was perfect, of course, and the mother flushed, and Krall frowned very briefly, but he addressed the child. "Elizabeta, we will play a game. You will put on this mask. It is magic and you will see . . . fairies and many, many wonderful things. You may feel a little unusual, but don't worry. There's a good girl."

"Sire . . ." Harriet said. "Surely there is some other way—"

"Shush, now, Mrs. Westerman," the duke said, raising a finger. "We have considered the matter and will not be questioned further." His voice was a deliberate singsong.

The mask was far too big for Elizabeta's face. Krall helped her tie the ribbons behind her head, but she still had to hold it in place with one small hand on the chin. It was an unsettling sight, the little body of the child in her pretty, gauzy pink dress, her feet turned out neatly at right angles to each other as if she were a dancer herself, then that huge mask with its wide knowing grin. It seemed almost obscene.

"It smells funny!" Her voice was high and nervous, muffled behind the wide wooden grin.

Krall laid one hand on her shoulder, watching her very closely. "That is part of the magic."

"I cannot see very well."

"Be patient, my child."

The duke shrugged and began to play with his dog again. Then the little girl's chest began to rise and fall more quickly. "Oh, my heart is thumping so!"

Krall swiftly undid the ribbons, and, touching only the edges of the mask, he laid it carefully to one side. Harriet heard Graves exclaim under his breath. The child's eyes seemed to have swollen in her head and her face was flushed.

"How are you now, Elizabeta?" Krall asked.

She tilted her head on one side and blinked repeatedly. She seemed to be breathing through her mouth. Her lips were parted. Something in the air in the empty center of the room seemed to fascinate her. Harriet was reminded of her housekeeper's cat chasing shadows in the salon at Caveley. Elizabeta lifted her right hand and tried, apparently, to catch at whatever she saw. It seemed to evade her grasp and she laughed. Whatever the girl was watching fell to the floor and she pounced on it, landing lightly on her knees. The rug was woven with tendrils and flowers. Elizabeta followed them with her fingers, then gasped and lifted her head.

"What do you see?" Krall asked.

"The flowers are growing, of course!" she said, without looking at him. "See, sir, they are climbing right up to the ceiling. Maman, Maman, do you see?" Her mother covered her mouth. "I never saw flowers grow so fast before! How I wish they were always like this!"

Harriet noticed out of the corner of her eye that the countess was watching now. The duke looked greatly amused.

"Do you see the fairies approach, Elizabeta?" Krall said.

She turned her head this way and that, then a sudden understanding came over her features. "Why, they are everywhere!"

"I think the Fairy King wishes to dance with you," Krall said.

Elizabeta suddenly blushed, then stood and took a number of light steps toward Graves and with a deep curtsey held out her hand.

Graves looked at his companions. Crowther gave a tiny nod of his head, and Graves took the little girl's fingers between his own and bowed.

"How does the Fairy King look, Elizabeta?" Krall asked.

"He is handsome and has a golden crown!" Graves lifted the girl's hand

and she skipped forward, lifting and dropping her arms, then returning and taking his hand again, they moved forward together. She spun again and returned to him. Graves tried to mirror her steps, but having none of her natural grace, nor the advantage of hearing whatever orchestra was playing to the child he was stiff and unnatural.

"I thought the King of the Fairies would dance beautifully!" the child said and the duke laughed. Graves frowned and the child saw it. "Oh, I have made him angry! His eyes are all red. Oh, they glow like the devil's!" Graves smiled and bowed. "He shall eat me!"

The duke began to laugh, but the child looked terrified. Her mother made a whimpering noise and tried to move forward, but Krall put out his hand to stop her. Graves looked up at Harriet desperately. Harriet thought for a moment then undid the ribbon at her neck and handed it to him. From it hung a paste flower of brilliants. She had worn it at Rachel's wedding. Graves took it and handed it at once to the little girl with a bow. She stopped crying at once and stared at it openmouthed. "He has forgiven me." She dropped to her knees again and taking Graves's hand, kissed his knuckles with absolute reverence.

The duke was still shaking with amusement. The little girl dropped Graves's hand and became quiet. Graves backed away a little.

"Elizabeta?"

She was tracing the flowers in and above the carpet once more. The Fairy King seemed forgotten.

"I'm dizzy," she said, her voice a little slurred. "I would like to go to sleep now."

Krall dropped his hold on the mother's wrist and the young woman swept forward, gathered the child up in her arms, and throwing a dark look at Krall, left the room. The duke managed to control his laughter.

"Well, whatever the effect of that mask, it did not mask her judgment of the dancing of milord Graves! Swanny, a purse for the mother and child, with our sincere thanks."

"Of course, Your Highness."

"I almost wish to see the fairies myself. Interesting. So Krall, is the mask a trap for djinns? Is it engraved with the Seal of Solomon?"

"It seems it is drugged, sire, as Mrs. Westerman suggested."

The Countess Dieth had got to her feet. "The child was coached! It is a lie to make you release Clode, sire!"

The duke had hold of his spaniel's forepaws and was making her dance back and forth on his lap. "Would you like to try the mask yourself, Countess? No?" The countess was silent. "I thought not. No, I do not think the child was coached. Poor Mr. Clode." He set the dog onto the floor and its claws skittered on the parquet as it retreated beneath the daybed. "Do you think someone might have wished to play a joke on Mr. Clode? Then perhaps the drug sent him mad, he killed Lady Martesen, and in horror at what he had done, tried to do away with himself. There. I have it."

Krall stroked his chin. "It seemed to me, sire, that Clode was still in some sort of dream when I first talked to him."

"So? Krall, are you doing damage to my theory? I was so proud." He examined them all in turn. "We could then say the death was accidental and our English friends could go home."

"I mean, sire, that if he realized what he had done, then cut his wrists, that would suggest his brain had cleared. But it had not. This was a murder of Lady Martesen and an attempt to murder Mr. Clode to conceal it."

"Oh dear, Krall. You doubt Clode's guilt, I see." The duke turned to Harriet and Crowther. "Hardly a day at the palace and already you have shaken Krall's faith. What a breath of fresh air and new thinking you are!"

Countess Dieth's voice shook slightly. "Ludwig, if Clode did not kill Agatha, then who did?"

The duke did not reply, but merely looked up at Krall. The district officer rocked on his heels. "I do not know who might have wanted Lady Martesen dead, sire."

"Krall, do you know you remind me of my uncle at times. Do you see how he did that, Countess? He asked his sovereign if he knows anything of the murder, but without *actually* asking!"

"Very crafty, sire," the countess replied. Her voice sounded hollow, defeated.

The duke frowned. "I have no idea, Herr District Officer, of anyone who might have wished her harm. Lady Martesen was well liked at court."

Krall bowed.

"Had her position at court not altered recently, sire?" Harriet said quietly.

The duke's smile became less friendly. "What a character you are, madam. It had. But Agatha was not a jealous woman. My betrothed had nothing to fear from her, nor had Agatha anything to fear by my marriage." Harriet looked at the floor.

The duke laced his fingers together and examined his knuckles. "So someone has been fooling us. How embarrassing. And not very nice to welcome our bride with a murderer running about." The room was silent but for the panting of the little dog under the daybed. Crowther stepped forward and bowed. "You may speak, Mr. Crowther. Do so carefully."

"Perhaps, sire, it might be best to keep the effects of the mask confidential at the moment. If whoever drugged it is convinced his secret is safe, he may be careless, reveal some sign of his identity."

"It would be embarrassing for Maulberg too, Mr. Crowther, as I am sure you realize, to release Clode the very second you arrive. Still. The little girl was very suggestible. Perhaps someone suggested the killing to Mr. Clode." He licked his lips. "But even in that case the mystery remains." No one spoke. "No word of advice, Countess? Chancellor Swann? You are both normally so full of helpful suggestions." The countess's face reddened under her powder as if she had been struck, but she did not speak. "Very well. We have just welcomed Mrs. Westerman and Mr. Crowther to our court. We wish our new friends to investigate these matters. For the time being, until matters become more clear, Mr. Clode will remain at Castle Grenzhow. Krall knows I think him very capable, but I am sure he would be glad of assistance in such a matter. Wouldn't you, Krall?"

"Very glad, sire."

The duke turned toward Harriet. "But perhaps my request alone might not be enough to hold you. I add to it that of your own king. Would you like to see the letter? The British ambassador brought it along with him this morning. Dear Lord, that man wears ugly shoes."

Harriet's throat grew rather dry. "Sire, your request alone would be enough to hold us here."

A corner of the duke's mouth lifted. "Clever girl. You shall have a copy of the letter in any case, to enjoy seeing your name bandied about in the correspondence of monarchs. See to it, Swanny." He looked carefully at his chancellor. "Are you cross I hadn't told you about my correspondence with Cousin George? Do not look so put out, my dear Swann. Am I not allowed a secret too from time to time?"

Swann bowed.

"What next, Swann? I assume I have a mountain of papers to look through?"

"There are a number of matters, sire."

"Very well. Krall, I assume from your horrible coat you do not intend to eat at our table this afternoon?"

"I wish to continue my attempts to discover the history of this mask, sire."

"You do work hard! You have every assistance?"

He bowed.

The duke looked about him. "Swanny, have some of the new musicians come in and play while we go through the papers, will you? Such excitement, I feel in need of a little calm."

14

Harriet all but fled the room and not until they were a hundred feet of gallery away did she speak. "Will you come to the castle, Crowther?"

"If you will excuse me, I think I should serve Clode better by consulting about the provenance of the drug on the mask."

"In other words you do not think you can stand another tearful reunion so soon," Graves said under his breath. Harriet smiled then found herself looking around guiltily. Something in the atmosphere of the palace made her fear she was in danger of being constantly overheard.

"What did you say to Krall as we left? He looked as if you had struck him," Graves asked Crowther. Harriet realized he was talking in low tones as well. Only a day and the palace had them fearing their own shadows.

"After asking him to come to our private room at his first opportunity, I said, 'I believe she drowned,' of course. What else would I say?"

"Social pleasantries have never been your strong suit, have they, Crowther?" Harriet said with a sigh. "Well, that explains the poor man's expression."

"At least I have not interrogated any despots about their amours today, Mrs. Westerman."

She grimaced. Their footsteps echoed up the corridor, which was lined with yet more classical statuary. Muses, heroes, and a smattering of dukes observed them as they passed. The Muses looked at them slyly over their shoulders. The heroes stared boldly and the dukes looked down their noses. "A fair point. Why did you not tell the duke about the manner of Lady Martesen's death?"

"I feared he might fetch in another child to demonstrate," Crowther said simply.

Graves shook his head. "That man almost frightens me."

"He is an absolute ruler, Mr. Graves. He has been obeyed his entire life.

Perhaps it is not surprising to find that produces a slightly . . . warping effect. Give Mr. Clode my best wishes." He nodded to them as if he intended to leave their side, but she put out her hand.

"Crowther, Rachel has been worried about Daniel. The state of his mind. This drug, do you think the effects might be long lasting?"

He paused for a moment, putting his weight onto his cane, his long fingers spread out over its silver head, and looked at their faces, all concern. "Not the drug itself, I think, given what Rachel has said. But you have been under fire in battle, Mrs. Westerman."

"A number of times on my husband's ships."

"So you have seen the effects, not on the body, but on the mind such extremes of fear and confusion can have?"

"More often than I would like. I think I understand you, Crowther."

"I fear I do not," Graves said.

"The effects of battle are cruel enough, Graves, but they are at least both understandable and shared. Even so, they can haunt men for years. Daniel's visions were his alone and included the bizarre murder of a young woman, the cutting of his own wrists, and being arrested."

"What do you advise, sir?" Graves's voice was low and serious.

"That we find out the truth behind his visions. We are haunted by what we do not understand."

"Then we shall. Come, Mrs. Westerman. Let us go and find our captured prince." Graves offered her his arm, Harriet took it, and they disappeared up the corridor. Crowther watched them go, then turned to search out his quarry.

He found Manzerotti at play in the rooms adjoining the ballroom that had been set aside for cards. The castrato noticed Crowther and at once handed his cards to a gentleman behind him and spoke to his companions. His soft cooing voice made each word a pearl.

"My nemesis approaches, ladies!" His French was as perfect as his English. The three women, middle-aged, heavily rouged and jeweled, hid their automatic smiles behind their fans. "Please allow the Comte de Grième to take my place among you."

Crowther did not smile, but simply watched Manzerotti get up from his chair and bow the count into his place with the same interest with which he would watch an exotic animal. He could not help thinking of the muscles and tendons of the body when he observed Manzerotti in motion; his physical grace was astonishing. The air seemed to ripple and part for him, allowing him to move through the world without the effort other mortals needed to shift their bodies from place to place. When he approached and made his bow, and Crowther returned it, Crowther felt his own body to be an inferior machine, unlubricated and fixed with cogs and gears more clumsily wrought.

"Mr. Crowther, have you had leisure to examine His Highness's Cabinet of Curiosities? Of course not. Let us have a look at them together."

Crowther followed him without a word through a set of heavy double doors into a room, octagonal in shape and lit from above by a glass roof and a series of high windows. The air tasted unused. Against each wall was a display case, paneled over with glass at its top, and set with narrow drawers below. Crowther organized his anatomical samples in something similar in his house at Hartswood, but his cabinet was a far more utilitarian object. These seven cabinets were wonders in themselves. Each was inlayed with mother of pearl into a themed profusion of life. The example to Crowther's right was smothered in inlays of flowers and vines that tumbled over each other, the stems seeming to thrust and grow under the eye. To his left, animals real and apocryphal clambered on each other's backs to peer in through the glass at the bones and preserved fragments of their fellows.

In the center of the room was a large table, octagonal also, and crowded with domed glass cases for larger curiosities. Crowther noticed the skeleton of a two-headed baby. It had been provided with an ivory violin and stood on top of a small mossy rise, one foot lifted as if dancing to its own tune.

"It was the current duke's uncle who created this room," Manzerotti said.

"Ludwig Christoph prefers living curiosities?" Crowther replied, but Manzerotti only smiled.

"He prefers the opera. Your rudeness is terribly clever, but not very useful, is it? Come now, Mr. Crowther, do I have to put a loaded gun in your hand too before we can talk like civilized men?"

"Would you?"

Manzerotti bent to examine the skeleton as he spoke. "I think not. You calculate more methodically than Mrs. Westerman. That makes you more dangerous in some ways. In truth, the more I consider it, the more I think you an exemplary pairing. You complement each other to an unusual degree."

"You heard of the demonstration?"

"Yes, I have already had a full report. You need not trouble yourself."

"Did you suggest using a child for the experiment?"

"Yes." He continued to stare at the two-headed baby. "Do you know, Crowther, I think the vegetation around this little monster's feet is actually injected lung tissue! Is that a kidney stone? My Lord, what imagination. Have you ever made anything like this?"

Crowther felt his mouth set in a thin line. "It is a work of Frederick Ruysch, I believe. And no, I do not build little tableaux." Manzerotti shrugged. "So the mask is drugged in some way," Crowther continued. "How did you know? Can you identify the substance?"

"Here is an instance. I am sure when next I meet her, Mrs. Westerman will want to ask me again of my general purpose here. If she can bring herself to do so, she will inquire as to the personalities and scandals of the court, then stare out of the window and wonder until her imagination proffers scenarios which her mind considers worthy of pursuit. You, meanwhile, latch on to facts. Hard, nuggety little facts. She is the artist, you are the craftsman. On balance, I doubt you'd have the imagination to create a horrid little tableau like this." Crowther did not reply. "The symptoms Mr. Clode displayed, and the manner they came on, suggested a certain substance to me. Something of which I have heard reports, but never encountered in the flesh, as it were. The fact that the rest of the party remained unaffected suggested the manner in which it was delivered. Do not blame yourself. I came to Maulberg from the south, reaching the border before you and traveling a little farther before I reached court. I therefore had longer to study my supply of papers. I am sure you would have realized the mask was the source of Clode's confusion before long."

"The substance, Manzerotti. How did you know it? What do you know of it?"

"I have made the study of drugs and poisons a pastime in the last years." He paused and lifted one immaculate eyebrow. "I am surprised a man who spends his time dissecting the dead curls his lip at such an interest, but of course, how foolish of me. Poisons are evil, sneaking, and covert, as I am evil. Is that how you figure it?"

"I do not style myself a theologian, Manzerotti, to speak of good and evil."

"Yet you are, in a way. I have no doubt that in your time investigating violent death in the company of Mrs. Westerman, you have delivered any number of stirring speeches on the greater good and the absolute value of truth." Crowther scowled. "I thought you had. You must realize that even a monster such as myself can contribute to that greater good when it suits me, such as giving Mrs. Westerman a little hint about the mask. Did you know there is a devil hidden in the organ of the cathedral in Leuchtenstadt? When the player pulls a certain level, he pops out to play upon his own little set of pipes, forced to sing the Good Lord's praises whether he wills it or no. Does the analogy please you?"

"Who arranged for those papers to be sent to you, Manzerotti? Who pulls the levers that control *you*? I suspect you function somewhat . . . independently."

"Perhaps. And like the little devil, sometimes I do not play exactly the tune my masters would wish." He seemed to brighten. "The composition of the poison on the mask I cannot swear to exactly, but I have thought it might owe its effects to the inclusion in the mix of a powder of one of the *datura* family."

Crowther brought his cane down on the polished floor with a sharp rap. "Yet you encouraged the duke to experiment on a child?"

"Hardly encouraged! Suggested in passing, and do be careful of the parquet, Crowther, I understand it was imported at great expense. You do know something of the subject then? But not a great deal. I imagine your expertise stops at identifying arsenic poisoning, and the effects of strychnine. A plant of the *datura* family must be ingested to prove fatal. The child would only have been in danger if she had started licking the horrid thing. Besides, I do not think anyone was particularly fond of her . . ."

"Manzerotti . . ."

The castrato's eyes seemed to darken for a second. "I hope you are not going to deliver a lecture on the sanctity of human life, Crowther. Such hypocrisy would surely choke you."

Crowther looked away.

When Manzerotti spoke his voice was light again. "Now, to cement this pleasant fellow feeling between us, have you anything to tell me? Has *your* expertise anything to show for itself?"

Almost against his own will, Crowther found himself replying: "She was drowned."

Manzerotti rapped his fingers lightly on the tabletop. Crowther wondered if he were trying to make the skeleton dance.

"Indeed? How fascinating! Are you certain? Of course you are, you would never speculate in front of me. No crime of passion this, then. Drowned on dry land . . . There's something almost ritualistic about it. There, Gabriel, you see? We can rub along. Dressed as a Goddess of the Moon, and drowned. Interesting."

"Manzerotti, what are you doing here?"

"Mrs. Westerman's spirit has entered the room at last!" He opened his arms wide and lifted his chin. "Was it the use of your Christian name conjured her? No need to frown so. Why am I here? Do not trouble yourself. It is largely a question of politics, so too dull for Mrs. Westerman and too abstract for you. As it happens, I believe Clode quite innocent and am curious to know who is to blame for the death of Lady Martesen. I am happy to offer you my cooperation therefore, for the time being."

Crowther looked into Manzerotti's face and his mind filled with images of flowers that poisoned and rotted from within those unfortunate enough to consume them. "And if our interests diverge, Manzerotti?"

"I will always dance to my own tune, Crowther. Your best hope is that they will not diverge. Now be not downcast, my friend! There cannot be many here who have the knowledge and wit to make that poison and who had the opportunity to treat the mask. Trust my expertise on that: whoever made that drug was instructed by an adept."

Having Manzerotti address him in such warm and encouraging terms was as much as Crowther could bear, and without speaking again he turned away and left him among the other exotics gathered together to amaze and confound in the duke's chamber of wonders.

15

Jacob Pegel was seated in the little square by the river with a book in his hands, enjoying the spring sunshine and feeling generally content. The corner he had chosen was out of the general run, but easy enough to find, and found he was, by the succession of dirty-faced boys who formed his army. They came to him with paper offerings, and news of where the paper was collected from and to whom it was to go. Only one note was sealed carelessly enough to allow its contents to be read without leaving a sign it had been tampered with. Pegel noted down its contents—again nonsense groups of five letters—then in front of the nervous-looking messenger charged with carrying it from one side of the town to the other, dropped it at his feet and stood on it squarely.

"Sorry, son," he said to the boy, who was looking at him outraged. "But you get an extra shilling for it, in case they box your ears for dropping it."

The boy took the coin and shrugged. It was a fair price for a beating. Pegel examined each letter carefully, made some notes, and then returned them to the messengers, who left with extra pennies in their hands. With their help Pegel traced the passage of the news of yesterday's attack through the town. It fluttered through the law faculty, among half a dozen philosophers, and circled via a couple of the more prosperous tradesmen to the vice chancellor himself. It circled once more, then fell softly on the doorstep of a house not far from Pegel's own, and the name on the note was not one with which Pegel was familiar. *Dunktal*. Interesting. The letters were all sealed, most with that curious mark of the owl. Pegel made more notes in the back of his book. Wrote down each name and direction and drew lines one to the other. By the middle of the afternoon he thought he had a fair idea of the names of Florian's secret friends and, roughly, the hierarchy of the organization. In his experience, bad news travels upward like a bad smell. The small boys who chose to play outside Dunktal's door reported that though the news had entered the house, it traveled no further forward. Jacob put his notebook into his pocket and sauntered down toward Herr Dunktal's front door.

Though she had spent as yet only one day in Ulrichsberg, the sense of relief Harriet felt when they passed out of the town was considerable. The road they followed wound upward along the path cut by one of the tributaries to the Neckar, climbing into the hills until the placid river by which they had started their journey had disappeared, and become a distant sigh in the valley below. On either side of them the forest stretched away, broken from place to place with columns of dark red sandstone; their edges softened with mosses and ivy, their silhouettes broken by new birch leaves. Scents of earth and water filled the carriage. Graves, freed from the palace, looked positively cheerful. Harriet glanced at Rachel, remembering their conversation of the previous evening and wondering if she had said everything she should have done.

Harriet remembered the first weeks of her own married life vividly, and with a certain amount of shame. She had loved James, and felt she knew him when they wed, but she recalled only too well the strangeness of first encountering the physical being of her husband outside the drawing room or the ballroom. The scent of him had been foreign, the sight of him stripped back to himself alarming. The physical side of marriage she had learned . . . to appreciate. She had been lucky. James had traveled the world before he met her and, he told her some months into their marriage, had once been the lover of an older woman, a widow. Though the idea that he had been as intimate with another as he was with her had troubled and scratched at her, she also recognized its advantages. He came to her bed wise, patient, and kind. His strangeness became familiar, his touch sought after, valued.

She had assumed that Clode, so handsome a young man, would have entered into marriage as experienced as James. She felt she had to blame herself. She had chosen to forget that Clode had been raised in a much more limited circle and was rather younger than James had been. She had also ignored the slight prudishness in Clode's nature, and in Rachel's. It had been a choice. Rachel had still been angry with Harriet for continuing to involve herself with the investigations of murder even in the weeks leading up to the marriage, and Harriet had found it impossible to do her duty and talk to her sister about physical love. Her cowardice had done Rachel and Daniel a disservice. After three months of marriage Daniel thought himself a brute, and Rachel judged herself as unnatural. Their affection was clouded by fear and embarrassment. Now they were separated by the horrors of the Carnival night.

Harriet remembered Rachel's face, turned away slightly as she drank her tea the previous evening. "Two nights before the Carnival, I asked him if he had never taken a lover in the past," she had said. "Harry, he was so angry with me. He asked if I thought he should take one now, as I was unwilling to perform my duties as a wife with good grace."

"Oh, my dear."

"That evening we were in company with Lady Martesen, and I know nothing passed between them but common courtesy, but I was so jealous. I stormed and cried and all but accused him of making love to her in front of me! He reassured me, and I was in such a passion I wouldn't listen to him. Then, well . . ."

"You can tell me, Rachel."

"Then it was a great deal better. But we were angry at the time and oh, Harriet, I was so confused the next day. I felt as if some sort of monster had been released, in us both. And I was frightened by it, and Daniel would hardly look at me, and then we went to the Carnival . . ."

"Did you notice the preparations in town?" Graves's voice called Harriet from her thoughts and back into the carriage.

"I did," she said, passing her hand over her forehead. "The princess's reception should be magnificent."

"Poor girl," Rachel said. "She is only fifteen, you know, and has never met the duke."

Graves crossed his long legs and stared out at the passing forest. "And now she will arrive in this murderous court with Manzerotti to sing her welcome."

"She is trained for it," Harriet said. "She will have wealth, power, influence."

"Do you envy her, Harry?"

"No, Rachel. I do not."

Castle Grenzhow was a structure from a less frivolous time. It brooded high over the river valley and watched the narrow road askance through thin windows. Only the eastern part of the castle had been maintained. The tower to the west had crumbled to a rotted stump, and beside it the remains of the manor house had dwindled to walls without floors or ceilings, a stone staircase that opened on empty air, halls of weeds and grasses. All was in pinkish stone.

The single track that led to the gate could be observed by the castle's remaining guardians throughout its last curving, climbing mile, and those in the carriage could feel themselves watched and waited for.

The castle, Harriet discovered when the carriage drew into the forecourt, had a more numerous population than she had at first thought. She had imagined Clode alone in a tower with one crooked guard to lock and unlock the door to his chamber. Instead the surviving part of the castle showed signs of being a thriving little community. There were several men on the gate and in the yard, and more supervising a work party down the slope. In the work party were perhaps a dozen men wielding pickaxes, all dressed in plain uniform work clothes. She could not help looking into their faces with alarm, and felt Rachel's hand brush her own.

"Daniel has not been forced to work," she said. "Here, as everywhere else, status is what counts. He has a room and his own clothes. These men," she nodded out of the window, "are from peasant stock."

"What are their crimes?" Harriet said, trying to pick out individual faces. None of the men were young, and all had the weatherworn skin of those used to outdoor work. None were fat, but none showed signs of malnourishment.

"I asked the same thing, Harry. Persistent drunkenness or theft. Some argued with their priests or the headmen in their village."

The carriage came to a halt and the door was opened by one of the scarlet footmen the court had provided to travel about with their visitors. An oppressive courtesy. A gentleman emerged from the heavy interior of the

castle to greet them with a broad smile. He was not the hunched and shuf-
fling jailer of Harriet's imaginings, but a figure wigged and frock-coated,
brushing crumbs from his waistcoat. Rachel made the introductions and he
smiled at them very pleasantly and asked after their journey.

"I am sure that all of Ulrichsberg is in a froth!" he said, gesturing with his
hands so broadly Harriet was afraid he might topple over backward. "A new
duchess! I have had her portrait hung up in my office already, next to that of
Ludwig Christoph. She is a pretty girl, but regal, I am sure you understand
what I mean—*regal!*"

"How is my husband, Herr Hoffman?" asked Rachel.

He shook his head. "Pleased to hear of the arrival of his friends, but I wish
I could get him to eat a little more. I had my own cook send up some of my
stew yesterday evening, so delicious it was. But he hardly touched it."

He blinked at Harriet and Graves. "The wind tells me you are already
sowing doubt about Mr. Clode's guilt at court."

"You are very well informed, sir," Harriet said, surprised.

"Fresh supplies and fresh gossip arrived only an hour or two ago, milady.
You have an early meeting with the duke, and Mr. Clode's friends leave it
looking hopeful. The Countess Dieth has a conversation with the duke, and
her reactions are observed. A scribe is asked to make a copy of a letter. The
tone shifts and without quite knowing why, we start to think Mr. Clode is
innocent. And I wanted to say, I am absolutely delighted about that. Such a
pleasant, well-educated young man, a little serious perhaps, but it has been
a pleasure to guard him. If you whip him away I shall have to hope the duke
finds some scribbler of seditious pamphlets to lock up here for a few
months, or I shall be deprived of civilized company. No doubt some young
man will publish something insulting for the wedding. I trust in that."

Graves opened and shut his mouth a few times before managing, "It is
kind of you to say you wish him freed, sir, if you would feel his loss so."

Herr Hoffman waved his handkerchief. "Not at all, milord Graves. I would
lose him anyway to the ax man, given the charge, and would much rather
see him go free! Do not worry about me a jot."

To that Graves had no reply at all, so merely bowed.

"Kleinman!" A rather stooped-looking creature appeared suddenly at his elbow in the doorway. "Kleinman will take you up. Such a delight to make your acquaintance. I hope I shall see you at one or other of the fêtes and celebrations in town. Perhaps I shall be delivering dear Mr. Clode back to you!"

"You are able to leave your place here then, sir?" Harriet asked.

"Oh yes, from time to time. Some of these fellows have been here fifteen years. If I unlocked the doors and gave them the key, they'd probably lock themselves up again at once. Really, where could they go?"

In spite of what Rachel had told her, Harriet had not been prepared to see Daniel so drawn. There was a gauntness to his features, and though he met them warmly, Rachel was right, he was still distant, still to some degree lost in that night.

"Harriet! Owen! How strange to see you here. What do you think of my first establishment as a married man?"

The room in which he was held was plain, but not uncomfortable. He had a little pile of books on his desk and a narrow view of the forest. The walls were the unplastered reddish stone of the castle, the only decoration a simple wooden cross above his narrow cot. Harriet preferred it to her own accommodation in court.

"I rather like it," she said with a brisk smile and took a seat on one of the wooden stools provided. She removed her gloves and handed him a letter. "From your parents, Daniel." His expression as he saw the handwriting on the envelope was both tender and pained.

"How are they?" he asked. "I feared for my mother's health—that the news might make her ill."

His deep blue eyes looked too large for his face. Harriet felt an overwhelming urge to bundle the young couple into the carriage at once and not let them out of her sight till they were pink with health again. "She is frightened for you, Daniel, of course, but I suspect she is stronger than you think. Verity intended to call on them again with her parents when they arrived from London. She will give them every attention and I think they will like each other."

"Yes, I think they will. However gracious you are to them, Harriet, my father still feels like a footman in front of you." He ran his hand through his hair and Harriet noticed for the first time gray hairs among the black. "He and Mr. Chase will understand each other. It is good of Verity to look to them. You have married well, Graves."

Graves was looking uncertain, something shocked by his friend's looks and tone. His voice was serious as he replied, "I know it, Daniel. And better than I deserve, much like yourself."

Clode dropped his gaze. "Of course, I did not mean," he put his hand out to Rachel, "you know I did not mean to imply . . ."

Rachel smiled and shook her head. "Of course not, Daniel."

An odd, clinging sort of silence fell over them. Harriet looked out at the forest through the open shutter. It filled the frame with spring green. So vast it seemed, waves hiding the landscape. It reminded her of the sea when they were out of sight of land, how it seemed to flow to the edges of vision.

"You have come to tell me about your reception in court," Daniel said. His voice was slightly hoarse, as if he had become unpracticed at speech. "Do you think they mean to execute me? Or lock me in a madhouse?"

"They will do neither," Graves said. "You will be returning to England with us, your name cleared and their profound apologies ringing in your ears. What is the matter with you, man? We have traveled for weeks and you greet us as if we'd just arrived rather inconveniently while you were writing epic verse or somesuch."

Clode almost smiled. Almost. "I thank you for coming, and I know you will do everything in your power to release me. But how can anyone, even Harriet and Mr. Crowther, find out the truth of that night? It must haunt me always." He folded his arms across his body as if cold. "I thank you, for Rachel's sake, but you can do nothing for me, I think."

"All that Crowther and Mrs. Westerman have done, and you show such little faith? In two months you'll be home and dancing with my wards till you are sick with laughing."

Clode turned sharply on his friend. "Laugh?" Harriet noticed that as he lifted his hand to his temple, the fingers were shaking a little. "You don't understand, Owen. I was parted from my reason, the horrors of that night . . ."

"No, I do *not* understand, and from what I saw of that little girl, I can only imagine. But it was a dream, Daniel. A nightmare, and you must learn to see it in that light, rather than brood."

"What little girl?"

"One who thought I was King of the Fairies. There, that almost made you smile! Your mask was drugged, my friend. We have just seen a demonstration this morning. A child wore it for a short time—and she saw all manner of things."

"So it was drugged?"

"Yes."

"But that does not prove I am innocent of doing Lady Martesen harm."

Graves was quite red in the face. Harriet felt a wave of affection for him. "From what I read, you were hardly capable of standing. Could you, in that state, pour water down a woman's throat till she drowned?"

"Drowned?" Clode lowered himself onto one of the rough stools in the room and stared at Graves, his mouth slightly open.

"Yes, drowned. You were drugged with your nasty mask—I can't believe you were fool enough to wear such a thing—and she drowned on dry land. Hoffman will be delivering you back to court within the day, I guarantee it. And you will look every silk-smothered devil there in the face like a freeborn Englishman! So there is a little parcel of facts for you and we have others to hand too if you will stop staring out of the window like a hero in a novel and act like a man. Do you have food here? Rachel says she always brings you delicacies and finds them untouched." He picked up a stool and placed it opposite Daniel, blocking his view of the forest. "And by the way, Manzerotti is in court."

Daniel turned to stare at Harriet. "Good God, Harriet! Is he . . . ? Have you . . . ?"

Harriet tilted her head to one side. "I was going to stab him with one of Mr. Al-Said's files, but he provided a pistol so I almost shot him instead. I hate to say it, but I think having the opportunity to do so, and not killing him, has done me a great deal of good."

Rachel smothered a shocked laugh. Clode was speechless. Graves plowed on.

"Now we have a mission, Daniel. We must think through every moment of your time in court before the Carnival and see who might have had a reason to try and murder you alongside Lady Martesen."

Daniel was looking confused and distressed, and Rachel put out her hand. "Graves, please! Daniel has been very ill."

Graves reached across the table and grabbed one of Clode's wrists, jerking it toward him. His coat sleeve rode up and the scar, thin and livid across his wrist, was exposed. Graves turned his hand back and forth. "Seems to be healing well enough. A year and you won't even have to wear long cuffs. Rachel, you have been too sympathetic. What Clode here needs is good food and a swift reminder of his duties."

"You think they aimed to kill *me*?" Clode said slowly, looking up at his friend.

"Don't be a fool. Lord, I've entrusted my ward's fortune to a babe-in-arms. *Think*, Daniel—if Colonel Padfield had not broken down the door, you would have died on the floor in your own blood. It was the merest chance saved you. Someone meant you," he released his grip to point at Clode fiercely, "*you*—to die there. Now who?"

Clode looked across at Harriet. "Is this your opinion too, Harriet?"

"Yes. In all particulars," she said very calmly, "and Crowther's too."

Clode shuddered and wrapped his arms around himself again. "Very well." Then he lifted his head and looked at Harriet. "You and Mr. Crowther are come like angels to deliver me, Harriet." The corner of his mouth twitched, and she saw something of his former self trying to return. She only smiled in reply, trying somehow in that smile to show both her faith and her sympathy.

"Do you have pen and paper?" Graves asked, looking about him. "I shall act as your scribe."

"No, Graves. Dear God, only years of close study have taught me to read your hand." Clode sighed deeply and shook himself. "Let Rachel write while you play drill master with my memory. But Manzerotti?"

Graves crossed his arms and tossed his hair back from his forehead. "Our concerns are with what happened *before* that devil arrived. Perhaps we will have a chance to shoot him later. Very well, let us begin. What are you looking at me like that for?"

"I think I am glad you are come, Owen."

Graves looked a little shy. "I promised your mother that I'd look after you. And Susan. If you come back all wan-looking and destroyed, it will only make her passion for you stronger, you know. I want you fat and balding before my ward is out on the marriage market, otherwise all men shall be compared to you and be found wanting."

"And we wouldn't want that, would we?" Daniel said.

"No, we damn well wouldn't."

The cell became a hive of activity. Harriet asked the guard at the door to send them up something to eat, then turned to see the younger people preparing to set to work. It was a moment where she felt the difference between them. They seemed eager, revived. She knew there was something desperate in their sudden energy, but thought it better they exhaust themselves. It would do them all good. They were preparing a sheet for each day that Rachel and Clode had been at court, then some fierce discussion ensued if it would be better to instead have a sheet for each personage encountered. Harriet felt weary, and wished for Crowther.

16

Pegel watched the house of Dunktal all afternoon. He thought of Florian coming to find him, then leaving disappointed, and felt a slight shiver of regret. However, his job was to follow the trail and this was where it had led him. A house that suggested prosperity, but not great wealth. There was a man in a green coat working at the window upstairs. It took an hour before Pegel recognized him as one of the men he had seen leaving the back room of the bar in Leuchtenstadt where he had first set eyes on Florian. He had left some hours before the others, so Pegel had not thought him important. It seemed he had been wrong.

He had expected some activity, some stirring within—but nothing came. The news of the attack on Florian did not seem sufficient to scare Dunktal into the streets. Jacob consulted his notebook again. The message had reached Dunktal, Dunktal had sent messages back, but none forward. Pegel wanted very much to get into that upper room where the man was working so assiduously, but he might be there for hours, days even. He needed to alarm one of the lieutenants enough that Dunktal would need to provide reassurance in person. He looked at the list of people who had sent to Dunktal. Three. Two men and a woman, the wife of the head of the law faculty. She lived on Charlottenstrasse. Now these friends of Florian obviously liked to think of themselves as the noblest of men. If a woman were threatened, surely Dunktal would not only send a polite coded note, he would go there himself—ideally in such a hurry he would forget to lock his door. But what manner of threat should it be? Nothing like the attack on Florian, of course, but it had to look as if it came from the same source. One of the odd little books of alchemy and allegory the Rosicrucians claimed as their manifesto would do nicely. Sent with no note. He tapped his pencil on his teeth and hid away his notebook, then sauntered up the road until he found a bookseller who had what he required, a cheap printing of *The Chemical Wed-*

ding. He had it wrapped and then found a boy at play among the gutters and handed it to him. "Fourpence to deliver it," he said. The boy looked suspicious. "And if they try and get you to say who sent it, tell them a man in a brown coat with a yellow wig. I'll be by and listening. Do as I tell you and there's another fourpence. Deal?"

The boy put out his hand.

It worked just as Pegel had hoped. The boy handed over the package to a manservant who disappeared back into the house on Charlottenstrasse. The boy began to slouch away, then the door was pulled open and the manservant reemerged and made a dash for him, catching him by the collar and lifting him almost off the ground. Pegel heard the boy whine out, "Yellow wig," then watched the gentleman look about him before striding back into the house. When the door was shut, Pegel beckoned the boy over and gave him the promised fee, then trotted back to his post outside Dunktal's house. The same manservant from the house on Charlottenstrasse arrived soon after him and was admitted. Five minutes later, and he and Dunktal were off again, and walking at a cracking pace.

The manservant had left first, with his hat pulled down hard over his wig, then Dunktal followed, locking the door behind him and tugging at the latch to check it held. Pegel reckoned he had maybe an hour.

There were too many comings and goings on the street to risk picking the lock on the front door, so Pegel slipped into the yard and up the back staircase. It was a risk, certainly, but the veranda had a low bowed roof on it that gave him some shade, and at this time of day most people's business faced forward, onto the street. There was a stout lock on the back door too, but Pegel was prepared for that. He pulled a long iron bar from under his coat and fitted it into the padlock. The only worry was the wait until he heard the rattle of a coach passing by, then he pressed down hard, and the snap of the lock was lost in the sparking rattle of iron wheels on cobbles.

District Officer von Krall did not keep Crowther waiting long, for which Crowther was grateful. He had underestimated Manzerotti's ability to shake him. He sat at his desk for some quarter of an hour trying to concentrate on what the castrato had said about the drug on the mask and recall what he knew of *datura*. Very little, he had to admit to himself. The only story he remembered with any clarity was of a doctor who had served in the American wars. He reported a case of a family, found by their neighbors sick and raving in the road in front of their farm. They claimed to see visions of Christ descending. Luckily their neighbor fetched a doctor as well as a priest. The latter prayed with them, while the former interrogated their maid of all work. The youngest girl in the family had been sent to pick greens for their midday meal, and the doctor found alongside their neat rows of vegetables a thorn apple bush. *Datura inoxia*. The doctor had done his best, but the little girl could not be saved.

The knock at the door came and another of the ubiquitous footmen bowed the district officer into Crowther's chamber. They exchanged slightly awkward bows, then Krall sighed and lowered himself onto one of the armchairs.

"Drowned? Truly? You're not blowing smoke in my eyes, Mr. Crowther?"

Crowther smiled. Krall's English was redolent of the docks more than the drawing room. He gathered some of the sheets from his writing table before taking a seat opposite him.

"I am not. The evidence is in the notes you yourself prepared, Herr von Krall." He pointed out the relevant passages and explained their significance. The district officer shook his head.

"I thought that professor was a damn fool."

Crowther sat back and put his fingertips together. "Your English is remarkably fluent."

Krall scratched his chin. "Four years in London."

"And your opinion of the English?"

"What? Oh, that they are like the Germans. All just wanting to be a little better than their neighbors. Why do you ask?"

"Simply curious." Crowther felt Krall's eyes travel over him, and the corner of the district officer's mouth lifted.

"Wondering if I'm prone to be prejudiced against you and your little group, more like." Crowther lifted his shoulders slightly. "No, Mr. Crowther. I am glad of your help, and too old to want the glory of finding out the truth of this nonsense myself. Shall we talk it through?"

They did, and by the time they had done Crowther was confirmed in his respect for his unpolished companion. The broken carafe on the floor was dismissed by them both. Krall had put his hand to his head and with visible effort tried to recall any scraps from his memory not already faithfully recorded in his reports that could be significant. There had been water in the smaller of the back rooms for the ladies to wash, and in a large basin that could have been sufficient to drown a woman in, if she were held with considerable force. But again, the lack of signs of a struggle gave them doubt.

"What if she were drugged also?" Crowther said at last. "There are substances that can cause great weakness, lassitude. If a man were capable of making a substance that could cause Clode's visions, he could also create something that would make a person weak, but that would leave no trace in the body."

Krall had his shoulders hunched. "Sounds more likely than Lady Martesen just holding still while someone drowns her. Indeed. If you are at liberty, Mr. Crowther, perhaps we might make a call on a gentleman of my acquaintance who might give us some help in the matter."

"I am willing." Crowther stood and picked up his cane.

"It will also give us the opportunity to get out of this damn palace," Krall added.

"In that case," Crowther said, "I am delighted."

"I'm sorry, Clode, what did you say then?" Harriet said.

"I mentioned that on the third evening, I was invited to attend a meeting of the local Lodge of Freemasonry, Harriet," he said, looking across at her. He already looked a great deal improved. "But of course, I can say nothing about it, other than that nothing remarkable occurred."

"Why can you say nothing about it?"

Rachel took the opportunity to set about mending her pen. "Harry, you know it is a secret society."

"Not very secret, Rachel. When Daniel's lodge opened the charity school in Pulborough, they had a parade! And the bookseller in town always has at least one pamphlet on display on the rituals and secrets of Freemasonry."

Daniel smiled. "It's different here, Harriet. The Catholic Church has banned membership, and though I doubt that bothers many Englishmen, it is a consideration here. There are any number of groups calling themselves Freemasons on the Continent, and very few of them bear much relationship with the English lodges. That is my understanding and experience. Some even admit women. But it is a useful way to meet people away from the court. One only encounters nobles there."

"Have you been to many meetings while in Germany, Clode? And don't look at Graves as if you need his permission to speak! I haven't asked you for any of your secret words of power." Harriet folded her arms. "I read one of those pamphlets once. I cannot say I was greatly impressed with the poetry of the drinking songs."

Graves grinned, and Daniel said, "Very well. I have been to several meetings of different lodges here and in Berlin. Various of the gentlemen I have met who have business dealings with the Sussex estate are members of one lodge or other. When they recognize I am a Freemason as well, they invite me along." He lifted his shoulders. "It is a sort of international gentlemen's club."

Harriet still had her chin in the air. "Like-minded men of business?"

"Never any harm in making friends, Harriet."

She sighed and sat back in her chair.

"Clode, have you come across any group calling themselves the Minervals in your travels?" Graves asked.

"No—why do you ask?"

"Just that during a lodge meeting I attended in London last year, there was a German fellow visiting, and he was full of dire threats about them."

"What manner of dire threats, Graves?" Harriet asked, putting her chin in her hand. Then, when he looked a little sheepish: "If you do not explain, I will tell Verity you were not helpful."

Graves cleared his throat. "I suppose it will be all right, in the circumstances. This chap had been at a conference in Wilhelmsbad in eighty-two, and he met some of these fellows there. They were recruiting from the ranks of the Freemasons, he said, and he became convinced they were intent on overthrowing the governments of Europe. He claimed they had spies and agents everywhere and saw chucking over the old order as a duty. Seemed a little crazed to me."

Rachel was arranging the papers disturbed by Graves's elbow. "In such a place as Ulrichsberg, I have some sympathy with them."

Graves was silent for a moment. "You know, Clode, if this plot against you had succeeded, we would have refused to renegotiate the bonds and demanded the repayment of the principal."

"That would have been foolish."

"Probably, but we would have done it. It might have been an embarrassment to Maulberg."

"You think a group of revolutionary Freemasons has been plotting against me, Graves?" Clode shook his head. "It seems unlikely, though between the wedding and the death of their chief privy councilor last year, I do not think they know what money is in the Treasury at all. It is said round court he once told the duke if he wished to put on the Carnival he had planned, he would not be able to feed himself the next day. And now that wise hand is removed."

"What was his name?" Harriet said sharply.

Clode looked at her curiously. "Count von Warburg, I think."

"How did he die?"

"There was a fire."

17

Pegel stood in the room in which he had seen the gentleman writing, and thought. If he was correct in his assumptions—and he was sure he was—the message he had sent had traveled upward and come to a rest in this place. Therefore here was the top of the tree, and it was very interesting Dunktal had not sent a message to some other town. Did he have any masters? That was just one of several rather pressing questions.

If there were crucial papers here, and that was what Pegel had come in to search for, Dunktal would not be so stupid as to leave them loose on his desk. He thought of Florian's terrible sincerity, his idealism. Did that extend up the organization too? If so, and given the apparent love of secrecy and symbols, all these codes and owls, it was possible the gentleman would leave the papers somewhere clever. Pegel had discovered that life was easier when people tried to be clever, since it often made them obvious. A clever code was far easier to break than a random one, a clever hiding place much easier to find than an unlikely one. He would have to assume that this gentleman would want his putative papers to hand. That meant this room. Good. Now for the clever bit.

The walls were lined with books—Lord, these radicals loved to read. Pegel stood very still, letting the details of the room shift and settle in his mind as he panned his impressions for gold. There it was. On the bottom of the bookshelf, crushed into the corner by any number of volumes on law, was a large, elderly looking Bible. If Florian was anything to go by, these people were not religious. Perhaps it was an heirloom of the family? Then surely it should be on display downstairs in the public rooms, not tucked up here. He teased it out of the shelf toward him and considered. It was certainly lighter than it should be. He picked it up and cradled it between his forearms.

"Open sesame!" he said in a deep voice, then gave a soft whistle. It was hollowed out, and a thick stack of letters and papers lay in the nest cut out for them. He grinned, considered, set the Bible down on the desk, then spent five minutes giving the room the look of a place speedily ransacked. He pulled out the desk drawers and scattered the papers, yanked out a random number of volumes from the upper shelves, and dropped them all so their spines snapped. The pages that had been loose on the desktop when he entered, he threw over his shoulder.

His ransacking done, he sat down on the floor with the papers from the Bible and sorted through them. Some were letters in plain language. Of these he noted down an idea of the contents, and names used; these were mostly classical pseudonyms, but one never knew where these things might lead, and each one was addressed to Spartacus. So Spartacus is Dunktal, he thought. The signatures were similarly unlikely, though Pegel grinned, his eyebrows raised, to see letters apparently from some of the Muses of antiquity. For Muses, he couldn't help thinking, they wrote ugly sentences. Some pages seemed to be instructions on the recruitment and training of members; others some of the central tenets of the organization. He whistled silently and made notes. Several sheets were in code and there were three longer documents that seemed to have been written by the same hand, and bearing the same date. They must be copied exactly and there was no way of knowing how much time he had. He set down his notebook, picked up the coal scuttle and emptied its contents down the stairs then shut the door, wedged a chair under it and opened the hatchway into the attic.

Thus, as prepared as he could be, he settled down to his work.

"An alchemist?" Crowther said coldly.

"Yes," Krall replied, and knocked again. "He is a good man. He was an apothecary."

"The drugs used on Clode are of a sophistication—"

"Bugger off!" The voice sounded from deep within.

Krall rattled the handle again. "Open up now, Adam, or I will break down the door."

"I said, bugger off!"

Crowther looked around the square while negotiations continued. So

even in a city as new as Ulrichsberg there were places that could look neglected. The house at which Krall hammered so vigorously looked like a
crabbed old woman surrounded by spring brides. Its windows were thick
with filth, there were tiles loose and greenery sprouted from the gutters.
The paint on the half-timbering was peeled. The houses on either side
showed what it should have been and it seemed to hunker and slump between them, neglected and resentful. Above the door was a faded emblem
of a unicorn.

Krall began to count slowly down from ten and a new storm of expletives
erupted from behind the low door. Crowther was a little gratified to realize
how many of them he understood. He had always thought German a
pleasing language to swear in. It had the proper supply of consonants. The
unseen owner of the house was proving himself to be an inventive user of
the linguistic tools to hand.

As Krall reached "Five" there was a screech and a wrench and the door
opened. The man who appeared behind it was an elderly, stooped creature
whose eyes were made huge by a pair of smeared glasses. He peered at Krall
over them and sneezed, then kicking the door open a little wider against
some resistance, spoke.

"Come in then." Noticing Crowther for the first time, he paused. "Who's
your pet?" He spoke clearly enough, but under his words was a faint high
wheeze; it was like a slow puncture in an organ bellows.

"This man is Mr. Crowther."

"Foreigner?"

"English."

"Explains it," he said, then tramped off into the gloom of the house. Krall
and Crowther followed.

The ground floor of the building was one low, continuous space but so
cramped with old furniture and broken oddments that the man in the eyeglasses had to lead them down a narrow path between the tumbling piles. It
was like a junk shop in a corner of the docks somewhere, a place where lost
remnants of better places went to die. Crowther saw chairs, dressers, tables
upended and balanced on half-opened packing cases; portraits thick with
grime set at an angle and half-hidden by the skeletons of chandeliers. Their

guide had now scurried ahead of them, more sure-footed and confident among the wreckage.

Krall said quietly, "Twenty years ago, Adam Kupfel—Whistler, as he is known now—was a rich enough man. He was an apothecary, and had a house outside Ulrichsberg worth envying. Now he lives in what used to be his shop, surrounded by the wreckage of his old home."

"What happened?"

Krall sighed. "He turned alchemist, and that turned him."

"How?"

"He always had a liking for all old books, and he found a thing in one of the bookshops of Leuchtenstadt one day—an old volume full of woodcuts and patterns and spells. It took some sort of hold on him. He spent all his money on similar works and turned the apparatus of his trade into a means of searching for the Elixir of Life."

"I am still unclear, Krall, what you hope to achieve by questioning a delusional recluse. What can he know of this drug, or who might have made it? These are matters of the real world."

Krall's eyebrows drew together. "I am not the first person who thought a recluse with unusual interests might yet do some good." Crowther felt his meaning, and his lips thinned. "Thing is, Kupfel was a good friend to me before this madness took him. My father died when I was just starting off in life, and without Adam's advice and guidance I'd have probably lost everything he left me. Many the evening I spent at his house while his son played on the hearth rug. He had the sharpest mind, and such learning. We would have been in a better state in Maulberg if he had taken the seat where Swann now sits, but such opportunities are available only to those of noble blood."

"I see."

"I doubt that you do. As to what he can tell us now, for all his madness no man within a hundred miles is as skilled with the methods of distilling and preparing drugs."

"Stop dawdling! Think I have all day to wait while you pick apart my history?"

Kupfel had to turn sideways to lead them into his lair, so close did the piles of refuse tumble together, but in the narrow opening Crowther saw a steady glow. As he squeezed through after their host he found himself in a more open space. It was as if they entered a cave carved from the walls of detritus around them. There was no dust here. Every surface was clean and bright. A fire burned evenly in a huge brick fireplace, and by its light Crowther saw the walls were lined with books. Desk and stool stood to the right, a pair of armchairs to the left, and behind them a door, part open to show a wall of glass jars and distilling bottles. Kupfel saw where Crowther was looking and went to shut the door, frowning.

"Sit down then, Benedict, you and your friend. Why do you disturb me? I was reading." He said the last with a vicious emphasis. Crowther noticed that Krall looked a little abashed.

"You have heard of the murder?" Krall asked.

"At the *Festennacht*? A woman, slaughtered by some hotblood."

"Mr. Clode's guilt is called into question."

"Hmm." Kupfel curled up in the armchair by the fire like an old dog and began to work his hands over each other. Crowther noticed they were covered in small scars and burns. There was a scar on his neck too that Crowther noticed only now as Kupfel twisted sideways in the light of the flames. It lapped his neck on the left side from collarbone to the underside of his chin, the flesh pink and puckered. Some sort of burn, certainly. Vitriol? Without willing it Crowther imagined a vessel exploding, the man turning away to shield his eyes and leaving the flesh of his neck exposed to the clawing liquid. The pain must have been indescribable, and the damage deep. No wonder his voice had that wheeze. How long had it been before Kupfel returned again to the fire? "How was she killed?"

Crowther spoke. "Drowned. Drowned without sign of restraint or resistance."

Kupfel bent over the fire and gently shifted one of the logs so it would burn more evenly, then, still stooped, he looked at Crowther. His glasses reflected the flames.

"Where did you learn your German?"

"Wittenberg University, largely."

"A man of the nobility then. A man of money, to study there. No wonder you talk my language as if you had that stick up your arse."

Crowther did not react and remained looking into the flames reflected on the smeared glasses. The alchemist put his head on one side, then the other. Once Crowther had seen a Persian tempt a snake from the basket with his pipe at a London fair. As he had watched the animal and the man, he had wondered who was influencing whom. The movement of Kupfel's head made him think of that snake again. There was a tang of sulfur in the air.

"I had heard in the chop shop that an Englishman and a widow had come here to declare the hothead innocent. You're no widow, so that makes you the anatomist then, I suppose. A man of science."

"I am. My name is Gabriel Crowther."

The reflection of the flames in the alchemist's eyeglasses hid his pupils, making him seem slightly inhuman. He bared his black teeth. It seemed he had no interest in Crowther's name. "Pah. Science. Progress! Man can be perfected, but by mystery. By the transformation of the stars he can live through time, raise the dead, become a god, know God." He leaned forward, and as he did so, the wheeze in his voice began to sound more like a hiss. His voice was not loud, but so insidious and intense it felt like a finger pressing on Crowther's eyeballs. He wondered, trying not to listen, what fumes hung around this place. The air was thick, the fire hot. "That is wisdom and it comes with sacrifice. Knowledge! Big word for little minds. In your cutting about of the flesh, have you ever found a soul? Found a thought, a dream? Found love?" He turned away again. "Of course not. You're merely picking through what you can see. You're like a man dabbling in a pool of ditch water thinking he examines the moon he saw reflected there. Look up, Mr. Crowther, look up!"

"I do look, Mr. Kupfel," Crowther said. "I look and observe, and I endeavor to understand. But I work with observable fact, not the babble of fantasy and imagination."

Kupfel waved a hand at him dismissively. "How can you understand anything without imagination? Your mind is too small for the Great Work. Too timid and wheedling. You seek little truths. An understanding. Which shows how little you comprehend."

He sniffed and wiped his nose on the back of his coat sleeve. "Why have you brought this man here, Benedict?"

"Mr. Clode—the man we all thought guilty: it seems some preparation was smeared on his mask. Confused his mind, made him see things. There is a suggestion it might contain *datura*."

"Have you brought it?"

"Yes."

Kupfel snapped his fingers and Krall produced the mask, carefully wrapped, from his bag and handed it to him. Kupfel sniffed it, and his face changed, stiffened. He looked between his visitors like a rabbit looking between dogs and deciding which way to run.

"You recognize it," Crowther said.

"Yes, Science Man. Did you say she went quietly . . . ?"

"She did, but this mask—" Krall said.

"Shush, Benedict. It's all one. No signs of drink? Laudanum? No bruising on the wrists?"

"No indication in the reports of anything of the sort. But you recognize the smell in the mask, do you not, Herr Kupfel?"

"I do. And I know the book where the instructions for making it are writ down. It is *datura* and some other odds and ends, not sure what works and what's there for the fun. Complicated. Very. Never managed to pick it apart entirely. One stitch wrong and the whole thing unravels. In the same book there's another receipt, one for a drug that can render people passive. Like dead, but not dead. It lasts some hours, perhaps a day then they wake up again, wander about, think it all a bad dream maybe. Unless you kill them for real. It's clever. Breathing is suppressed, heart hardly to be felt, the limbs stiffen. They look dead enough to bury. But they live. Poor bastards."

"What book, Adam?" Krall said, leaning forward. "In what book are these things writ down?"

Kupfel looked up. "Mine. In my book."

Pegel was on the last page of code, and thought he might actually make it. He had started to sweat and he had to concentrate hard to make sure he made no mistakes in the transcription of the code, but he was close. There was a very soft crunch of footstep on coal on the stair. He thought for a moment of risking it and finishing, but with a wrench he placed the letters back into the Bible and slid it back into its dark corner. The steps on the stairs were getting closer. Fools—they must realize they were making a noise, why not charge at the door? He reached for the hatch to the roof and hauled himself up, then dropped it behind him and looked around the narrow loft. He had been hoping for something bulky to hold the hatch shut. Quickly now. There, a trunk. Lighter than he would have liked, but needs must. He dragged it over just as the door went below. There was a shout of rage. He saw the trapdoor onto the roof and stepped from beam to beam to reach it, used the crowbar to snap the lock, pushed it open, and clambered out.

"He's on the roof!"

Damn. They had someone on the street below. He looked back into the attic and almost at once the trunk jumped and bucked as the people in the room below tried to force their way up. He clambered up and swung himself over the apex of the roof so he would be hidden from the street. His feet slipped and scrabbled for purchase. Downward was no escape. He headed to his left, flattened against the roof and holding onto the overlapping slates with his fingertips. He had waited too long, but his foolishness might also be his rescue, for it was getting dark now.

"Thief! Thief! On the roof!" More than one voice now on the street below. He had to move a lot faster. Be bold, Pegel, he told himself. Just let go with your right hand. Speed, momentum. You know about these things, they might help you fight gravity long enough. With a roar he pulled his hand free and began to run like a man crossing a scree slope, throwing each foot forward and on as it started to slip. The gap between this roof and that of the neighboring house was small, hardly a stride. He hoped mathematics was as solid as he believed and leaped, then kept on running. His pursuers were on the street.

"There, there! He's jumped to the next."

As long as he kept on the back side there was still a chance. Another leap, another life lost on his score. He glanced right. A veranda leading backward along a larger courtyard. Could he make the jump down? Only one way to find out. He landed awkwardly. Physics was one thing. Biology another. His ankle twisted and he gasped, and slipped; the flesh on his palm tore, but he found a hold, drew himself into a crouch, and, keeping low, stumbled north. The voices of his pursuers were fading, but they'd work it out soon enough. The veranda ended and he clambered up the gutter and around the edge of the next roof. Thank God town dwellers never look up. He couldn't put any weight on that right ankle without wanting to scream. Well, you wanted excitement, he thought, and paused. The gutter pipe looked sturdy, and between these two houses was a narrow passage. It was too dark to see what lay below him, but he guessed he'd find out soon enough. He lowered himself down and with his left foot managed to find a foothold on the sill of an upstairs window. Now the right had only to hold him for a second while he moved his hands. Letting go with his right hand was the hardest thing he had ever done; the gutter wanted to hold him away from the wall and tip him downward. For a second it seemed all was lost, but his poor torn fingers managed it and he found himself clinging to the wall and gasping in air like a fish on a slab. He slithered a little farther down but instinct made him scramble for a hold with his right foot, and it buckled. Gravity grew bored with the game and flung him into the darkness below.

The Alchemist wrapped his arms around himself.

"Adam, you know of these drugs?" Krall asked. "How?"

"Old memories, old methods. The time before I started on the Great Work. I traveled in my youth, Benedict. You know that. You knew me then. You probably thought me happier then than now, poor fool. I sought truth and understanding, like that man there." He nodded at Crowther. "Thought I'd find it by wandering about asking impertinent questions. It was a shaman I met in Marseilles. He'd traded his way out of slavery and made a fortune on the Dominican Islands. He sold the drug to whores who worked the docks. It would leave their client without movement or speech, then they would rob them. They would wake confused." Kupfel stood and stirred the fire again. "I thought it might be of use when people needed to be cut for the stone. He gave me his supplies and promised he could arrange more if I wished."

"And?" Krall asked.

"And I tried it, of course. It can be taken in a liquid. Colorless, a little bitter but not foul. I paid a servant to cut me when the drug had been taken to see if it stopped pain along with the ability to move or speak." He shuddered and his voice grew lower. "It was hell. I lost my understanding, but not my sense of fear or pain. It was as if all the demons of the night had been released against me as a punishment for my arrogance. My memory was weak afterward, but I was for some hours convinced I had died and been damned. I thought the flames were around me and a cut made along my arm was one of a million made by the hot knives of satanic slaves. Better by far to face the blade with a clear mind than in that condition. The supplies and the notes for the method of preparation I shut away." He looked into the flames. "The angel drug is a preparation from the same shaman."

"Angel drug?"

"The one smeared on that mask." It still lay in front of the fire, grinning up at them with empty eyes. "He used it in his ceremonies to let him see his gods. Taking it was like communion to him. He left me a rich and happy man."

"You have not prepared these compounds recently then?" Crowther asked.

"Not for twenty years."

"Where are your notes then, and the supplies?"

Kupfel wrapped his arms around himself more firmly. "Stolen."

"By whom?"

"I do not know. The children here tell each other stories about me and from time to time the braver ones have broken in to search for my stores of gold. I noticed they were gone this winter, along with some books, and bought better locks with my son's charity."

"You were not concerned that such dangerous items had been taken?"

"No. How could the thief have known what he was taking? And in any case, my notes are always coded. Only someone who knew my ways of working could make any sense of them."

"And who knows your ways of working?"

"No one. I wish for no disciple."

Crowther sighed and sat back in his chair. "Yet it seems you have one."

Kupfel waved his hand at Crowther as if he were a figment in the air he could disperse. "Someone else has met my gentleman from Marseilles, or one of his followers."

"Indulge us, Herr Kupfel. Could you write a list of what was taken?"

The alchemist looked at Krall, and on his nod hunched his shoulder and made his way to the writing desk. As he wrote he murmured, "I still dream about that night and its horrors. Better to be poisoned, hanged, broken on the wheel than that. If this drug was used, that girl died surrounded by her worst imaginings, convinced that God had forgotten her." He put his palms together. "He had not, child, He had not."

Darkness. Darkness and filth. Darkness, filth, pain, and oh, by all that was holy, the stench! Pegel managed to open his eyes. He could see by the stars glimmering between the gutters above him that it was full night. He tried to raise himself, but his hand slithered and a wave of sickness washed over him. He lay back again for a moment and groaned as quietly as he could. He must have been unconscious for an hour at least. Perhaps the smell had finished what the fall had started. Still, he had been lucky. The gap between the houses where he had fallen was obviously a dumping ground. Shit-covered straw. Food scraps, broken rubbish, potato peelings. Didn't these people have pigs to feed? The students must be keeping them all in ready money if they could throw away food. Still, it had broken his fall and he had avoided landing on anything that might impale him. He thought. At this exact moment it was difficult to tell just what his injuries were.

He tried to raise himself again, and this time managed to lift his head and struggle to a sitting position. Every bone in his body ached, but none seemed to be broken. Something stirred in the darkness and a rat ran over his right leg. He drew it back with a hiss, then had to bite his forearm to prevent himself from yelling out loud. The spasm dulled, and breathing heavily, he slithered through the mulch until he could find ground firm enough to stand on, then pulled himself upright on the broken edge of a barrel. He hobbled to the end of the alley and peered out. Everything quiet. A candle or two in the windows, but shadows enough. He brushed off his coat and breeches as best he could. He would get to his attic. He would have to pick up help on the way; he could not possibly haul water up the staircase with his ankle ballooning. Still. That was for later. First he had to get home, shadow to shadow, darkness to darkness, and have a look at what he had found.

Crowther had returned to his room from the alchemist's cave in a thoughtful state of mind. He had developed a habit of writing out his thoughts as they occurred to him when considering complexity, and he turned to his pen now. The time it took to form the words on a page slowed his thinking just enough to stop his mind skittering off into speculation. One word at a time, one sentence, to form a thought and follow it. This was how he built his arguments. The visit to Kupfel had not humbled him as such, since he saw Kupfel in some ways as a relic of a previous age, but his simple question, if Crowther had in the many human bodies he had dissected ever found a soul, was a serious one. It had hovered around the edges of Crowther's study from the first time he took a knife in his hand and began to use it as a tool of investigation. He normally tried to ignore it.

The workings of a living being were both miraculous and coarse: the speed and accuracy with which humans saw, moved, reacted compared with the weight of flesh slippery and dead. What was it that created life in matter? Kupfel was right in his suggestion that Crowther's studies had given him no answer to that. The difference between the living human and the corpse seemed initially so small, unless great violence had been done. It was no different than his pocket watch wound and ticking, and his watch stopped. The cogs and wheels were all still present, and ready, it appeared, to function as they always had. Yet there was no key to turn, no way to make the heart move again once it had ceased. Did life come into being as a result of motion? As the sense of wind on his face came to him when he rode on a still day, did thought—life—form through some effect of the movement of blood? Was that life? Was the soul a smoke generated by a body moving in the world; rubbing up against it? If that were true then must animals, having blood and brains, also have souls? Did Mr. Al-Said's creations, which had so impressed Harriet, having movement, have life?

He looked down; he had ceased to write. The quill remained between his fingertips, waiting for him. There were mysteries enough in the pattern of muscles that controlled the movement of his hand over the page to employ his mind. Let alchemists, philosophers, and mechanics experiment with the rest. He sensed he was being watched and turned to see Mrs. Westerman in the doorway, smiling at him.

"You haven't moved in some time, Crowther. I feared you had wound down."

"Good evening, Mrs. Westerman. How is Clode?"

"Confused, and he has been very afraid, I think, that he might have had some hand in the killing of Miss Martesen under the influence of that drug. Graves did something to convince him it could not be so, and got him to eat. Then they spent two hours attempting to discover who might have tried to kill him. I have never seen Graves so covered in ink."

He smiled. "Did they reach any conclusion?"

"There was nothing obvious, of course. No business dealings he thought crooked, nor did he call unexpectedly on any gentleman to find a knife in his hand."

She came into the room and took a seat in one of the armchairs by the fire. He watched her move, easy and unselfconscious where he felt so often stiff, unsure. "Rachel and Graves will go out to the castle again tomorrow."

"And you, madam?"

"I have not decided yet; they certainly need no assistance to spill ink. Crowther, is it very wrong of me to occasionally find our friends who are in the first flush of youth a little exhausting?"

He picked up the pages and began to read what he had written. "You are almost twenty years younger than I am, Mrs. Westerman. For the sake of our friendship, perhaps I should leave that question unanswered."

He glanced at her sideways; she laughed softly, then began to pull at one of her red curls. "I have just had an interesting visit from Colonel Padfield," she said.

"Indeed? Did he supply you with any further suspects?"

"That would have been good of him, but no. He asked me if he and his wife might have our blessing to employ Michaels in some quest of their own."

"Michaels? How did you answer him?"

"That Michaels was his own master and might do as he wished, naturally. It seems the colonel learned that Michaels is fluent in the local tongue, and Rachel has spoken highly of him."

"But he gave you no clue as to the mission?"

"None. But I rather suspect it is to do with his wife. Something mysterious in her past. But I must save my imagination for our own concerns."

Crowther sat back in his chair and lowered his chin. "Curious."

"Indeed. Michaels has agreed to call on Mrs. Padfield in town tomorrow. But for now come and have supper with us, Crowther, and tell us what you have learned."

Pegel did not find help. He clambered up to his rooms slowly and in pain and instead of the blessing of warm water he had to rely on the curative powers of the remains of a bottle of red and clean clothes. The ankle was sprained, not broken. If Florian came tomorrow would he have the sense to connect the man running over the rooftops with his injured friend? Best take that one head on. He removed his notebook from his filthy coat and hid it behind a piece of loose skirting board. Not the best of hiding places but all he could do at the moment. He managed to light the fire then lay in front of it like an old gun dog, his arm a pillow and the rough woolen blanket Florian had slept under the night before his only covering.

PART IV

18

Doubt can drift through corridors like a woman's scent. It passes in a touch from one being to another; a question asked, or even the idea that a question has been asked, can circulate without facts to carry it or definitive news to push it from place to place, but nevertheless it leaps from one to another like an infection. The day Harriet, Crowther, and Graves arrived in Maulberg, everyone knew that young Mr. Clode had murdered Lady Martesen and attempted to kill himself in remorse. Shocking, of course. But done, enclosed, over, tied up, and tidied away. This morning, without being able to say quite why, everyone was less sure. The question opened up like a wound, and at once the next followed. If he was not guilty, then who was? Many tried to dismiss the question, to ignore it, but it troubled the corners of their minds. Gentlemen paused in the middle of their correspondence to stare out the window; they found they were not listening to their stewards. Ladies ceased to hear their maids as their hair was dressed, and gave their orders in a manner distracted and unsure. Servants raised their eyebrows at each other as they passed in the corridors, shook their heads in the courtyards, and the question spread, knocking at the doors with the milk seller, carried out of the dress shops and perfumiers, coming home from the market with the fish and potatoes till it landed finally on the lap of a middle-aged woman sitting in the kitchen of a neat little house on Bergman Strasse.

Mrs. Gruber was alone and expected no company that day. Her mistress had left Ulrichsberg after the funeral for her sister's house in Hamburg with her little son and the best plate. Her only duties in the past fortnight had been to catalog the contents of the house and see it protected from dust and sunlight until the final decisions could be made. The will had been read and confirmed her master as a man reasonable and fair in death as in life. His family were content and the servants had all been left with a little something to keep out the cold. Mrs. Gruber thought she might go and live with her son, perhaps invest the money she had been left, and that she had saved, in the business he was beginning to grow. He and his wife had offered her a home in the past and told her they would be glad of her help with the book-keeping. There was a good chance of growing old peacefully and secure there. Well. There it was. She would not be sorry to leave Ulrichsberg. But now the question had crept in through the keyhole and she wondered how to answer it. There was, after all, no help coming to her master now, but then again . . . He had been generous. He had been kind. He had put business her son's way, and even if he could be short-tempered at times when the gout was eating him up, a little careless in the friends he made and brought to the house sometimes, he deserved *something*.

She decided to take a walk. She would put on her hat and spend a little part of the morning in the fresh air, and if the chance came to speak her mind, so be it.

The third person Mrs. Gruber exchanged good-days with that morning was her niece, who worked as a maid in the palace: the young girl was delighted to interrupt her morning's comings and goings to gossip with her aunt. They talked about the preparations for the wedding and after speculating about what share in the entertainments they might expect, the girl chatted about the English who had arrived, friends of Mr. and Mrs. Clode. Her aunt asked her if they seemed friendly or respectable people. Her niece confirmed it and told her in great detail about the strange Mr. Michaels who was now in residence in the fake village and who spoke the dialect of the region like one of them. Mrs. Gruber nodded, made her decision, and within half an hour of this conversation was knocking on Mr. Michaels's door. Half an hour later she found herself seated in a private drawing room of the palace with Mrs. Westerman, Mr. Crowther, and Mr. Michaels as support. She was given tea, treated with great civility, and left glad she had come. When she sat down to her modest lunch some hours after that, back in the kitchen of her dead master's house, she was not sure if she had done the right thing. Part of her thought His Honor would want to be left in peace. But she had learned how a question can lead one in strange directions. The image of Mrs. Westerman's open smile and schoolgirl German stayed with her the rest of the day. Mr. Crowther's eyes, she noticed, were ice blue like her master's.

As soon as Frau Gruber had left them, Harriet and Crowther went in search of Krall. They found him surrounded by paper in a cloud of tobacco. He greeted them happily enough.

"I have traced the mask! It seems it was not tainted before it arrived in Oberbach—Padfield's housemaid tried it on to amuse the footman and suffered no ill effects." He realized the English were not listening to him with the attention he had hoped for.

"The Honorable Diether Fink," Crowther said at once.

Krall drew heavily on his pipe then wafted away the smoke as if it had come as a bit of a surprise to him. "A good man. Banker and adviser to the court. Died in his bed some two weeks ago. The duke himself rode before the coffin. What of him?"

"You did not feel that another suspicious death following on that of Lady Martesen was of significance?"

Krall rubbed at his forehead with his fingertips. "Suspicious? It wasn't suspicious. He choked. His doctor hooked the nut that killed him out of his throat himself—he told me so. A tragic loss, of course. But people die and he had reached a fair age."

"His wrist had been cut," Harriet said. "Deeply. Then cleaned and bandaged."

Krall dropped his hand to the table and stared at her. "His wrist? *His wrist?*" His eyes narrowed, making Harriet think of the rocks overhung with vines she had seen on the road to Castle Grenzhow. "How do you tell me of this?"

"His housekeeper came to see us," she replied. "She saw the wound as she was laying him out. There was no other mark on his body."

Krall hunched his shoulders. "His wrist? Yet cleaned and bandaged? You trusted the woman?"

Crowther nodded. "She seemed quite respectable, and kept apologizing for troubling us with her fancies. Is the fact Lady Martesen's wrist was injured widely known?"

"No, no . . . I don't know. It seemed an unimportant detail. The gossips had plenty to feed on. No, I don't think it was widely known. Why did the woman wait to speak till now?"

It was Harriet who replied. "She had been uneasy about it since the morning of Fink's death, but when she heard there was some doubt after all about Lady Martesen's murderer . . ."

"I see, I see. Well, my humiliation is complete. Damn that incompetent sawbones. How could he not notice?" Krall sank his chin into his chest. His craggy face had grown red and his fists were clenched. He said in a lower voice, "What else?"

"That there were no servants in the house that evening, but there were signs Fink had a guest."

"That I had heard. No one knows who . . ."

"That did not strike you as suspicious?" Crowther said.

"Fink had plenty of guests!" Krall exploded. "The man loved his whores—half the bastards in Ulrichsberg are his! There was no surprise he chose to entertain on the quiet while his wife was in Strasbourg. I heard because the other gentlemen liked to say that at least he died content. And why should we look? We had Lady Martesen's murderer safely locked up. Were it not for Mr. Clode's connections and nationality, we would probably have condemned him already."

Harriet moved to the window. As the day of the arrival of the new duchess approached, activity in the palace seemed to continually increase. As she watched, a number of gentlemen, musicians by the shapes of the cases they were carrying, were crossing the yard in the direction of the Royal Opera House. A man in green and gold was directing an overladen cart under one of the archways. "It must be related. From her description, the wound was not accidental. I believe whoever killed Lady Martesen killed this banker too." She felt the fabric of the curtain hangings with one hand. Thick material, heavy and the color of blood. "Two killings of members of the court. Was Clode merely a convenient scapegoat then? The attack on him incidental?"

"I think not," Krall replied, rubbing his temples. "Whoever killed Lady Martesen went to some trouble to drug that mask, then lead Mr. Clode to the scene. It would have been simpler to drag in some fool from the streets. He would have had no rich friends to support him, no ambassador to force us to keep him safe. Two . . . two targets. What is the phrase?"

Crowther twisted his cane. "Kill two birds with one stone, I think is what you have in mind, Herr Krall. Mrs. Westerman, the answer must be locked in with Mr. Clode. He must give us a list of those people he met at court since his arrival here and his dealings with them."

"Graves and Rachel will return to the castle today to continue his interrogation. And you and Herr Krall are right: whoever has performed this killing is clever enough to know a peasant would make a better scapegoat than the agent of an earl."

"We cannot be sure that Fink *was* murdered," Krall said, almost to himself. "Some coincidence, some accident."

Crowther watched him steadily. "I do not think you believe that, Herr District Officer."

"No. I do not." Krall kept his chin low. "What am I to tell Swann? The cortège of the princess arrives at the border tomorrow morning. She arrives here the day after. Well, it is too late for her to go home now. As long as news doesn't reach them before they are past the borders of Maulberg." He brought a fist down on the table. "Damn this to hell."

He looked up at Harriet, a slight air of challenge in his eye, but she made no sign of offense or distress.

"What if Lady Martesen were not the first victim?" she said instead.

"What?" Krall said, distracted. "What do you mean, madam?"

"I mean, whoever has done this has managed to throw sand in our eyes most effectively. Perhaps they have tried and succeeded before. Have there been any other deaths in the last few months?"

"People do die, Mrs. Westerman."

"Yes, Herr Krall, but I am talking about members of the court and ignoring any case of long illness, or falls. Fire, for instance."

Krall looked at her suspiciously, but said nothing.

"Fire, Mrs. Westerman?" Crowther asked.

Rather than give him any answer, she turned to Krall, her head tilted to one side.

"I believe," Krall said wearily, "Mrs. Westerman might be referring to the death of Count von Warburg. He was indeed killed in a fire at his house just before Christmas."

"The circumstances?" Crowther said shortly.

Krall looked a little angry. "There was a fire and he died. Just before Christmas! Von Warburg had supped at court and returned to his own house. The maid woke in the night smelling smoke; by the time she knew what she was about, the whole of the top floor of the house was ablaze. Luckily for her, she slept in the kitchen. They managed to save the neighboring houses, but there was nothing much left of Warburg's place. It was assumed he had gone to bed drunk and the candle had caught on the bed-hangings."

"And that might be exactly what happened," Crowther said.

"It might well be," Harriet replied, "or it might be another murder concealed."

Harriet saw her friend close his eyes briefly. This was exactly what Crowther hated most. When he had a body, or a collection of facts to examine, he was content, focused. This sort of speculation frustrated him, made him feel lost in the fog.

"Was the body examined?" he asked.

Krall turned to stare out of the window. "The upper story collapsed. There was not much of a body to bury, let alone examine."

He then groaned slightly and put his head in his hands.

"You have remembered something else?" Crowther said, perhaps unnecessarily.

"And then there was Bertram Raben," Krall said heavily.

Harriet folded her arms. "Yes?"

"A suicide. It seemed. In January. He was a serious sort of fellow, a writer and poet, a young man but well thought of. He wrote for our newspaper here. We thought perhaps this fashion for suicide which has swept the country in recent years had finally caught up with us. But something was a little odd about it to me."

"We are all attention, Herr District Officer."

"I happened to be in town, and my colleague asked me to look in. Well, there was his room, papers everywhere, of course, and him just sat in the middle of it, opposite the door on a straight-backed chair. Thought it was an odd place to choose to die. Why not the easy chair by the fire? And there didn't seem to be enough blood."

"Interesting."

Krall stood up and leaned on the desk, his shoulders up. It cost Harriet some effort not to back away. "This is madness," he growled. "Yesterday I had one woman dead, and her murderer under lock and key; now you want to persuade me I am looking at four murders and no suspect."

"We cannot waste time with nostalgia, Herr Krall," Harriet said in slightly clipped tones. "Now to whom can we speak about these gentlemen?"

19

Having done his duties at the palace, Michaels made his way into the town. The market square was swarming with workmen who were building stands on three sides; they looked as if they aimed to dwarf the cathedral. He paused to watch them work and thought after a few minutes of observation that he would trust them enough to sit there, were he invited. Not that he would be. These were the stands where the nobility of Maulberg would wait, carefully ranked and placed to watch the arrival of their new duchess in two days' time. Michaels rolled his shoulders and set off at an easy pace for the house of Colonel and Mrs. Padfield.

On his arrival he was shown into the library. It was a rather grand name for a modest room, about the size of the third-best private parlor at the Bear and Crown. He mostly used it to store furniture that needed mending. Michaels sometimes thought houses were built with libraries in order to provide a place for men such as himself to be received. His thick beard and rough coat were not in keeping with the delicate decoration of a fashionable lady's salon, but he had become too powerful a man to keep standing in the hall.

He had come to Maulberg to assist his friends, knowing that with his guidance they would cross Europe a great deal more quickly, and he aimed to speed their return in the same way. He was happy to leave his business in the care of his wife and thought it might be a chance for his eldest son, a boy of fifteen or so, to step out from his shadow. His time in Maulberg he had intended to spend in looking around at the land his mother had been born in, see how the locals managed their horses and their brewing, and find out if there were any interesting opportunities in which to invest his growing wealth. Still, the mysterious request for an audience from these friends of Mrs. Clode's was intriguing. And he was at liberty while Mr. Crowther and Mrs. Westerman harried out the truth from this place.

Mrs. Padfield did not keep him waiting long. She was a good-looking young woman with a pointed chin and round eyes that seemed to bulge a little from her head, and though she was slight, her movements were quick and her orders to her maid brisk.

"Did anyone see you come in?" she asked at once.

Michaels affected a slightly befuddled surprise. "No, ma'am." In front of this thin-edged woman, he thickened his accent a trifle. Her bright little eyes danced over him as he shifted from foot to foot and turned his round hat in his hands.

She watched him for a few moments longer, then laughed. "All right, Mr. Michaels. No need to play the yokel with me." He kept his eyes low, though he let a smile lift the corner of his mouth. "The palace gossips say you are a wealthy man, and one to be treated with respect. Mrs. Clode has told us of your authority in your village."

He looked up at her. "What do you want of me then, madam?"

She took a seat and nodded to the chair opposite. "Sit down, please, Mr. Michaels. What I am about to tell you is known to only one other person, my husband, and to my shame he learned of it only two nights ago. I have decided to take a great risk in sharing this with you. I hope Mrs. Clode is right, and you are a man to be trusted as well as respected."

Michaels sat, but made no comment, asked no further question. She sighed and turned away from him. "When we met I told my husband that before I arrived in Ulrichsberg, I worked as a governess. That I came here in search of work. In truth, between the ages of twelve and twenty I helped my sister and uncle trick the rich into giving us their gold, and that is how we ate." Her words came out quickly toward the end, and as she finished she looked him boldly in the eye, her chin in the air.

He pulled on his beard. "What manner of stealing? Can't see you raiding travelers at twelve, and someone's taken pains over your education, haven't they? No one bothers to teach a pickpocket or a housebreaker lady's manners."

She nodded. "The man who called himself our uncle took me and my sister from the orphanage in Leipzig and trained us to be mediums for the spirit world. We had a talent for it."

"You're some manner of witch then?"

She smiled and shook her head. "More an actress. It was all theatrics, a keen eye, a few tricks. Imagine a young girl, all dressed in white in a dark room with my uncle murmuring incantations, telling you all your secrets and giving you messages from your dead friends and enemies. I grew used to the sound of gold coins rattling on the tabletop."

Michaels had met a fair number of tricksters and fools in his time, but his skepticism must have shown on his face. She reached over and touched his hand and he looked up. Her voice became very soft. "Your son is quite well, Michaels. He has had a more gentle start than you did, but he has your eye for people. Trust him. He will not grow soft because he did not have to earn his first money with his fists." She sat back again and laughed at the expression on his face. "Worth a coin or two?"

"Fair play, lady. I'm impressed. You have a talent for reading people. How did you know of my son?"

Still smiling, she picked up an ivory puzzle ball from the table at her side. It was a narrow tower with a ball on top, pierced and carved to show another ball within, also pierced, also containing another. "Mrs. Clode mentioned your family. Your history as a fighter is written in your face and hands if you know how to read it. It doesn't always work. We'd arrive in a town where there were enough bored rich nobles, and set about milking them with tales of their future, their dead loved ones. Once we'd made a few too many mistakes, my uncle would sweep us off to the next place. An unsettled life. But he fed us and clothed us, gave us an education and never tried . . ." She shrugged.

"So what happened? Ran out of towns, did you?"

"Not quite. But my sister was ambitious. She heard that there were nobles ready to pay through the nose if you could convince them you knew the secrets of alchemy. But my uncle was getting old and did not like the risks. When he got sick, she ran off with half our money, and half our jewels. Beatrice is her name. Sharp as a pin. Hair black as a crow's wing. She was proud of it. Made her stand out among all the fair-haired peasants and the powdered rich." She moved the puzzle ball so the ivory spheres turned and clicked against each other.

"What happened to your uncle?"

She smiled sadly, and Michaels wondered what she was seeing. "I looked after him. Saw him buried decently." Her voice lost its softness. "Then I came looking for her. I'd had a letter from her saying she was in Ulrichsberg, calling herself Beatrice Lachapelle, and that she had found a magus—someone to teach her. I met the colonel when he arrived at the hotel where I was staying here."

"And of your sister?"

She shook her head. "Not a trace."

Pegel woke and stretched very carefully. Bruises mostly, he thought. He'd have rather done three rounds with his pet giant than take that fall again. The ankle was bad though. Well, he had to spend the day organizing the papers he had got anyway. What was left of it. He had slept long and hard and the sun was already at its height. He looked at his right palm. Torn, ugly, and dirty. He needed food and watering. He got slowly to his feet, hobbled over to the window, and opened the latch. There was a pair of boys playing below him. He whistled, and after a good bit of miming and a coin that glinted in the sunshine, he heard small steps thundering up the staircase.

By the time his window rattled with a pebble hurled by Florian, his dirty clothes had been carried off, his wounds washed, and his ankle was supported on a mound of blankets. The brighter of the two children he had held on to as a servant for the day. When the pebble struck, Pegel sent him to see who it was.

"Fella."

"What sort of fella, genius?"

"Yellow hair and all very la-di-da!" The boy performed a little mincing walk across the window and Pegel tried not to smile.

"All right, go and fetch him in then."

He went without a word and when he returned, presented Florian with a flourish. "Here he is! What do you want me to do now then?"

"Bottle of wine and a bit of bread and cheese from Mother Brown's. Go on then!"

"They ain't going to give it to me for free, are they?"

Pegel shrugged. "Fair point. Florian, give the boy some money, will you?"

Florian reached into his pocket automatically and handed the child a couple of coins. The door slammed and his wooden soles clattered down the stairs like a drum roll.

Florian had been staring at him openmouthed. "Jacob, what on earth happened to you?"

Pegel crossed his arms and lowered his chin, looking sulky. "I met your friend in the brown coat again. He was running up from Fluss Strasse in a ripping hurry, but that giant wasn't with him so I thought I'd try to have a word. Judged it wrong. He threw me over, turned my ankle."

"Oh Jacob, I'm so sorry. Did he hurt you badly?"

"Oh, I'm fine, don't fuss! He just got lucky, had some momentum built up. I could have taken him, no problem, otherwise."

Florian came over and placed a hand on his shoulder and squeezed it. For some reason Pegel's eyes stung a little. "What time of day was this?" Florian asked. "I came looking for you yesterday."

"Out walking most of the afternoon. Clears my head. I was just coming back—it was dark, or getting there, I suppose."

Florian picked up a chair from the other side of the room and brought it over so he could sit with Pegel at the desk. He leaned forward, his elbows on his knees, and looked deeply into his friend's eyes. "A most terrible thing. It seems this man had found his way into the depths of a . . . society of friends of which I am part."

"What society of friends?"

"The ones I told you of the other night. Men ready to rule, ready to guide us to a better future."

Pegel scratched his head. "Those dreams—you saying they're real? What are you going to do? Hang all the dukes? Kill the kings?"

Florian smiled. His face really did glow when he talked of these things. "There will be no violence, Jacob. Our people will take positions of power in every court and country in Europe. We will convert to our cause those rulers who can be reasoned with. The others we will control, then educate their heirs. Slowly, all of this," he waved his hand, taking in the attic, but

Pegel supposed Maulberg, the empire, "all this will wither away and once again people can live as nature intended."

"You're mad."

"Inspired! But it is vital that secrecy is preserved until the world is ready. Vital. And now, somehow, someone has done what no one thought possible and identified the leader of our group in Leuchtenstadt." Pegel scratched behind his ear in hopes of hiding a slightly smug expression. Florian, however, had turned to watch the blue spring sky through Pegel's huge window. "It is such a closely guarded secret, only two or three people know his name."

"You do not know your own leader?"

"It is much safer so! I know only the names of two or three members of my own rank, and then there is my guide in the rank above. He will decide when I am ready to be initiated into the next rank, then pass my advancement over to another man who will guide me to the next stage. I told you, secrecy is vital."

"Sounds like the army. What's your rank now then?"

Frenzel hesitated. "Master Knight of the Chosen Company of the Elected." Pegel snorted. "Jacob! This is very serious!"

"Too bloody right it's serious—look at my ankle!"

The stairs gave notice that food was arriving and Jacob's young butler slapped it down on the table. "What else?"

"Nothing for now. Go and run about in the square and scare the old ladies, or whatever it is you do," Pegel said. "Stay within earshot, though. I may want you later." And when the boy stayed where he was: "What?"

"Retainer."

Florian reached into his pocket and pulled out yet another coin. He placed it in the boy's hand, saying, "Look after my friend."

The boy grinned and began to run the coin back and forth between his fingers. "I'll wipe his arse if you carry on paying like that."

Pegel grinned. "Not required. Now sod off, there's a good boy." As the lad went on his way again, Pegel noticed that Florian was blushing slightly. Good Lord, this man was brought up in a nunnery, he thought, and felt a stab of affection.

"The house of this man, our leader here, was broken into last evening. His papers were searched. That man must have been fleeing the chase when you encountered him."

"I wish I could have stopped him."

"If the thief had found anything of value we should all be ruined, our project at an end. Our leader here is in constant communication with a network of superiors, our leaders across Europe."

Is he now, Pegel thought. He said, "The thief had no luck then?"

"No, the significant papers were very cleverly concealed, and found undisturbed."

Pegel shifted in his seat to try and ease the ache in his leg. "So you know who the leader is now then?" Florian shook his head, and Pegel rolled his eyes.

"But it'd be so simple to find out! I told you, that fellow was running up from Fluss Strasse when I had my 'encounter' with him, as you call it. All you need to do is wander down that way and ask in a casual manner whose house was broken into last evening, and there you go! They're probably all talking about it."

"Jacob, you don't understand. The society requires loyalty, obedience. I shall be introduced to him at the proper time."

"I thought you were a brotherhood. How can you be brothers if all these layers of secrecy are required?"

"It is for the greater good."

"Greater good! Well, if you say so. So are there other bands of merry revolutionaries—sorry, visionaries—elsewhere in Maulberg? Do you actually have a chance of doing any good, or have my sacrifices been in vain?"

Florian shook his head again, and Jacob thought of a young horse, troubled with flies. "Oh no, Jacob. I told you much good has already been done. The leaders of our group first came together almost seven years ago. There are many of our mind who hold high positions at court in Ulrichsberg. So I have been told."

"But you don't know who?"

"Of course not."

"Can we eat?" Pegel said, apparently losing interest. "Healing makes me hungry."

"When I talk of the greater good, Jacob, I mean something real. It's not just an idea. I have something to show you. I thought of it as soon as I saw the equation you wrote out, and well . . . after what we've been speaking of." Florian reached into his pocket and took something out of it, then held it between his fingers, hesitating.

"Oh, give it here then." Pegel took it and looked. It was the small medallion struck in silver. On its face was an owl holding open a book. On the pages were legible four letters: *PMCV*. On the reverse was an outline of the state of Maulberg.

"Confident lot, aren't you? Claiming Maulberg for your own already."

"It is just to show where we are from," Frenzel said earnestly. "There are many places in Europe where our members hold great power."

"Hmm. What does PMCV stand for?"

"Per me caeci vident."

"'Through me the blind shall see.' Interesting claim. Now you said you thought of it when I wrote out that equation. Does that make me the owl? Yet in talking about your owl it sounds like you think me blind."

"You just need to be led toward the light, Pegel." Florian looked confused suddenly and made to reach for the coin again. "I shouldn't have given it to you; they are only for those who have taken the oaths. Give it back."

Pegel held it out of his reach. "Hang on there, you can't give a man a present then snatch it back."

"Please, Jacob, it was a stupid idea." Pegel looked at him. There were tears in his eyes.

"All right, all right. *Per me caeci vident*, eh?" He ran his finger over the raised body of the owl, then passed it back to Florian. "Then talk, owl, and I shall eat."

Michaels set down the letter on the table. It was the short note from Beatrice that had brought Mrs. Padfield to Ulrichsberg. "So you think this man Kupfel is the magus she wanted to learn from?"

"He's the only alchemist in town."

"You haven't been to see him yourself?"

"I intended to do so, but by the time I had found out his name, an attachment had formed between Colonel Padfield and myself. I did not want to risk his affection, which was foolish. I find I have married a generous man. And then . . ."

"What, lady?"

She smiled briefly, sadly. "I was sure she would come to me. I married under my true name, and we always read the papers wherever we lived. She would have seen I had married well and come to pick my pockets. She has not."

Michaels stroked his jaw. "She could be anywhere by now. What's to say she's not in Spain, telling fortunes there?"

"If you find signs she had gone there, I will not ask you to follow. But I am sure she would have written. I can only think she either has married very well indeed, so wishes to keep our past as secret as I do, or she is dead. I would like to know which. I hope you will help me, though I know there is no reason why you should."

He considered, and thought of his wife and son, the mantelpiece in the kitchen where the family liked to spend their time with its pewterware laid out. "That ivory puzzle ball you were playing with—I think my wife would like it. If I find you certain word of your sister, I'll take that for her."

"Very well."

Michaels got to his feet and his greatcoat knocked against the table and made the teacups rattle. Mrs. Padfield stood also and rang the bell for the maid.

"Why now?" he asked. "You lived with the not-knowing all this time. Why confess all to your husband, then me?"

She clasped her hands loosely in front of her. "I think I have been looking for a way to tell my husband the truth for some time. I am . . . very fond of him. Then I heard a man like yourself had arrived in court and it gave me hope."

"Any other way to know her, other than the name and the hair?"

"She had a plain gold cross with her name engraved on the back. A boy she liked gave it to her many years ago, and I never saw her without it after."

The maid curtsied at the door and Michaels made to follow her. Mrs. Padfield offered her hand and Michaels caught the maid's blink of surprise. No wonder she couldn't go looking for herself if offering a hand to a man like him made the servants curious. "Thank you, Michaels."

He nodded and followed the maid out of the house.

It was a small and extremely inky child who opened the door. Harriet had elected after their discussion with Krall to find out what she could of the writer Bertram Raben, and Krall had directed her to the shopfront in one of the smaller squares of Ulrichsberg where his works had been printed and sold, and where the official newspaper of Maulberg was written and printed. It was suggested that to avoid the sneers of the court, Harriet should take her maid. It irritated her, but when she saw Dido's delight at an outing, even if it were walking three paces behind her mistress to a newspaper office, she felt more at peace, and a little guilty.

Harriet asked for Herr Dorf and the inky child jerked his head toward a young man in shirtsleeves standing behind a desk in the back of the room. It was a crowded space and Harriet had a general impression of paper, noise, and tobacco smoke. Four or five men, rather sloppily dressed, shouted instructions or requests back and forth. The man to whom they wished to speak looked up briefly and seemed to be in the process of readying himself to speak to them, when another man of roughly the same age, but double his girth, thrust a sheet of paper under his nose. He spoke German, but with such weight on each of his words, Harriet found she could understand him reasonably well.

"Look at this, Dorf! Look! Four princesses at the gala and the names of three of them are spelled wrongly! It will have to be altered, or we shall have all of the cats about our ears."

"Then speak to Flounders, Kurt. And you could learn to write more clearly." Dorf's voice was calm but sounded deeply weary.

"I think you should tell him."

"I am sure you can express your displeasure strongly enough. Look, we have a guest." He crossed toward Harriet and made a bow. He was perhaps the same age as Graves and had a particularly long face. He reminded Harriet of her favorite saddle horse at Caveley, a patient beast.

"How may I be of assistance?"

She bowed her head quickly and spoke in French. "I wished to speak to you about Bertram Raben. I understand you knew each other well?"

Herr Dorf looked a little confused. He moved his hand across his forehead and answered in the same language. "Indeed, we were friends. He was one of my best writers. You are Mrs. Westerman, are you not?"

She admitted it and could see the questions forming behind his eyes, but he was too careful to give them voice at once. Instead he turned and fetched his coat from the back of his chair. "Let us take a turn around the square. There is no chance at all of us being uninterrupted here."

The day was bright. They began walking side by side; Dido took her place behind them and a little separate, looking around her with a wide grin.

"You seem much occupied at the moment," Harriet said pleasantly once they had fallen into step.

"The wedding, of course. We are producing lists of all the various attendees, the speeches, and every human who can hold a pen has written some sort of verse for the occasion, it seems."

"What sort of material did Herr Raben write for you?"

"All manner of things," Dorf replied. "Odd bits of gossip from the court for the daily news sheet. Longer pieces of opinion on literature or politics. We did a couple of those as short pamphlets. People knew he had friends at court, so they read what he wrote with interest. They sold quite well. He was a logical thinker and had a fine turn of phrase when he put his mind to it. He seemed to enjoy his life."

"Yet he committed suicide?"

Dorf looked up at her sideways. "So I believed—until you walked into my office, Mrs. Westerman." She smiled and they walked a little farther in silence.

"Would you know of anyone who would wish to do him harm?"

"No man picks up a pen without making enemies. But no, nothing that would mean—"

"Herr Dorf, forgive me, but you do not seem shocked that I am asking about Raben. Why is that?"

He came to a halt and Harriet noticed that they were outside his office once more. "I wondered if it might be a robbery at first, as his watch was missing—but then there was money untouched and in plain sight in the room. Still I did not think Bertram would have killed himself, Mrs. Westerman. I know we can be terribly wrong about our fellows, but I have never been quite able to believe it."

Harriet frowned at the earth in front of her. "Did he write about the Freemasons? Did he have enemies there?"

Dorf looked surprised. "He *was* a Freemason. He wrote against some of the lodges, who he believed had forgotten the central ideas of brotherhood and charity in their search of esoteric mysteries. The Rosicrucians he thought fools, and said so."

Harriet pondered this. "You would say he had influence in court?"

"He did. He was well-liked there. Do you think that might have been why he was killed? Some intrigue there?"

"I can hardly say."

"One moment, Mrs. Westerman. We were talking about my friend, a prominent writer certainly, but no more. And, I presume, about Lady Martesen . . ."

Harriet looked at him; he had the long dark eyelashes that reminded her again of her horse. She suddenly missed Caveley very much. "Dieter Fink, Count von Warburg."

His eyes widened. "You think there is something suspicious in those deaths also?"

"I do," she said simply. "Well, certainly in Fink's case. Of Warburg, I do not know as yet. But do you see what I am suggesting? A banker, a writer, a first lady of the court. It begins to look like a campaign, does it not?"

"And you asked about Freemasons because . . . ?"

"Mr. Graves heard rumors in London of a group called the Minervals. They were said to have revolutionary aims and to be active in this part of Germany. I wondered if they were conducting a campaign against Maulberg."

Herr Dorf gave a little snort and nodded to himself. "That *is* a coincidence. Minervals? One moment. There was a gentleman who wished us to publish some rather wild accusations about an organization of that name. I thought it was ridiculous, but I may still have the papers. You are in luck, the gentleman wrote in French."

"What happened to him?" Harriet asked.

"Disappeared off to Strasbourg in a cloud of indignation, I think. Will you wait a moment while I try to find it?"

Harriet was happy to do so.

Michaels found Kupfel's house easily enough, then lit his pipe and leaned into the shadows to consider. There were two other shopfronts opening onto this particular square. From one drifted the smell of meat cooking, and there was a steady stream of people coming and going from the doorway, their midday meal wrapped in scrap paper, steaming in the cold air as they dispersed again into the streets. When it looked like the rush had died down a bit, Michaels shifted himself out of the shelter of his corner and went in. It was a low room, dark with steam and smelling strongly of onions, but clean enough. There were two or three tables about, and he took a free seat in a corner, ordered liver and onions and made himself comfortable. The girl who fetched and carried from the kitchen gave him a smile, and he touched his forehead to her, but until he had eaten and was alone in the place he made no attempt at conversation. He knew it would come. No one ran an establishment like this unless they had a friendly sort of nature. They would be sighing and stretching now, glad the hardest work of the morning was out of the way and just in the mood to find a stranger interesting.

"Like it?" the girl said as she took away his plate.

"Just like Mother used to make," he replied with a grin.

She frowned briefly. "Not from round here, are you?"

"You've got a good ear, miss! No, I was born and raised in London. My mother was from here though, that's how I know the language."

"London!" The girl sat down at once and put her elbows on the table. "I've heard of London. Is it true anyone can get rich there and end up in a carriage?"

"Some do, I guess. I've got the blunt to pay for one myself now. But I like to ride and my wife would sooner walk."

The girl hugged herself. "My! How did you get so rich?"

He scratched his chin. "Prizefighting got me started. After that, horses and their care."

She laughed. "No good to me then. Horses make me nervous, and I can't see me fighting for money."

An older woman appeared through the door to the kitchens, wiping her hands on her apron, and the girl twisted in her chair. "Here, Mum, you'll never guess. This fella is from London, though he talks just like a real person."

Michaels tipped his hat and got a friendly enough nod in return. "Thank you for the liver and onions, ma'am."

She looked at the empty plate on the table and lifted her chin. "Nice to see good cooking appreciated. You look like the sort of man who's a pleasure to feed."

Michaels shrugged and studied the tabletop. "Not sure my lady wife would agree with you, ma'am. She says it's like having a pack of wolves to tend."

The cook looked pleased. "Sure she doesn't mean it, Mr. . . . ?"

"Michaels, ma'am, just Michaels."

"We wives love to tease our menfolk almost as much as we like to feed them. I'm Mrs. Valentin, and this is my daughter Gurt. Now might you like a little something to settle that in your stomach? I brew a Schnapps that can take the nip out of a fresh morning."

"That'd be a real treat, ma'am." Michaels pushed out the chair and bowed.

"Such nice manners! Gurt, go and fetch the flask and shut the door, then maybe Mr. Michaels can tell us how he comes to be in Ulrichsberg."

20

Frau Gruber thought her excitements for the day were over and was glad of it when there was a firm knock at the door and the tall thin figure of Mr. Crowther appeared on the step. He reminded her of the priest in the village where she had grown up, with his formal German and the severe glint in his eye. She had hoped that she had got past the age where a man could make her feel nervous, but this one did. He was so unlike her old master, his belly busting out of his waistcoat and his laugh of brandy and tobacco.

He said he wanted to talk to her a little more, and was invited in. Not wishing to receive him as if she were mistress, but feeling the kitchen would be inappropriate, she ushered him into her master's study and went to fetch a little of her own stock of sweet sherry. When she returned he had his cane under his arm and was flicking through one of the master's books. He turned as she came in and went about arranging the liquor and glasses on the table, but remained with the books till she invited him to sit.

"You are most kind, madam," he said, and she felt herself blush.

"How may I be of assistance, sir?" she said as she poured out the wine. Lord she was sounding like her old priest now. If her niece came in and heard her talking so fine she'd laugh her silly head off.

"Will you tell me, madam, anything you can remember of the last day of Mr. Fink? I am sorry to discomfort you in any way, but such was our amazement this morning, we did not make detailed inquiries."

She sipped her wine a little gingerly. "Discomfort," eh? Might just be his German but it sounded like he'd heard about the whores. Lord save me, she thought. In for a penny.

"His Excellency had breakfast at home, as always was his custom. He then did some work here." She pointed at the desk and they both looked at it for a moment.

"Did he receive any visitors at that time?"

"No, sir." She nodded and was about to sip her sherry again when she saw her glass was near empty. Mr. Crowther saw it too and made to pour her another. He really wasn't so bad, after all. She noticed his glass was still full, though.

"He went to the palace for a time, then came back about two and had his dinner here."

Mr. Crowther took a sip of his sherry and gave a look as if he approved of it. Man just needed some feeding up.

"I have heard there were signs that he also had visitors in the evening."

Some of the jollity left her. He did know about the whores. "He did love his wife, Mr. Crowther. But men . . . I don't think she minded, really, and he was always very sweet to her when she came home."

"I do not judge," he said.

She looked at him sideways, taking in the black clothes, the thin face, and the still-brimming glass of sherry. Like hell you don't, she thought.

"I said good night to His Excellency as he went back to court, sir. And before you ask, there was no bandage on his wrist then. I'd have seen it as I helped him on with his overcoat. I go home at ten, and I always leave a little something out. Wine and nuts or the like." She felt her eyes fill with tears and fumbled in her pocket for a handkerchief. "Then I came in at six the next morning, as ever, to make sure the girl had the fires going. Poor child, she'd gone in and found him there on the bed, half-dressed and blue round the lips. I sent her for the doctor, but it was too late. He was cold. There were two glasses and the decanter by the bed—and the nuts, of course. Poor fellow."

He waited and she found herself carrying on talking, just as if he was a priest and a friendly one. "Once the doctor had been I cleaned him up and took away the glasses. That's when I noticed the bandage on his left wrist. He liked his undershirts long in the arm. That's why you couldn't see it at first."

"Were there any other signs of . . . activity?"

She shook her head. "No, sir, and that was the other odd thing. He never usually . . . entertained in that room. That was the bed he shared with his wife, you see. He never . . . with other women there. Out of respect."

She reached for the handkerchief again. By the time she had recovered herself it seemed Mr. Crowther was ready to depart. She thought of the little owl fob and wondered if she should mention it. She also wondered if she had made too much of a fool of herself already with her talk and the sherry, but at that moment Mr. Crowther happened to smile at her, and thank her for her hospitality.

"There is just one other little thing, sir," she said.

"Oh, that's nice of you! To take trouble after a cousin you've never met." Mrs. Valentin had no family of her own other than Gurt, so she saw a large one as a blessing. Michaels knew there was no point in pretending he hadn't traveled here with Mrs. Westerman, Graves, and Crowther. It was only his reasons he twisted a little to help his current ends.

"Your mother's niece? You think she was here?"

"Last word I had. And that I got by accident. My mother was no writer, nor her sister neither, but her girl Beatrice must have picked up some schooling. She sent a letter to my mother and that got held by the barmaid in the inn we used to live at. She's a sweet old duck. Known me since I was all scabs and bones. I always go and visit when I'm in London, and when I was up selling horses there last year, she put it into my hands. Didn't know what to do with it, truth to tell. Not much of an address on it, but when I heard of Mr. Clode's troubles and that Mrs. Westerman and Mr. Crowther were coming out, seemed like God giving me a push, you know."

Mrs. Valentin nodded sagely. "The ways of providence, Mr. Michaels, the ways of providence . . ."

"What's she like, your Mrs. Westerman?" Gurt said, leaning forward. "I heard she shot a spy!"

"Gurt . . ." her mother said.

"What, Mum? Peter said she had a look of a devil about her. He helped carry her luggage yesterday."

Michaels looked at her. Her eyes were light blue, and some of her blond hair had escaped from under her cap. She looked eager as a puppy. "Don't think she shot a spy," he told her. "Helped catch some once, and shot another fellow up north. And if she did, I know she had good reason for it. She's a good woman."

"And what of this Mr. Crowther? He that cuts up dead bodies? Is he an alchemist too? I saw him going into Whistler's place yesterday."

"Did you now?" Michaels said, placing that snippet in his pocket like a windfall. "No, Mr. Crowther don't believe in magic. Whatever his business was there, wasn't that."

"And this cousin of yours worked for old Whistler?" Mrs. Valentin asked politely.

"Not sure as sure, ma'am. Just said she was working for a man used to be an apothecary. They told me at the palace about this place."

"There are two others, retired apothecaries still breathing in town. All made a fortune stirring up vats of powder and paint for the court. But I know them. Never had a girl in the house that could read. What age would she have, Mr. Michaels?"

"Born well after my mother left for England. No more than twenty-five now. I'd like to help her out if she can be found. I was still poor when my folks died. Be nice to do a bit of good if I can."

"And Mr. Crowther? Does he cut up bodies with his sword stick?"

"No. Uses a special knife though. He brought it with him."

Gurt shivered, delighted. "So I hear that maybe the lawyer didn't do it. What do you say, Mr. Michaels?"

"I'd stake my life on it, Miss Valentin. That boy is innocent as you are."

"Lord, poor fella!" Gurt said, her eyes wide.

"Could it have been two years ago, Mr. Michaels?"

He nodded. "I suppose that was when the letter must have been sent."

"There was a girl . . . Gurt, do you remember? Dark-haired little piece. Used to come and get a chop for Whistler every Saturday and charge it to his son. Had that dark blue dress I thought was just the color for you. Wasn't her name Beatrice?"

"Oh, that it was!" Gurt rolled her eyes. "What a little bitch she was!"

"Gurt!"

"I'm sorry, Mother, but she was so. And I'm sorry for you, Mr. Michaels, if that's your niece. You know, twice I saw her sweetheart a shilling out of one of the fellas to pay for her supper, then she'd charge it to Whistler's account anyway and walk off with the coin in her pocket and her nose in the air. And the manners on her! She'd make the empress herself, God rest her soul, look humble." Gurt widened her eyes and tilted her head a little to one side. "Honest, Mr. Michaels, if that's her, don't pay her no mind. Sure we can find you another girl to spend your money on if you fancy it?"

Michaels suppressed a smile, though he noticed a definite cooling in the air, as if a draft had just come in from the angle where Mrs. Valentin was sitting.

"Sorry to hear that, miss. But I still have a duty to my poor mother. What became of her?"

Gurt crossed her arms and sat back in her chair looking sulky. "No notion, I'm sure. She was here through the spring and summer, then pouf! Gone away! I asked Whistler if he'd got sick of her and blown her up in one of his experiments. He looked at me as if I were stupid then ran away. But you might ask Simon. They seemed friendly. You'll find him hammering for the blacksmith off Ludwig's Platz. She took a coin or two off him, and he don't part with them easy."

"Or there's the son," Mrs. Valentin continued. "Theo Kupfel. He sells ointments and perfumes on Karlstrasse, and pays them that wait on his father."

Michaels got to his feet. "Thank you, ladies. You've been very kind to a stranger."

21

Michaels would probably have gone straight back to the palace to see Crowther and find out why their paths had crossed at Whistler's door, except his way took him along Karlstrasse, so shrugging his shoulders he pushed open the door of the perfumers, and stood slightly stunned by the smell of rose water as it clanged to behind him.

It was a large shop, crammed with dainty-looking porcelain and glass jars in gleaming and glowing display cabinets. Three neat young women, gleaming and glowing too in their way, stood behind the counter, all engaged in what looked like intimate conversation with ladies whose elaborate hair and impractical costumes marked them out as nobility. There were a number of vitrined display cases on chests scattered about the room. He leaned over and examined the one nearest to him: silver-backed brushes and minuscule combs resting in velvet boxes, and to his left a display of snuffboxes, each one crowded with painted cherubs and chariots. His nose began to itch. There was a sign above the counter, the writing in gold leaf: KUPFEL'S MIRACLES FOR LADIES AND GENTLEMEN. ELIXIRS OF YOUTH AND VITALITY, BY APPOINTMENT TO THE COURT.

The prettiest of the young women standing behind the counter gave him a long look and rang a tiny little bell by her side. Michaels felt as if he were the bear from his own inn sign, ungainly and unsure on his two hind legs.

A door to the back of the shop opened and a man, probably some years younger than Michaels, appeared. He was very thin and pale. His hair was pulled up off his head at such an unnatural angle it must have been stiffened with sugar water, and he wore his breeches so tight to take a seat must be impossible.

"Can I help you?"

Michaels was briefly distracted by the thought of breaking off a portion of that reddish quiff and eating it like barley sugar.

"I said, can I help you?"

Michaels dragged his eyes to the man's face. "I want to ask you something concerning your father. If you are Theo Kupfel, that is."

The man gave a dramatic sigh and exchanged sad and weary smiles with his shopgirls. "What has he done now? More explosions?"

Michaels shrugged. "No, nothing that I know of. Thing is, there was a girl working for him a couple of years ago who I think might be a niece of mine. Dark hair. Pretty. Goes by the name of Beatrice."

"Apologies! No idea! I must have hired a hundred girls to try and look after my father, and most of them can't take his manners for more than a fortnight. So sorry, bye bye, off you go!" He made a little shooing gesture.

Michaels wandered over to the counter. "I'm in no hurry, son. She stayed a fair while longer than that. I'll just have a look around until you've had a chance to think."

He stuck his finger into one of the pots and lifted it to his nose. It made him sneeze. A bell jangled and a woman in red silk opened the door. Michaels smiled broadly at her. She retreated. The women already in the shop began to cast slightly nervous glances at him while their servers waved colored powders at them like matadors trying to attract the attention of a bull.

"Very well," Kupfel said sharply. "I shall tell you what I can remember. Out the back, if you please."

Michaels followed him and noticed one of the shopgirls shaking her head sympathetically as he went.

Michaels sat down on one of Kupfel Junior's spindly little chairs rather more heavily than he needed to and was glad to see its owner wince. He leaned up against his desk and folded his arms across his narrow chest.

"Beatrice? It does ring a bell—she lasted a few months, now that I think of it. Though I can't tell you much about her. And we're very, very busy with the wedding around the corner. Everyone wants to look their absolute best for the arrival of the new duchess."

Michaels shifted his weight from side to side on the chair and grinned as if

childishly amused by the little squeaking noise it made. "Very well!" the per-
fumer almost screeched. "If you can just stay still while I think."

The squeaking stopped.

"She was prettyish, I suppose, for a common girl. That black hair. I even
offered her employment in the shop, as I was a little shorthanded, but for
some reason she preferred to go to my father."

"He had no one at that time?"

"His last girl gave notice the day before Beatrice arrived at my shop. Said
she had come into some money and meant to go and marry on it, but that
she had a cousin willing to take the place. That was Beatrice."

Any thoughts on the convenience of the arrangement, Michaels kept to
himself.

"And you had no complaints of her?"

He shrugged his shoulders and Michaels noticed they were padded.
"None. Then she was gone and gave me no notice. First I knew of it was my
father turning up at the shop demanding to know where his dinner was. I
suppose I would have owed her wages for the last month, but she made no
effort to collect them."

"That not strike you as unusual?"

"Young girls can be flighty."

"See much of your father, do you?" Michaels asked, looking about him.

"Our relations are a little strained. Not surprising, given his eccentricities.
I took what he taught me of his arts and have created the best cosmetics in
Europe. Do you have a wife? I have a skin cream that will make her look as
fresh as she did on the morning of your marriage! I can create scents to
charm a hermit from his cave, rouge that looks as natural as the blush on a
rose. I make the world a better place and he despises me for it. He thinks
himself superior because all he has become is scarred and poor, while I am
rich."

He tossed his head and Michaels stood up. The man looked as if he were
made of china, his pointed little chin aiming at the air, his ridiculous quiff.
This is what has come of his father's lifetime of work then, he thought.
Money enough to stuff a man's shoulders with horsehair.

"He taught you then?"

"Not as such. I never spent enough time curled up over his damned books to be thought worth teaching. But I watched in my youth and that's how I learned. He talks to himself as he tends his furnace."

"Thank you. But I like the way my wife looks right now." Michaels turned toward the door. Kupfel stood holding out his hand.

"Perhaps if you could leave by the back way? We wouldn't want you to have another sneezing fit, now would we?"

22

Crowther had not yet returned to the palace, and Rachel and Graves had once more headed up toward Castle Grenzhow. Harriet tried to read, briefly, and considered to whom she should write, and what she could or should say, then picked up her cloak once more and headed for the gardens. Her footsteps took her toward the automata makers. Her theft of the file was not mentioned. News of the demonstration of the mask had drifted up the hill toward them too.

"I had thought there was an agreement to not let that news out," she said, accepting a glass of tea from Sami.

"Mr. Manzerotti is a keen collector of works such as ours," Adnan said. "He knows we are friends of Mrs. Clode's and while examining our wares let a few details slip. We of course gave him a very reasonable price."

"What did he buy?"

"The caged songbirds."

"Naturally." Harriet thought of Manzerotti and wondered whom he was working for now. The King of Prussia? Why not. He was a powerful man who would of course be interested in a state such as this, squeezed in between the kingdoms of Austria and France. She tried, as she watched Adnan work, to think like a king. To have Maulberg strong must be to his advantage. If Austria were to absorb it, Prussia must feel threatened, but if Prussia were to try and claim it overtly, then Austria would protest. Poor Maulberg, she thought, all these great powers grouped around it, watching each other, laying a claim for influence. Then these Masons with a revolutionary bent. Did they exist? And if they did and did manage to destabilize Maulberg, didn't they realize they would be swept away in the flood as France, Austria, and Prussia tried to rush into the gap? She sighed.

"Mr. Al-Said, explain this marriage to me."

Adnan set his file to one side. "Mrs. Westerman, I am a Turk and a commoner. Why do you believe I can tell you anything of the matter?"

Harriet picked up one of the brass keys in front of her and spun it between her fingertips. "For just that reason. You and Mr. Sami have been here nearly two years, but you have observed, not been drawn into it all. How did you come here?"

"We knew that the duke liked to spend generously on items such as ours. We had hoped to tempt Count Frenzel too." Adnan blew the fine metal shavings away from the brass disk on which he worked. They glimmered. "He once had a reputation for buying works such as ours, but as far as we know, he has not bought anything from us yet."

Harriet lifted up the key and smiled with artificial brightness. "What makes this place tick?"

"Same as any court. Gossip. Intrigue. Alliance. Influence. Power," Adnan replied.

"Power. A strange concept in a state with an absolute monarch."

"Indeed. It can bestowed and whipped away again at any moment. People contort themselves in many ways to try and capture it, retain it."

"Explain."

"They watch each other. They impress or indulge each other. Some buy amulets from any fakir who comes through the city that promise to make them invulnerable."

She smiled and sat back a little. "Do they really?"

"Oh yes. When money and influence pass so quickly, so . . . whimsically, people will cling to whatever they can convince themselves will help them."

"This marriage is important, is it not?"

"Yes, I think it is. The princess is the only child of the Elector of Saxe Ettlingham. It is not a large kingdom, but it has tactical advantages."

"And it borders Maulberg."

"Indeed. The duke has some interests in it through his mother's family. In agreeing to marry the princess to him, the elector has named the duke his heir."

"So Maulberg should rejoice? Yet the wedding negotiations seem to have been carried out very quietly."

"Indeed. Six months ago when the duke announced his betrothal, the news fell on the court like a thunderclap. The duke seems to have kept his secret even from his most intimate friends."

"Why?"

Adnan examined the air above her head. From outside Harriet could hear a cuckoo calling. She had never liked the birds since she first heard the stories of their breeding. Creatures that grew fat on the labors of others.

"I think he likes to surprise. He has such a love of spectacle, to drop this coup of a marriage into the court . . . pleased him, I suspect."

"How was it arranged then?"

"Colonel Padfield seems to have had a hand in the negotiations, and Count Frenzel."

Harriet rested her cheek in her hand, placed the key on the workbench and spun it on its axis with a fingertip. "Why do I feel not everyone is delighted?"

"I cannot say why you feel what you feel, madam."

"Mr. Al-Said . . . ?"

"A shift of influence, of power perhaps. Also, the princess has been granted the great indulgence of bringing a number of gentlemen from her own court and placing them in positions of power here. Some members of court also wished the duke to marry a different princess. One with less powerful friends."

She watched him work a few minutes more, finding the patience and exactness of his movements deeply calming. "I can see why my sister has found refuge here, Mr. Al-Said."

"I shall tell you what I have told her, Mrs. Westerman," Adnan said. "Remember it is a false refuge. We are still in the grounds of a palace, not lost in the woods."

Harriet had intended to read the papers she had received from Herr Dorf in the quiet of the gardens on leaving the Al-Saids, but as she emerged into the spring air she found Michaels outside, in conversation with the metalworker Julius. The latter was in full conversational flow, speaking in the local dialect. As soon as he noticed Harriet he switched to French and made his bow.

"Mrs. Westerman! Delighted to make your acquaintance. I understand you gave up a rather pretty necklace yesterday. Would you like to commission a replacement? I shall make you something so charming you will be glad you gave the first away. Gold and emeralds to bring out the color of your eyes. What do you say?"

She shook her head. "Is there anyone who doesn't know the details of the demonstration?"

"I rather suspect the duke is preparing the court for Clode's return from Castle Grenzhow by letting little details slip. How about a gift for Mr. Clode? A snuffbox, perhaps. Enameled?"

"The duke is still considering whether to release Clode. I would not want to presume, and in any case I have not come to Maulberg to spend my housekeeping."

"Another serious lady! Thank the Lord not all of your sex can refuse me so easily. I should starve." He frowned for a moment. "What about an Athenian Owl! Perfect emblem for a seeker after truth such as yourself, and I've already . . ." He suddenly blushed. "Forgive me. That would be tasteless in the extreme."

Harriet shook her head, confused. "You shall not tempt me, but why should it be tasteless?"

His face was still very red. "I did make one before, but it was for Lady Martesen. She wore it often. The idea of offering you a replica, in the circumstances . . . I apologize, I have no idea what I was thinking." Harriet felt rather sorry for him.

"No need to mention it further, sir. And you are quite a salesman. Now do tell me, what were you saying to Michaels so excitedly when I interrupted you?"

He looked grateful for the chance to recover himself; his voice became lower and softer. "Only how glad I was when the Al-Said brothers arrived in court and took up residence here. The servants from the palace had been sneaking into the building night after night to amuse themselves with parlor games and ghost stories. I don't begrudge them some entertainment, but sometimes the women would let out a shriek that would wake the dead. Certainly woke me anyway." He cleared his throat. "But you have both had more than your fair share of my nonsense now. Good day, Mrs. Westerman, Michaels."

He nodded to them both and returned to his workshop. "If he can control his tongue, I think that young man will do well in life," Harriet said, watching him retreat

Michaels grunted. "He thinks too well of himself, if you want my opinion. I asked him who the people were who came up here, and all he had to say was 'servants,' as if anyone without a title has no right to a name of their own." He glanced at her sideways. "No need to grin at me, missus. I doubt you like this setup any more than me. Never realized how easy I had it in England till I saw all the bowing and scraping goes on round here."

"I can't imagine you ever bowing to anyone, at home or here, Michaels. Yet you would not ride in the carriage with us, or dine with us on the road, and when you come to Caveley you come in through the kitchen door."

"I like the fresh air, and my boots are always dirty."

She sighed. "I suppose I should be grateful you didn't say you know your place."

"Maybe you should." He winked at her.

"Enough! I know better than to fence with you. What news then, Michaels?"

He shrugged his shoulders. "Some dribs and drabs. But it seems my path and Mr. Crowther's have led us the same way. That needs thinking on. I'd be willing to come and chew it over with you both, if you're at liberty."

They found Crowther in his room, and when Michaels had finished telling them what he had learned, and they in turn told him of the uses Kupfel's drugs had been put to, Michaels hissed between his teeth.

"It makes me worry for the girl," he said. "I've no doubt that it was she who took the books and supplies, but she was all cons and flummeries, not murders. I reckon she's passed those poison notes on to someone else, and I wonder what has happened to her now."

Harriet put her chin in her hand. "I fear you may be right. Is there no way of finding out where Beatrice went?"

"Maybe. There was a boy here who liked her, we had a word or two as I passed him coming back, and though I don't think he knows much, I reckon he knows a little more than he's saying. I just haven't found the right way to wind him up to talking. I'll ask around here too. Sounds like my Beatrice could have been caught up in the spirit nonsense that Julius made mention of."

"Good luck, Michaels," Crowther said. "It seems you might have the best chance of running this matter to ground for now."

"We'll see. Plenty of riddles for all of us." He paused. "So Mrs. Padfield's been hanging on and waiting till someone like me came along that might help her, trying to keep this quiet."

Crowther nodded. "I understand. I can see no reason we need let it be known that Beatrice was Mrs. Padfield's sister. What say you, Mrs. Westerman?"

"The same."

"I meant to tell you, Mrs. Westerman," Michaels said, turning to her, his voice soft. "If you wish it, I will throttle that Manzerotti for you. I could make it back to England on the quiet."

She studied her hands.

"Thank you, Michaels. But no. If I cannot kill him myself, I will not send another to do it. Find this girl and her poison book. And we shall try and discover who has been making such use of it."

When he had left, Harriet showed the papers she had collected from Herr Dorf to Crowther. He read through them and put them aside with a sigh. "Nonsense."

"It does read like the work of a madman, does it not? Secret societies working in the heart of government. All assertion, no evidence. Thank goodness we have news of this poison book, or I should think myself lost indeed."

If anyone knew who used to go to the village to see spirits, they weren't saying. Michaels couldn't blame them. Sneaking off after hours like that would be enough to lose you your place; better to play dumb and say you had never heard of such a thing, especially to a stranger just rolled in. He gave up soon enough and stepped into town to wait for the boy to finish at the blacksmith's. He timed it nicely; after half an hour Michaels spotted the boy emerging from his workplace and slouched forward.

"Can I buy you a brew, lad?" he said, nodding toward a doorway nearby.

Simon looked suspicious. The offer of a free drink is a difficult one to refuse on any occasion; however when your feet are sore with standing and your bones ache with hammering iron all day, such a refusal is all but impossible. He nodded, and they went into the tavern together.

A keen-eyed boy just clambering long-boned into his teens brought them beer, and Michaels pronounced in its favor.

"You know I want to talk to you more of the girl Beatrice," Michaels said, once he had sunk half his drink in a single gasp. Simon sipped his as if he thought it might be bad.

"You said you were her uncle."

"That why you clammed up on me?"

"She told me she had an uncle, but he was dying or dead. You look pretty bloody healthy to me, and for all Gurt or her like say of her, I trust Beatrice over you."

Michaels grinned into his beer. "Thought that might be it. You were more friendly with her than others knew, eh?"

Simon didn't answer, but hunkered over his tankard.

"Did she tell you she had a sister too? Two years older than her, taken out of the orphanage with her by the man they traveled with. It's on her account I'm asking."

"Why say you're an uncle then, and lie to folks you're asking trust from?"

"It's a fair question." The smoke in the place was so thick you didn't need to light a pipe yourself, just taste your neighbor's tobacco for free. Michaels examined the young man. Hard eyes, and thin-faced. He wondered if Beatrice had seen him as a fellow spirit. Like appeals to like, after all.

"All I can say is, the sister married well. Wants to know why Beatrice hasn't found her out to feel how deep her pockets are, but she doesn't want to risk asking around her herself now."

"Who is she?" His face was hidden by the tankard, but Michaels could still see his little eyes glimmering through the fug and fall of his fringe. He leaned forward till his face was only an inch away from the other man's, and spoke quietly and carefully.

"You don't want to think of playing that game, lad. You tell me something that helps, and I'll see you won't suffer for it. But don't get thinking." He put his hand on the boy's elbow and twisted very slightly. Simon hissed in pain. "Now maybe your little rat's mind is thinking who it might be. Maybe you're thinking I'll leave Maulberg soon. Well, I might. But I won't leave the lady unprotected, so even if you do work it out and try and force a penny from her, you'll have to watch your back every night for the rest of your sorry little life." He leaned back again and patted the boy's shoulder in a friendly way. "Be smart. Take the easy money and smile. Two thalers now, if I like what you say, and five more if I find something worth finding." It would take the boy two weeks to earn that in the general run.

He rubbed his elbow. "All right. What do you want to know?"

"For two thalers down? Bloody everything."

He considered. "She wasn't that friendly to begin with. Held herself apart, you know? Then one night I found her round the back of Whistler's place sitting on a barrel and crying her eyes out. Thought she'd fly when I saw her, but I showed her a couple of magic tricks. Made her smile. After that we seemed to bump into each other a fair bit. Nothing much. Just a bit of conversation and a laugh at the end of the day."

"She liked your tricks."

"Yeah, you know, just pulling a coin out of her ear, that sort of caper. Funny thing is, she never wanted to know how I did it. I asked her why and she explained that that always spoils it. Told me a bit about her sister and uncle then."

"And what of her work for Whistler?"

"Said she wanted to learn the tricks of alchemy, but that she'd bribed her way into working for a fool who was actually trying to do it—make the Elixir of Life and all that—rather than fake it. She was bitter that she'd spent good money to get the position. Said it was money wasted. All books. No cons."

"So what did she plan on doing then?"

"She was a smart one." He smiled and scratched his ear, the hard glitter in his eyes softening now. "The next time I saw her, she said that she reckoned she could still get her money's worth out of it. He had some book of his own and she'd worked out the way he had of writing in it. Thought it could be sold with the bits and pieces wrapped up with it. Then she'd picked up some learning from the other books, copied out pictures and signs, a few spells and incantations and stuff. Cut out others. Said she was making her own book of magic, and when she found the right mark she'd twist him for everything he'd got."

"What happened to the books she cut the pictures from?" Michaels asked. Simon shifted in his seat. "You burned 'em in the forge, didn't you?" The boy said nothing.

Michaels looked about the room. Voices were beginning to warm up and the laughter was getting louder. Three or four men of about his own age with their backs to the wattle walls were singing a song to the vine and toasting it in vats. He knew the feeling from his own place. A good night, open pockets, and no trouble.

"Beatrice was still wanting to take a step up from the occasional session seeing spirits, then?"

"Suppose so, though she did them now and again for the servants up at the palace." He sounded a little more eager to speak now. Get away from those mangled books burning in his master's fire, no doubt. "Said it was a good way of getting information out of them on the sly. She weren't one to give up on her dreams easy, Beatrice. She thought if alchemy was a washout, best thing to do was find a rich family with a hole in it and draw them in. Stay with them, give them the good news of their loved ones, find a bit of treasure for them, then settle in and rob 'em blind."

"Still don't see how—"

"She thought she could arrive a pauper and leave a lady. Find a grateful old man with wealth to leave behind him to the girl who had been such a comfort, who had summoned angels to visit him and let him talk to his lost ones again."

"Did she tell you she was going?"

"Yes, the day before."

"When?"

"Late summer, near two years ago now."

"Where was she headed?"

"Didn't say precisely." He supped his drink again and looked away. Michaels sighed and counted out two coins from his purse onto the table. "She took the road to Oberbach."

PART V

23

Krall did not know why he had been summoned to the Mirrored Hall of Ulrichsberg Palace, but when he found Chancellor Swann there in his shirt-sleeves, gray-faced and alone with a candle in his hands, he began to suspect.

He had been woken, dressed, and then guided to the chancellor by Wimpf, who had taken the role of his personal servant while he was in the palace. As they approached, Krall found the chancellor surrounded by a hundred broken images of himself. Together they filled the room like a crowd.

Swann wasted no words on greeting Krall, but only nodded and swung open a hidden door on the wall behind him, sending their gathered images dancing among one another in the candlelight till they were legion. Wimpf disappeared back into the shadows.

"This way," Swann said. The hidden door led to a long corridor, unadorned, and crimped and bent by the rooms between which it snaked. Krall had a sense of being lost in the entrails of some great beast, or finding himself cast suddenly in an abandoned mine. Even in the light of the traveling candle he could see doors and panels to his left and right. From here surely all the court could be observed, reached, secretly. He wondered about his own rooms. After some minutes Swann came to a halt with his hand on a latch to his left. The candlelight made him look a great deal older; his shoulders seemed to have acquired a stoop since they had seen each other a few hours before. There was a light gray stubble across his chin, and his cravat was only carelessly tied.

"Krall, are you loyal to the state you serve?"

"Yes, Your Excellency," Krall said, frowning and irritated by the pantomime.

"And your sovereign?"

"My sovereign is the state I serve."

Swann seemed to consider this a moment before he continued. He handed the candle to the district officer and, pushing open the door, gestured for him to enter.

It was one of the smaller guest chambers. Krall stepped forward. Countess Dieth was seated in the middle of the room on a straight-backed armchair in a full court gown of plum silk, her chin down like someone sleeping over their book. Her left hand hung loosely, pointing toward the floor. Her stillness. In his first confusion, it took Krall a moment to realize she was dead. "Huh . . ." he said and crossed slowly toward her, his steps heavy and awkward. Her dress pooled out around her feet. Krall lowered his candle and with his right hand gently lifted her chin.

Her face was white with powder, her cheeks rouged, but around her mouth was a flurry of dark specks, coal dust on snow. He brought the light closer. Her lips were covered in what looked like soil, loose dry soil. Krall looked around him, but the room was clean. Her eyes were open, bloodshot, empty.

"When was she found?" he said, resting his palm on her cheek. Quite cold.

"Half an hour past," Swann said, his voice rather thick. "A maid had cause to enter the room. I was summoned, and on seeing the body, ordered that you be awakened."

"What cause?"

"District Officer?"

"What cause did the maid have to enter this room in the thick of night? Countess Dieth has a house in town—why is she not there?"

"I do not know."

Krall tilted the countess's face back and carefully opened her mouth. It was full of dirt. He breathed in deeply and with great gentleness closed her jaw and let her head tip forward again. There was soil caught in the bodice of her gown and in the folds of her skirt. He struggled with the impulse to clean it away, to make her neat again. Then he held the candle to cast some light upon the lady's wrists. The left had been slit and the hand was bloody.

The candle moved back and forth. There might have been some blood on the dress, but he could not be sure, given the deep color of the material. The polished floor was apparently quite clean, no signs of drop or spray. He frowned.

Krall lifted the candle above his head and walked slowly around the body. The room was very much like his own, one of the apartments provided for the favorites of the court when their sovereign wished them near at hand. Not large, but luxurious, the wood all polished or gilded. Thick hangings tied around the bedposts. The fire had not been lit. The basin and ewer on the washstand were empty. He thought of his own chamber in the palace. Every night he had spent there, when he entered the room, the coals had been burning in the fireplace, fresh water to wash in. Normally wine and a little something to dull the appetite under a cloth. There was a small table set up to the body's right, with decanter and glass set upon it. Both empty.

"Mr. Crowther and Mrs. Westerman?"

"Retired early and have not left their rooms since. Neither has Mr. Graves, nor Mrs. Clode."

"Forgive me, I meant to suggest they should be summoned."

"I see. You think this is the work of the same person who killed Lady Martesen?"

"And Herr Fink. And possibly Raben and Warburg as I mentioned to you this evening—no, yesterday, I suppose it was." It felt natural to speak low. "It seems likely, don't you think, Your Excellency?"

Swann turned away slightly and put his hand to his forehead. He was trembling a little, Krall noticed. He had never seen Swann display any kind of emotion before. "But those crimes were concealed. The madman provided us with a suspect for Lady Martesen's death and made the others appear accidental."

"Perhaps he was not so mad then as he is now," Krall said. He caught sight of something and the candle moved quickly through the air, fluttering in the draft, then steadying again. On the back of the door to the west wing corridor was chalked a design in red. A circle with lines through it, drawn over a triangle.

"Do you recognize that, Your Excellency?"

Swann did not look, but remained with his chin tucked low. "Death has come in at our window, into our palaces," he mumbled; "it strangles our children in the alley, our youth in the street."

Jeremiah, was it? Krall thought. So the chancellor had developed a talent for quotation along with his stoop. "It is almost light, Chancellor. Will you wake the duke and tell him?"

"It is my duty. First I must dress."

"The duchess arrives tomorrow. You will wish to keep this quiet a day or two."

Swann looked up at him. "We might wish it, but I fear it will be impossible."

"There might be rumors, but it is not impossible surely—for you, Chancellor? Unless the duke wants this known too."

Swann straightened his back, something of his old manner managing to reassert itself. "He will not. The servants can be threatened into silence. Countess Dieth's people in town will be told that she has retired to her country estate. People might assume, given the relations the countess once had with the duke . . ."

"Mr. Crowther will not be able to examine the body here."

Swann's mind, it seemed, had woken at last. "The Lady's Chapel is being redecorated in honor of the new duchess, but it is not yet finished. The works have been halted while the craftsmen complete her apartments and the preparations for the theatricals. It can be sealed and guarded."

"Good."

"I have two men awaiting orders."

Krall stroked his chin. "Let her be carried there then while it is still dark, and have the men that carry her guard the chapel. Then send Wimpf to collect Mr. Crowther and Mrs. Westerman. If that seems fit to you, Your Excellency."

"A sensible idea."

Krall returned to his study of the strange diagram on the door. "How many people sleep in the palace, do you think, Your Excellency?"

"Perhaps a hundred or more. Certainly more if you include the quarters of the coachmen and stablehands, and the Ducal Guard."

Krall set his candle down on the mantelpiece where its light sent the shadows of the room's fine furnishings, its gilded mirrors and molding, skipping and dancing. "The palace is not in my jurisdiction, Your Excellency."

"Nevertheless, given the similarities, I ask you to investigate." Krall did not answer at once. "We are united in our wish to know the truth, Krall."

"I am glad to know that." Krall had been feeling like an old man these last years, but staring at the design on the wall he realized he was enjoying a sensation he hadn't felt in some time. He was curious. "You may call your men, sir," he said. "Then, with your leave, if you will send the maid who discovered the countess to me and ask Wimpf to wake Mrs. Westerman and Mr. Crowther. Perhaps he might take them their coffee and something to eat before telling them what is afoot. I will wait for them."

"Whatever your wish, District Officer." There was an edge in Swann's voice again, but Krall made no move to show he felt it.

24

Harriet was used to waking early, usually before any of the servants came to her room, so when she woke to the sound of movement beyond the draperies around her bed, it was with some confusion. It was still dark. At first she thought she was in her bed in Caveley, but the nap of material on the sheets around her felt unfamiliar. Then it came back over her in a familiar flood, the dispatch, the journey, the splendor of Maulberg, that she had had Manzerotti in front of her and a gun primed in her hand, and yet she had not shot. She groaned.

"Madam?"

She struggled up onto one elbow and twitched open her bedcurtain. "Dido? This is early even for you."

Her maid was lighting the fire. Harriet's nightshift slipped from her shoulder and she pulled it around her again. The air was still chill.

"Sorry, madam, but one of those footmen is outside wanting you. Said the name Krall?"

"He is the law officer in charge of the case."

The maid got to her feet. "That'll be it then. He's brought you coffee and rolls and gone to wake Mr. Crowther, poor man." Harriet smiled. The longer Dido spent in her service, the more she sounded like Mrs. Heathcote. "There's something wrong, madam. He was white as a sheet."

The white-faced footman, Wimpf, looked as if he intended to retreat when he had shown them to the room in which Krall was waiting, but the district officer beckoned him inside before closing the door and speaking. The room was soft with early light; gradually the colors and shapes were revealing themselves.

"I apologize for the hour, Mr. Crowther, Mrs. Westerman. Countess Dieth has been killed. Her body was discovered here by one of the maids early this morning. Her left wrist was cut and her mouth filled with earth."

"Where is the body?" Crowther said at once, looking about him as if Krall might have concealed her behind the draperies.

Krall yawned, and covered his mouth. "Countess Dieth has been taken to the Lady's Chapel. We could not wait to move her, Mr. Crowther. This must be kept quiet for now and she needed to be taken somewhere appropriate in darkness. I will lead you there in a while, but I wished you to see this room as I found it. I hope you will indulge me."

They looked a little suspicious. Well, good for them if they did. They inspected the small space in silence, a candle each to help guide them through the softening shadows, Mrs. Westerman lifting the skirts of her dress as she moved. They were like ghosts. Some marking on the arm of the straight-backed chair in the center of the space caused a few murmured comments to pass between them. Krall sat on the high bed as they made their investigations. His feet did not quite touch the floor. At one point he felt in his pockets for tobacco and tinderbox, but reconsidered and with a sigh replaced them. Wimpf again made a movement as if to leave the room; Krall again motioned him to stay.

"Do you mean to mock us, Mr. Krall?" Crowther said at last.

Krall blinked. "Mock you, sir? That was certainly not my intention. Why would you suspect such a thing?"

It was Mrs. Westerman who answered. He decided he liked her dress. "The lady was not killed in this room," she said calmly. "It seems the body was moved here sometime after her death."

"The killer placed the body of poor Dieth here *after* her murder?" Krall asked, his head on one side.

"No, I don't think so, Mr. Krall. I think she was found somewhere else, then placed here before you were summoned. That decanter was brought in from wherever she was found. It has its twin on the table. I suspect that design on the door has been copied for your benefit. See how hesitantly some of the lines are drawn? This is a bold killing, and that is not boldly drawn."

"But how can you say the countess was not killed here?" Krall asked.

Crowther answered him. "The blood. The chair comes from this room indeed, one can see in the rug the marks where it has been moved to this position, and there is blood on it—but not such a stain as would result from a wound fresh-flowing. Only flecks that must have been dislodged when the body was brought here sometime after death, when the blood had fully dried. The floor is clean. No blood whatsoever there. Where could the body have been found, that it needed to be shifted in this way? What could have been more humiliating to the court than finding one of its own slaughtered inside the palace itself? Mr. Krall, I cannot believe this fooled you for an instant. Nor could you have hoped to fool us."

Krall considered the ceiling with the contented look of a man hearing exactly what he wanted to hear, then he turned to the footman and began to speak in German. As he did, he could hear Mr. Crowther whispering a translation to his companion.

"The gentleman and lady wish to know, Wimpf my boy, where the body was first discovered. Where was it? Who ordered you to carry it here?" The footman opened his mouth, but Krall continued, "I know your family, boy! I thought a couple of thalers and a few friendly words might make you my eyes and ears in the palace, but you've been bought already. You've been watching me, haven't you, you little devil? Was she still warm when you lifted her?"

"How—?"

"You had red chalk on your sleeve when you woke me. Stuck out rather, that, boy—you being so clean as a rule. That picture on the wall is your work, is it not? Sure you copied it right?"

"I, I . . ." Wimpf stuttered, but Krall held up his hand.

"Remember before you speak, lad, that I answer only to the duke. Now tell the truth. Your parents are good people. I cannot believe they brought you up to lie."

"I f-found her . . ." he stuttered out at last, "in the temple . . . I went to Major Auwerk and he came back with me, then he told me . . . He carried her. I thought he meant me to, but when I went to pick her up, he told me not to touch her. He carried her here. I brought the table. Then he went to Chancellor Swann."

He looked very afraid. Mrs. Westerman stepped forward and put her hand on his sleeve, saying in halting German, "Yours is not the fault. The district officer will see you get no hurt."

Krall doubted if he could guarantee such a thing entirely, but Mrs. Westerman's words calmed the boy a little, and he smiled up at her timidly. He seemed to have shrunk in his livery.

"What temple, Wimpf? The Temple to Apollo in the gardens? Is that where you found her?"

He shook his head violently, blinking his lashless eyes. "I cannot say—it is a great secret."

Krall had never had much use for secrets, and now his patience left him. Grabbing the servant by his gold and scarlet coat, Krall flung the boy onto the floor by the bed, then stood over him with his fists balled. He heard the silks of Mrs. Westerman's gown shift, but neither of the English moved to stop him.

"*Now!* If you want to leave this room as you entered it—tell me now!"

The boy scrambled backward and found himself cornered between the end of the bed and the wall.

"It's hidden! It's hidden! You can only get to it by the back corridor. It's just a room with a few chairs in it, that's all. Like a cupboard almost. I call it the temple. It was my joke." Krall took half a step forward. "I clean it. When I am told to. Maybe two dozen times over the last two years. Major Auwerk asked me to, he asked if I was to be trusted. If he puts the key in my hand, that means I am to clean it. I clean there when everyone else is asleep and return the key."

"What does he pay you?"

"Nothing! Only since I started I've been promoted twice. I wanted him to know he could trust me. And now I have betrayed him . . ."

Krall continued glowering for a second, then stepped back and rolled his shoulders. "He betrayed you first, boy. Major Auwerk has the key now?"

"Yes."

"So you went to clean the room. How much work is that, usually?"

"Not much. Glasses and a bottle or two. The chairs and so on to put back in place. Sweep and dust."

"How many?" The German Crowther spoke was a great deal better than

Mrs. Westerman's, though as he spoke Krall could almost smell the dusty air of a university lecture hall.

"How many what, my lord?"

"How many glasses?"

"It changed. Never more than seven. There are only seven glasses in the case."

"Today?"

"None used. All clean."

Krall heard Mrs. Westerman whisper something to Crowther, and he said, "Mrs. Westerman wishes to know if this decanter and glass were in this temple. And if you include them in your count."

Wimpf's fingers were digging into the rug underneath him. "The decanter and glass were there—I've not seen them before. The seven glasses are nice. Special. Wine goblets. Countess Dieth was sitting in a chair in the center of the room facing the door. I just came in and she was there. I thought she was sleeping, but then I saw her hand. I was scared, I ran out to Major Auwerk's room in the barracks and told him. The decanter and glass were on a little table next to her. Just as they are now."

"And the picture?" Krall asked.

"On the back of the door like here. The chalk was still on the floor. I copied it properly. The major checked."

"So, facing her when the door was shut? I see." He rubbed his chin. "Right then, Christian, on your feet and straighten yourself out."

The boy leaned on the bed as he got up and winced. Krall realized he must have thrown him quite hard and found he did not care. He reached into his pocket. "Here is paper and pencil. Draw the room as you saw it. And draw a plan of how to reach it." The boy hesitated. "Do it, Wimpf, if you want to keep that head on your shoulders."

"Young man," Crowther said, "how much blood was there?"

The boy shook his head. "Not a great deal, my lord. A few splashes under her hand. I cleaned it all up."

They watched him as he drew with shaking fingers. After a few minutes he laid down his pen and Krall examined the sheet—clear enough. "Not bad. Stay out of the major's way today. I suppose you were asked to keep an eye on me and my English friends? Then as far as he is concerned, that is what you are doing. Avoid him until I get word to you. Now out you go."

Wimpf paused at the door. "Mr. District Officer?"

Krall held up his hand. "I don't know, boy, what will happen to you. I can't see into the future. But don't despair. I doubt your fate will be any worse than the usual mix."

They watched him leave.

"Good God!" Harriet said when the door had shut. "You knew all along, didn't you, Herr Krall?"

"As Mr. Crowther said, madam, I am not stupid. There was the smear of chalk on his sleeve, and the maid they told me had discovered the body has the wits of a peahen. Can't believe Swann didn't spot this nonsense." He sat down on the bed again, well satisfied. "I suspect young Wimpf thought me a bit of a country cousin, as do most of the people at court, so I thought I'd make use of you and all your cleverness. He might have kept lying to me. It worked too."

"Who is Major Auwerk?" Crowther asked.

Harriet was studying the symbol on the door. "He accompanied us from the border, Crowther, at the head of that party of hussars. What his role is in this . . ."

"We'll find out soon enough—he won't be going anywhere," Krall said. "Now, I am afraid you had better see the countess."

There was light enough now. He blew out his candle.

25

Michaels liked the farmland around Oberbach. As the light of the new day found him he was letting his horse amble along the valley with a pipe in his mouth and a sense of cautious approval. The wooden houses he could see from the road were neat, their gardens well-tilled, and the fruit trees that hung over his way were showing the signs of cheerful new growth. Walnut. Apple. Almond. The chimneys of the farms were already pushing wood smoke into the first sunlight and he thought contentedly of the morning scenes playing inside. The wife at the fireplace, a child at her skirts and her kitchen clean. His own wife would also be up and working at this hour. She was efficient and quick in her movements, sometimes she hummed at her work, and sometimes not. He would walk out around the yard, see to the horses, and scan the hedgerow for something pretty to bring back into the kitchen. He had told his son to bring his mother the first primrose he found. He hoped the boy had remembered, trusted he had. He felt it likely they were thinking of him now and felt a solemn happiness.

Michaels entered the town itself from the north, and by the number of travelers he nodded to on the road, suspected he was arriving on a market day. Women walked along the verges in pairs with baskets over their arms, their aprons washed to a startling, public whiteness. The old town gate under which he rode was hung with baskets of spring flowers and the main street had the look of a place recently scrubbed clean and smiling. The death of the lady during Carnival had left no visible scar. The old houses in the square looked confident and prosperous. Their half-timbering was outlined in red and green, and the shutters were all folded back. The newly built town hall with its wall of tall windows seemed designed to flatter its citizens, not cow them into obedience. It was a proud little place, bustling already, speaking of a group of people who had money enough to satisfy their hungers, then were in the habit of looking around them to see what could be improved.

After two hours of wandering through the marketplace and complimenting the women on their produce and the men on their stock, Michaels thought that if he had ever to leave his own place in Hartswood, he could do a lot worse than taking over the stable where he had left his horse and settling here among these handsome, homely streets and pleasant faces. There had been talk of this last year having been all cruel weather, and the fat on the animals being hard come by, but there were both buyers and sellers enough, it seemed to him, and the local wine was a sweet and delicate thing and had much to say of sunlight and rich soils. He had also realized, with regret, that the trail of Beatrice did not reach here. People stopped in their work and folded their arms to consider, but one after another they shook their heads.

"We get people passing through often enough," one woman selling eggs from a basket over her arm told him. She was red-cheeked and cheerful-looking and wore a shawl around her shoulders Michaels's own wife would have coveted. "But a young girl on her own would have been noticed and looked to."

"It would have been two years ago . . ."

"It's not a big town! If she'd stayed here, worked here at all, we'd know her face. A girl with black hair, who liked to wear it loose, would be noticed in an hour! Mostly the strangers we see are men traveling about for one reason or another."

"She had a fancy to go into service in a great house," Michaels said, turning his round hat in his hands.

"Why come this way then, rather than stay where she was among all the court and their nonsense?" She spoke almost affectionately, as if the duke was a child to be indulged with pretty toys, and shifted her basket so her hip could take the weight of it. Michaels only shrugged. She pursed her lips, thinking, then lifted a finger. "There are a few places beyond the village of Mittelbach. Estates with fancy houses. You might ask of her along that road. Take the north road back two miles or so, and you'll see the turn to it

heading up the hill, to the west—lies just past old Hahn's farm. He has five
pear trees below his house coming into flower. You can't miss the way."

A man passing in homespun, a pair of rabbits slung over his shoulder,
heard her and laughed.

"What's the fella ever done to you, to send him to Mittelbach, Maud?"

"Keep your nose out of others' conversations, Georg, or expect to have it
snipped off!" Then she turned back to Michaels with a blush. "Though he's
right enough. It's a mean little place. Their pastor does nothing but drink
and their headman's a devil."

Georg did not seem to be overworried about his nose. "The blacksmith
has an amulet—you know, got the hair in it of that robber who killed three
travelers in Gottingen in seventy-nine. Means he can't be vanquished by any
man. He deals out the beatings the headman prescribes. Almost killed a
woman there last year."

"*Did* kill her!" Maud replied. "A chill like that would never have carried
her off if he hadn't knocked the health out of her. And she was no adulteress,
just had a jealous husband and a friendly disposition. There, you see? We all
know each other's business round here."

"Why don't they complain to the duke?" Michaels asked.

"Not his people. It's the land of one of the imperial knights, surrounded
by Maulberg, but not Maulberg, you know? There are a few up that way. A
big house, some land, some grand fella who acts like a king and spends all
that can be dragged out of the soil on silks to wear in another man's palace.
They don't care what happens to the people as long as their stewards roll up
with a bag of coins once a quarter."

Michaels thanked her and offered her a coin from his own bag. She
laughed at him. "No charge for a chat, brother. Keep your money and buy
one of May's cheeses with it; you'll get nothing worth eating in Mittelbach."

Harriet was becoming accustomed to spending time with the dead, but
that was not the same as being unfeeling in their presence. Countess Dieth
was much her own age, and in her interviews with Krall about the death of
her friend, she had answered like a woman of passion and intelligence. Harriet remembered her expression when she had understood the effect of the

mask—her fear—and suddenly the death of this woman seemed to fall hard on Harriet's shoulders. What could she—*should* she—have done yesterday? It seemed to her now that she had spent half the day wandering the palace grounds. She had not *pushed*.

The doors closed behind them, and Harriet hesitated halfway up the short aisle. It was not a large chapel, but beautiful in its light and proportions even if the floor was messy with dust and wood shavings. Harriet was flanked by carved stalls; she saw the small organ, its pipes freshly gilded, on the south wall, the pulpit to the right, and there the countess lay, like a sacrifice, on a table covered with white linen set before the altar. There were candles at her head and feet, but the day was bright enough now to make them unnecessary. She was lit by the morning sun coming through the stained glass of the east window. Her plum-colored dress was patterned with the red, blue, and yellow of the arms of Maulberg. Pushed against the walls was a pair of scaffold frames. Harriet looked up to where the frescos on the ceiling had been abandoned partway through their painting. Christ in the center, fully colored and robed. Around Him, any number of angels faded into outlines and bare plaster. Harriet noticed that the color of Christ's robe was the same as the countess's dress. He had His arms held out wide.

She took another step forward and watched as Crowther opened one of the countess's eyes with thumb and forefinger. Krall took a seat in the stalls.

"Was she suffocated with the earth in her mouth?" Harriet's voice sounded hollow, and loud to her in the empty space.

"Suffocated, I think," he answered, without looking up. "The earth may have been placed in her mouth after death however. If, when I open the body, I find there is soil in her stomach and throat, then we may conclude..."

"I understand."

Crowther moved to the other side of the body and stooped, apparently examining the left wrist. As she watched him, he became suddenly still, frowning, then he let out his breath and turned away. She had never seen him give any sign of distress or discomfort in the company of the dead; his normal attitude was a quiet curiosity.

"Crowther, what is it?"

He stood aside.

Trying not to think of the living woman, Harriet finally stepped forward and looked carefully at the body. There were lines around the eyes, across the forehead that Harriet recognized from her own mirror. Then she examined the skin around the throat, the uninjured wrist, the nails on that clean right hand. No bruising she could see at all. No nails broken, no sign of restraint. It was just as they had been told of Lady Martesen's body. She thought of Kupfel's drug. The soil in the mouth. There was unlikely to be a ready supply of soil in the temple any more than there had been a convenient method of drowning Lady Martesen in the haberdasher's back room. Whoever had done this had brought his tools with him. So he had planned these embellished killings; he did not slice the wrist, then change his mind.

She stepped around the countess's head to her left side, feeling like a traveler ordered by her guidebook to examine the peculiarities of a certain effigy, and turned her attention to the injured wrist. The deep slash had let the flesh separate to expose the meat and matter below. The hand was blackened with blood. It had run from the wound and across her palm, then traveled along the fingers. Its course was easy to read. The thumb was clean. She spoke as she thought. "The blood on the hand suggests the heart *was* still in motion when the injury occurred, does it not? This is a flow, a wound in living flesh." She glanced up at him and Crowther nodded. "We had thought the lack of blood might mean these wounds to the wrists were made after death, but it cannot be so." She remembered what Krall had said about the place where Bertram Raben had died. That there was not enough blood. And no mention of *any* blood at all at the scene of the death of Herr Fink.

"That footman talked of blood in the room where she was found. You translated the word he chose as 'drops,' if I remember." Crowther nodded again. "That does not suggest the quantity of blood that would result from this wound. It must have poured out. There should have been pools of it." The wound must then have been inflicted, and allowed to give forth a profusion, before the victim's mouth and nose were sealed and her heart ceased to beat. *So where in the name of God was the blood?*

It came to her like knowledge remembered, a simple fact she had always known, but had forgotten momentarily. She felt her own blood begin to roar in her ears, and thought of an account Crowther had given her of an execution he had attended in Germany, of people crowding around the trunk of a freshly executed criminal with their cups held high to catch the blood that flowed, outpourings of the final beats of a heart that did not yet know itself dead.

"Oh God, Crowther. Whoever did this *collected* their blood."

Turning away, she walked quickly into the darkest corner of the chapel and put her hand against the wall. For a moment she hoped she might be able to control the clenching in her stomach, but as if it wished to taunt her with a separate will, her mind filled with every incident of bloodletting she had ever seen. With the eyes of a child she saw the door to her father's room open and the local doctor emerge cradling a bowl of bright red from his regular spring bleeding; she found herself on the red-painted orlop deck of her husband's ship assisting the ship's surgeon among the shattered and struggling victims of a surprise attack from privateers; she was watching blood pool on the floor of the Great Chamber at Thornleigh Hall; she was bent over her husband while her skirts soaked in his blood; she was watching some man, a bowl in his hands, patiently collecting the flow from Countess Dieth's unmoving, pliant fingertips. She struggled for the door, wrenched it open, and stepped in to the courtyard, panting hard.

Crowther watched her go, but knowing what was in her mind did not follow her at once.

"Mrs. Westerman is a clever woman," Krall said softly.

"Yes, she is. And it is both her gift and her curse that what she understands, she must also feel," Crowther replied. "Whatever good we have done in the past, at moments such as this, Mr. Krall, I wish to God it were not so."

26

The contrast between Mittelbach and Oberbach was stark. Turning off the road back to Ulrichsberg seemed to drop Michaels back into another age. One would have thought this country had been crossed by warring troops only months ago rather than twenty years in the past. It seemed a land whose people had been torn from it, and not returned. Though the rising ground to the north of the track showed signs of having been cultivated in the past, the terracing was only visible as ripples in the undergrowth. A few ancient, struggling vines curled up the remains of the poles. Near Oberbach they flourished, here they were broken and wild. The first house he saw was a ghost, the door hanging off and the garden all brambles. It was like the enchanted villages in the stories his mother used to tell him, and he approached the huddle of dwellings expecting a witch.

No witch. Instead he saw chained to the flogging post in the mean village square a boy, not more than ten years old. A woman was crouching by his side, weeping and trying to wash the child's wounds. The punishment was fresh; across the boy's back Michaels could see the open wounds of whip blows. Six of them, and deep enough to scar. The boy was unconscious, his weight hanging from his wrists. The manacles looked too large for him. He was like a child in his father's coat.

Michaels dismounted and led his horse to one of the buildings. There were two men standing outside with pint pots in their hands. They were watching the woman trying to support the child's weight so the manacles would cut into her son no more, their faces blank.

"What's the offense?" Michaels said quietly.

The man nearest turned and looked him up and down. He was shorter than Michaels by a head and his shape reminded Michaels of the snowmen his children had made in the churchyard that winter. They had lined the path to the church door, annoying the vicar and amusing the gentry. He had beaten them for the impertinence, but not hard. The snowman removed his pipe from his mouth and spat on the ground.

"Whelp was caught stealing."

"Will no one help her?"

"And risk a whipping themselves? No fear. Let her look to him. He is to be let down at dusk anyhow." Michaels looked up; the sun was not yet near its heights.

"What did he steal?"

"Water from the river, maybe. Headman asked the widow to keep house for him, but she's too proud to fulfill all her duties."

The other man laughed quietly to himself, then caught the expression on Michaels's face and stopped.

"What's your business here?" the first man asked.

"Looking for someone. Woman, perhaps came through here two years ago, maybe stopped near here a while. Black hair, she wore down."

"She ain't here no more. Never saw anyone like her." His answer was a bit quick and Michaels saw the other man's eyes flick right and left.

"Is that so? Who does the whipping?"

The man nodded toward the forge. Michaels set a coin on the table. "See that someone feeds and waters my horse."

He stood for a while considering the woman and child. To intervene might prevent him making any further search for Beatrice. He remembered his offer to Mrs. Westerman to kill Manzerotti and disappear into the forests and make his own way home. He thought of his wife and children in Hartswood. He didn't want to make the life of Mr. and Mrs. Clode more difficult, but he couldn't unsee this, and there'd be no real point in going home at all if he couldn't look his family in the eye. He realized in truth the decision had been made before he even started to think on it. He crossed the square and walked into the smithy the man had nodded at. He found hammer and chisel on the workbench and turned to go, when a shout stopped him.

"What the hell do you think you're playing at?" A man his own height and wider by some margin came lumbering out of the back of the building, pulling his breeches closed. A young thin-looking woman followed him, smoothing her skirt. She slipped past Michaels and turned the corner without looking back. Michaels considered the man. His head was shaven and there were veins pulsing around his neck. His flab hung in bags at his waist, but his shoulders were broad, his arms long, and his hands heavy-looking. Again Michaels thought of his mother's fairy tales.

"Just borrowing these," he said, and walked out of the house. He heard the man shouting behind him. He sounded confused. Michaels lifted the hammer and chisel as he walked; he saw the woman's face, frightened and tear-streaked. She held up a hand as if to ward him away, but before she could move further he placed the chisel on the chain and struck it. It split apart and the ends ran free of the ringbolt with a satisfying clatter. The woman took the boy's falling weight and Michaels heard the child groan. He had just enough time to turn and duck under the hammer blow aimed at his head. The blacksmith staggered.

Michaels stepped away from him, and the blacksmith charged again. Michaels waited, then again danced away from the blow. The blacksmith was panting.

"There now, you're just wearing yourself out, fella," Michaels said. "Not used to hitting people who ain't been tied up first, are you?"

In reply, the blacksmith dropped the hammer and charged at him head down, but this time he was ready for Michaels's dodge and twisted enough to grab him around the waist. Michaels went down, but managed to squirm out from under the blacksmith's falling body and scramble to his feet. The blacksmith's left hand shot out, caught Michaels on the ankle, and pulled him down again. Michaels kicked out hard with his right leg, bringing his heel down on the blacksmith's face, and felt the nose break. The man roared with pain and let go of Michaels's ankle. Michaels threw himself across his back, got his arm around the man's throat, and pulled. The blacksmith's arms paddled in the dirt and his eyes bulged.

"Which arm do you use for your whipping?" Michaels spoke through clenched teeth.

"Get him off me, you bastards! Get him off!"

"No one's coming, fella."

"I'll kill every bastard one of you for this! Fuck you all, fuck you all to hell!"

There were people watching from all sides now, silent, expressionless.

"*Which arm?*" Michaels punched him sharply in the kidneys so the blacksmith yelled and writhed.

"Left! *Left*, you son of a bitch."

Michaels paused for a second, remembering the hammer blow. "Nice try." He stood and dragged the blacksmith through the dirt to the stone steps leading up to the flogging post, then knelt on his back and yanked his right arm out so the forearm rested between the two lowest raises. The blacksmith yelled out again but Michaels drove down with his open palm and felt the bone snap. The blacksmith screamed. Michaels stood, spat onto the dirt, and watched for a moment. Then knocked some of the dust off his coat and turned to go.

"Murderer . . ." the blacksmith managed. Michaels paused.

"What's that, fella?"

"You heard." The words came out between sharp pants. The blacksmith's face was yellowish-white, like milk on the turn.

"Bollocks. It's a clean break. You'll mend."

"You've murdered me, I tell you! If you go now, they'll kill me," he hissed.

Michaels looked around him. A couple of sour-looking youths had emerged from the buildings around them to watch the fun. One had a shovel in his hand. His face was pinched and he carried his head forward and his shoulders high. There was a glittering in the air and Michaels knew the taste of it. Normally when a fight was done, tension fell away, it was the same lightness that came after a thunderstorm. This air, this sense of heaviness, meant violence to come. He cursed under his breath and crouched down. The blacksmith's cheek was pressed into the dirt, the fat of his face forcing his right eye closed.

"You got any friends here willing to shelter you?"

His left eye glittered with hope and he spoke quickly, his words flickered with spit and fear. "The pastor's—Pastor Huber . . . His house is down the track past the forge."

Michaels looked at him. The man was worth nothing, and to take him would rob the growing crowd of its revenge for all the beatings he'd given out. He thought of his wife again, remembering an argument they had had about some business in Hartswood. "You're not God, Michaels!" she had said.

"We're going now." He got the man's good arm over his shoulder and hauled him up, thanking God he hadn't broken the bastard's legs. He felt the crowd watching him, jealous, angry, but it was leaderless now. If one man had stepped forward and claimed the blacksmith, the rest would have followed, but no one did. "We don't run, we don't dawdle," Michaels said, and taking as much weight as he could, half-dragged the blacksmith from the square.

27

After some minutes breathing in the fresh air, Harriet found that Crowther had joined her. He stood a few feet away from her, leaning on the head of his cane and watching. It was typical of him, she thought, to remain at hand, but not approach her too solicitously. Rather he waited until she had recovered enough to speak. At last she lifted her head and looked around her. It was still early. The entrance to the Lady's Chapel lay in a small enclosed courtyard, high-walled and hardly overlooked. There were a number of neat piles of workmen's tools and a stone bench against one wall. Its plainness was a relief in comparison to the rest of the palace, and the slight chill in the air was welcome. The two men guarding the chapel doors kept their eyes on the empty air in front of their noses.

Crowther saw her lift her head, and nodding toward the bench, he crossed the space between them and offered his arm. She took it and let herself be guided. As soon as they had taken their seat he reached into his coat pocket and produced a document, much decorated with ribbon and seals.

"What is that?"

"The order for Daniel's release."

"Krall gave it to you?"

"He procured it while we had our coffee and had it in his coat all the time. I feel as if it is a reward for having spotted the trickery in the placing of the body."

She took it from him and traced with her fingertip the impression of the seal of Maulberg. "How strange. We came all this distance to obtain this. I should feel elated, should I not?"

He began to twist his cane between his palms. "We came to save Daniel, yes. But we also came to know the truth. To find out what has happened."

"Where is Krall?"

"He has gone to fetch my knives for me."

"Did he say anything to you about this mysterious chamber?"

"He seems to think it was a place for confidential meetings. That is his speculation, at any rate. He asks us to let him interrogate Major Auwerk himself." She nodded. "It seems we were not the countess's first visitors, Mrs. Westerman. The duke came and sat vigil with her as dawn came up."

Harriet sighed deeply. "I will never know what is meant here, and what is true. Do you trust Krall?"

Crowther shook his head. "I don't think I trust anything I see here. My instinct is to think Krall honest and well-meaning, but that is my prejudice. I see the show and fakery of the court and do not like it. Therefore when I see Krall looking ill at ease among it in his old coat, I am disposed to like him. There is no logic in it. Do *you* trust him, Mrs. Westerman?"

She smiled slightly. "You put faith in my instinct, Crowther? I have learned to my cost it is not so accurate as I would like, but my feelings are as yours on the subject."

She pulled one of the ribbons on the release order through her fingers. She could hear the usual shouts and orders coming from the other court-yards now. The palace was waking.

"Have you ever seen anything like this murder, Crowther?" she said at last.

"No, Mrs. Westerman. I imagine few people have."

"I cannot help remembering what you told us of Kupfel's drug. I wish he had not told you about the continued suffering of those rendered passive by it."

"May I suggest you do not dwell on the subject? Whatever hell they passed through, their sufferings are over now."

She did not reply at once, then: "Why does he want their blood, Crowther? I had been almost seduced by Graves's talk of revolutionary Freemasons into thinking these killings had some sort of political intention behind them, then the blood and that symbol. This is some manner of ritual."

"Freemasonry is all ritual, in my opinion. It makes the members feel they are more than some ordinary drinking society, but this is a step beyond anything I have heard imputed to any branch of Masonry I know of. No mention of collecting blood, or smothering people with earth."

"A pity. It would have made life rather more simple." She sat forward and put her chin in her hand, tapping Daniel's release order against her skirt. "The elements. We have three of the four: water, earth, fire, possibly, if Warburg *is* another victim—what of air?"

"It is a very easy thing to smother a person who is incapacitated. Close the mouth, pinch the nose. In the absence of any other of the four elements at the death of Fink and Raben, I would suggest that this insanity could say they were killed by air, or rather, the lack of it."

"It has a rather twisted logic to it." She stared at the flagstones in front of her. "Why do people perform rituals? Make sacrifices?"

"To gain some advantage, some blessing from the gods."

"I read a rather colorful account of instances of human sacrifice in my father's library," she said. "Peoples who were in the habit of killing prisoners or their own kin for success in wars or some such."

He smiled. "I am surprised your father let you read such things."

"Oh, I was forbidden to do so. But he often forgot to lock his study door. Crowther, if these are sacrifices, these victims with rank and position, I feel that whoever is offering them must be asking for a very great favor from his gods. And there is another matter," she went on. "If we are right, and the blood is being removed from the place of killing . . ."

"We *are* right. The blood flowed, the blood is no longer there. Ergo, it has been removed."

She lifted her hand, impatient at the interruption. "Then perhaps we are not seeing the ritual, but only a part of it. He is doing something else with the blood."

"I see."

At last she stood and smoothed her skirts.

"I mean to track down this symbol that was on the door, Crowther. And put the order for Daniel's release into Rachel's hands."

"You will tell them of the murder of Countess Dieth?"

"I shall."

"It is to be given out that Countess Dieth has gone into the country."

"Naturally. The new duchess arrives in state tomorrow morning, does she not? Poor child." She turned away. "I shall leave you to the countess. I wish I had had the opportunity to speak with her further." She bit her lip, then without another word, left him.

The priest, Huber, opened his door himself, but when he made no move to stand aside, Michaels gave it a firm push and dragged in the blacksmith. The priest stank of brandy, though if they were fumes lingering from the night before or he had started again, Michaels could not say. He saw a simple parlor with a sturdy-looking chair in it, so dropped the blacksmith there.

Huber looked baffled, and Michaels paused, wondering what explanations he should try and give. Then he simply walked out the door again. Let them sort it for themselves. It was possible they would come after him, but Michaels had not given his name, and it didn't look like anyone would be seeking that hard for justice on the blacksmith's behalf. Still, it would be best not to linger. He walked back up the track again, knowing the rabble would not turn on him now the blacksmith was put away. As he entered the square he saw the young man with the shovel in the forge. It looked as if he and his friends had found the blacksmith's strongbox, and were trying to break it open. The woman and her child were gone. He went to untie his horse. His mount had felt some of the violence in the air and was blowing hard through her nose. He put a hand on her neck and murmured to her. The words weren't important, but she needed the touch, the steadying from him. He felt her muscles beginning to relax a little.

The skinny girl he had seen at the blacksmith's came running up and slid to a halt at his side. Her eyes were a little vacant and the bones at her collar stuck out like a bird's.

"They said you were looking for the witch."

Michaels continued to stroke his horse. "Looking for a girl, bit older than you, might have come through here two years ago."

"She had black hair. Never seen hair like it. Devil must have spat in it to make it so shiny."

"You know her then?"

The girl began to chew at one of her fingernails. "She wandered round here from time to time. I saw her. Three times." She held up three fingers to show him, her nails bitten and dirty.

"Where was she staying?"

"Dunno. She's dead. Came with her head held high and no nod or smile for anyone. Time one. She was a witch. Saw her out in the fields. Time two. Then I saw the devil himself burying her. Time three. She's dead. Just before the first snow."

Michaels nodded very slowly. "The devil, you say? And where did he bury her?"

"By the waterfall."

"Where's that?"

She swung from side to side so her thin skirts swished around her ankles, chewing her thumbnail and staring at him. "Path goes up from old Rebecca's place. You passed it if you came in from the big town. Steep. Your horsey won't like it. You'll have to walk."

Michaels ran his hand through the horse's mane. It snorted and shook its head. "How come you saw it?"

She kept swinging from side to side. "I like it there. Here is not nice. I only come when I am hungry. Would you like to know what the devil looks like?"

"I think I should."

She stopped swinging and gave a little skip, speaking so fast Michaels could hardly keep pace with the sense of it. "Like a man! Tall and thin with a long black cloak! I hid in the bushes and watched for a while, then the devil made me sleep, so I never saw him disappear. I liked her hair. I made a wreath for her, even if she was a witch. I am glad the devil buries his servants somewhere pretty. Maybe I should work for him."

Michaels slowly took a coin from his pocket and put it out toward her, but she stepped away as if he'd held out something foul. "They'll only beat me for it."

He put it back into his pocket then swung himself onto his horse. She watched him.

"He'll have to go away now."

He turned and looked at her with a frown. "The blacksmith?" She nodded. "That any hurt to you?"

"No." She was chewing her finger again.

"By the waterfall, you say?"

"I think maybe I'd like to be a witch."

"Even though you see what happens to them? Better learn your prayers." She wrinkled her nose and made a tsking note in her throat.

"Do you know where she was going? When she first came through the village?"

"Westways," she said, then turned to walk off, now dragging her feet.

Michaels gently pressed his horse's flanks with his heels. An hour later he was back with the egg seller in Oberbach. He tipped his hat to her. "What's your priest like here, sister?" he asked quietly.

28

Harriet delivered the warrant for Clode's release to Rachel and Graves while they drank their coffee. They were delighted to have it, then shocked into silence by her news of the murder of Countess Dieth. When she explained the symbol to them, Graves mentioned that he had met the gentleman in charge of the library and offered to accompany her there and give her an introduction before leaving for Castle Grenzhow.

"If you can wait, Rachel," he added gently to her. Rachel had taken the order for Clode's release from the table where Harriet had placed it, and held it tightly between her white hands. She gave a quick nod.

"I think I have a little courage left. Go. I can wait a while longer."

Harriet went around the table to sit by her sister and covered her hands with her own. Rachel did not loosen her grip around the order. "Rachel. We can leave. We can go now and leave all this behind us. Return to Hartswood. Ask and we shall follow you without question."

"That letter from the ambassador. The King of England has asked you to assist Maulberg."

"Damn the king," Harriet replied with a smile and her sister flinched.

"Harriet . . ." Rachel closed her eyes for a second. "No, Crowther is right. Daniel's best chance of leaving these horrors lies in finding out the truth. If we run now, they will follow him."

"They might follow him in any case, my love."

She nodded again. "They might, but we must try. Work it out, Harry. I know you can, but please, try and work it out as fast as you can. Now go to the library. I shall rest until you are at liberty, Graves." She stood and left the room rather quickly. Harriet watched her go.

The library was not housed in the palace but, to demonstrate that it was available to all respectable people, had been built on one side of the town square. Graves and Harriet left the palace and found themselves among the preparations for the reception of the new duchess. The stands for the nobility had been completed and were now being dressed. Great bolts of cloth in blue and green hung from their sides, swagged layers of it separated the levels of the stands, and along the upper level ran a forest of flagpoles. Everything glittered.

"What must that material have cost?" Harriet said, her brightness rather forced. "I hope they donate it to the poor afterward. You could make a new coat for every man in Pulborough with that material."

"I was thinking the same, though the effect might be a bit strange, don't you think?" Graves replied. Harriet smiled, mentally repopulating the market town with blue damask. "And now we have shown ourselves to be what we are."

"What is that?"

"Not nobility, Mrs. Westerman. We have thought about what things cost and shown ourselves up terribly as a result."

"It doesn't seem to bother you greatly, Graves."

"I've never been prouder of being the owner of a shop. And of course, my friend is about to be released. I am ready to forgive myself and the nobility most things." He frowned. "Lord, should I be so lighthearted with that poor woman lying dead? How quickly we can forget what we don't wish to think of. Earth in the mouth . . ."

"Crowther told me not to think about the manner of death more than I have to, and I think I shall do as he suggests, Graves. Our repulsion does her no good."

"And it is given out she is only sick . . ."

"I wonder if it will be believed."

"Most likely people will think she has decided to remove herself from court while the new bride settles herself at the palace, and will praise her delicacy." He looked at Harriet with steady attention. "I fear, Mrs. Westerman, you are on the trail of someone very dangerous. He has killed and covered his tracks with repeated success, and now he has murdered in the palace itself. Part of me feels I should insist we leave for England at once."

Harriet saw the countess's face in front of her again. "Rachel has told us what she thinks, and she can be just as stubborn as I. Nor do I think Clode will be persuaded to leave until we find who made the attempt on him."

"I understand. Here, we are arrived."

"It's a handsome building," Harriet said, looking up at the portico.

"And open to every subject of the Duke, whatever their station. Now let us see if we can find Mr. Zeller."

In fact, Mr. Zeller found them almost as soon as they had entered the building. He was a rather round man whose dress would have been regarded as old-fashioned when the library was first built. He walked with his head held forward and tilted down to some degree, and swung it from side to side as he spoke. Harriet was reminded of a turtle in search of green shoots. His eyes were squeezed half-shut throughout their conversation, and he kept his shoulders hunched. Harriet was not sure if it was the atmosphere of the library, or the carriage of the man, but she fell naturally into a low whisper.

He led them through the main hall of the library into an office lined with books in locked cases and invited them to sit at the library table.

"Our reserved collection," he whispered, glancing around as if he feared the books themselves might be listening. "The more . . . rare, esoteric volumes of our collection are held here so we may study those who wish to study *them*. No one is allowed to consult them without a letter of recommendation from their priest, and one of the faculty at the university at Leuchtenstadt." He shuddered as if delighted. "A fascinating collection of texts claiming magical knowledge among them. My friend Adolphus Glucke would say they should all be burned, but then he's a rationalist. He says they lead men down false paths, and of course, some men do disappear into their shadows. For myself, I value them as history. A record of the attempts of great minds to try to understand our world. Now what is it you have to ask me?"

Harriet put a piece of paper in front of him. "My friend Mr. Graves has spoken to me of your erudition, sir. What can you tell me of this symbol—its derivation and uses? And also . . ." she presented another list, the books taken from the alchemist's laboratory, "do you have copies of any of these works to hand?"

He took the sheets from her and gave a satisfied snort. "Ah, Mrs. Westerman! Fate must have prompted me to lead you into this room! I hope you have some little time at your disposal."

Crowther had never performed an examination of this kind under guard before. Krall sat on one of the pews at a safe distance, puffing his pipe and with his back turned. Outside, the two guards remained. Crowther wondered what they had thought of Harriet's distress. Crowther did not normally cover the face of the corpse as he worked, yet this time he did so. Did the horror of her death mean she merited this particular attention? He wondered who would prepare the body for burial and who would scoop the earth from between her jaws. With a sort of weary acceptance he decided to make that task his own.

"What will happen to the countess when I am done here, Mr. Krall?"

Krall kept his back turned. "This afternoon a carriage will stop at a little out-of-the-way place between here and the countess's estate near Leuchtenstadt. A lady, apparently taken very ill with fever on the road, will be carried in. The house will be cleared to save the inhabitants from infection. Her private doctor will attend her, but she will die tomorrow evening. The doctor will insist she completes the journey to her estate in a closed coffin, again to avoid infection, and she will be buried at the parish church the next day." Crowther nodded and began his work.

It was with great sadness he saw earth in the stomach and throat. Of Kupfel's strange drug of pacification he could find no sign, and no other sign of violence on the corpse other than the wound on the wrist. There was nothing that would speak to him. He noticed that her nails were very short. He could still smell rose water on her skin.

"There is no need to turn round, Krall," he said at last. "But could you have water fetched please, and fresh linens."

The waterfall was indeed a pretty place. Michaels had led the priest and Georg up the track, having told them his only clue was the word of a simpleton, but they still came readily enough. The priest of Oberbach was a man of about his own age who said at once he thought it his duty to go with them, and Georg was happy to lend his shovels and his sweat for the price of a drink.

The path to the base of the waterfall was narrow and overgrown. Where it reached the base of the falls it widened out into a flattish space where a small party might watch the waters tumble down in stages, veils of white spume rushing from one stage to the next over granite edges. The banks were thick with bright green moss and bracken beginning to unfold. Spring seemed to be advancing more quickly here.

The priest sat on a flat rock on the edge of the clearing and removed his glasses to polish the spray off them. "This used to be a favored spot for courting couples when I was a child," he said, hooking them back over his ears and squinting up the slope to where the head of the falls was lost among the beech and brambles. "After the war it became the fashion for the young people to meet more under their parents' eye and parade around the square. I wonder why that was?"

"Too many bastards and six-month babies bred in the woods," Georg said, yawning. "And Gertie, who used to live in the farm by the track before Rebecca, was a bitter woman! No one could walk by without her offering some spiteful comment then running into town to tell everyone who had passed. It became a byword for a girl having a bit of a slip, you know. People used to whisper that she'd been 'taken to the falls.'"

"Oh, I see," the priest said, smiling. "Look—herb Robert! Spring will come, after all."

Michaels paced the edge of the clearing. "She said that she left a wreath on the grave."

Georg poked at the ground with his shovel. "The bank is too steep for burying on the other side. If the girl is here she's within thirty yards east of this spot. Now the brambles are thick and old, so let's look for where they ain't."

"Shall I . . . ?" The priest looked up at them.

"No, Father," Georg said. "You take your rest here and look at your flowers. We'll call you if we find anything." Then he added more quietly to Michaels, "You know God loves you when He sends you an honest landlord and a blind priest. You sweep to the right, me to the left."

It took some forty minutes before they found it. Michaels had to work hard to focus his eyes as he went. He wondered if the villagers had betrayed him, murdered the blacksmith, and decided it was safer to blame him for the death than pass it off as accidental. He should have abandoned Mrs. Padfield's sister and simply ridden out until he got back to England. To stay so close to that mean little village on the word of a simpleton and for a stranger . . . He could have reached the coast and arranged for word to be sent back to Mrs. Westerman. What did these deaths mean to any of them? They had enough to spring Clode from prison, and surely that was all that was needed. They could let the court look to its own and head back to where they were wanted. He put his hand to his beard and pulled at it. Not that he had any right now to curse someone for interfering. He had seen that child all bloody and acted because he had a back broad enough, an arm strong enough, and all his conviction. Well, Mrs. Westerman and Mr. Crowther had the learning and the smartness, their way of going about in the world, and they had their convictions too.

He frowned. There was an old trunk fallen a yard or two away, propped up on its own stump and bleached. Something hung on it, a woven circlet of twigs and reeds with the remains of rotted flowers dotted around it, held like a murderer's body in the cage to decay in public. Behind it lay a rockfall spotted over with bracken and bramble and new saplings struggling for their chance at light with greedy new leaves. There was something wrong in the way the soil lay. He felt a turn of sadness in his stomach and called Georg to his side.

"What do you think?"

The man came and fiddled with the scarf around his throat. "I'll fetch the shovels."

As soon as they felt the soil with the blades they nodded at each other. The priest had come with Georg, and was knocking the brambles away from his coat with his Bible. He noticed them pause.

"What is it? Have you found something?"

"Not yet, Father," Georg said, moving the earth in shallow bites. "But we will. The earth here has been dug."

They worked slowly, and from their first sight of a snap of fabric, got on to their knees and used the shovels as if they were trowels. Michaels had thought to bring the priest along only because he knew it was right to have some sort of authority in the place as they did this work, but now as the patch of fabric became a dress it was a comfort to hear his voice reading quietly from the Book of Psalms. He was very different from the drunkard in Mittelbach. No smell of brandy on him, but a weary sweetness in his manner that Michaels felt as something like a blessing.

Michaels began to work along the dress, loosening the soil until he realized he was not feeling vines now in the earth under his fingertips but human hair. The priest paused. She had been buried facedown.

Sitting back on his heels and wiping the sweat and muck from his eyes, Georg said, "She needs a box to put her in, and we'll need a few extra hands to manage her back along the way." He stood and brushed the soil from his knees. "Will you come back with me, Father?"

"No, no," the priest said quietly. "I'll watch with Mr. Michaels over this poor soul." The dress was a dark blue.

29

Harriet returned to the palace with a fierce frown drawing her eyebrows together and Graves staggering under the weight of a number of volumes. He placed them carefully on the little writing table in her room and gingerly stretched his fingers.

"I hope you made more of that than I did, Mrs. Westerman," he said.

"I can hardly say, Graves," she said, taking the first volume from the pile and turning the pages. "Alchemy again. These drawings are very beautiful, are they not? But they seem to me to be fairy stories for adults. With so many meanings available . . . it is like some drug for the imagination. Everything has a dozen possible resonances and so a manner of significance to every creature on God's earth."

Graves drew a circle on the polished surface of the little walnut side table next to him. "An alchemical emblem of life and balance scrawled on the wall where a woman is murdered."

"There is ritual in these murders, Graves. Why drown a woman on dry land, or choke another with earth in the confines of the palace, if it were not vital to the killer that they die in such a manner?"

"A sense of the theatrical?" Graves said. "A demonstration of power? There is something grandiose here, don't you think? Overblown? I saw a production of *Caractacus* at Covent Garden in seventy-six where the gold of the setting overpowered the music so completely, they might as well have not bothered giving it voice at all."

When she did not reply, he looked up. Mrs. Westerman was a little too casual for him in her handling of the rare texts of the sovereign's collection; she had in her hands a volume he suspected of being a survivor of the Renaissance, and was holding it at arm's length and turning one way and another. "Do treat those poor things carefully, Mrs. Westerman," he said in a pleading tone.

Harriet turned the book toward him. It was open at a double page showing a variety of strange-looking symbols, pentangles studded around with astronomical figures picked out in gold and red.

"Beautiful," he said.

"Do you think so? Perhaps, but this one"—she tapped one in the center of the right-hand page—"I am sure I have seen this somewhere before."

Graves realized she was already alone with her studies so stood to take his leave. "Are you sure you will not come to the castle?"

She looked up at him. "No, I think not. I must read." She flashed him a tight quick smile and returned to her books.

Crowther found Harriet some time later, still surrounded by the volumes from the library, but with a light in her eyes. She became still while he told her of the body of Countess Dieth and what he had learned from it, but when he asked her about the fruits of her own labors she became quite animated again.

"These are fascinating, Crowther," she said. "In another hour I shall have the secret for making gold from lead."

"I had quite enough of alchemy yesterday, Mrs. Westerman. Do not tell me you have turned mystic?"

She smiled. "It is strange, many of the books Beatrice took were not about alchemy as such, but more about magic generally. Spells and seals. Ways to become invisible, discover secrets or treasure. No, I have not turned mystic, but there is beauty here, and such imagination."

"It is nonsense," he said.

She raised a hand and let it fall again. "Powerful nonsense, if you believe in it. I have also been thinking of Kupfel's shaman and his ingredients. Many of the men who sailed with my husband knew the waters round the Dominican Isles," she said, "and they feared what they found there. They would tell legends of men brought back from the dead and made to serve the magicians that summoned them. If one were ever allowed on the ship, they said the spirits of the sea would rise up in rage and drown everyone on board. Do you see what I mean, when I say belief gives these things power? Perhaps those men were people who had been treated with some of the strange remnants Kupfel has gathered together. He thought himself in hell when he took the paralyzing drops; whatever Clode took made him see devils. Many men might think they had died and been summoned again from hell." Crowther nodded reluctantly. "I thought them only stories that sailors tell, like the kraken and mermaids. Horrible to think there might be some truth in them."

"But why, Mrs. Westerman? Why have these individuals been chosen to suffer such torments and then be killed in such a way?"

"Are you encouraging me to speculate, Crowther?" She was teasing him, but he could not help that.

"I suppose I am to a degree. I will try not to do so again."

Her eyes danced then she turned toward the window again and became serious. "Opportunity? This madman wants blood, so he takes it where he can and then performs his strange killings. That might answer for those earlier deaths—men who lived on their own. But what could be more difficult than killing in the middle of the palace! It does not answer."

She put her chin in her hand and drummed her fingers on one of the volumes on the table. Crowther watched her. It had, he admitted silently to himself, become one of his pleasures over the last years to watch Mrs. Westerman think.

"Let us suppose we are right about those previous deaths. These are all individuals who had great influence with the duke, or in the case of the writer, some influence on the general society. Could they be political assassinations? But then this element of theater in the deaths, the ritual . . ."

Crowther picked up one of the volumes from her pile and began to turn the pages as he spoke. "A performance, but a private performance; a ritual, but it has some purpose. The removal of the blood . . ."

"Blood has great significance in all these volumes, it seems to me. Though they normally ask that the magician use his own. There then follows a great deal of chanting."

"Of course blood is significant," he said. "Every child knows blood somehow contains the spark of life, and that if we lose enough of it we cease to be. But what led you into these paths, Mrs. Westerman? This symbol?"

"And your list of what was pilfered from Herr Kupfel. The librarian,

Zeller, was intrigued by our little design. He says it is an emblem of alchemy." She took one of the volumes from behind her, opened it, and turned it to face him. The picture was a complex one filled with figures and symbols. A crown, a salamander, a bearded face, but the central form of a seven-spoked wheel placed over a triangle seemed identical to the design chalked on the door to the room where the countess was murdered.

"It seems very like."

"It is, isn't it? And it appears in one of the books stolen from Kupfel. Shall I explain the symbolism of the original to you?"

"I don't think that is necessary," Crowther said, studying it. "The spokes are the seven stages of alchemy, each also related to one of the seven heavenly bodies; here are the four elements; the three points of the triangle are labeled body, spirit, and soul. It is like one of Mrs. Bligh's fortune-telling cards, full of great, but somewhat imprecise, meanings. What is it, Mrs. Westerman?"

"Just that I was at some pains to commit to memory the seven stages of alchemy."

He smiled.

"Seven stages, just as there were seven glasses," she added. "Now what else, seven ages of man, days in the weeks . . .'"

"Celestial bodies, as I said. By the old count."

"A number of some significance then?"

"Most of them are."

She leaned back in her chair. Crowther noticed for the first time the remains of a meal among the books. He hoped the books would be returned to Herr Zeller unstained.

"But do you not think, Crowther, you would have to hate someone very much to kill them in this way? These people were not chosen at random. It feels . . . like revenge." She twisted her mourning band on her finger, thinking of Manzerotti.

"Mrs. Westerman, give me your hand." Crowther spoke quite sharply, so she put it out to him at once. He took it between his own and twisted up the mourning band to the knuckle. In the three years she had worn it, the ring had made itself part of her. The space below was a little paler than the rest of her finger and slightly indented. Crowther's touch was dry and cool. "I am a fool," he said.

"Probably. May I have my hand back?"

"Hmm . . . yes, of course. Countess Dieth wore no rings. Necklace, eardrops, yes, but no rings when I examined her, yet she had a band on her flesh like yours."

"So she did wear one."

"Habitually, as you do that mourning band for Captain Westerman. Yet it was not on the body."

"So the killer might have taken something more than blood?"

"Perhaps."

Harriet rapped her fingers on the veneer of her desk. "Could you make out the shape of the ring?"

"Thicker than your band."

"I wonder if the duke will see me," Harriet murmured. Crowther had raised his eyebrows at her. "He was often in company with Countess Dieth. Perhaps he remembers it, and in any case I have the desire to know our host better."

"Be careful, madam."

"There is food in the parlor, Crowther. Eat."

Harriet was forced to wait some minutes in the anteroom and was wondering if perhaps she was wasting her time, given the number of gentlemen in court dress who also seemed to be waiting to see their sovereign, but it was not long before the door to the duke's study was opened again, and a gentleman almost smothered by the splendor of his cravat beckoned her inside.

Though the room in which she found herself was far too grand for anyone but an absolute ruler to call it a study, it was a far more domestic space than any other she had seen in the palace. The colors were the brown and green of leather volumes, and the space was broken up with small groups of chairs and tables. The duke was bent over his desk while Swann hovered behind him, placing one document after another in front of him for signature. Christoph Ludwig looked up as she entered, then beckoned her forward.

She heard a movement behind her and saw that Manzerotti was present, curled in the armchair like a cat. She remembered the duke's request for music as he worked the previous day and wondered if Manzerotti had been required to serenade his present patron's signatures.

"Mrs. Westerman!" the duke greeted her. "I thought you would be on your way to Castle Grenzhow by this time."

"My sister and Mr. Graves have left to collect Mr. Clode."

The duke did not look up. "I feel like a pharaoh in Egypt, such a plague seems to have struck my advisers. I hope that releasing Clode will lift the curse. Did she suffer?"

"I am sorry to say it, sire. But yes, she did."

The duke was silent, staring at the page in front of him. He was absolutely still for some moments, then, as if he had been suddenly reanimated, lifted his head.

"Ah, here is an uncomfortable case, Mrs. Westerman. I'd be delighted to have your opinion on it." Harriet wondered, not for the first time, if she should have listened to Crowther. "A young woman is accused of killing her husband. From the accounts the lawyers have prepared it sounds rather as if he deserved it. He was a known drunk, a bully, and she was often seen bruised in the village."

"What does she say, Your Highness?"

"That he was beating her, she used her cooking pot to defend herself, and down he went."

"Your subjects surely have the right to defend themselves against attack."

"That depends on who is attacking them, Mrs. Westerman. A man rules his wife, as I rule my people. If the people disagreed with the way I ruled them, would you say they had the right to rise up against me?"

"You, sire, are neither a drunk nor a bully."

"You are a loss to your diplomatic service, Mrs. Westerman." Harriet smiled, wondering with what disbelief her husband would have heard that opinion. She thought of Manzerotti behind her and touched her mourning ring again like a talisman. "The district officer of the area—not Krall, my dear, I have thirty-four—the law faculty at Leuchtenstadt and my Privy

Council all recommend execution. Surely if I only imprison her for a year or two that will be seen as weakness on my part?"

"Mercy, sire."

He blinked at her. "Swann, the lovely Mrs. Westerman recommends mercy. Is your heart still of stone?"

Harriet saw a flash of irritation cross Swann's face. "A crime against a husband is a manner of treason, sire. If you will be merciful, do not agree to her breaking on the wheel, but she must certainly die."

The duke smiled lazily. "One would think after all these years, Swann, you would have learned not to say 'must' to me. We have failed to protect our friend Countess Dieth, so this is our penance. We will be merciful to this girl. A compliment to the fairer sex. An indulgence."

He passed the paper back to Swann unsigned then pushed himself away from the desk a little.

"The gentleman at the door said you have something to ask me, Mrs. Westerman. Ask it."

"Thank you. Did Countess Dieth wear a ring, sire? There seemed to be a mark left on her hand to show she did, but there is no sign of it."

He frowned briefly. "She did, a sort of signet ring engraved with an owl. I never saw her without it. How strange that it is missing." His long-fingered hands went to his neck. "Lady Martesen also had a similar device—a jewel she wore at her neck. Swanny, do you remember?"

"No, sire."

"I teased her about it when I first saw it. They were cousins, you know. I asked them if it was some family emblem."

Harriet heard a stir of silk behind her as Manzerotti shifted in his seat. "Did she explain it at all?"

"I don't remember. It made her blush, you see, Mrs. Westerman, when I asked, and Aggie always looked so beautiful when she blushed." His smile faded and he put up his hand to take another paper from Swann. The chancellor did not notice for a moment, and it was not until the duke had clicked his fingers that a fresh sheet was offered to him. The duke began to read.

"Your Highness?"

"Yes, madam?"

"Might these attacks be aimed at you, sir? This loss of people . . . of importance to you."

He put down his paper and watched her for a few moments. "If an assassin can kill Countess Dieth, he could kill me. He has not done so. Therefore I am not a target. No one in court, other than myself, is ever indispensable, but in two days Maulberg will be more secure than it has been for years, and in all likelihood better advised. Do not bridle, Swanny, you know I think the world of you, but we need fresh blood, fresh thinking."

Harriet dropped her eyes and curtsied.

"Thank you, Mrs. Westerman. Glance to your right as you leave. There is a little Caravaggio of St. Catherine there of which I am quite fond. Find who is responsible for the deaths of the women, and it is yours."

The doors were opened for her, and she paused in the anteroom for a moment, realizing her breathing was uncomfortably rapid. She wondered if the duke had been teasing her when he called her a diplomat. She had just lifted her chin again when the door behind her opened and closed once more and Chancellor Swann emerged. Without preamble he took hold of her elbow and led her into a quieter corner of the room. The waiting gentlemen harrumphed into their collars and stared about them.

"Chancellor Swann?"

"Krall has spoken to me of the major," he said simply. Harriet looked up into his face; he seemed to have aged in the last days. There were shadows under his eyes, and they flicked from side to side as he spoke. "It is my habit to take a walk in the garden between the hours of four and five o'clock. Perhaps you and Mr. Crowther would like to meet me there."

His manner surprised her, but she nodded. "Certainly, Chancellor."

He hesitated as if about to say something more, then retreated once again into the duke's audience chamber.

Harriet found that Crowther had taken her advice, had served himself from the warming plates and begun to eat. He had been joined by Krall. The contrast between the two men made her smile. Crowther took no pleasure in his food, and whatever was put in front of him seemed to regard it as a necessary inconvenience. Krall had filled his plate and was busy trying to empty it again. Harriet waved them back to their seats as she entered. Crowther looked at her, but she only slightly shook her head. Krall had already returned to his food.

"The district officer has spoken to Major Auwerk," Crowther said.

"Meetings were held in the room from time to time," Krall said, dabbing at his mouth, "between some friends of the duke who wished to meet away from the public gaze. However, the major never attended himself. Countess Dieth would ask him to leave the room unlocked and clean it afterward. He was willing to hold the key, but must have thought the cleaning below him, so employed Wimpf and put in a good word for him from time to time."

"What friends?"

Krall pushed away his plate. "The major says he did not know, but that he trusted the countess absolutely."

"And do you believe him, Herr District Officer?"

"I do. I sense he would have loved to know who met there with the countess—"

"Seven glasses," Harriet said. Krall ignored the interruption.

"—but that he did not. He was glad to hold the key though. The countess had great influence and I am sure she helped his rise through the ranks. He is young to be a major. I have called on the countess's servants in town. They did not seem altogether surprised that she had decided to spend some time at her country estate. Her maid said they expected as much when she returned to the palace last night. She told them a servant had arrived with a summons. She then instructed Auwerk to leave the door unlocked after supper." He stood. "Forgive me. I must make the arrangements I spoke of earlier. I fear I shall be of no use to you for some hours."

They watched him go and Crowther told her how the murder of the countess was to be concealed. She wrinkled her nose, but said nothing. "What news from the duke, Mrs. Westerman?"

"The countess wore a ring with an owl on it. Lady Agatha wore a necklace with one too. And Chancellor Swann wishes to speak to us. What is it, Crowther?"

"The owl. Fink had a fob with an owl design—it went missing when he died."

Harriet frowned. "Good Lord. Can it be coincidence?"

Crowther shook his head. "I doubt it, Mrs. Westerman."

30

By early afternoon frustration and hunger had driven Pegel down the stairs and out into the streets of Leuchtenstadt, leaning heavily on a staff his diminutive manservant had filched for him from one of the neighbors' woodpiles. He was beginning to doubt his ability to break the code. Pegel was used to excelling, and had come to enjoy it. If he left now with the names he had collected, his belief that the man in green, Dunktal, was Spartacus, leader of the Minervals he had come to hunt, then he would be praised and rewarded. If he rode into Ulrichsberg with the coded messages made readable he would impress a man thought unimpressible. He would be able to ask anything. But he was not sure he could do it. He kicked at a pebble and it danced into one of the gutters that ran along the street.

He stared into the water; it was one of the many channels that ran along the streets of Leuchtenstadt. It was an aspect of the old town that appealed to him, these little rivers flowing in the gutters. He was told by his landlady, with a wink, that if he stepped in one he'd marry a Leuchtenstadt girl. He doubted it. He chewed a pastry still warm from the oven and, to avoid seasoning his food with his disappointment over the coded messages, he began wondering idly if it would be possible to describe the motion of water in the language of mathematics. A thing so simple that was also so complex—was there a key? A way to unlock? His thoughts became wordless and he looked up from the water to the cathedral spire. Dark red, yet so light, so apparently delicate was the structure, it seemed to lift away from the earth and take the body of the cathedral with it into the air. Pegel liked the earthy sense of humor of the stonemasons who had carved the waterspouts around the flying buttresses, the frogs and demons, the spitting woman and hanging arse, what private revenges or jokes had they built into the stone? Was the woman the wife of the man who carved her? His mother-in-law? Pegel was sure that no one could resist folding themselves into their work. It was another reason he preferred mathematics to literature. Less personal. He dusted the last of the pastry from his hands then became still. Surely it could not be so simple? Would they use a phrase so readily bandied about as a key? It was certainly memorable. In his excitement he leaned on his right ankle, and the joy of inspiration gave way to a stream of curses.

Swann was waiting for them by a shallow pond surrounded with high beech hedges. In its center stood a statue of a young boy, one stone leg bent, pouring water from a giant conch into the pool below. Harriet was glad of her cloak. The naked statue made her feel cold. She thought of the new duchess, wondered what her life had been up to now, which of these many statues would become her favorites, or if she would claim the right of a new bride and have them replaced with her own fancies.

Swann did not greet them. He had been seated on a stone bench examining the boy, and now he stood slowly and came toward them.

"The duke has enjoyed this winter," he said as he joined them. "There was an ice fair once a week, with skating on the grand lake, and each of these little garden rooms was made into a grotto where the guests could retire to warm themselves. We burned enough fuel each evening to warm a village for a month."

Harriet frowned. The straight-backed servant of the duke had never spoken to them in this way before, and there was something strange in his tone. Something lost and floating. A sheen of sweat lay on his brow.

"Chancellor, do you know of this group who met in the secret chamber?" Crowther's voice was quiet. He sensed something out of joint here too. Swann was carrying a cane. He placed it in front of him and leaned on it, swaying a little forward and back. His eyes were unfocused, looking up over the fresh-clothed beech hedge into the solid gray sky.

"The last summer was cruel, this winter worse. We will need guidance. Help. And my sovereign thinks only of how he loves to skate."

Harriet examined his profile. He seemed to see something other than the world they saw. She had only just heard the duke talking of the need for fresh blood among his advisers. He had arranged an advantageous marriage. These did not seem the actions of a man who thought only of skating. "Your Excellency?" He turned his hooked nose slowly toward her, and she thought of a man sleeping, trying to wake. "Chancellor Swann? Were you one of the seven people who met in that room? Was Lady Agatha another? Was Fink?"

Swann frowned and waved his hand. "We have done much good. Now we are hunted."

He staggered slightly; the cane slipped away from him and twisted on the gravel. Harriet reached out to put a hand under his elbow and guided him back to his seat on the bench. He sat rather heavily and a silver flask clattered from the folds of his cloak.

"Crowther! He is unwell. Help me."

He sat on the other side of the chancellor and lifted the man's chin. "Swann! Swann—can you hear me?" The man's eyes were half-closed and his hands were beginning to twitch. "Who is being hunted?"

He blinked and managed to turn his head in Crowther's direction, looking at him as he might a particularly stupid child. "It is all for the greater good. We shoulder the burden of control for the greater good." A thin thread of saliva hung from his lip.

"Crowther, we must get help."

"A moment, Mrs. Westerman. What do you mean, Swann?" Crowther took him by the shoulders and shook the man. A little sense flickered into Swann's eyes again

"I serve the secret superiors. We obey. For the greater good."

Crowther snapped his fingers in front of Swann's swimming gaze. "For God's sake, Crowther," Harriet hissed.

"Why did you summon her last night, Swann?"

His voice was becoming slurred. "There was no meeting. We did not meet."

"Crowther! Now!"

"Yes, Mrs. Westerman! Go, fetch help. And Manzerotti."

Harriet set off across through the hedges and back toward the palace at a run. Crowther let Swann slump against him. He could hear Harriet calling out, her shouts bouncing off the cold stone and amazing the statues.

Swann was half-carried into his chamber by Crowther and one of the footmen while Harriet followed with his cane and flask. As they let him fall onto the bed Harriet heard the clip of heels on the wood floor and Manzerotti appeared in the doorway; he paused there a moment to take in the scene.

"My dear Mrs. Westerman, Mr. Crowther, what on *earth* have you been up to?"

Crowther disentangled himself from Swann's flowing cloak; Harriet saw him flinch as his injured shoulder jarred. He turned first to the footman. "Salt, water, a basin. *Now.*"

The man turned to go, but Manzerotti put a hand out. "First, give me your gloves."

The servant looked amazed, but stripped them off and handed them to the singer before running for the door.

"He was distracted, but able to walk and speak some fifteen minutes ago," Crowther said. "Then his speech became slurred and he was no longer able to stand unassisted."

Manzerotti nodded.

"This fell from his pocket," Harriet added, and handed Manzerotti the flask.

He took it, now wearing the footman's gloves, unstoppered and sniffed it. "Nothing obvious." Harriet undid her cloak and began to undo the buttons at her wrist. "Keep your gloves on, Mrs. Westerman," Manzerotti said sharply. Harriet became absolutely still, remembering the mask for the first time. He set the flask down and bent over Swann's body. He was murmuring and his lips were a little blue.

"Your assistance, Mr. Crowther."

Crowther managed to lift Swann into a seated position while Manzerotti removed cloak, hat, and wig. Harriet took the chancellor's hands and pulled off his black gloves. It was awkward, the hands loose, but still twitching from time to time, her own fingers made clumsy by her gloves. They came away. The skin of Swann's hands was mottled and red.

"Gentlemen."

Manzerotti and Crowther paused to turn toward her. Then looked at each other.

"It may be a symptom rather than the cause, but he must be washed," Manzerotti said. Crowther nodded. The footman returned and Crowther began to mix salt and water. His hand hovered over the glass by the chancellor's bed.

"A different glass," Manzerotti said to the servant, "more water and flannel."

Harriet shifted to begin unbuttoning Swann's waistcoat. She noticed that it was beautifully made, and on each button, a half-shade lighter than the black velvet that covered them, was embroidered the arms of the House of Maulberg.

The footman was back again. "Shall I get the physician, sir?" he said.

"If you must," Manzerotti snapped. The footman backed away, bewildered, then, noticing the gloves and cloak on the floor, bent down automatically to pick them up. Manzerotti's arm shot out. "Don't touch them."

Crowther put the fresh glass to Swann's mouth and forced the contents down his throat. Almost at once his stomach began to heave and Manzerotti sprang out of the way. Harriet managed to get the basin under Swann's head almost at once. It started to slip in her hand and she felt Manzerotti's fingers around her own for a moment to steady it. Swann vomited up liquid and bile, and she heard Manzerotti tut as his sleeve was splashed. Then he moved Harriet out of the way as he took Swann's forearms and plunged his hands into the other bowl of water.

Swann groaned. Crowther tilted his head against his own chest and poured more of the salt water down his throat, and at once new shudders ran through Swann's body and Harriet gripped the bowl. Crowther took a cloth from the stack that had been brought in and wiped the vomit and spittle from Swann's face.

Harriet set the bowl on the floor and staggered back toward an armchair, suddenly aware of her own labored breathing and the thudding of her heart. Manzerotti glanced toward her. "Mrs. Westerman, if you would be so kind?"

She nodded and struggled to her feet, then took the bowl in which Manzerotti had washed Swann's hands. He began to dry them with another cloth. She knelt and removed Swann's shoes.

"Well?" Manzerotti asked.

Crowther had tilted Swann's head back and opened his right eyelid with thumb and forefinger. Harriet could hear the chancellor's breathing. Heavy, rasping. It made her own lungs sore just to hear it.

"I don't know," Crowther replied. "He's not dead yet. There is nothing obvious in the vomit. If some substance has been ingested through the skin, perhaps it can be sweated out." Harriet retreated again and the two gentlemen manhandled Swann under his covers. She noticed that Manzerotti lifted out Swann's hands and laid them on top of the sheets. Crowther banked up the fire. Then they took seats on either side of her and all three watched the figure in the bed.

"It is Swann's habit to walk in the garden every day at this time for an hour or so," Manzerotti said; his light high voice sounded almost soothing. "It is usual that he ask not to be disturbed."

"He asked to see us."

"Lucky that he did. He would most certainly have died otherwise." Manzerotti stripped the footman's gloves from his hands and threw them in the fire as he spoke. Without further comment Harriet and Crowther did the same with their own. Harriet watched hers burn with regret. She had intended to give them to her maid when they returned to England. The fire caught and crisped the leather, making the fingers curl together. Then they waited in silence for the court physician.

31

By the time Georg had come back with another man, a bedsheet taken from his own house, a wide plank, and a number of ropes, Michaels had cleared the rest of the earth away from the body. Her legs were curled up under her dress. He laid the donated linen over her, and then tried to push it into the soil below. The color of the earth around the body was changed, darker, thicker somehow. The body rolled back into his arms like a lover sleeping and he found himself staring into a death's head. There was a leathery skin clinging to parts of the skull. The long dark hair was loose, seemed unattached to the skull, but rather laid over it. The dress was thin and stained dark along the length of the body. Michaels held himself still. He thought of what the boy had told him, tried to make her alive again in his mind, laughing at simple magic tricks, worrying a system of magic of her own out of the library of the alchemist. They had taken their chances, she and her sister. Now her sister had a house with a library in it and a reputation to protect, and this girl's path had led her into the forest and the earth. He saw the glint at her neck, the little gold cross Mrs. Padfield had told him of. He lifted the remains up in his arms, placed them on the board, and folded the cloth around her while the priest continued to pray. He hoped she'd died quick and not known the blow was coming.

Harriet did not have long to recover herself from the shock of Swann's collapse before the duke himself arrived. She, Crowther, and Manzerotti stood and the duke nodded to them, remaining just inside the door with his spaniel in his arms and with Colonel Padfield and Count Frenzel at his side.

It was Frenzel who spoke first. The skin around his mouth was white.

"Who has done this?"

The duke looked at him askance. "I rather think you have stolen my line, count," he said. "However, I feel sure if our guests knew, they would tell us.

Reymen?" His personal physician scurried past him to the bed and took Swann's wrist in his hand.

"Weak, sire," he said eventually.

"Will he live?" the duke asked. The physician looked hopefully at Crowther and Manzerotti. Neither man moved.

"I do not know, sire."

The duke studied Swann's thin form on the bed for a long moment. "Time will tell, I suppose." Then he turned on his heel and left smartly. Half-crouching, the physician followed him and his advisers.

"What are we to do?" Harriet said, then caught her breath, realizing she was now including Manzerotti in the *we* she spoke.

The singer stood and bent over the bed to examine the hands. They looked as if they had been burned. "I think it *was* the gloves." They still lay on the floor by the bed, looking both dead and malevolent. "We cannot leave him unguarded. Whoever poisoned them may try again as soon as we leave. Your sister is something of a healer, I think, Mrs. Westerman?" Harriet stiffened, and though Manzerotti did not turn around he must have felt it. "No, we have not been gossiping and swapping receipts, madam. Colonel Padfield mentioned it."

"She makes and sells some household remedies in our village," Harriet said at last.

"That must be excuse enough. Let her come, her husband and Mr. Graves. They will make less convincing nurses, but better guards. He must not be left alone."

Harriet nodded.

"We should also send for Herr Kupfel. Though I doubt he will come willingly," Crowther said. Manzerotti turned and raised one beautifully groomed eyebrow. "It is likely that the drugs that disoriented Clode and rendered the victims passive came from his collection of receipts. Where there are instructions for the creation of two dangerous drugs, there are probably instructions for the creation of several more."

"I agree. Where are these papers now?"

"Stolen at some point. With some of the elements needed to create them, and a number of volumes on alchemy and magic ritual. Kupfel might know some manner to ease the workings of whatever did this to Swann."

"Fascinating," Manzerotti drawled, studying the frayed flesh on Swann's hands. "That is a collection of papers I would give a great deal of gold to see."

Harriet shuddered and she stood to hide it. "I will go to Swann's offices. Perhaps he has left some sign of what he meant to tell us. I assume it will be given out that the chancellor is merely indisposed."

"You should not curl your lip, Mrs. Westerman. It does not suit you. Yes, I imagine so. Do you think they will let you riffle through his papers, dear lady?" She could hear the smile in Manzerotti's voice.

"The duke has asked us to look into these matters. I go with his authority."

"But you speak German so badly . . . Still, perhaps it is better that Mr. Crowther and I keep vigil here and you give yourself some other occupation around the court." He looked at her, his head on one side. "We would not want to ruin our present good understanding by spending too long in each other's company now would we?"

She had no answer for him and turned to leave the room. As she went she heard his low laugh and felt her cheeks burn.

32

The pane rattled once, then again. Pegel shut his workings into his notebook and put the originals into his jacket before going to the window. He saw Florian below, looking up at him from under his thick blond hair, shielding his eyes, and smiled. He opened the window.

"Come on up!"

Florian waved and trotted off to the rear of the building, and Pegel had plenty of time to place his notes and papers behind one of the loose tiles of the roof slant before unlocking the door and taking his seat again. The stairs creaked, and Frenzel was in the room, smiling a little shyly with a paper-wrapped parcel in his hands.

"That for me?" Florian nodded. "Do I get to keep it this time? Hand it over then."

As Jacob ripped off the paper Frenzel said, "Where have you been? The professor keeps asking for you."

"*The Wealth of Nations!* Very nice. I didn't know it had been translated."

"A friend of mine."

Pegel hobbled across to his own bookshelf and pulled a number of papers from between the books.

"Give the professor this, with my compliments. It hasn't been published yet, but Laplace is a friend of mine. He explains it all pretty clearly."

Florian took it a little doubtfully. "What are you doing?"

"Just working on a little idea. As you know, you can't ask a man to discuss it when he's in the midst of a new idea. Might all just dissolve in front of me if I do."

Florian shrugged in the direction of the door. "I suppose I should . . ."

Pegel looked at him, poor little rich boy in search of a friend. He suddenly knew what he would ask for if his idea for the codes worked.

"Sorry, old boy! Don't go." He stood up and put a hand on Florian's shoulder. "Just a bit out of sorts today. Got a letter from my father. He says my mother is ill and wants me to come home and settle down. Take up the law and all that."

"I'm sorry about your mother, Jacob. Is there any danger?"

"She's always ill. The old man just wants me where he can disapprove of me eye to eye is the meat and measure of it. Come and sit for a bit. You never mention your family. You get along?"

They took their seats side by side on the worn settee. "I hardly know my father," Florian said at last. "I remember my mother a little. She died when I was five. My father never had anything to do with me when I was a child, then he sent me away to school. He married again, a kind woman but she died too, soon after giving birth to my little sister."

"You have a sister?"

He shook his head. "Born dead. Mostly I lived with my aunt and uncle after that."

"What sort of place is it, your father's?"

"Old. It used to be a nunnery. It has a cloister still and the dining room is where the church once was."

"So you *were* brought up in a nunnery!"

"What?"

"Sorry, nothing. Sounds very grand."

"Very cold. Courtyard after courtyard and not a room in the place of a convenient size. But fitting, I suppose, for an imperial knight."

Florian talked for some time, and listening to his stories of the children he played with, the landscape, the gardens, Pegel let his mind rest. He was happy. Florian was the son of an imperial knight. Pegel's work would lead to a number of arrests, but if Florian could be got out of the way . . . Off the lists. Off lands where the duke's word was law. Even if his friends gave his name, it would be easy to bluff his way out of it. Yes, Pegel could save Florian from himself—*if* his master would let him.

Crowther watched Manzerotti bending over Swann's hands for several minutes. The fire had been banked up and the room was becoming oppressively hot. Crowther's thoughts were growing foggy and thick, and a thin layer of sweat was beginning to burst out of his pores. He felt like an old creature, cornered. He stood and crossed to the window and found there, like a cold movement in the fug, a whisper of healthier air. He placed his hand into it, letting the draft slice over the pulse in his wrist.

Crowther felt that he was growing old. He had dedicated his youth, his maturity, to study and to the avoidance of other people, but he believed now that the only work of any real significance he had accomplished had been in the company of Mrs. Westerman; had been done since she had dragged him out of his study and thrown him among other people. The ghosts of his own past had glowered over him for thirty years; in her company they were exorcized. He smiled, feeling the cold air over his wrist. He had tried this winter, perhaps fearing that Mrs. Westerman wanted to return to her domestic concerns, to rediscover his zeal for his own private study. The readiness with which he abandoned it at her request was demonstration enough that he had not been particularly successful. He did not mind the years he had wasted; rather he was glad, even as he felt the pressure of his age, that he had not wasted them all.

Now Manzerotti was watching him. The castrato looked as comfortable and composed as ever. The drama of Swann had left Crowther feeling ragged, and he envied Manzerotti's ability to retain his poise so completely. Crowther wondered if it was a result of being stared at for his entire adult life. Perhaps he had developed some thicker skin that allowed him to ignore both the adoration and the suspicion with which he was regarded. An animal adapting to its environment. Perhaps the poise was trained into him from his earliest age, just as the music was.

"Did you submit to the operation willingly?" he asked as the thought formed in his head. For the first time he saw something like a spasm of emotion cross the castrato's face, but so fleeting and slight was it, a moment later Crowther could not swear to having seen it at all.

"No. I did not. I come from peasant stock, Gabriel. My family were as ignorant and mean as the rocks from which they tried to drag a living. I sang at church with the other children, the priest recognized my talent and suggested to my parents that there was money to be made. They leaped at the chance to make some easy gold from one of their brood."

"I am sorry."

Manzerotti looked up at him and smiled briefly. "How strange—I believe you are. But you should not pity me. I am terribly rich now, you know, one way or another. How nice it is to chat, Gabriel." He dropped his eyes. "You realize, we are not very different, you and I. If what I hear is to be believed, and my information is usually very good, it is the sins of your family that made you a recluse. Thus you are a man with no sons to follow him, just as I am."

Crowther turned away slightly.

"My friend Johannes volunteered for the operation. He was eager. He saw it as a chance to serve God. Then when his voice failed, he chose to serve me."

Crowther recalled the last time he had seen Johannes, Manzerotti's assassin, heard the crow-crack of his mangled voice. It had been in a room as hot as this but in a hovel, not a palace. He had stuck a knife into James Westerman's belly, then Crowther had in turn left him to be torn apart by a mob. Crowther did not shy away from the memory, and he felt no shame about letting the man be murdered. Nevertheless he found himself speaking. "He died proclaiming your escape, your invulnerability, Manzerotti. He said you were his voice."

Manzerotti was silent, then nodded slowly. "I was a cruel and unforgiving deity. But his devotion was absolute and, as you see, his faith was not misplaced."

For some time the only sound in the room was the ragged breathing of the chancellor.

"Shall we be successful in sweating the poison out of him?" Crowther asked at last.

"It is one strategy among others, but I shall be easier when your alchemist has examined him." Crowther watched the castrato take a cloth from the basin at the bedside and carefully wipe the chancellor's hands again, then discard the material he had used.

"Anything of the murder of Countess Dieth you wish to confide in me, Gabriel? As we have become so confidential? You see, I know she is not in the countryside." Crowther clenched his jaw. "Ah, not yet. I understand. It is my turn to offer you something, is it?"

He washed his hands and took a seat by the fire once more, his attitude more businesslike. "Very well. You know I am not here simply to fill my pockets singing for the duke, though he is a fine judge of opera. I am interested in Maulberg, Gabriel, because over the last five years there have been a series of minor . . . events that have begun to look suspicious to my eyes."

"To your eyes, Manzerotti, or to the eyes of those who employ you?"

"I have no intention of naming my employer, so for the moment you must think of us as one. Do you wish me to continue?"

Crowther nodded reluctantly. "I do. What manner of events?"

"Nothing serious in themselves, but a pattern of minor illnesses and ailments. Nothing as violent as this, or as exotic as the other murderous attacks. Some of the victims have held position at court, others have been visitors to Maulberg on business either mercantile, military, or diplomatic. I suspected, and in the past few weeks have confirmed, a pattern in these troubles."

"Interesting. You believe the duke has a pet poisoner?"

Manzerotti turned toward him, and blinked his black eyes. "He would not be the first sovereign to find such a person of use."

"Have you been of such use?"

"Tush, Gabriel. So crude! I would not tell you if I had been. I do not think the duke himself has commissioned this poisoner."

"Why not?"

"Dear man, I have my reasons. No, I think someone has been acting without the duke's authority, occasionally on Maulberg's behalf, mostly on their own."

"Poisoners who have a tendency to be civic-minded."

"Occasionally. Once or twice a man with claims on the Maulberg Treasury such as Graves has become rather ill here and left to recover their health before they could recover their money. But one case might serve as a more typical example. An architect from the French court was passing through Ulrichsberg and was made welcome in the usual way. The duke took a liking to him and they spent some time closeted together discussing plans for a new palace—nothing on this scale," he raised his hand to the magnificence around them.

Crowther put his other wrist into the thin draft and felt his blood carry the cooling through his arm. "You have my attention, Manzerotti."

"Their discussions reached beyond architecture; the duke was observed reading books that the architect had recommended. The architect then became ill."

"Indeed."

"Yes. He recovered after some weeks, then became ill again. After that, he returned to France saying he did not find Ulrichsberg conducive to his health. He tried to continue his intimacy with the duke by letter. He received no replies."

"Interesting."

"Isn't it? There have been other occasions. My little inquiries have taken me far afield. Have you been to St. Petersburg? Lovely city. Then Vienna. But when news reached me of a member of the court actually murdered and some rumors of the distressed state of the Englishman accused, I decided to come to the source of these incidents. It is also interesting to note, Gabriel, that Colonel Padfield has his own house and servants in town, and Count Frenzel still spends most of his nights on his own lands."

"The men who helped arrange the current marriage. Yet these murders of Countess Dieth and Lady Martesen . . ."

"And the others. Yes, I have heard of your interest in the recent accidental deaths too. They are on a very different—how may I say it—scale. I agree. And they are of a much more recent date. The petty poisonings in which I am interested began several years ago, long before that interesting little poison book was taken."

"Would it surprise you to learn, Manzerotti, that there is some sort of hidden meeting chamber within the walls of this palace?"

"No. It was built by the uncle of Ludwig Christoph. There are slightly secret passages all through the building. But it is no longer in use."

"It is. And Countess Dieth's body was found there."

Manzerotti raised an eyebrow. "By whom?"

"A footman who has orders from a Major Auwerk to clean the place. He informed the major, who put the body into one of the grace and favor bedrooms before he summoned Swann, Krall, or ourselves."

"The major did that?"

"Then Swann asked to meet Mrs. Westerman and myself. I believe he knew something more of that secret room than even Major Auwerk did."

"Fascinating. What a nest of vipers this place is," Manzerotti said with a yawn. "It makes me long for the Opera House. Well, Gabriel, now we have begun, perhaps you had better tell me everything you and the lovely Mrs. Westerman have discovered."

It took some time. Crowther could not remember when he had spoken at such length to anyone other than Mrs. Westerman. At some point during his narrative, the door had opened and Harriet herself had entered the room and taken a seat quietly between them, only motioning for him to go on. He concluded with a mention of the ring, necklace, and fob in the shape of owls. Then he turned toward Harriet. "Did you discover anything, Mrs. Westerman?"

"Only this." She held out a sheet of paper toward them. It was folded twice and contained a series of groups of five letters. Crowther examined the broken seal. An owl.

"Do you think Swann learned something of this group and meant to tell us?" Harriet asked as he looked at the seal.

Crowther handed the paper to Manzerotti and sat back. "Then he was poisoned to prevent sharing his knowledge? Possible."

Manzerotti sighed. "Codes are such a frustration. Without the key we do not know if this is an instruction, a warning, or a request of some sort. Nor do we know if it was addressed to Swann or found by him." Having given Harriet a brief account of the reasons for his presence in Maulberg as he had described to Crowther, Manzerotti continued, "A little club. These owls— interesting. I doubt that they are merely enthusiasts for the theater or some-such. Who are the members, I wonder? Shame we cannot turn out the pockets of every person at court in search of owls."

"A cabal," Harriet said.

"So it would seem, my dear," Manzerotti replied.

Suddenly Harriet got to her feet and crossed to where Swann's hip flask sat on the mantelpiece. She nodded to herself then handed it to Crowther.

"Another owl. So Swann is certainly part of this group," Crowther said, passing the flask to Manzerotti. The latter studied the engraving a moment, then set it down on the table in front of him.

Harriet remembered Swann's muttered words in the garden. "And now they are being hunted."

Manzerotti smiled very faintly. "It seems so. Gabriel tells me you have thought of revenge when you have seen the pantomime of these crimes. Their viciousness. I wonder if you are right. I know of many little plots and shufflings here, but that does not mean I know them all." He looked at his watch. "The moment for the triumphal return from Castle Grenzhow approaches. I think I had better remove myself from the reunion. Though I am delighted to see the handsome Mr. Clode released, perhaps it would be best if he didn't discover us here, so intimate." He stood. "My dear Gabriel, Mrs. Westerman." He bowed. "Such a joy to spend a little time with you both. You must come and hear me sing this evening. Not only because it will give you pleasure, but I think you had better start asking who else Swann's little clique has damaged, don't you agree?"

Pegel examined his stack of purloined messages and rolled his shoulders. It was a simple insight, that people could not resist writing themselves into what they created, and it had been the case with many codes and ciphers he had come across in the past. He had written out the square before Florian had interrupted him. Now he wrote out that phrase above it. *Per me caeci vident*. Then knocked out the repeated letters. *Permcaivdnt*.

"Well, let's see if that's true," he said, and began.

He pulled out the first of the letters and moved up and down the square guided by his keyword. The first two groups of letters were nonsense, but then the words began to unfurl. His excitement was touched with regret; the search over, his weariness was gaining the upper hand. The pompous idiots! If they'd chosen something at random, he might never have found it. The first paper contained instructions on how to indoctrinate new members to the order. Slowly. Guiding them into habits of obedience and secrecy through their readings and discussions. Offering them help, approval, admiration, friendship, punishing any who left their order with scandal and hatred. The second contained in a series of numbered paragraphs, some of the philosophy that Florian had shared with him. That to return the world of men to a happy state of equality and peace, property must be abandoned, borders between nations removed, and a group of enlightened individuals would then guide the people like Olympians. The document didn't actually mention Olympians, but that's what it seemed like to Pegel.

He sighed deeply and put down his pen. Surely there was no sensible man alive who would believe this nonsense. And yet . . . If it were revealed little by little, dressed up with the proper ritual, and when people encoded their letters, they seldom allowed themselves any great, persuasive flights of rhetoric. Perhaps these rather bald statements could be made to sound glorious in the words of a skillful orator. But could there really be, as Pegel's master suspected, members of the Minervals in positions of real power in Europe? He started on the third sheet, and the neat little groups of letters unfurled into a name, then the name of a town and a title, then there was another . . . He had his answer. His master had been right.

Pegel got up from his chair and checked that the lock was turned in his door. He was returning to his chair when he changed his mind again and dragged a stool in front of it as well. As he sat down he noted that his fingers were shaking. There were Minervals in power all across the empire—and he had the list of their names.

33

Harriet left Crowther to guard Swann while she went to greet Daniel and tell her friends of Swann's illness. Their discussions were interrupted on numerous occasions by court officials knocking lightly on the door to offer their congratulations to Clode on his return and express their pleasure in seeing him. When she asked if Clode, Rachel, and Graves might watch over Swann, they responded with such enthusiasm Harriet suspected that the continual exchange of polite platitudes was having as severe an effect on their tempers as it had on hers.

"You were right to say that Clode would not want to leave until this business was cleared up, Mrs. Westerman," Graves said. "We suggested to him that we could leave at once and he was most emphatic in his refusal."

Harriet and her brother-in-law exchanged glances. Daniel was looking better than he had two days before. There was some color in his face and he had lost a little of his hunted look.

"Harriet," he said. "What you have told us . . . I—this madman did not collect my blood also?"

She put her hand on his sleeve. "No, I think not, Clode. He seems to be after the blood of these individuals alone."

Daniel smiled briefly. "I find that oddly comforting."

Harriet had on her lap the product of her friends' work in Castle Grenzhow. There were a number of sheets in Rachel's neat handwriting, each one carefully dated with a series of visits and meetings. "Lord, Daniel, you kept yourself well-occupied here. I assume if anything had appeared to you that was particularly strange, you would have mentioned it by now."

"We have written down everything, and I see nothing suspicious," Daniel said.

Harriet began to read more carefully. "You saw something, Clode. Something that made you seem a danger to this creature and his plans. I wish we knew what we were looking for."

"Murder will out, Mrs. Westerman," Graves said, and stretched his arms. "I am going to rest for a while if Mr. and Mrs. Clode will take the first part of the evening at Swann's side. Fine way for you to celebrate your reunion."

When Rachel and Daniel entered the chamber of Chancellor Swann to relieve Crowther, they found he was not alone with the patient. Herr Kupfel had arrived at last. Clode and Crowther were still shaking hands, with great warmth on both sides, when Kupfel patted him on the sleeve.

"I need things."

"What can I do for you, sir?" Clode asked.

The alchemist rattled off a list of equipment and ingredients in a mixture of French, English, and German that made Clode's head spin. "I shall do my best," he said doubtfully and Kupfel rolled his eyes and shuffled back toward the bed again, where he stood, staring down at Swann's sweating, sleeping form.

"Don't worry, Daniel. I think it best if I go. They know me in the kitchen and gardens," Rachel said, a little wearily.

Kupfel turned to her with a look of deep suspicion. "You remember the list?" he said at last. His accent in English was heavy, as if the words had to be spat out individually like rocks.

Rachel repeated it back to him. "Would you like the creeping Jenny fresh or dried? It is just coming into flower, but I know the cook has a store from last season. She takes it for her cough."

"Creeping Jenny?"

"*Lysimachia nummularia.*"

"Fresh."

Rachel simply nodded. Her husband and Kupfel watched her leave, a little openmouthed. Crowther smiled.

Evening, and Harriet found herself once more changing her costume. To listen to music in the court, it seemed, required a different standard of dress than was thought seemly during the day. It was lucky that Dido had been insistent about the proper number of dresses, gowns, gloves, and jewels that were necessary for residence at a foreign court. Harriet said so, and Dido grinned. "It is a pleasure to dress you up nice from time to time, Mrs. Westerman. You're never out of riding dress at home, and before then, of course, it was the mourning clothes—such dull colors." She put her hand over her mouth. "I'm so sorry, madam."

Harriet shook her head. "Don't worry, Dido. They *were* dull colors. James said so himself when I wore them for my father."

"I wish I'd known the captain better, madam," she said. "Everyone is full of stories about him at Caveley. He sounds like a good man."

Harriet looked at herself in the mirror. The dress was cut quite low and showed off the length of her neck and the paleness of her skin.

"He was, Dido, and much loved by his family and his friends." She turned and smiled at the maid. "But it is just as you said before, my dear, about travel. We must make our own stories now."

Harriet met Crowther in the concert chamber. He raised his eyebrows when he saw her and nodded in approval. Having enjoyed that minor triumph, Harriet wondered where to begin. Most of the people in the room were strangers to her. She thought of Mrs. Padfield: perhaps she might be able to offer some insight into old stories that could have driven someone to wreak a terrible revenge. Tomorrow morning, she would return to the Al-Saids' workshop and see what other threads they could offer. She and Crowther joined the Colonel and Mrs. Padfield as the company began to take their seats. They shook hands and Harriet was glad to notice the colonel looking at his wife with affectionate admiration.

"Lord, what a crush!" the colonel said, a little loudly. Mrs. Padfield put her arm on his sleeve and he blushed and said more quietly, "So many strangers here for the wedding."

His wife was looking around the room. "Yet I do not see Glucke, do you, my dear?" The colonel shook his head. "Strange," Mrs. Padfield continued. "He is such a lover of music."

Harriet smiled. "That is the gentleman who keeps cats, if I remember rightly."

"Indeed. But he is almost as passionate about opera. He helped design the Opera House, and I have never seen a man so delighted as the day he heard that Manzerotti was coming here."

They found their places but, frustratingly, Harriet found herself next to the colonel rather than his wife.

The duke entered, alone apart from his dog, and once the room had risen to greet him and all had taken their seats again, Manzerotti strolled out on to the stage and bowed. Seeing him on stage was somehow worse than sitting with him in Swann's chamber. The leader of the opera band played a shimmering clamber of notes on the harpsichord, the violinists began a rhythm, dancelike, neat and tripping, then Manzerotti began to sing. It was as beautiful as ever. Light, dancing over the air rather than through it, a thing as perfect and fleeting as the glimmer on the crystal chandeliers. Harriet felt her lungs compress. It seemed so very wrong to take pleasure in his music, but her body simply ignored her objections as she was lifted and fell with it. She raised her fan to cover her eyes. What would it be, to know such perfect lightness?

The aria ended to the usual storm of applause, and with a bow to the duke, Manzerotti made way for the dancers. Crowther saw something in Harriet's expression and turned his head toward her, saying softly, "You cannot blame yourself, Mrs. Westerman, for the effects Manzerotti produces."

Colonel Padfield, who was seated on her right, was obviously one of those gentlemen who saw instrumental music as an invitation to general conversation. "Amazing thing, power of music, isn't it, madam? And the fairer sex are particularly prone to it, I believe."

"Indeed?" Harriet said, steadying her breathing and wishing him in Hades.

"Oh yes," he said comfortably. "There was a woman here at the court some six years ago, before my time, you know, who was so taken with some Italian violin player she made quite a fool of herself. Apparently the duke was on the point of putting her under his protection, but she couldn't resist her passion for the fiddler. Had to leave court under a cloud, of course, and her son was taken away from her. Then the sovereign's eye landed on

Countess Dieth. There was quite an amusing anecdote about it. When they told the duke what the lady was up to, apparently he said, 'But I have estates in Italy, and I play the flute very well!'"

"They removed her child from her?"

"Lord, they had to! She was the widow of one of the officers, and the son was a godson of the duke. Couldn't let him be raised by such a woman."

One of the dancers was lifted across the stage in a series of leaps that seemed designed to show off her form rather than advance the drama to any degree that Harriet could understand, but the general applause provoked drew Colonel Padfield's attention back to the stage once more. Harriet closed her eyes briefly and thought of her son and daughter at Caveley. She knew what she was capable of if they were under threat. She wondered.

Kupfel received the basket from Rachel with a suspicious eye. He riffled through it, then placing it on the floor by the fire, said only, "Good."

Clode took a seat next to his wife.

"Rachel, how did you ever manage to gather all those things in an hour?"

She yawned for she was tired now. "I made some friends among the servants and learned something of their cures. The nobility thinking you a murderer gave me the opportunity for some study."

Clode removed his hand from her arm and Rachel bit her lip. She was becoming as outspoken as her sister. She glanced at Herr Kupfel. He was on his knees in front of the fire with the basket at his side. He was quite still and Rachel realized, with a slight shock, that he was praying. It had never occurred to her to pray before she started similar work. Kupfel brushed something from his eye, then picked up the saucepan and the crock of milk.

Manzerotti began his second aria. Harriet let it carry her. She did not know the piece, only that the music seemed to rage as it rose, then in a moment became slow, thick, and open, grieving alongside the hautbois before becoming a battle again. His audience applauded and the duke rose and walked to meet him on the stage. Manzerotti went down on one knee to kiss his hand.

"Revenge and love from *Flavio*! Most appropriate." The duke looked pleased. "That is the opera you will be giving us tomorrow, I believe."

Manzerotti got to his feet and bowed. "It is, sire."

"An opera that touches on the responsibilities of ruling a kingdom." The duke turned to the audience. "Even musicians have the opportunity at court to lecture their sovereigns and be paid for it." There was a ripple of sycophantic laughter.

"I will do all in my power to give you pleasure, sire," Manzerotti said. Harriet heard a woman sigh lustily behind her.

"Very good, songbird." The duke removed a large diamond from his second finger and handed it to him. "See that you do."

Kupfel had left as soon as he had completed his work, his head lowered. The remnants of his cure lay scattered where they fell. Rachel had tidied them as best she could. Now she and her husband sat in silence watching Swann sleep.

"He seems a great deal easier," Rachel said at last. "I wish I knew what Mr. Kupfel was about." She crossed to the bed and checked the bandages wrapped around the chancellor's hands. They were greasy with the preparation Kupfel had made over the fireplace. She had watched him cover the skin with egg whites, then his strange custard of herbs, milk, and oil.

"Rachel . . ." She turned toward her husband. He looked very young. "Why did he choose me—whoever did all this? I don't understand what I did."

She returned to him and sat at his feet. It was how she used to sit with Harriet when they talked late at night at Caveley. She realized even as she settled that she had never sat by his side in this way before.

"I hope the answer lies somewhere in those notes we have made. Harriet will work it out. She has that fire in her eyes. I feel myself as if we are lost in some magical tale."

"What do you mean, my dear?"

"Do you remember Jocasta Bligh's cards, the ones she uses to tell fortunes?"

"Of course. When last we met, she threatened you with five children."

Rachel laughed softly and felt Daniel's hand on her shoulder; his touch was tentative, unsure. She reached up and took it in her own, lifting the back of his hand to her mouth and kissing it before laying it back in its place.

"I think this man is a poet, of sorts," she went on. "I mean, these deaths, these death scenes are like little horror plays. And everyone circling round this seems like characters from Mrs. Bligh's pack of cards. The Page who found Mrs. Dieth; Kupfel is a Hermit if ever I saw one. Perhaps Harriet is Justice now! There is even an Emperor in the shape of the duke. Is it not strange? When you begin to look for such things in the world, they appear everywhere."

"I think each one of us tries to make a story for ourselves. To understand the pattern of life."

"You are right. Daniel, I hope the story we make will be a happy one."

"From this time on, Rachel." He was silent for a moment, and she looked up at him, the line of his jaw beginning to shade with stubble, the shape of his throat. "And what of me? Where am I in this fairy tale of yours?"

"I thought of the Fool, the first card in the pack. The beginning of things."

"My costume? Of course. Do you think that might be why he chose me?" Daniel said, breathing out. "That was all? Because I looked like the illustration on a pack of cards?"

"Perhaps that was enough."

Daniel was quiet a long time. "Do you think me a fool, Rachel?"

"No, but I think we have both been foolish, don't you?"

"I think I have married a clever woman."

"Of course you have, but perhaps not very wise. Daniel . . . that letter you wrote to me the morning after you had been arrested . . ."

"I apologize for it, Rachel. It fell from me—no wonder you thought me deranged, that you were frightened of me."

"No, Daniel, that's just it. It was a little wild, but my dear I should have said this the moment that I came to see you at Castle Grenzhow . . ."

"But I behaved as if you were a stranger making a social call. I wanted to let you see I was no longer mad, or at least that I had some control."

"I know, darling, and I was a fool not to tell you to stop being an idiot then, but I was so afraid for you. But let me finish: when you spoke in that letter of me being disgusted with you, frightened of you, I swear to you, Daniel, it was never so. The drug made you think such things. I have always loved and trusted you." She twisted around so she could look up into his face, hopeful, unafraid. "Darling, whatever strangeness has marked the beginning of our marriage, I swear there has never been a single moment where I have been frightened of you, or disgusted by you. I swear it, Daniel, on those five children Jocasta has promised us."

He got down on his knees beside her and took her in his arms.

34

The audience began to make its way into the supper chamber. Harriet took Crowther's arm and turned to the colonel.

"What happened to the lady?" she asked. "The one whose son was taken away?"

Colonel Padfield shook his head. "I haven't a clue, madam. I am afraid I have told you all I know of the matter. One moment—Doctor von Reymen?"

The duke's physician turned toward them and Padfield continued in French. His words were fluent enough, but spoken with an English accent so uncompromising, Harriet felt herself smile. "Do you remember the story of that young woman who wanted to run off with the violinist? Mrs. Westerman has just asked me how the story ended. I have had to confess, I don't know."

Von Reymen came closer to them and looked around him as he approached, as if delighted to be observed in conversation with them. Harriet was sure she and Crowther would do nothing to enhance Reymen's reputation. The colonel's stock, however, was obviously on the rise.

"Ah yes! I remember it well. You must always come to me for the tittle-tattle, *mon* colonel, I have been at Ludwig's side so long. Kastner was the lady's name. The fiddler Bertolini. Well, I say lady. Her French was not well, not well at all. She was sent away and her son, Carl, was enrolled at the Ludwigsschule, here in Ulrichsberg."

"Was she never allowed to visit him?" Harriet asked.

"She might have been in time. But after the first year, there was no one to visit! An outbreak of fever came to the town and the child was one of the eight who died. Very sad, of course, he was a brave little chap. But no doubt she was glad of his death—so much easier to find a new rich protector without a child."

Harriet clenched her jaw. It was probably a good thing that Crowther intervened to ask, "You attended the child? Did he tell you nothing of his mother?"

"It was a terrible time, milord. I had no time to chat to him, there were so many taken ill. Now there was a man, the drawing master . . . Durnham— Dreher, that was it! He must have taken a liking to the boy, since one often found him at the bedside. None of the other masters seemed to think the child would amount to much."

Harriet closed her eyes, thinking of her son Stephen, the terrors she had felt whenever he was ill, and the death of her first child half a world away. The memory of it still lay vivid and black in the core of her.

"Mrs. Westerman?"

She opened her eyes to look at Crowther and he nodded to the far corner of the room. Krall was standing by the double doors, waiting for them to notice him. His brows were drawn tightly together.

Crowther bowed toward her. "I think you may have to change your dress again, Mrs. Westerman."

Krall had told them only that Adolphus Glucke had been found dead; he then waited in their private parlor, staring ferociously at the fire as Harriet and Crowther dressed to leave the palace. Harriet did not speak to Dido as she changed her clothes. She tried to remember what had happened since she first dressed that day in the darkness: Countess Dieth found, her mouth full of earth and her ring with the owl symbol missing; Clode's release; and the discovery of Swann staggering and senseless in the garden. A fragment of the aria Manzerotti had sung had stuck, repeating itself in her brain, and again and again she saw the image of a young boy dying of fever and separated from his mother.

Adolphus Glucke was not provided with an apartment in court, but in common with several other senior members of the Privy Council, his house was only a short stroll from the grounds. There he had lived with his books and scores, unmarried, a little aloof but devoted to the service of the duke and Maulberg. His home was one of the first in Neue Strasse, a tall, narrow building that reminded Crowther of those built in Soho Square or Portland Place for families coming to spend the season in Town, and not concerned if they were a little cramped. The height of the frontage gave Crowther the impression he was being looked down upon. He turned; the view was much the same that he had first had of the palace, yet, set to the west of the market-place as it was, Glucke's house seemed to be looking at it slightly askance. The street was dark and quiet, and Krall hurried them up the steps and into the hallway, glancing about him as he did so. At the bottom of a steep internal staircase was a small group of people. Krall barked and glowered, and it was established with reasonable quickness that they were Glucke's housekeeper, who had discovered him, and her daughter and son-in-law to whom she had run; also the member of the Watch, who had just begun his work of singing out the hours and biblical quotes when she gave him the news. Mr. Glucke's footman was the last of the group.

"Has the body been touched?" Krall asked. Crowther began to translate the exchanges from German to English for Mrs. Westerman.

The son-in-law stepped forward. "We didn't like to, sir. All looks so strange we weren't sure what to do beyond call the Watch."

"You did well, son. Right, one step at a time. Mistress Schneider, tell me what happened. Start at the start and go slow."

Mistress Schneider smoothed her apron and wet her lips. For some reason Crowther liked her. She seemed young to have a daughter full-grown and married. He was reminded of his own housekeeper and wondered, briefly, how she did.

"Shall I start in the morning, sir?" she said.

"Whenever you think best," Krall replied, lifting his eyebrows.

"Mr. Glucke was at court, as he always is in the mornings with the Privy Council, when there was a great banging at the door. I opened it to find old Mr. Kupfel on the doorstep."

"The alchemist?" Harriet whispered to Crowther. He nodded but kept his eye on the housekeeper.

"Did he visit here often, mistress?" Krall asked.

She hesitated. "He used to, sir, but these last years it's been more his son that comes. Not in the morning, though."

"Mr. Glucke buy a lot of face potions, did he?"

She shook her head, unsmiling. "Young Mr. Kupfel has done very well, sir.

He is even spoken of as a future Mayor of Ulrichsberg. Mr. Glucke was often visited by the better people in town, those who have not the rank to attend court."

Krall scratched the back of his head. "I understand you, mistress. But it was Adam Kupfel came this morning? Do you know what his business was?"

"He wouldn't share with me, now would he? No, all I know is he seemed to have worked himself into a rage. He said he'd wait for Mr. Glucke in the study, and beyond getting me to give him a plate of something hot, that was all his talk with me, and even that cost him so much twitching and sneering you'd think I was a dog not to be trusted without a muzzle."

"How long did he wait?"

"It was an hour till Mr. Glucke came back—so early in the afternoon. Then there were voices raised."

"Raised loud enough for you to make any sense of what was said?"

"Two words only from Kupfel. My master always spoke low. They were 'thieves,' and 'fools.' I thought maybe the children had been riffling through Kupfel's junk again."

"And then?"

"Kupfel stormed out in the same mood he arrived in. I gave my master his meal."

"He did not dine in court?"

"He only sups there from time to time, sir. The food is too rich for him. The food *was* too rich for him," she corrected herself. "The master asked me to come in and clear away his plate, then he went down to the cats."

Crowther stopped translating and looked at Krall with his eyebrows raised. The district officer sighed and turned to them. "Mr. Glucke was a scholar, but he had his quirks. He had a fancy for cats—used to have them in the study while he worked. Unsanitary, I always thought it, though they are pretty enough. He's always had a dozen or so of them at any one time."

"Ah yes," Harriet said to herself. "The mechanical mice."

"Then what?" Krall said to the housekeeper.

"Then nothing, District Officer. I knew he was going back to court in the evening, but time was getting close for his usual hour of leaving, and there was no sign or sound of him. I knocked and got no answer, so I went into the garden round the back and looked in through the window. I could see him sitting there, but he didn't move when I knocked. The only things that were moving were the cats, and they seemed . . ."

"Seemed what, mistress?"

"Seemed strange, sir. They were all gathered round him. I thought he was ill so I fetched my son-in-law here to help William knock down the door, and then we saw . . ."

"So the door to the study was locked from within?" Crowther asked.

"With the key left in the lock. The garden door was locked too, though there was no key in that."

"Thank you, mistress," Krall said slowly. "I think it best if we go to the study now."

Crowther did not move. "Madam, this may sound a little unusual, but did your master have anything with an owl on it?"

The housekeeper frowned and was shaking her head, when the footman touched her shoulder and whispered to her.

"Of course—on his watch, sir. On the case."

"Thank you."

"The cats?" Krall said suspiciously.

"Still there, sir. We left the door to the garden open, thinking they'd be off, but they don't seem to want to leave him."

Adolphus Glucke was seated in the center of the room; he had been a thin man in late middle age. With a slight shock Harriet realized he was the man she had seen during their first evening in Ulrichsberg, the one who had reminded her of Crowther. His body had slid forward slightly in the chair and his head was tilted back. He could have been sleeping off his beer on a tavern bench, except his left hand was covered in blood. On his lap was curled a large snow-white cat. Another wound its way in a regular figure of eight between his feet. The room seemed full of white fur and a low throb of purring. Krall entered first. Harriet and Crowther followed more slowly, looking around them at the unfamiliar chamber. It was smallish and square. The wooden floor was covered with red and black rugs, a little threadbare in places. Three walls were covered in books. The fourth was dominated by a French window; the night air blew softly in through it, carrying the scents of the garden. Tasteful, forgettable landscapes hung on either side of it. The desk had its back to the light.

Crowther crossed to the body and looked into Glucke's upturned face. The cat on his lap turned its head toward him, put back its ears, and hissed. Crowther ignored it. Glucke's mouth was filled with earth. It was as if the head had been held back in its current position and the dry soil poured in until it overflowed around his cheeks, leaving a haze of particles over the skin. Around the eyes it was darker, as if it had turned to mud. Crowther felt a chill run through him; the man had been crying as he died. One of the cats was pushing against Glucke's hanging hand as if wanting to be stroked. Crowther hoped they had been this close to him as he died, that somewhere under his suffering he had felt their comfort.

"It is the same," he said.

She was standing by the window.

"The killer must have come and gone through the garden," she replied after a pause. "I wonder why Glucke let him in."

"Someone he knew, must be," Krall said.

"Someone he did not think could be a threat," Harriet added. "Crowther, could you close the door?"

He moved away from the body to do so, and the cat on the body's lap settled again and began to knead the thigh of the corpse, purring. The same symbol was chalked on the white paint of the door. Triangle, circle of seven spokes.

"He has done it," Crowther said. "Unless Swann survives. Seven wine glasses, seven spokes. Seven victims. His work is done."

"Or she," Harriet said softly. "But Swann has not been bled."

Krall looked around the room, following the progress of another of the cats over the top of the mantelpiece. "I shall have a look along the path. Perhaps the killer dropped a visiting card, though more like I shall just find the key to the garden door thrown into the shrubbery."

Crowther heard the hopelessness in the man's voice. "We will find who did this, Krall. He will make a mistake, leave a mark behind he doesn't mean to."

"Perhaps. But this . . . A disgusting, humiliating way to die."

Crowther had no comfort to offer. "Were you acquainted with Glucke?"

"A little. I believe he recommended me as district officer in Oberbach when I handed my business on to my son-in-law."

His tone suggested he had no more to say on that. Instead he ran his hand through his hair. "It all comes too fast. I must speak to Colonel Padfield and Count Frenzel immediately."

"But first we must go straight to Kupfel and discover why he was so angry this morning," Crowther said.

"In time. For the good of Maulberg, and the duke, this crime must be concealed."

"The duke?" Harriet said. "Why should this be concealed just to protect him from embarrassment?"

Krall turned on her. "The duke is a good man, appointed by God to guide us. He shall be protected."

"From whence this enthusiasm, Krall? Until this morning you have been rigorous in your honesty, your pursuit of the truth," Crowther said. "You questioned the duke in our presence."

Krall's face flushed red. "Twice a month the gates of the palace are opened, and anyone—*anyone* who wishes it—may petition the duke in person. He greets the people as his children and cares for them. He listens to what they say and he acts. It drives his advisers mad half the time. But he does it."

"But the palace, the Opera House," Harriet objected. "All the luxury of the court . . . the duke does nothing but indulge himself!"

"How long have you been here, Mrs. Westerman? Three days? Four? But you think . . ." He turned away for a moment, then spoke again, more slowly. "Do not be fooled by the manner in which the duke presents himself to the world. There is not an inch of ground under his authority he does not know. And the land under his authority flourishes. He will not be made vulnerable, not by the actions of some madman. The extravagance of the court is the gilding on something real. Something of value."

There was no sound in the room other than the low rumble of the cats purring.

Harriet crouched down to stroke one that had decided to rub up against her. As she put her hand out to it, she noticed it had dried blood streaked across its white back, and she recoiled slightly. "Forgive me if I spoke hastily, Mr. Krall. You are right, we know little of Maulberg. Conceal the murder if you must, but surely, for the good of the duke, you must find who is responsible. May I have the map of the secret chamber that Wimpf drew? Perhaps there is something useful there. We will be discreet."

The district officer hesitated, then drew a paper from his pocket and handed it to her. "Agreed. But you *will* continue to act with some discretion or I will have you and your party thrown out of Maulberg. I have my arrangements to make." He left the room, and in a moment they could hear his voice upstairs barking out commands.

Harriet examined the paper in her hands as she spoke. "I had no idea he was so devoted to the duke."

Crowther was watching the door through which Krall had disappeared. "I think it may have come as a surprise to Krall himself."

Harriet placed the paper in her pocket. "Go to Kupfel. I shall examine the secret chamber."

Crowther looked concerned. "I shall go to Kupfel, but Mrs. Westerman, you cannot go looking for the chamber alone."

"Why on earth not?"

"I hate to state the obvious, but there is a killer at court."

"I begin to suspect there are several of different sorts. I shall take Graves."

"And now, Mrs. Westerman, you are forcing me to sound like your sister. You cannot wander the palace at night alone with Mr. Graves. Though I know your sister has courage, she cannot be a sufficient guard. Clode himself is still weak—and in any case, they must guard Swann."

Harriet might control her temper with Krall, but she did not with Crowther. "Then what *would* you have me do?"

He closed his eyes for a moment and leaned his weight onto his cane.

"Take Manzerotti."

35

Pegel sat back in his chair. He was uncomfortable. Normally when he looked up from his work he linked his hands behind his head, crossed his ankles, and thought about what he wanted to eat next, but tonight he stood slowly and looked down at his notes with great unease. He took a step away then returned and swept the papers into one of the drawers, slammed it shut, and turned the lock. Then he headed toward the main door of his room to release himself. His momentum carried him until he had the key in the lock, but then he turned back, gathered up the papers once more and folded them into his coat pocket. There were three places in the room he had prepared for papers to be concealed, but now the messages were translated into plain language, none of these places seemed sufficiently secure. He was almost angry with Florian and his little group for making their codes simple enough for him to unpick. He didn't want to know all those names, whatever profit it might bring him. The thought of the money stilled him for a little while. Money of his own. It would be enough for him to establish himself somewhere with a decent university. He could stay there, in one place, teach mathematics and pursue his own studies. He might even be able to make a friend he could keep.

As soon as the idea formed he thought it nonsense. He was not the sort of man who could afford to lead a settled existence. Better to dance through people's lives, blow smoke in their faces and disappear while their eyes were still smarting. Damn these papers! It was no good. It was simply too dangerous to leave them lying around as they were. He must burn them, take the originals, and translate them once more in front of his master. He unfolded the pages and looked at the names. He had watched some of them and thought them good men. Fools, of course, idealists too protected by their position to see how the world really worked, their eyes so fixed on some distant lofty goal they probably hadn't even noticed when they stepped off the edge and into the abyss. The papers burned and curled in the grate and he prodded the ashes into nothing. He wondered what would happen to them. Some of the smoke got into his eyes on this occasion. He would ride out as soon as it was light.

There was a light knock at the door and Harriet opened it to find Manzerotti leaning on the frame, a candle in his hand.

"I received your note, as you see, Mrs. Westerman. I do hope you haven't reconsidered your decision not to shoot me dead."

She turned back into the room and he followed. "Frequently. But tonight I am asking you to examine this chamber with me."

"How exciting! Secret passageways, darkness. I should be delighted, of course, but, flattered as I am, why is not Mr. Crowther or Mr. Graves at your side?"

She kept her back turned. "Crowther has to visit Herr Kupfel, and Graves is on watch at Swann's bedside. Rachel and Daniel need to rest."

"I am sure the happy couple would be delighted to continue their vigil?" he asked innocently.

"Perhaps, but Mr. Crowther feels it would be unwise of me to be found alone at night in the company of Mr. Graves."

"Whereas a being such as myself? We eunuchs are a useful breed."

"It is nonsense to worry about such things in these circumstances." She breathed deeply. "I thank you for coming."

"Gabriel loves you very much, I think, Mrs. Westerman. I am sure to make the suggestion was as distasteful for him as it was for you to comply."

She hesitated briefly then picked up the map Wimpf had drawn from the table. "Why do you call him by his Christian name, Manzerotti?"

He shrugged. "Because it irritates him, but he knows that to order me to call him by any of his titles, real or imagined, would make him ridiculous. He is a vain, proud man. It is a nature I understand, being both vain and proud myself." He took the page from her and examined it in the light of his candle. Harriet guessed he must be about her own age, but his face was as smooth as her ten-year-old son's. "I think the most discreet way we can let ourselves into these passageways is through a doorway on this corridor."

"Why were they built, Manzerotti?"

He tilted his head to look at her. His expression was almost affectionate. "Your naïveté is one of your great virtues, my dear. Do try never to lose it. In palaces such as these the great do not want their servants on view unless they are liveried and as superb as the gilding. I am sure they were built so the lower servants could go from room to room without offending their masters by breathing the same air. Shall we?"

Crowther knocked on the door with the head of his cane. There was a shout deep from within.

"Who is it?"

"The Englishman."

The door was shuffled open. A little. "What? Why are *you* here? I heard the Watch call midnight already."

"Will you not let me in? Do you not wish to know how Chancellor Swann does?"

There was a moment of doubt on his face, but the door was dragged open enough to allow Crowther entrance and he once again followed the alchemist's stooped back through the junk to the comfort of the back room. Crowther did not wait for an invitation to be seated.

"Why were you arguing with Glucke?"

Kupfel remained standing, staring at the fire. "None of your business. How is Swann?"

"Still more asleep than awake, but much improved, I understand. His hands are less inflamed. Glucke was murdered this evening."

Kupfel turned around at that, his mouth open and his face suddenly pale. Crowther realized he had not known the power of the blow he was delivering. "What? Glucke?" Kupfel sat down heavily in his armchair and began to cry, covering his face with his hands. Crowther felt a spasm of pity. Kupfel raised his head. "Was it? Was it . . . like the woman?" Crowther nodded and Kupfel howled. His face was red now and running with tears; he gulped and wiped his sleeve across his face. "Oh God, oh God . . . I wish I had never met that man. Never asked . . . What suffering I have brought among us."

Crowther stood and poured a brandy from a dusty-looking carafe on the desk then handed it to his host. Kupfel took it and drank. Crowther poured a glass for himself and tipped it down his throat. He had never been a man who drank. It had marked him out in his youth and made his fellows suspicious of him—confirmed him in their eyes as a dry eccentric even at that age—but confronted with Kupfel's animal grief he reached for it. It burned, but he felt its warmth. Kupfel stopped crying, but he rocked back and forward in his chair, and Crowther discovered that he grieved for him. What strange beings he found himself in sympathy with these days.

"You went to see him, Kupfel. You thought he had stolen the book, did you not?"

"I thought he had got someone to steal it for him." Kupfel's voice was small and cracked, the wheeze underlying it more pronounced.

"Did whatever harmed Swann come from the same volume?"

Kupfel's face was crumpled and lined as if it had been scythed and folded. He held his empty glass in his old hands, and Crowther could read in the scars on the fingers years of toil and work with heat and substances corrosive and violent. "No. It was not in that book."

"Did you believe Glucke had killed Lady Martesen?"

"No, no. Never. He was a good man. No, I believe he got his hands on the book then gave it to a man of no scruples, a man ready to harm, to corrupt anyone who stood between him and power."

Crowther was profoundly tired; he knew there was something in the words of the old alchemist that would make him understand, something important, but it slipped from him. Kupfel thought the book had been stolen by Glucke; they knew the book had been stolen by Beatrice so Kupfel was wrong, and therefore his anger with Glucke meant nothing. He must sleep.

"The book was stolen by your serving girl Beatrice," he said. "We are trying to follow her path."

"The maid? Impossible!" Kupfel looked into the fire. "A girl? You think her capable of understanding it?"

"Yes."

Crowther put his hand on the little alchemist's shoulder, and to his surprise the man reached up, seized it, and held it with his own, speaking with sudden enthusiasm, even through his tears. "I am so close, English. So close to the Great Work. Once that is complete, the Elixir, I can treat any ill, I can cure anyone who is harmed by what I have learned." His voice was intent, a little desperate.

"You cannot raise the dead, Mr. Kupfel."

He slumped again. "It has been done. Perhaps I might, but I would not. I cannot save Glucke now. No one comes back from death . . . *whole*."

They moved slowly along the corridor, the candles dancing shadows up the walls. Harriet noticed that Manzerotti smelled of bergamot. He seemed to have no animal scent of his own. He had handed the map back to her as soon as they closed the door to the passageway behind them and allowed her to lead the way. She wondered what her husband would think of her now. He wouldn't understand it, of that she was sure, but would he forgive her? Would he have continued to love her, had he lived? He had been gracious in his letters when news of the events of 1780 had reached them. He knew that she had saved Lord Sussex and his sister, or helped to at any rate, but she sensed that he had reservations, that he was not convinced that she had needed to step so far outside of the role nature and society had given her. She occasionally argued with him in the privacy of her own mind, claiming it was his own fault. Taking her with him on his tours abroad in the early years of their marriage had meant she developed this core of wilfulness, of unconventional thinking, a love of adventure. But that would have been unjust. One of the reasons she had married him was the smell of salt and foreign climates on his skin, the stories of his adventures, and she had campaigned to join him. Whatever strange quirk in her nature that meant she was here now, feeling her way through the darkness with Manzerotti behind her, had been born into her.

"Here, I think," she murmured.

Manzerotti handed her his own candle and felt for the handle. "Locked."

Harriet felt her eyes sting. "Of course it is. I am a fool. Wimpf said Auwerk had the key and I never even thought—"

"Do not worry, dear lady, I have another advantage over Mr. Graves as a companion on this venture." Manzerotti reached into his jacket and produced a soft leather roll. It was the same sort of thing that Crowther used to carry the tools of dissection with him, but much smaller. He untied it and showed her within a number of slim metal tools, each a subtly different shape and size.

"Lock picks? How did you know?"

"A lucky guess, my dear. But I try to be prepared. I am also carrying a knife and a large quantity of money."

"You know how to use these, of course."

"Of course. How do you think I always manage to know a little more than I should? But I had the best teacher when I was young—hunger. The boys who had been castrated were a little better fed than the rest at the school where I was trained, but only a little. There. The pantry at Padua was a great deal better guarded than this."

He pushed the door open. At first Harriet could make out nothing but the checkerboard design on the floor, but as Manzerotti moved around the room, lighting the candles that hung against the walls, each with a brass panel behind it to throw forward what light it could, the room began to take shape before her.

It was a square chamber, with a number of chairs placed against the wall and one larger chair at the north end. The case with the glasses in it was located on the sideboard by the door. Harriet opened it. Seven, all identical and arranged in a circle. She took out one. It was engraved, as Wimpf had said, with a pattern of vines and flowers. He had not mentioned that there was also an owl cut into each glass.

"What do you think they spoke of here, Manzerotti?"

"Power, I suspect. Imagine, Mrs. Westerman, this little group with their owls: if they had simply been courtiers wandering in the gardens making their little plots, then they are ordinary. But here they are a secret little group of seven, meeting in their own secret little room. It gives them a sense of their own importance. Some people have children to stave off their mortality, some religion, and some create these rituals of their own."

"But not you?"

"I am a breed apart, Mrs. Westerman, you know that."

"Music?"

He smiled. "Very, very occasionally. I enjoy what is beautiful and original, and so very little is."

She fitted the glass back into the case and closed it. "Do you know of a musician named Bertolini, who was employed here some years ago, Manzerotti?"

"Yes, but he was neither beautiful nor original. He is Kappelmeister in Colburg now. He leads a band of competent musicians in a competent manner. What of him?"

"I heard this evening that he was involved in a scandal here some years ago. It ended badly for the woman involved. She was separated from her child, and the child died."

"I am not sure I understand, my dear. What threads have you been pulling from the air?"

"I was told the duke was thinking of putting this lady, Kastner was her name, under his protection when the scandal broke out, then after her banishment his attentions alighted on Countess Dieth. Suppose this little cabal wanted one of their own in the ducal bed and they slandered this woman to remove her. She is sent from court, her child is taken from her and dies. That woman therefore had reason to hate her enemies to such a degree she might take this . . . *revenge*." The word choked her, and she found herself staring at Manzerotti, but seeing only her husband. She remembered suddenly the feel of her children's hands in her own the day of James's funeral. She stepped back from him, fumbling for the chair behind her, and sat down. He lowered himself onto one knee in front of her. She felt a sickness in her throat.

"Mrs. Westerman . . ."

"Do not speak."

"I must."

She placed her hands over her ears, but could not block out the sound of his voice.

"I have done many things that you may think immoral, but I gave no order that any man, woman, or child should die in London. I ordered that a body be removed and concealed. That is all. Johannes's devotion to me was very powerful. It had become unmanageable by the time we arrived in London."

"I shall not hear you—you are the devil himself."

"Johannes acted to protect me, but *not* by my command. Do you think I would be the man I am today if such slaughter were my usual modus operandi?" His voice was low, urgent.

"Why did you not tell me this before, at once when we met, if it is true?"

"You would not have believed me."

"Why should I now?"

He was still kneeling before her, looking at the floor in front of him. "You know me a little better now. I should have killed him before we left France. I am sorry, but he was my friend. I told myself he was under sufficient control." She covered her face and heard him move; he had taken the chair next to her own. "Forgive me."

"Never. Even if you did not give the order, it was still you who told Johannes that my husband might be able to identify you. I shall never forgive you."

He sighed. "That is your right." He waited until her breathing began to steady and then spoke as if the exchange had not taken place. "The woman you speak of cannot be your murderer; you need someone who can move about in plain sight. Someone to whom Glucke would open his door. Either this merry band gave someone else a motive as powerful, or someone is taking revenge on her behalf."

Harriet's blood beat in her brain, her exhaustion slowed her thoughts. She held up her hand. "Mrs. Westerman?" She did not speak to him, but after a few moments picked up the candle from the table and placed it near to the paneling behind them. There was a draft coming from somewhere close to her that carried some strange foreign smell. An astringency. She stood.

"Never speak to me of London again, Manzerotti. Never mention my husband in my hearing." He lowered his head. "Now help me shift these chairs." He did so swiftly, setting them in the center of the room while Harriet moved the candle flame to and fro. The flame held steady. She wondered if she had imagined it, but then she felt it again on her left hand. She moved the candle once more and the flame fluttered and bent toward the wall. Using it as her guide, she brought the candle closer. There was a keyhole. It had a thin wooden covering over it, that had been left not quite straight, allowing that thread of air into the room. She ran her hand over the carved uprights in the paneling. It was possible that the edge of a doorway might be concealed beneath them. She felt Manzerotti's breath on her cheek.

"Very good, Mrs. Westerman."

This lock took rather longer than the first. Manzerotti, after an initial examination, actually removed his coat. She watched him as he worked and wondered if she believed him. The more she thought of it, the more likely it seemed. He was subtle; the murders in London were not.

As he worked, he never swore or showed any sign of frustration. The only indication that he had found it anything of a challenge was the nod he gave to himself as something deep within the wood clicked. He pushed the door with his fingertips. It was beautifully weighted. To conceal its edges behind the decoration it was particularly wide, yet it swung slowly open even with that most gentle pressure. He stood at the doorway looking over his shoulder at her. Without his jacket his figure looked almost girlish, and his forearms showing where he had pushed up his sleeves were as white and hairless as his cheek.

"That smell," she said.

"Yes. I would think it wise if we were to avoid touching anything in this room," he said, and moved aside to let her join him in the doorway. It was a far smaller chamber, almost a closet. A narrow bench ran along one wall and on it were a number of innocuous looking glass jars. In front of them was a brown leather folder. Manzerotti produced a knife from his pocket and flicked open the cover with its blade.

There was a diagram of a series of circles, each labeled in flowing copperplate. Harriet counted the row of jars. She craned forward slightly to read, then she reached out for one of the jars. Manzerotti, apparently without looking up, caught her wrist with his left hand.

"A moment, Mrs. Westerman." He turned the page. A number of paragraphs in the same florid handwriting. "The names may be innocent but the potions are not." He tapped the knife on the page as he released her, and Harriet read: *Nausea, vomiting, and evacuation of the bowels. To be ingested. Will not be detected in highly peppered dishes.*

"And here."

May be applied to clothing: will cause a painful rash wherever it touches. "This is foul."

Manzerotti's voice sounded angry when he spoke. "Yes, it is, and my employer and I take it very seriously. I am in your debt, Mrs. Westerman. This is certainly the lair of the poisoner I am searching for, though Herr Kupfel's most powerful secrets did not end up here. There is no sign of the drugs used on Clode or the victims of bloodletting." He turned another page. "Nor anything that would nearly kill Swann either. But it is unpleasant enough. Until we sort out who is who in our catalog of poisoners, may I give you some advice—advice you might pass to your friends here?"

She would not look at him, but nodded.

"Caution. No poison is completely invisible. Drink only when you see others drink. Eat only from shared plates. As for clothing, remember, Mrs. Westerman, you noticed a scent that came from the poisoner's chamber. That must be your warning. May I also suggest that none of you put clothes on your person that feel cold to the touch. Sometimes articles are chilled, that on being warmed by the skin give off their poison. And now, madam, perhaps you will allow me to escort you back to your chamber?"

PART VI

36

Harriet slept very deeply for those few hours. She dreamed of walking through her own gardens at Caveley and finding there not her friends or children, but Manzerotti laughing at a wound in his belly, the duke introducing his spaniel to her as his new wife, and Crowther locking her into a room in Caveley she had never known existed with the Countess Dieth, who wore the mask of a harlequin on parade. Stephen was sitting at a desk in the corner of the chamber, but instead of working at his mathematics Harriet found her son drawing a strange talisman again and again. His movement was mechanical, and when he looked up at her his eyes were made of glass. She found herself outside her house again. A man in a long black cloak and mask was chalking symbols on her door. Her children emerged from the door hand-in-hand. She called out to them and began to run toward them, but Graves appeared, caught her around the waist and began to drag her into a carriage. The footmen were dressed in the livery of the Palace of Ulrichsberg. She fought, but Graves slammed the door on her. She threw herself to the window and called out to Stephen and Anne; they made no move toward her but stood to either side of the man in the black cloak and mask, holding his hands.

She woke to hear the maid moving around the room and the clink of china. Her forehead was damp. She slid out of bed and Dido bought her a dressing gown. She held it for a moment and breathed in deeply; nothing but the smell of lavender and the coal burning in the grate. She drew it over her arms and the small hairs on her arms prickled. The coffee was set out beside the fire. She poured it into the waiting cup then closed her eyes.

"Dido, do you make my coffee yourself in the morning?"

The girl looked confused. "No, ma'am. The trays for all the guests are made in the kitchen this side."

Harriet looked at the tray in front of her. Rosewood, inlaid with the arms of Maulberg in mother-of-pearl, little displays of flowers and laurels in the four corners. "Is this the tray that I had yesterday? Is it marked for me in some way?" Dido was frowning, trying to make sense of her. "It is so charming," Harriet continued, lifting the cup. "I wondered if all the guests have the same."

"All the trays are the same, ma'am. I'll say this for this place—they know how to run a kitchen. The cook makes dozens of trays with coffee and a roll. Plenty with chocolate, which is very nice, though I know you've not a sweet tooth like Mrs. Clode. I arrive at the hatch and say, 'Coffee and roll,' and they hand me a tray. The maid behind me says, 'Coffee and roll,' she gets a tray."

Harriet sipped her coffee gratefully. "Thank you, Dido. I'll wear the same costume as yesterday, if you would be so good as to lay it out."

"The marriage?"

"I shall not be attending the court festivities. I'm sorry, Dido, you won't have the opportunity to bind me into court dress today."

Once Dido was finished with her, she sat down at her desk and drew toward her the various volumes selected for her by Mr. Zeller, the books stolen from the old alchemist, and tried hard to think of nothing but what was in front of her. There was a lifetime of study here. Harriet found herself sinking into the manuscript paintings. She imagined the patient hands of the scribes as they drew and colored these borders to the pages with daisies and vines. In the center of the page in front of her, a king wandered through a landscape that reminded her a little of Keswick—low lands between great hills. He wore long golden robes edged with fur, a crown, and he carried his scepter and orb with him. Behind him in the marshes, in the curl of a rushing river, falling over itself past woodland, was another king, drowning. An old king. He still wore his crown, but the hand he held above the waters was empty and his beard was long. It seemed to be a promise of eternal rebirth. She turned to another, a French translation of a book written in German by a man who claimed to have discovered the secrets of magic in his wanderings through the lands of Egypt. He stated, matter of factly, that with his magic, a dead body could be raised again and made to walk about for seven years; in fact, one of the dukedoms had been run by such an animated corpse until the heir was old enough to rule as he should.

Harriet put down the book and wondered how many people around her believed such things. She had been amazed last summer to see in Keswick how the beliefs in old magic still pulsed through the hills, but that was among the common people. Did such belief really pool in people of her own class, in the ranks above her, to the degree that a person would kill for ritual purposes? She took up the book again. Incantations, calls to angels and demons . . . Each spirit seemed to be as carefully ranked as the officials in the palace; each had its own role and specialty, its proper term of address. There were repeated warnings that if not called with their correct titles and attendants, they would be deeply offended.

She found again the image she thought she had recognized. It was quite different from the one chalked at the death scenes of Countess Dieth and Glucke, but it nagged at her. She spent a few minutes trying to understand the Latin words below it, then she sighed and, book in hand, made her way to Swann's chamber where Graves maintained his bedside vigil. The chancellor was asleep, but snoring. His color was much improved and his sleep seemed peaceful. Graves clambered to his feet as she came in, but she waved him back and without preamble, said, "Graves, do you read Latin?"

"Of course," he said. "It's a little rusty, but part of every gentleman's education, you know."

"Not to be wasted on females, however. Can you translate this?"

He took the book from her and started to read, his left hand moving back and forth through his hair as he did so.

"Not fair, Mrs. Westerman. This is not Ovid, you know. This is medieval Latin. Quite different."

"Can you translate it?"

"Well, the fact that it's nonsense doesn't help either. Let me see. Blood, life. That's fairly simple: blood is life and by this blood can life be summoned from the other . . . region, maybe? Realm perhaps. Does that sound likely?"

"It does. Can you read any more?"

"To fasten the spirit within the statue use this seal and the . . . incantations . . . to . . . I think these are names of spirits. Do you want the list?"

"No." She took the book back from him and frowned over the symbol. It was based on the Star of David—she had thought at first that explained her sense of familiarity with it, but there was something more to it than that. She had seen this before somewhere, or something very like it, with its intricate mix of curls and lettering, circles within circles. So much more esoteric, more learned than the folk magic she had encountered in the Lake Country. But then this was magic for the scholar, to dazzle the rich and reading classes, and thus it needed to be steeped in all these layers of learning. If too many people understood it, it would seem cheap; just as they collected the complex and rare in their cabinets of curiosity, or paid enormous sums for the delicate complications of Mr. Al-Said's automata. She straightened and looked at the picture again. *That* was where she had seen it, pinned to the wall in his workshop among the keys, brass disks, and paper faces!

"I must go up to the village."

"Do you wish me to come with you?"

"No, and Crowther should rest. I shall ask Rachel."

"Very well, but you must take mercy on me at some point. Guarding a sleeping man is very dull work."

37

Michaels had spent the night at the house of the priest of Oberbach, having seen the girl's body laid in one of the side chapels of his church. As dawn broke he mounted his horse and the priest handed him the reins.

"However she died, Mr. Michaels, you have done a good service to her soul in bringing her here. She rests with God now."

Michaels ran his fingers through the horse's mane. She shifted and tossed her head a little. "I don't know how well she will rest, Father. It seems she was much caught up with things of darkness." The birds were acclaiming the day, and around the neat garden of the priest's house flowers opened, insects moved from bloom to bloom. Spring was opening up, full of the promise of summer coming.

"Be that as it may, I believe in a God of mercy, Mr. Michaels. I shall pray for her."

Michaels touched his fingers to his hat, and turned his horse out toward the road.

The Al-Saids were early risers. Their breakfast had already been cleared away and they were at their twin workbenches when Rachel and Harriet arrived. Sami was using the smallest pair of tweezers Rachel had ever seen to add plumage to a bird an inch long; his brother was working opposite, bent over a miniature lathe with a file in one hand. They welcomed the sisters, and Sami set about making tea while Harriet explained why they had come.

Adnan plucked down the paper with the design and looked at it. "Peculiar how, when one has had an object around for a little while, one ceases to see it. I am very sorry, Mrs. Westerman, but I do not recognize it."

"I do!" Sami took it from his brother's fingers. "It should be with my papers rather than yours, Adnan. Such a curious thing—I meant to try and find out what it signified, but we've been so busy making birdcages for every woman in court. The gentleman who paid us so much for Nancy wished it to be painted on her body, under the clothes. I think he must have commissioned something from Julius too, you know, Adnan, because I saw the same symbol on his wall. I meant to mention it to you."

"The metalworker?" Harriet asked.

The brothers nodded.

"And who is Nancy?"

Adnan lifted his shoulders. "My brother names all our automata, Mrs. Westerman. He refers to the walking model we made last year, which was named after a young woman who refused to dance with Sami once in London."

Harriet put her hand to her forehead. "I . . . Can you tell me more about this walking automaton? Who bought it?" The two brothers frowned. It was a strange effect; Sami's face was more rounded than Adnan's, his nose smaller, but the frown was exactly the same. Harriet wondered how often her expressions or habits made it clear she was Rachel's sister.

"It grieves me to say, Mrs. Westerman, we cannot tell you the name of the person who commissioned us," Adnan said. "We never met our client. All instructions came by letter, unsigned and by hand through one of the palace servants. We received a payment on instruction, and at the halfway point in our work, and then on completion."

"An unusual way of doing business," Harriet said.

"Very," Adnan agreed, "and not an arrangement I would usually enter into, but I was too tempted by the idea of trying to build what I was asked to create in his letter, and the gold he gave me on account suggested he could pay for it."

"It was such a wonderful idea!" Sami said. "An automaton, life-sized, who could dance. Only a madman like my brother would even attempt it, and only a genius like him could achieve it."

Adnan looked a little embarrassed. Harriet sipped her tea. "How on earth did you manage it, Mr. Al-Said? It sounds impossible."

He lifted his hands. "Just as the writing boy you liked is the illusion of intelligence, Mrs. Westerman, so the dancer is an illusion of willed movement.

The figure is a woman, and she has but one dance, a slow minuet. She is wearing a long dress so you never see it, but in truth her feet do not leave the floor. It would be impossible for her to stand if they did." He shrugged his shoulders.

"Like this," Sami said. He scrambled into the space between the workbenches and the shelves covered with faces, eyes, and brass keys, then he stood very straight with one hand raised, the other at his waist and his nose in the air. Rachel laughed. He wrinkled his nose at her, then resumed the pose and took two slow rhythmic steps forward, his hand still raised as if holding his partner by the fingertips, but he held his foot very low and level over the floorboards. "Imagine that under my foot is a wheel," he said. "It appears as if my leg lifts and carries the foot forward." He tilted his head toward his imaginary partner and blinked.

Harriet shook her head. "Can she turn?"

Adnan nodded. "Have you ever skated on ice, Mrs. Westerman?"

"I have," she said.

"The movement is similar." Sami continued his mime, turning as he slid over the wooden floor and took two steps the other way, then he dropped the pose and pushed his hands deep into his pockets, hunching his shoulders. "It was cruel, to have us build such a wonder then give her away where the world cannot admire her. Poor Nancy. I miss her."

Adnan's eyes were slightly clouded. "We shall build another dancer, Sami. We have all the designs—and the money, of course."

"We deserved a pension for that work. Though I admit," he smiled at Harriet, "the gold did help pull the sting a little."

Harriet was looking at the leather folders piled at Adnan's elbow. "May I see the designs? What did she look like?"

Sami clambered over the worktop and launched himself at a pile of his own papers. "Adnan's designs of the wheels and levers will mean little to you, Mrs. Westerman, but let me show you this . . ."

He became, briefly, a flurry of activity, sorting through his own piles of drawings and sketches, then drew one out. The paper showed the figure of a woman dancing, seen in profile, and another sketch showing her looking out of the paper back at the viewer. It was not a girl's face or figure. Harriet would guess the woman to be a little younger than herself, and she was not beautiful, but pretty. Gentle. "Are these your work, Mr. Al-Said?"

Sami shook his head. "No, the drawings came with the commission. Then the talisman you noticed. That was to be painted on the front of the torso, but out of sight, under the clothing, as I said."

"The clothing too was specified," Adnan said. "In fact, it was provided. It came with the money and the notes as to what the model was to do and how."

Harriet put her fingers to her forehead as if she could massage the thoughts out of her brain. "Provided? Surely . . . I am alone in suspecting . . . ?"

"That we were re-creating an actual woman? Yes, Mrs. Westerman, we suspected that. I am afraid I did not know what to think. An artist paints living people, a sculpture has living models."

"But you add movement, does that not make your creations something different?"

Adnan put his elbow on the table and his chin in his hand and gave a lop-sided smile. "I do not know, Mrs. Westerman. Suppose this is the re-creation of a woman lost to our client, or even a portrait bought to compliment her, what harm could it do? It is only an automaton. Even if it is a rather wonderful one."

She continued to stare at the portrait. It had life in it, even this simple piece of paper. "Was there anything else unusual about this commission?"

"There was hardly anything *usual* about it. One more element, perhaps; there was a stipulation that there be a gap in the torso." He took his turn at his own papers and held out a sheet toward her. It showed a space, neatly measured eight inches by eight.

"For what could this be?"

"I asked, of course, since leaving that space made a complicated work more complicated still. The messenger simply said it was required. That was his answer to any question asked."

"Who was the messenger? One of the servants of the palace, you said. Do you know his name?"

Adnan pinched the bridge of his nose. "Wolf, William . . . no, Wimpf! That was it, Wimpf."

Harriet's pace was a little too hot for Rachel as they returned through the garden. She felt a clutch in her stomach and came to a halt.

"A little sickness, Harry. If we could just sit for a moment?" She fought the swell of nausea. "Talk to me, Harriet, give me something else to think on. Why are you so interested in this sign, the automata?"

Harriet put her arm around her sister's shoulders and thought of her own times of pregnancy. That strange yellow nausea that came so violently, then left her, that first glorious moment when life stirred in her. "That design came from one of the books stolen from Kupfel along with the poison books. Below that was mention of some manner of ritual using blood. Now I wonder at the secrecy with which the model was commissioned."

"The servant they mentioned, Wimpf—he is the man who cleaned the secret room for Major Auwerk, is he not?"

"Yes, though of course he must serve the needs of any number of people at the court during the day."

"I see."

"Do you believe him, Rachel?" Harriet asked suddenly. Rachel realized she had been waiting for the question.

"Manzerotti? That he did not order James's death? I cannot say. It is plausible, I suppose. Do you?"

Harriet put her hand to her face. "I simply don't know, my love. Part of me feels it does not matter. Whatever I do, whatever revenge I might dream of taking, I can never bring James back." She suddenly froze. "Oh my Lord . . ."

"What is it, Harry?"

"The automata, the rituals, the blood. There was a sentence in one of those volumes taken from Herr Kupfel's about fixing a spirit in a statue. But the lady was banished, not killed, it was her *boy* that died. We must get back to the palace and talk to Crowther and find out about the woman in the picture. Could it be the widow, Frau Kastner, driven from court, and if so, is she alive and where did she go? Are you recovered?"

"Just a moment more, please, Harriet. My head is spinning."

The sisters sat together in silence, then, just as Rachel opened her mouth to speak again, Harriet held up her hand. There was the sound of footsteps close by on the gravel and on the other side of the hedge, Harriet heard Manzerotti's voice; he was speaking in French.

"You have done very well, you will leave Maulberg a rich man. I think I could have named the names on *this* list . . ."

"How?" The person to whom Manzerotti was speaking sounded rather put out. It was the voice of a young man.

"They are dead. All but one of them."

"Good God. The Circle of Seven? Those closest to power in Maulberg? What a blow to the Minervals."

"You sound sorry for them. Do you wish to sit, does your ankle pain you?"

"It's not a problem as long as I don't forget and put my weight on it too suddenly. You should have seen me, clambering all over those roofs like a damn squirrel. Honestly, Philippe, then waking in that muck. Lord, I thought I'd never stop stinking."

Harriet realized she had never heard Manzerotti's first name spoken aloud before; she didn't even think he had one. Rachel's hand lay in hers; she squeezed it gently.

"But look here," the unknown voice continued. "Are these other people in danger?" They heard the sound of paper being unfolded, jabbed at.

Harriet heard Manzerotti's soft laugh. "Now you have given me their names, yes, I think they are in quite a lot of danger, don't you?"

"That's not what I mean, and you know it."

"What is your concern?"

"Florian."

"Oh yes, the young man of whom you have made such exemplary use. A young man at his studies in Leuchtenstadt. No, I don't believe the murderous hand will reach to him. What the duke will do to him when he learns he is part of this society, I cannot say."

"I want to get him out of Leuchtenstadt." Harriet heard Manzerotti sigh and there was a rustle of clothing as he took a seat on the other side of the hedge. She caught Rachel's eye. Her sister looked uncomfortable. Drained as she was, Harriet still smiled. It was typical of her sister's strict codes of behavior that she could feel it was wrong to eavesdrop on the conversations of a spy.

"You have become sentimental, my boy?"

"Let me take his name off the list—they'll never know. And get him to his father's place till all this dies down. He's just an infant! All ideals and softheartedness, with no idea what he is caught up in."

There was a short silence before Manzerotti spoke. "I think the same might be said of you, Pegel."

There was no reply.

Then: "I shall consider it."

"Thank you."

"Let us return to the palace, Jacob. I would like you to explain what you have been about to a widow of my acquaintance and an anatomist."

"I don't understand."

"I know."

The footsteps retreated. Rachel looked up at her sister. "It rather sounds as if we should be making our way back too, does it not?"

"Indeed it does. I hope we will hear from Michaels today."

"He will have found her trail, Harriet. No one is more capable. But I fear learning what he has found at its end."

38

Harriet had time only to tell Clode and Crowther what she had learned in the village before a note arrived asking them to meet Manzerotti in Swann's office. Rachel and Clode went to release Graves from his watch at the chancellor's bedside. When they were admitted to the chancellor's office Harriet did not see the castrato, but instead a young man in a dark blue coat sitting in Swann's chair. He had his feet up on the desk, his hands linked behind his head, and his eyes closed. His face was rather bruised. As they entered he opened one eye and looked at them both carefully, but made no movement.

"Manners, Pegel." Manzerotti's voice spoke slowly from the window where he leaned, half-watching the activity in the courtyard. The youth rolled his eyes and sighed lustily but stood, rather awkwardly, nonetheless, and made a bow. "This, Mr. Crowther, Mrs. Westerman, is Jacob Pegel."

"Delighted," Harriet murmured and examined the youth more closely. He looked away.

"Pegel is a . . . friend of mine, who has a talent for discovering all sorts of interesting information."

"Another spy then?" Crowther asked, and Harriet saw Pegel blush under his purple bruises.

"Ignore Mr. Crowther," Manzerotti said. He joined Pegel behind Swann's desk and put a hand on his shoulder. "His manners are worse than yours. Tell them."

"If you wish it, Philippe," the youth said rather stiffly, then he continued in rapid, rather rough-edged French. "I have got my paws on a mound of information about a group active in Maulberg. Call themselves the Minervals. I have lists of their members and a number of instructions going back and forth in cipher, and I've had a look at a fair few of their letters in plain text. They have a presence in various states in Germany, but they are most proud of the stranglehold they have over Maulberg. I have a note from last year speaking of Maulberg as a paradigm for the new world order."

"How did you break the cipher?" Harriet said.

He shrugged. "I'm cleverer than they are."

Crowther took a seat. "Are our victims on your membership list? Or do the instructions include their death warrants?"

Pegel glanced at Manzerotti.

"Mr. Pegel," Crowther said with a slight drawl, "I assume that what you have discovered from your espionage has a bearing on the murders in Ulrichsberg. I cannot believe we have been dragged from our coffee merely to hear you boast."

Pegel looked at him with his head on one side and folded his arms. "Look, Mr. Crowther, all I know of you is that you are a competent anatomist, you left one of Manzerotti's men to be torn about by the mob—Johannes was his name, I think—and you were just quite rude to me. What gives you the right to sit down and look at me as if you are settling in for an interrogation?"

Harriet had never heard Crowther being spoken to in that fashion. He looked at Pegel as if he had two heads. He then put his fingertips together and opened his mouth to reply.

"Forgive Pegel, Gabriel," Manzerotti said quickly. "He is very tired." He then turned toward the boy. "Pegel, my dear, Johannes did work for me I do not think I would ever ask of you. He also killed a number of people, including this lady's husband."

"Oh."

"So you see, you cannot blame them for taking against my old friend."

"And I am a great deal more than competent," Crowther said.

Pegel unfolded his arms and clasped his hands behind his back instead. Then cleared his throat. "The members of the organization call themselves the Minervals, as I say. There is, or rather was, a circle of seven individuals at Maulberg who seemed to hold the reins of the state."

"And their symbol is the owl," Harriet said.

Pegel rocked on his heels. "Err, yes." Harriet thought she saw Manzerotti's mouth twitch into a smile.

"And am I right in thinking the names of those seven are our victims and Chancellor Swann?"

"Yes. Honestly, you are good!" Pegel said, grinning at her.

"But this marriage was not their design, was it?" Crowther said. "Even before someone began to kill them in this foul way, they had begun to lose their influence. Their control. So what made things go so terribly wrong for them?"

Pegel sat down again at the desk and started to rub his right ankle. "They spilled some ink on that subject, as you can imagine. There were words about the influence of 'John Bull.'"

"That must be Colonel Padfield," Harriet said, and she saw Manzerotti nod.

". . . and of the Toy Man."

"The Toy Man?" Harriet repeated. "Count Frenzel, I suppose. He did collect automata once, the Al-Saids mentioned it."

"They are referred to by only those names. Then, toward the end of the year they speak about the unfortunate losses in their circle. Remember, Mrs. Westerman, I am talking about letters written in plain language. Only when they wrote in code did they name names, state facts."

"But they did not see those deaths as suspicious?"

"As I said, the word used was 'unfortunate.' What has been said since you threw the cat among the pigeons, I can't say."

Crowther examined his cuffs. "The note Mrs. Westerman found in Swann's office?"

"From . . ." Pegel glanced at Manzerotti. "A gentleman in Leuchtenstadt. A suggestion of whom to approach, and hopefully recruit, in the party arriving with the new duchess. It seems events here have come too thick and fast for news to get to Leuchtenstadt."

"How did you manage to discover so much about them, Mr. Pegel?" Harriet asked.

"Oh, a little playacting. Best way to get an idea of an organization is to make it think it is under attack. They recruit among the various orders of Freemasonry, so I made them think one of those orders, the Rosicrucians, were cutting up rough." He shrugged.

Harriet got to her feet. "So what is their aim?"

"In general? Oh you know, a new world order, universal brotherhood and justice, no property, no states . . . that sort of thing."

"That certainly would be new," Crowther said dryly.

Pegel gave a snort of laughter and Harriet found herself thinking he could only just be out of the schoolroom. "So who gives the orders, who leads?" she demanded. "Swann said something about 'secret superiors.'"

Manzerotti straightened and left his post at the window. "You must indulge the performer in me on that point. You will know of them soon enough. It's really *quite* entertaining. But then I do have a rather dark sense of humor."

Harriet looked at him steadily and he smiled, showing his white sharp teeth, then she turned back to Pegel. "And once they held power in Maulberg, Mr. Pegel? What did they do with it? There is no universal brotherhood here."

Pegel had the trick of youth in that his mood seemed able to switch in moments. He suddenly looked faintly miserable. "They did what everyone with power does in my experience, Mrs. Westerman. They spent most of their energies trying to hang onto it. I imagine they told themselves that others of their kind were moving into positions of power in other states, then these 'superiors' would give the word and the New World Order would magic itself into being."

"As lead magically transforms to gold," Crowther said darkly.

"That's it exactly, Mr. Crowther!" Pegel said, and in his enthusiasm leaned on his bad ankle and winced. "And just like alchemy, you end up with lead and a nasty smell." Even the corner of Crowther's mouth twitched at that.

Pegel was still grinning at the idea when Harriet spoke again. "I suspect someone is taking a very personal revenge, Mr. Pegel. Are there any references to them having done great damage to anyone? Did you see the name Kastner mentioned anywhere?"

He shook his head. "Mostly petty shufflings, as far as I can tell. Though after the deaths of Raben and Warburg, they talked about how cleverly they had avoided the danger posed by the carpenter's daughter. It was as if they wished to encourage themselves. Whatever the plot was, they seemed to think they had been very clever."

"I wonder if that was Frau Kastner."

Manzerotti nodded. "Kastner derives from a word for carpenter."

"So they *were* responsible for her slander. What a thing to boast over," Harriet said quietly.

"They are as arrogant as any aristo in some ways," Pegel said, looking oddly distressed again. "For God's sake, they even struck little medals with the owl on to hand out to lower-ranking members." Harriet was quiet, thinking of the woman separated from her child. "I have some two hundred and fifty names, and if we can seize the papers I had to leave behind, I think we may uncover more." He hobbled across the room and took a seat opposite them, balanced on its edge; his left leg bounced up and down as he talked. The contrast with the feline grace of Manzerotti was marked. "Not just in Maulberg, of course, all over Germany and Austria."

"That is a great number of people to be keeping revolutionary secrets," Harriet remarked.

"That's just it, Mrs. Westerman—I don't think they all are. They often recruit from within the ranks of Masonry, then just like in Masonry you ascend through ranks of the Minervals, and new secrets are revealed to you at each stage."

Crowther leaned back in his seat and crossed his legs. "And how does one ascend through these ranks?"

"Reading! And taking any number of impressive-sounding oaths. Also, a great deal of essay writing, the aim of which seems to be that the adepts convince themselves they should give up their will and conscience to their elders."

"How did you find them, Mr. Pegel?"

"I met a man in Strasbourg. He had flirted with them, joined the lowest ranks, then decided he didn't like it. They slandered him all over Leuchtenstadt, he said. It meant he had to leave and find work elsewhere. I suspected he was exaggerating, but now I am not so sure."

Harriet frowned. "I wonder if that was the man who tried to get Herr Dorf to publish his article?"

Manzerotti pulled a watch from his waistcoat. "How time does fly when discussing these conspiracies. May I suggest, my friends, that if you have anything you wish to ask Chancellor Swann, you do it at once. It will soon be time for my little show."

They stood, Manzerotti a little more slowly than the rest. "But you won't say anything to spoil my fun, now, will you?"

39

When he arrived back in Ulrichsberg, Michaels found the place in a state of excited delight. Bunting hung from the windows and the roofs were on fire with the flags of Maulberg and Saxe Ettlingham. He rode slowly around to the rear of the palace, stabled his horse, then walked through the gardens to the fake village that was his billet. There he found Mr. Graves sitting on a bench by the ornate little well, warming his face with his eyes closed. Hearing footsteps, he opened them, and sprang to his feet.

"Michaels! How are you? I have come to escape the sickroom and imagine myself back in Sussex. You aid the illusion. Did you find the girl and the book?" He noticed the landlord's expression. "Ah, no happy ending there, I take it."

Michaels shook his head. "What's this about a sickroom? Any hurt come to our friends?"

"No, no," Graves said immediately. "Come and take your rest and I shall tell you what has happened since you left."

"I should go and have words with Mrs. Westerman."

"They are closeted with Chancellor Swann. Clode has been sent from the room like a schoolboy. Rest a moment. Let us exchange our news."

"Her name is Antonia Kastner," Swann said, then turned away from them and the paper Harriet held out in front of him.

"She was the woman banished from court?" Harriet asked.

"Such behavior is not tolerated here. There may be an understanding between persons of rank, but a musician . . ."

Harriet attempted to control her temper. She had not exactly promised Manzerotti not to throw Swann's hypocrisy in his face. The temptation was strong.

Swann settled into his pillows. He looked more like he had when they first saw him. Imperial. Self-assured, even in his sickbed. Harriet had not expected Swann to clasp them to his bosom and call them his saviors, but his failure to show any sign of gratitude rankled. His next words did nothing to improve her opinion of him.

"Musicians! A useless set of people, and all morally dubious. I know the duke has a passion for opera, but I cannot see it. The tone of the court would be much improved if they were all expelled."

"You know her son died while they were separated? Where is she now?"

He remained silent. There was movement in the corridor. Harriet felt her cheeks redden. She had an overwhelming desire to see Swann suffer.

"Adolphus Glucke is dead," she said. Swann had only the chance to look at her, shocked, when the door was swung open and the duke, already dressed to receive his bride, entered Swann's chamber. He was in a coat of brilliant white satin embroidered with golden tendrils, birds, and flowers. His waistcoat was solid silver thread. Even the beauty of Manzerotti, who stood at his shoulder with Colonel Padfield and Count Frenzel, was cast into temporary shadow. Harriet and Crowther moved away from Swann, and the duke nodded to them before taking his seat by the sick man's bed. The chancellor struggled to straighten his posture.

"Calm yourself, Swanny," the duke said. "I am glad to see you so much recovered, but you will need your strength."

"I congratulate you on your wedding, sire. It is most kind of you to visit me on such a day. It is an honor."

"Congratulate me, do you? An honor, is it?" He watched his chancellor. "Have I always been such a disappointment to you, Swanny?"

"Sire, I . . ." Swann was losing his poise; he looked at the faces of those around him in confusion.

"Shush, now." The duke spoke very softly. "You have had care of me since I was a child. Care of my education, my training. I have my ways, but I know my people and love them. Do you think you did such an appalling job you had to turn traitor?"

"Your Highness, I do not understand."

"I told you to be quiet, Swann. You see, I thought you believed I had improved these last years, but that was not so, was it? It was just you and your little cabal who thought you held the reins so securely, I could be indulged and gently manipulated, rather than bullied into behaving, as you used to do. Is that what the Minervals taught you?"

Harriet watched Swann's face. When the name of the Minervals was spoken, his skin went gray. It was as if he had aged in front of her in moments. His bandaged hands began to pull at the sheets and he blinked rapidly.

"Sire, you have been lied to! It is all lies!" His voice was harsh and dry and there was a yellowish bile on his lips. He licked them convulsively. Lifting one bandaged hand, he pointed to Padfield. "Why do you listen to that oafish Englishman? And Count Frenzel, you are a fool. You believe yourself an expert on every subject under the sun, when it is clear you have no capacity for real study."

Count Frenzel went white. "You ridiculous little monster."

The chancellor began speaking more quickly, his voice rising. "That eunuch is a spy, sire! I know he has worked for Austria in the past. You are being lied to!"

The duke sighed and leaned back in his chair, turning his foot. His shoes were white too. The heels golden. "I am a duke, Swanny, I have been lied to all my life. And as for my songbird, do you really think he would be in this room now if I did not know of his other talents? Of course he is a spy—he is *my* spy."

Harriet looked at Manzerotti and he shrugged slightly and smiled at her.

"I have felt something wrong here for a long time, Swanny, but I did not know whom I could trust. The arrival of Frenzel last year and Padfield the year before was most opportune. They were fresh, and though I could not know their loyalty, or their abilities, I knew they were untainted. They became my way of acting, and knowing that I could act. It was the King of Prussia who recommended Manzerotti to me, by the way. He and I have become quite friendly."

Swann seemed smaller, as if he were shrinking among the bedclothes. "Sire, Christoph, my friend—I admit it. Some of your closest friends, we created a small informal association, to guide, to quietly assist. We did it all for Maulberg."

The duke continued to make little circles with his foot. "'The governors of nations are despots when not guided by us. They can have no authority over us, who are free men.' Recognize that? One of the key assertions of the Minervals. You arrogant fools. An informal grouping? I could laugh if I weren't so disappointed. You are too German for that. I have learned a great deal this morning about all your ranks and titles." He stood suddenly. "You almost made my state a laughingstock with your petty intrigues, your drugs and plots."

"All to Maulberg's advantage!"

"Or your own! Anyone who looked as if they might become close to me driven away, and your incompetent meddling in affairs of state. How stupid are you, that you believe the best way to conduct policy is with a poison ring. You thought of your own influence first, your pleasure in intrigue came second, your duty to the good of the people a poor third."

"No, our loyalty to Maulberg—"

The duke balled his fists. "I *am* Maulberg." Swann twitched away from him. "Do you hear me, Chancellor? *I* am Maulberg." He leaned forward, and putting his hands on the bed and bringing his face close to Swann's, he said: "These unknown superiors of yours, Swanny. Do you know who they are?"

"Men of wisdom . . . of great power."

The duke shook his head. "There are none! And your Spartacus, the man to whom you and the countess and the colonel and the rest bowed down, your fountain of knowledge, your link to these great unknowns—Spartacus is a junior, *junior* member of the law faculty at Leuchtenstadt! The son of a farmer. A radical who himself wrote every law of the Minervals, all your ceremonies and initiations. There *are* no superiors! Lord, did he know how to make you dance, you and your precious circle of seven here. It's all non-sense. Shadows and secrets and the theatrics of a charlatan. And now someone has run you all down and is punishing you. You are like wild pigs in the gulley. No idea where the shots are coming from."

"But sire—"

"Whatever this horror that pursues you, you summoned it yourselves." He stood upright again and straightened his cuffs. "You are to leave my territories and you will never return. You are banished, sir."

"Christoph, we only wanted the best for everyone. I am the last of our circle left alive, I have spent my life serving you, will you not help me now? I have been loyal . . ." His voice came out in a dry whisper.

The duke did not look at him. "Not loyal enough, Swanny. You might have told yourself you had high ideals, but once you had your cabal in place, you thought only of your own power. This marriage is the best thing possible for Maulberg, but you and your friends feared it because it would decrease your power here. You wanted a puppet and a state to rule. In the end, your loyalty was to yourself." Harriet thought of the duke as she had first seen him, playing with his dog, or at cards with his courtiers. She wondered just how long he had been playing a part, creating a fiction so he could move unseen in his own palace. "Count Frenzel—you have the lists. Draw up the warrants, please. I will sign them—and Colonel Padfield, I trust you to see them executed." Frenzel bowed; he was still a little white around the lips. At last the duke looked back at the shrunken figure on the bed. "When you leave, leave quietly. If you are here in the morning, your estates will be forfeit. Good-bye, Swanny." He turned to the door. Swann held up his hand and called his name, but the Duke did not alter his pace and the door shut behind him.

Harriet and Crowther remained where they were. When Swann put his head into his hands, Harriet stepped forward and placed a hand on his shoulder. He shook her off and glared at her. "Get out, you witch! Get out, you whore, and take your pet with you. Get out. I would rather die than be comforted by you."

She was so shocked she felt unable to move, but found Crowther's grip under her elbow and realized she was being guided from the room. She couldn't help looking back at the ruined old man on his bed, sobbing into his fine linen.

40

They retreated to their salon. Harriet's color was high, and as Crowther told Graves of what had happened in Swann's chamber, she walked back and forth across the room, her skirts flicking and tumbling around her.

"I can hardly believe it!" Graves said. "Did you suspect it, Mr. Crowther? That Swann was one of the group?"

"I did. A man who has spent his time that near to absolute power . . . He would not be the first to think he could wield it better than his master."

Graves opened and closed his mouth a couple of times before saying, "You must think me hopelessly naive."

Crowther smiled at him. "It sits rather well on you, my boy."

Graves sighed. "I have been looking through our notes while Mr. and Mrs. Clode rest to see if I can find any trace of the name Kastner. I can find none."

"Swann confirmed that Antonia Kastner is the model for the automaton," Crowther said. "But he claims to know nothing of what happened to her after she left here."

Graves sat back on his chair and rubbed his eyes. "No mention of an 'Antonia' either. Perhaps Julius knows who commissioned him for this item with the same design. I saw him this morning. He invited me to watch the festivities in the square, so if you want to find him, I would do so there." He pushed the papers on the table about a little hopelessly. "At any rate, I want to know what it was that he made that had this symbol on it."

"I don't care," Harriet said suddenly. Graves looked up at her rather stunned, though Crowther's face showed no emotion.

"These Minervals! The duke is right, they brought this on themselves. Let them suffer. They deserve these miserable deaths. To take that woman's reputation, to forcibly separate her from her child . . . Let whoever is taking revenge on her behalf finish his work with that miserable chancellor! I shall toast his success as we leave this poisonous place."

They were silent. Graves began to say something, but Crowther made a gesture to silence him. Crowther then turned to the window, placing his hand against the pane of glass. The courtyard outside was full of movement, servants running to and fro, carriages and horsemen clattering over the cobbles. "If you, Mrs. Westerman, had dedicated your energies to revenge after your husband's death, the world would be a poorer place. These are not actions you should admire or wish to emulate. And what of Clode?" Without wishing to, Crowther found himself thinking of Manzerotti and his gibe about Crowther's great speeches on truth or justice. "Come, Harriet. If these deaths prove anything, it is that revenge is death itself."

"Would it be wrong to kill Manzerotti?"

"It might not be wrong, but it would do no good. Nothing you can do will bring your husband back to you."

Harriet sat down at the table and covered her face. Graves stood up slowly. "I also have some news. Mrs. Padfield's sister Beatrice is dead. Michaels found her body and is gone to give Mrs. Padfield news of it. I shall return to my post guarding Swann. This killer's work is not complete while he lives. And whatever Swann has done . . . no one should die like that."

"You have had the lion's share of the watching, Graves," Crowther said, though he kept his eyes on Harriet's bent head.

"Daniel and Rachel are resting together. I would not wake them." He left quietly and for a while the only sounds in the room came from the servants passing by in the courtyard outside. Crowther remained standing, watching Harriet and leaning on his cane. She made no sound, but he saw the teardrops falling on the polished wood of the table. "If there were any way known to man or God, Harriet, that could undo the hurt that was done to you . . . To bring James back . . ." He thought of the alchemist, his boast that he could bring back the dead, and stopped. He thought of the blood, the rituals, the woman talking to spirits among the servants, the seal that fixed a spirit in a vessel.

Harriet raised her head. "Oh, Crowther, that's just it. You see it, don't you? It is not *just* revenge. I'm certain that poor woman is dead, and some madman is trying to bring her back."

Harriet was very quiet as they made their way out of the palace. She was a still point among the frenzy of excitement around her. It seemed the duchess's arrival was imminent and the city was putting on a brave display for her. The stands were filled with the nobility, all splendid in blue and gold. Along the lower ranks of the stands were a large number of ladies and gentlemen visiting from other courts and therefore not in the duke's own colors; they provided an ornamental border to the stands.

The women were in colored and embroidered silks, their hair worked high, and the faces in the stands, male and female, were all powdered and rouged after the French fashion. Harriet, glancing up, was reminded of a display of porcelain dolls in Pulborough. On a whim she had bought the least unfriendly looking of the display for Anne. Her daughter had seemed delighted with the present, but treated the doll with a sort of superstitious awe. Her rag doll was dragged around with her wherever she went, while this porcelain monstrosity was named Margaret, at Crowther's suggestion, and placed high over the nursery. Anne and her rag doll occasionally brought it interesting pieces of gravel and set them at its feet like nervous worshippers before an idol.

There was a small stage at the center of the square with a pair of high-backed, thronelike chairs on it, a cluster of less impressive seats in front of it, and a small reading lectern. A number of musicians were being given some last-minute rehearsals from the court composer.

Every other available space in the square and throughout the gardens leading up to the palace itself was filled with the citizenry of Maulberg. All were in their best and jockeying for position in a good-humored fashion. Whatever rumors might be flying around about the sudden spate of illnesses among the members of court, the atmosphere was of expectant good cheer. There was a stir in the mass of people at the front of the palace and a group of horsemen began to clear a way down the central path. An open carriage painted in silver and red drew up in front of the central portico. The duke emerged and stepped inside accompanied by three visiting princes all in blue military uniforms.

They began to make their way down through the gardens, and the people started to cheer. The duke raised his hand and waved. The trumpeters on the dais struck up a fanfare.

"There he is!" Harriet exclaimed, and for a moment Crowther thought his companion had been caught up in the excitement of the moment, but he found that rather than pointing at the duke, she was pointing at a young man with red hair and a slightly dirty coat on the edge of the crowd, some twenty yards from them. They jostled their way over and Harriet put a hand on his sleeve.

"Mrs. Westerman!" he said with a grin. "I've come to see the fun. So glad to hear Mr. Clode is out of the hole. Saw Mr. Graves up at the village this morning."

"Julius, have you made something recently with a design on it, a little like the Star of David, but with words, letters on it?"

"You mean the djinn bottle? That was about a year and a half ago."

The crowd around them roared, so Harriet had to raise her voice.

"The djinn bottle? Why do you call it that?"

"Well, the design you mentioned is a bit like one of the Seals of Solomon. You know when he built the temple in Jerusalem he was supposed to have used enslaved spirits to help him. Then he sealed them in brass vessels, and the Templars found them during the Crusades . . . then ran off with them to become Freemasons in Scotland. Or was that the Holy Grail?" He was straining on his tiptoes to see over the crowd. "Ooh look, the duchess's coach is coming!" A fresh blare of trumpets rang out. A coach built more for show than travel and all in gold was drawing up to the stage. The horses all wore golden plumes that must have made them the envy of some of the women in the stands. Around them, everyone had a handkerchief in the air and was waving it furiously.

"What was it?" Harriet said, tugging on Julius's sleeve.

"Just a large brass bowl with a domed cover. The whole thing looked like an ostrich egg, with that design repeated on it round the edge. Fits together very neatly. The engraving took forever. Ahh, here she comes."

The door to the golden carriage had opened and the steps were let down. A thin figure in blue and gold appeared, and the cheering increased in volume. "Oh, that's a nice touch—look, she is bending down to kiss the ground of Maulberg, and wearing our colors." The crowd seemed to agree. The roar and cheers reached a feverish clamor. The duke stepped forward and took his bride's hand to lead her to the stage.

"Who commissioned it?" Crowther bawled in Julius's ear.

"Eh what?"

"The djinn bottle! Who commissioned it?"

"No idea. It all came through one of the footmen at the palace . . . Wimpf. Peculiar job, but I was well paid for it."

The duke led his bride to one of the thrones and took his seat beside her, still lightly holding her hand. She looked so young. The three princes who had come with the duke and a number of other dignitaries who had emerged from the retinue of the golden coach also took their places on the dais, and a young man was ushered up to give a speech. A hush fell, and the man began to speak in Latin.

"Top scholar at the Leuchtenstadt, that lad," Julius said to them, and tucked his thumbs into his waistcoat. "What a great honor. He'll have a medal to show his grandchildren. After the recitation they will sign the marriage certificate then return to the palace for the gala. There is to be a public feast here too, you know. A lion's head pouring wine. Three roast oxen."

Harriet was turning away when she felt a touch on her arm. "Michaels! I am glad to see you."

He nodded. "Happy to find you in this crowd, Mrs. Westerman, Mr. Crowther. I have been looking for Mrs. Padfield, but she is not at home. Do you know where I might find her?"

Julius turned away from the scene for a moment. "Good to see you, Michaels. She is in the stands there with all the court ladies fluttering their fans at the new duchess. You'd do best to wait for her back at their home. They will all have to change their dresses again for the gala." Michaels shoved his hands into his pockets and looked grim. Harriet began to move to the edge of the crowd and Michaels and Crowther followed her.

They walked until they could find space enough to speak. "What news, Michaels?" Harriet asked quietly. "We heard from Graves that the girl is dead."

"Been in the ground a good long time," he answered. A couple of young men jogged past them toward the crowd, singing as they went. Michaels watched them pass before continuing, "No sign of Kupfel's papers, or her book of odds and ends. She was buried near a waterfall between Oberbach and a nasty little place called Mittelbach."

"You are sure it is her?" Harriet asked. The crowd behind them gave a great roar of approval; it rolled and rocked between the buildings.

"I'm sure."

"My congratulations on finding her," Crowther said quietly. "How did she die?"

"It was luck, is all. As to her death, the back of her head was smashed. Strong arm and a rock, I think." There was another cheer and the crowd began to applaud. The air crackled and boomed with the sound of a volley of gunfire.

"The military salute," Harriet said, glancing over her shoulder. "The marriage contract is signed. Who owns land in that area, Michaels? What are the important houses? Did you hear the name of Kastner?"

"No, Mrs. Westerman, can't say I did. There are plenty of healthy farms and a good number of men who've done well in Oberbach and have built a house—they might any of them been a temptation to young Beatrice. Mittelbach is part of the estate of Count Frenzel. You might ask him." The crowd was beginning to disperse. "I owe that woman news of her sister. I had better be waiting for her when she comes back to change her frock. Good luck to you both." He turned away from them and was swallowed into the crowd.

Harriet leaned on Crowther's arm. "I wish Krall were here. He could frighten an answer out of Wimpf. Do you think we might manage to get a name from him?"

Crowther shook his head. "No doubt Krall is still busy protecting the duke. We might get some intelligence from Wimpf, but Krall would do a better job of it, I agree. We have another line to follow though, Mrs. Westerman, if you are not too exhausted."

"I am quite well. What do you mean?"

"The school."

41

Herr Kinkel was far, far too busy with the arrangements in the east wing to see the signing of the marriage contract. The back quarters of the palace were a frenzy of movement. The new duchess's retinue had to be accommodated, their baggage stowed correctly, their servants billeted, and everyone required hot water. However, he did notice Wimpf helping the stooping figure of Chancellor Swann into a waiting carriage. The blinds were drawn down. Strange. Strange too that rather than slamming the door and letting the carriage drive off, Wimpf got up behind as if to travel with the chancellor. Where could they be going? Still such a frenzy; he had even seen old Kupfel wandering around court yesterday. If Theo had to press his father Adam into running errands, he was pushed indeed. Herr Kinkel wondered about this for almost five seconds, the complete time available to him, then the housekeeper almost knocked him from his feet, staggering along the passage with fresh linens in her arms, after which he returned to more pressing duties.

Rachel sighed sleepily and put out her hand. Her fingers brushed her husband's chest and she felt her hand being taken and his kiss on her palm. As she opened her eyes, she found him watching her and smiled. She let her hand rest on his jaw for a moment.

"Did you sleep?" She moved closer to him.

"I did—and better, I think, than I have for some time."

She laughed and tucked her head under his chin. "As did I." Perhaps for the first time, lying there, she realized what her sister had lost when James Westerman was killed. She thought of Harriet, her restlessness. It had been in her long before James had died, those first years of marriage they shared, sailing over the oceans till she had been forced to remain in Caveley, for Stephen and Anne, for her. Then to lose James, that bond between them that kept part of her soul out in the winds and weather even while she remained in Sussex. She knew she was like Harriet in many ways, but she did not share that restless nature. It was what divided them. Her arm lay over Daniel's side, she could feel it rise and fall with his breathing. To live with him, to bear his children, to face the coming winters together in their own home and among their friends was all the adventure she wished.

"Daniel . . ." She tilted her head back so she could watch his face as she told him. "I believe I am to have a baby. Are you pleased?"

Some time later they found Graves in the parlor and told him their news. He wrung their hands so hard Rachel had to protest.

"Please, Daniel, defend me! Graves, you will tear my hand off!"

"Lord, I'm so delighted!" He almost danced away from her, then his smile faltered.

"What is it, Graves?" Daniel said, looking a little more serious, but keeping his hand on Rachel's shoulder.

Their friend grimaced and folded his arms across his chest. "Only that I wanted to tell you what has happened with Swann. Great dramas. These Minervals have been exposed by Manzerotti and some child genius." Rachel smiled to herself. For all his responsibilities, Graves had something of the child in him still. "All the victims of these gruesome murders were on the list, some inner circle of seven treating the duke as a puppet and trying to make Maulberg a breeding ground and haven for their philosophy. The duke is trying to handle it quietly, but I had some words with Colonel Pad-field. He expects to detain a number of people during the celebrations this evening."

Rachel was amazed. "Manzerotti was working for the duke?"

"He was. All the time. Seems the duke did not want a group of revolutionary poisoners running his state for him."

Daniel frowned. "One moment, Graves. There have been six victims. Surely the attack on Swann was something different. Rachel, should you not sit down?"

"Daniel, I have only this minute got up. So these Minervals were influencing Swann? Flattering him? Using his closeness to the Duke . . . ?"

"He was a fully paid up member," Graves said, opening his arms wide. "Crowther thinks I am naive not to have suspected it, but Padfield was shocked white too. Swann is banished!"

Daniel sat down rather quickly. "My God. I shall think every man I meet a revolutionary now. Where are Harriet and Mr. Crowther? Are they guarding Swann?"

"No, they've gone charging off to see if Julius can let them know who ordered those strange commissions. The automaton is certainly modeled on that poor lady, Antonia Kastner. My dear Mrs. Clode, are you sure you should not sit down? You are rather pale."

"Did you say *Antonia* Kastner, Graves?" she asked.

"I did."

Clode took her hand. "What is it, my dear?"

She looked at him, her eyes wide. "Oh Daniel! I do not think it was you that saw something you shouldn't have done. I think it was *me*."

The Ludwigsschule was formed around a wide courtyard on which the pupils could be taught the basics of military drill. It was deserted. At the entrance provided for pedestrians under the wrought-iron gates they were met by an elderly gentleman who lifted the latch for them and asked their business.

"We wish to inquire about a child who died here some six years ago," Harriet stated. "I am afraid we have not an appointment."

The gatekeeper scratched his neck and looked suspiciously at them. "Today?" he said. "A child six years dead and you wish to inquire for him on the afternoon of the duke's wedding?"

"We come directly from the duke," Crowther said. The man opened the gate and shuffled aside to let them in before slamming and locking it again. "They are watching the opera now at court, aren't they?" he offered by way of conversation as they crossed the vast expanse of the drill yard at his comfortable pace.

"So I understand," Harriet said.

He led them through the main entrance and a roar of noise fell over them in a torrent. It seemed to be coming from a grand hall to their right, and as if to confirm it, the gatekeeper was almost knocked off his feet by a dozen boys of about ten years of age, all dressed in blue coats with black trimmings and wigged, racing in that direction. The adults followed them through an arched entrance and around the edge of a high and spacious hall filled with the clamor of some five hundred boys aged between ten and fifteen.

Harriet could not at once understand how the seating was arranged. She assumed the boys would sit together according to their age, but some of the youngest sat with their elders. Some boys had epaulets, others did not. She asked the question of Crowther who translated it, and the answer.

"Rank, Mrs. Westerman. The boys are seated according to their rank. The head table is reserved for the princes who are schooled here. The seats lower down the room are for those not of noble stock."

"They begin their education in such matters very early, Crowther."

"I have seen a woman of rank kiss the hands of her niece and call her Illustrious Highness, when the niece in question was a child of three years old. Yes, they begin such things early."

There was a raised dais at the far end of the room where the professors of the institution were gathering to dine under a flattering portrait of the duke. He had been painted wearing a gaudy version of the blue and black coats of the pupils. Crowther bent toward their guide, then said to Harriet, "Ludwig Christoph founded this school ten years ago and pays for about half the students to attend. Sons of his officers, by and large."

The gentleman who sat directly below the portrait of the duke had noticed them approaching, and as they were led toward him, left his seat to join them below the steps to the dais.

They made their introductions and Crowther repeated that they had come from the duke himself. The headmaster, a Mr. von Bieber, frowned, but nodded.

"I have been master here only five years, I am sorry to say. I know, of course, of the outbreak of fever at the time you mention. Eight children died, but I do not recall their names. Kastner, you say?"

There was a gentleman just taking his seat next to them. Overhearing them, he turned. A native German by his accent, he addressed them in French, however. "Headmaster, I knew that boy. Carl Kastner?"

The headmaster looked deeply relieved. "Thank goodness—thank you, Herr Dreher. Perhaps you could take our guests into my study and answer any questions they may have. If we do not get food into the boys soon, I fear for our safety."

Herr Dreher gave a curt nod and stood, then invited Harriet and Crowther back the way they had come. All at once, silence fell in the hall. Harriet turned to see that the places at the head table, apart from that of Herr Dreher, were now all taken and the headmaster had got to his feet. The boys had their backs straight and each looked directly ahead.

"Stand."

The boys stood up in a single movement. The headmaster gave a nod, and one of the boys at the head table began to recite. "*Benedic, Domine, nobis et donis tuis quae ex largitate tua sumus sumpturi . . .*"

Harriet's footsteps seemed horribly loud to her as they retreated to the back of the hall again. The grace ended to a general "Amen," barked out with youthful vigor from the diaphragms of each boy.

"Eat!" the headmaster said, and there was a great clatter of cutlery.

"I cannot help thinking of the Al-Saids' automata," Harriet whispered to Crowther.

"I felt sorry for the boy from the moment he arrived. He was very unhappy here." Mr. Dreher spoke French well enough, though his accent was strong.

"You were one of his teachers," Harriet said.

"Yes, and one of the few who didn't beat him every other hour. Did you notice the little pieces of paper many of the students wear in their collars?" Harriet nodded. "It is a list of the child's misdeeds. The duke on his visits, or anyone who wishes to, may stop a boy and read his tally at any time. Carl was reprimanded continually for malingering, or for womanish behavior."

"Womanish behavior?" Crowther asked.

"He missed his mother, and cried for her, then was beaten for it." His lip lifted slightly. "We are supposed to be making soldiers here."

"Do you know where his mother was?"

"I didn't at the time. Everyone knew *who* she was and the story of the scandal, and of course the boys beat him for that too. In his shoes I might have ended up hating my mother, but he talked of her whenever he had the chance. He was convinced she was coming for him."

Harriet thought of her son and felt a mixture of such rage and fear, she did not know how to frame another question. Crowther asked, "And later?"

"I went to see the child when I heard he was sick." The slightly casual air of the master had disappeared. He looked at the floor in front of him. "He was very ill, and he knew it. But he wanted to have his things sent to his mother, and asked me to take them."

"And where was she?"

"Living at the house of one of the imperial knights between here and Oberbach. She sent a message to Carl that he had a new papa and they were coming to get him soon. The night he died he told me the name was Frenzel and asked me to take his Bible to her." As he paused, Harriet became aware of the sounds from the dining hall. Boys, voices chattering like starlings. She longed to see Stephen. It was an ache in her. Frenzel. Of course. Only a man who had bought automata in the past would commission something so complex from the Al-Saids, would think of that as a vehicle. She struggled to listen to Herr Dreher. "Poor woman. I had thought she was some courtesan and Frenzel was simply her new protector, but when I went there . . . She was a gentle lady, devastated by the loss, of course, but she was so desperate to talk about the boy. Kind. Noble in nature if not in name, I would say. And I don't think she was just Frenzel's mistress either. Even if no one knew it, I think they were married."

"And was Count Frenzel there when you spoke to her?" Harriet said, still amazed.

"Watched her like a hawk. She was kind to him, even in her grief, but he watched her so jealously. I was shocked when I saw him in court again. I thought there would never be a time when he allowed her to leave his sight, and he could not bring her here, of course."

"I suspect the lady died," Harriet said gently.

"Ah, I am sorry to hear that. Sorry indeed. During her delivery, I suppose?"

42

"It was two days after we arrived," Rachel said. "Do you remember, Daniel? You wanted to talk to Count Frenzel about investing in the business of one of his tenants."

"I remember," Clode said. "He was as unhelpful as possible." He searched among the papers on the tabletop and handed one to Graves. "We went to his country estate. For a man with his position in court, he spends a lot of time there. It was a foggy day."

Rachel nodded. "I walked in the gardens while you and Frenzel talked. He left his servant—Gunter his name was, I think—to guide me. A funny old man. He had a beard down to his knees and hardly a tooth in his head, but he was very wise about things that grow. It was a cold, damp sort of day, but the house was wonderful. Converted from a nunnery, I believe. We were talking of planting and medicinal herbs, as far as my German could manage. He wanted to tell me something, but I couldn't understand it."

She put her hand over her eyes. The memory had come back very vividly now. The gray stone of the house and the muted February colorings in the garden. Dark greens, soaked soil, and fog in the air. "He was showing me one of the beds and trying to tell me what grew there, then went off to find a dried sample in the kitchen, so I was left on my own." It had been so quiet. She remembered the shape of her footprints in the dew on the lawn, the silence, the fog blurring the edges of everything, muffling any noise. "I walked round the wall into the next garden and there seemed to be a grave there."

"In the gardens of a house?" Graves said, leaning forward.

"I know. It made no sense. It was like one of the garden rooms here at the palace: a bench and a patch of lawn with a stone in the middle of it where the duke would have placed a fountain. I went up to look, and there it was. A flagstone inscribed with the name *Antonia*, and dates. May God forgive me, I thought it was for a favorite horse."

"No second name?" Crowther asked.

"None."

"And the dates?"

"I cannot remember exactly. I think there were twenty-seven, twenty-eight years between them. That is why I thought a horse, rather than a dog . . . The later date on the stone was seventy-eight, I think."

She could see it again now. The simple square stone in the center of the lawn. There was a piece of turf cut away in front of it and she had bent down to inspect it: it had been freshly dug. Sandy soil. She thought of the soil in the mouths of Countess Dieth and Herr Glucke.

"Then the servant found me. He seemed rather upset to have discovered me there."

"Angry?"

"No, not angry." She thought of him stooped, and his insistence on leading her away at once. His nervous, flickering gaze. "He kept glancing up at the windows of the house."

Clode put his hand to his forehead. "Count Frenzel spent half our interview looking out of the window. And he was certainly in a foul mood by the time it ended. My dear, why didn't you tell me?"

Rachel remembered her husband getting back into the carriage, his handsome face flushed, and slamming the door to behind him. "Frenzel was not the only one to leave that interview in a foul mood, Daniel. You lectured me about the uselessness of such people and the general inequality in Germany until we arrived back in Ulrichsberg, and then we had to go to supper in the court."

Daniel looked rather guilty.

Graves looked between them. "Do we know where Frenzel is now?"

"He must be around somewhere. Shall we go and find him?" Daniel said, looking happier than he had in days. "I think I have strength enough to knock him down. Then Krall can arrest him." He spoke very evenly then stood up to ring the bell. Before the ring had quite died, there was a scrape at the door, and a footman was bowing to them. Rachel smiled at him.

"Hans, good afternoon. I know he is terribly busy, but could you ask Herr Kinkel to step round and see us for a moment?"

The footman retreated and Clode felt a flowering of pride that his wife knew the names of the people who served them. It was typical of her. Then he frowned.

"Graves, a moment. I cannot keep pace—who guards Swann now? We are here, Harriet and Mr. Crowther are still in town."

Graves sat back on his chair. "Be at peace, Clode. We need not be distracted from hunting down Frenzel. A letter arrived for Swann. He threw me out saying Duke Ernest of Gotha had offered him refuge." Graves glanced at his watch. "He rattled out of here some hours ago."

Swann could not stop himself weeping. Each time he managed to control himself, some new memory would appear and the rage and grief would break over him again. He only hoped that by the time they stopped for the night he would have clawed back some of his dignity. It was a moment before he realized that the carriage had come to a halt. Some delay on the road. He reached into his pocket and pulled out the flask of brandy that Wimpf had handed him as he closed the doors, traced the engraving of the owl with his thumb, then drank deeply. Still the carriage did not move. He hit the roof with the head of his cane. His arms felt strangely weak, his cane made nothing more than a dull tap. His vision began to swim. He heard a voice outside—Wimpf's—what was *he* doing here? "Seems the chancellor has been taken ill again, coachman. Will you give me a hand getting him into the house?" What house? Where was he? He began to hear a whispering, a chattering in his ears. Voices, many voices. Fingers were beginning to pluck at his clothes, fingers he couldn't see. He tried to brush them away, but his hands would not move.

The gentleman in the green coat enjoyed the gala extremely. Herr Dunktal had worked very hard, and despite the accidental losses suffered among the court at Ulrichsberg, he was confident that with Swann as chancellor, they would replenish their higher ranks from the adepts. He even had hopes of making some converts to the Minervals among the new retinue brought in by the duchess. A different marriage might have been preferable, but if he could recruit in Saxe Ettlingham, his tendrils of influence would begin to curl out of Germany and into France. The attack on one of his promising younger followers by an agent of the Rosicrucians and the subsequent ransacking of his home had been discomforting, but great men such as himself faced these obstacles from time to time and overcame them. He stuck his thumbs into his waistcoat. It was an opportunity to remind them all of the need for secrecy, for security. The papers were all safe, and if they were discreet, the Rosicrucians would bother him no more.

It was delightful to watch this spectacle anonymously knowing that he, he alone, an apparently modest man of middling rank in the university, held such influence, such power. He began to walk through the crowd, searching about for any sign of his Minervals. Amusing, that they would never think to even speak to a man as unimportant as himself. Yet they would obey the commands of Spartacus without question. For the most part. He had heard that Countess Dieth had removed herself to the country, which had not been his advice. He began to search the crowd more methodically. It dawned on him that he had not seen Swann either during the celebrations, nor Adolphus Glucke. He started to experience an unusual and unpleasant sensation—the feeling that he was not entirely aware of everything that was going on. His collar began to feel a little tight. A large, squareish gentleman in military uniform appeared at his side and asked his name. His English accent was very strong. Dunktal gave his name somewhat hesitantly. The military man introduced himself as Colonel Padfield, and Dunktal realized that this was one of the men who had managed to arrange the current wedding behind the back of the Minervals. Colonel Padfield suggested he might like to accompany him away from the crush. Herr Dunktal understood that it was not a suggestion that he could refuse.

43

Pegel had swept down upon Florian in a frenzy and all but dragged him from his house. Florian had been confused at the idea that he must, at once, accompany Pegel to the home of his father near Mittelbach. Pegel's explanation—that the Rosicrucians were after them and they needed to lie low for a few days—was dramatic, but also baffling, given how phlegmatic Jacob had been till now. It was only when Pegel appealed to him as a friend, his eyes open and apparently wet with tears that Florian had started to be convinced. He had tried to explain that he hardly knew his father, but Pegel was adamant. Astonished, Florian agreed.

The ride had shaken Pegel's ankle till he thought the pain would drop him from his horse. He could see the anxious glances Florian was casting in his direction as they rode. At least the injury gave him an excuse not to speak. Pegel pulled out his watch and glanced at it. The Masonic symbols of order and brotherhood had begun to irritate him. He threw it into the hedgerow.

"Jacob?"

"Not now, Florian."

The duke's men would be raiding the addresses provided by this time, discreetly walking professors, tradesmen, and gentlemen out of their offices and homes, a polite but firm hand on the elbow. Pegel recalled the duke's pale face as he gave the orders, the various advisers bowing to him, gathering lists of names. With that thought in his mind Pegel sighed and looked up and found they had arrived.

Florian's home was splendid. A sprawling mansion had been created on the remains of the nunnery. It was a fairy tale sort of place of towers and spires, red-tiled roofs and what looked like an extensive series of walled gardens. They rode in through the gates into the first courtyard and dismounted. Before Jacob had managed to clamber down from his horse, a servant in the livery of the Ulrichsberg Palace appeared from the stables.

"Christian!" Florian called out delightedly. The servant approached, and Jacob looked at him closely. He seemed much of their own age.

"Master Florian! What a surprise—your father will be delighted to see you. Are you well?"

"Very! My father is here? I thought he was up at Ulrichsberg toasting this wedding."

"He comes back here whenever he can."

Florian turned to Pegel. "Jacob, this is Christian Wimpf. His mother was my nurse after I lost my own. We grew up here together! But you have a position at court too now, do you not? Why are you not there?"

"I was accompanying another guest here."

"How is your family?"

"Well, thank you, Master Florian. Count Frenzel has provided for the building of a new barn, and they have taken over the lease of the Ekert farm. But here is your father."

He stepped back with a slight bow, and Pegel turned to see a handsome-looking man in his forties striding out toward them, arms open. Jacob felt a sudden spasm of jealousy. His father never looked pleased to see him.

"Florian! What an absolute wonder you are here."

Florian looked a little amazed. His father embraced him.

"I hope we are not disturbing you, Father. I did not think you would be here. I hope—I hope you are well, sir."

The count still had hold of him. "I am very well, my boy. And you are always welcome here, now more than ever. How perfect it is that you come today—how wonderfully Providence plans every detail."

Florian looked bemused, but recovering slightly said, "This is my friend, Mr. Jacob Pegel. A fellow student at Leuchtenstadt."

Pegel bowed and found himself clapped on the shoulder with such enthusiasm he almost stumbled. "But you are so much more than that! Aren't you, Mr. Pegel? We were not introduced this morning, but I was there when you explained matters to the duke. I am proud to have you here, my boy." Pegel opened and shut his mouth. There had been a number of people in the room . . . "And you are a friend of my son's? Wonderful! Now I know why you are here. You are consideration itself. So much better for Florian to be out of Leuchtenstadt while the faculty and student body are purged of these Minervals! They are so many that Florian must have acquaintances among them." He became serious. "Good of you to remove him at such a distressing time." Pegel became aware that Florian was looking at him, his mouth slightly open. "Yes, your friend is a hero of Maulberg, Florian. Now come, I shall take you up to your rooms myself. Is that all your luggage?"

He turned to lead the way into the building and skipped lightly up the main staircase then turned to the left. Pegel followed with his eyes down. He had known he would have to tell Florian some time, but he wanted to explain over a bottle of wine. Later. Not have it dropped on him like this. He could feel the anger and pain coming off his friend in waves.

If the count noticed the distress of the two young men, he gave no sign of it. "Here you are," he said, opening the door. "Your mother's room for the time being, I think. Now, you boys rest and I shall have Wimpf bring you up something to eat and drink. I'll just turn the key on you . . ."

"Father?" Florian said with an embarrassed laugh.

"A few matters I must take care of, Florian. Then we can all be together." He squeezed his son's shoulder. "I am so pleased you are here, my child. And your friend."

He was out of the door in a moment and the key turned.

Pegel tried to talk to him, but Florian would not look at him. Wimpf brought food and wine, and Florian only stared at the floor while Jacob ate. His face was pink with rage.

"It was you," he said at last.

"Yes."

"Why?"

"Because doing so will make me very rich."

"Is that the only way you have to make money? With a brain like yours?"

"No, but it's one I have come to enjoy."

"I thought you were my friend."

Pegel threw down the remains of a chicken leg. "And so I have been! You are not locked up in one of the duke's cellars now, are you? I owe a favor to the most dangerous man in Europe now, because I decided to save your skin. And I lied to a duke in getting your name off that list. I wonder if Daddy would have been so pleased to see you if he knew you were up to your neck in this Minervals crap."

"You expect me to be *grateful!*"

"Well, I didn't know your father was going to lock us up instead." Pegel got to his feet and began to pace the room. "Enough of this. I will not wait on your father, Florian! I cannot sit still behind a locked door. What sort of man is he?"

"I hardly know," Frenzel replied miserably. "He has always been a man of strong passions. I have never seen him like this, though. He has never been affectionate with me before. Even when my stepmother was alive . . . I met her only once, at the wedding."

There was a gentle scraping at the door. Not the sharp rap that Wimpf had used, but a cautious whispering call. Frenzel went to the door. "Who is it?"

"Master Florian? It's Gunter, sir."

"Gunter! How are you? Lord, I wish I could see your face. Can you open the door?"

"That devil Wimpf has taken the key. I am only to give you this. You are to read it." A thick bundle of papers appeared under the door. Florian picked it up. "I wish you hadn't have come, Master Florian. He's taken a turn for the worse."

"Look out for yourself, Gunter. And the other servants."

"There's only me and Cook left now. He sent the others away when that girl first came."

"What girl?"

"I have to go. Be careful."

Whatever doubts Pegel had had before, that overheard conversation dispelled them. He opened the narrow window of the bedchamber as wide as it would go. Florian was at his shoulder almost at once. "Jacob! What are you thinking of? The drop is too far."

"I won't sit here like a chicken ready for the pot, Florian. Stay here and read your letters if you want." Pegel stripped the linens from the bed and began to tie them into a rope end to end. Still far too short for the drop, but it would at least take twenty feet off it. He tied one end to the bedpost and pulled it with all his strength to test the knot.

"Do people really make ropes out of sheets?" Florian said, slightly amazed. "I thought they only did that in novels."

"I have never done it before, but it seems as good an idea as any."

"You don't often have to escape from your treachery out of high windows?"

Pegel spun around at him. "You are a bloody fool! And the worst sort. The sort who so believes in his own high purposes that he's forgotten most of the world is blood and stink, and most people are blood and stink. You'd be as much use in an actual revolution as a nun in the Grenadiers. Your only purpose, your *only* use is to feed each other's delusions about your ideas for the greater good. You're a naive idiot and why I risked my neck to get you out of Leuchtenstadt, I have no idea."

"Neither do I! All my friends betrayed, everything destroyed. Our plans set back a dozen years. You have brought misery on a nation, Pegel!"

"Shut your jaw, you self-important little fool. Some madman has hunted down the Minervals in Ulrichsberg. That secret circle of seven at the court are wiped out! And what did they do when they had power? Poison anyone who threatened it, and slander some poor woman so they could plant one of your little friends in the duke's bed."

"What are you saying? That's not true. That can't be true!"

"I've read the letters. Her name was Kastner."

"Kastner? That was my stepmother's name before she married my father."

Pegel hardly heard him. "Now get out of my way." Pegel clambered up onto the window ledge and pulled a loop of the improvised rope around him. As his foot pressed against the ledge his ankle screamed at him, but he set his teeth.

"What's to stop me cutting the sheet and sending you to your death?" Florian said, desperation in his eyes.

"You haven't got the guts," Pegel said simply and began to lower himself down the wall.

At the end of his rope, he hesitated. It was still perhaps ten feet left to fall, then a long sloping roof leading into one of the internal courtyards. He found himself wondering what would be better, to further injure his right ankle, or to risk his left and aim to fall on that side. He closed his eyes and let fate decide. He landed on his side, then slid down the deep slope of the roof. Even as he fought for a grip on the tiles he felt a certain peace. It was as if he was watching the whole from above. *I wonder what will happen now?* some calm, mildly interested voice asked in the back of his head as he tumbled forward, his chin scraping and bouncing, the wounds on his hands opening up. He rolled off the guttering and something hard struck him at the base of his skull.

My child,

This is a love story. I know that when you have read these pages you will understand this. Love gave me life, love took it away. Love gave me the power I now have. With it, I serve love.

Your mother and I were married to join two houses, two estates, never two hearts. She was a good wife to me in the brief years of our union and I grieved for her sincerely, though I could not then understand the fierce passion of loss that you felt as a child. How can one imagine what one has never felt? I thought you weak and unreasonable and I fear you must have seen that, must have felt it. I hope others were more generous to you than I. Is it any comfort to you to know that I have experienced all the horrors of grief since then? And in feeling them have thought of you?

I remember your delight in my automata; the minutes we spent watching them together were the happiest we had as father and son, I believe. It was such a pity that you never would understand that these little wonders were far too precious for a child to touch. In time, had you been obedient, I would have let you turn the key, or start the mechanism. To steal the little walking figure I imported from Spain and all but destroy him in your attempt to see how he moved was not a crime I could forgive. But I regret that sending you away deepened the rift between us.

Do you know your stepmother pleaded for you? Not that she was your stepmother then, simply a widow of narrow means living on the charity of our neighbor, some cousin of hers. She heard of your crime, and of your punishment, borrowed a horse, and rode alone up to my gate to try and convince me that your foolishness was a sign of a curiosity to be encouraged. She did not manage to do so. I see her now striding back and forth across the room, in a passion that a weakling child such as you be sent away from those he loved. I should have been shocked, disgusted even by such a display, but instead I longed for her to stay. You went to school the next day, and I went to her. For the first time in my life I tried to please a woman. We were walking in her cousin's gardens the first time I made her laugh. It was not that first day, or even in that first week. I cannot remember how, only that it was against her will, angry as she was still for my treatment of you. Grieving as she was for the wrongs done to her. But I remember the surge of joy I felt at the sound, at my victory. That simple little wedding day we shared was the happiest day of my life. I think you liked her. You would have loved her.

It is a matter of regret to me that you never knew your stepmother. I hope you believe me when I tell you it was through no fault of hers. She often suggested you return from school or take some visit with us rather than with your mother's relatives. In truth I was jealous. Any look, any smile of hers that fell not upon me I felt lost, stolen from my store. I did not want her to try and win your affection, I did not want to see her affection spent on you. Such a terrible happiness is love. Such an impossible gift to bear. At that time I was even glad rumor had driven her from court, because it led her to me. She knew she had been conspired against, though she did not know who had done so, and suspected it was because some of those close to the duke had seen he favored her. Fools. She would never have accepted Ludwig Christoph as her lover. She was too noble, too good. They slandered her, destroyed her reputation, and separated her from her son for nothing.

Her pregnancy delighted her. She talked of giving you and her own boy a brother or sister to care for. I convinced myself it would change nothing if the child lived. The house was large enough, the household had servants enough and the village wet nurses, but perhaps one corner of my mind hoped from the beginning it would not survive. I did not wish to see her love divided; how could I accept only a share of her heart, when the whole was not enough? Yet she flowered as she grew, took delight in the child's quickening. She was seated at her sewing when she felt it first, that strange stirring beneath the skin. Life somehow appearing within her, trapped within her belly some flame, some spark. We reach toward these images of fire when we talk of life; how deadwood stirs into sound and movement, and she cupped it in her hands and gasped. Such a simple thing to women, but what sacrifice, what learning, what bargains with devils and angels it requires from a man.

And there was the matter of her first child. Oh, if I have sinned against you, my son, how much more did I sin against that poor boy. She was desperate to bring the child home. She was sure his constitution was weak, that he would not survive without the care of his mother. I told her I had written to the duke to request the boy be allowed to live with us. I told her I had petitioned him in person. I told her he wanted the child to complete the year at the school. I told her I would petition again. I did none of this.

In truth nothing prevented me from collecting the child on the first day of asking, except that I did not want him here. I grieved to see her suffer, I suffered just as much to deny her, but it still seemed in the passion that held me, preferable. There was an outbreak of fever at the school. If then we had heard of the danger perhaps I would have finally relented. I do not know. The officials at court were informed, but no one there thought to get word to his poor disgraced mother, and the first we knew of any illness in the place was when one of the teachers made the journey to my home carrying the news of his death and his few possessions. Can I describe that day to you? She had not been allowed to write to him, by order of the duke, though I discovered she had managed to bribe Christian to convey to him the occasional note. They were love letters. Love letters that showed a depth and strength of feeling never present in her affectionate manner toward myself. I think my dislike of him deepened to hatred then. I am ashamed of that. The letters told him of our marriage and promised, with what fervor it was promised, that his mama was coming for him very soon. How did I know these things? How did I come to read them? Because the child had stored the letters in the lining of his Bible. Each one had been folded and unfolded, reopened and reread so many times they were in danger of falling apart. The teacher had found them, and thought they should be returned. I cannot say if that was a kindness or a cruelty. It is strange how the simple fact that the fold in a piece of paper has worn through almost to nothing can tell so clear the story of a boy's hope, his loneliness, his longing for his mother.

Her despair was complete. But she would not let the man leave until he had given up the last, briefest, most incomplete memories of her child. Such was her hunger to hear his name, even the story of his illness and death was longed for. He and the teacher had said their prayers together, and he said that if he did not recover he would join his father in heaven and wait for his mama there. She covered her face when she was told that, and I saw the man look at her with wondering eyes. He thought, of course, that she was a whore and would be spending eternity in hell for her sins. I wonder if he told the child that before he blew out the candle and left him? By morning her son was dead.

The pains came upon her the next day, far too soon. Four and twenty hours after they began the accoucheur came to me again, less sanguine, more severe. I did not let him speak, but went to her at once, past the tutting maids, the outraged nurse. She was whiter than the linen on which she lay, her hair loose around her and soaked in her sweat. The light in her eyes was too bright. She used all her strength to speak to me. She took my hand, she swore her love and she begged me to make her doctors save the monster that was killing her. My last words to her, and hers to me, were of love. In the antechamber I told the doctor to destroy the child if there was any chance that doing so would save her.

It was probably dead already. The cord was wrapped around the neck, but it would not go alone. Cheated of its own life it took hers. The nurse lied to her, she said. Told her as she bled out her last that she had a healthy child and needed only to rest. The woman meant to comfort me with a vision of my darling going happily to her rest. A fiction. My wife was no fool. She knew she had brought forth death and it had fed on her. This is what they did. Those little schemers, those poisonous diplomats with their lies, their slanders. They killed her son, they killed her daughter, they killed her.

They tried to prevent me entering the room. A butcher's den. Doctor and nurse bloody to their elbows, and the bed crimson, rags soaked in blood across the floor, basins full of red water. Her nightgown soaked in it. I threw them out and would not let them touch her till morning, but sat by her side, her head cradled in my arms begging her to open her eyes. I promised every-thing, I swore everything, I prayed that I would go mad, and for a while I feel I might have done so cradling my dead love, my dead self in that bloody chamber.

Florian put aside another page with shaking fingers. "Oh, God, Father! What is this?"

44

Pegel was seeing stars. Real stars. It had grown dark. He thought they were pretty. Sometimes he became so obsessed with the mathematics of their movements, the steady passage of the planets among them, that he forgot that they were also very shiny. After a while it occurred to him that this might not be the best use of his time, and he began to grope about him in the dark. He could see the shadow of the roof from which he had fallen. It was not far. The back of his head was very tender; he felt the place that hurt most. It was sticky with blood, and he realized he felt rather sick. What had he landed on? His vision swam a little. The woodpile? No, bundles of straw and twigs, with a frame of logs on top of it. His head had hit against part of the frame when he fell. He raised himself up. He was still a few feet off the ground. He slithered down from the heap as quickly as possible before stumbling away a few steps, sat down smartly as his ankle failed, then slithered away until he found his back against a wall. He was in an internal courtyard, stone walls on all sides, stone flags on the ground. He had been lucky to have had his fall broken. But what was this bonfire? He thought of the frame on top of it and struggled to get some sense out his pounding, spinning brain. Florian had said Kastner was his stepmother's name. He tried to remember every detail about the murders Manzerotti had seen fit to tell him. Ritual. Some sort of revenge? A woman drowned, another with earth in her mouth. Every one of the circle in Maulberg bar Swann murdered. *Swann* . . . Wimpf had just accompanied another guest here. Christ! Jacob had a nasty suspicion that he'd just been saved by falling into Swann's funeral pyre.

Krall returned to the palace in a grim state of mind, but satisfied that the deaths of Countess Dieth and Adolphus Glucke would be thought natural. Glucke's servants were loyal to Maulberg, and the housekeeper had been firm in her agreement. "Can't be how he's remembered, can it, dying that way? If we say it's a fever, people will remember the good of him."

Krall found Swann's chamber empty and then had a few minutes of conversation with Colonel Padfield that left his mind swimming. He made his way to the private parlor of the English, where he found Mr. and Mrs. Clode and Mr. Graves in a state of some excitement and waiting for the return of Mr. Crowther and Mrs. Westerman. He was glad to see the young Englishman free and said so. They shook hands, then he shook his head over the mysteries behind these murders and wished aloud that he was able to tell Clode who had done him such harm. The English pounced on him with a flurry of information. He was so far flummoxed that he found himself lighting his pipe without asking Mrs. Clode's permission. Count Frenzel? A second wife? Blood rituals?

"Where is Frenzel?" he asked.

"Returned to his estate, so Herr Kinkel tells us," Mr. Graves said.

"Strange," Krall said, and drew on his pipe. "I know he spends much time there, but the duke is only married an hour. What of Swann? Where is he?"

"He received an offer of sanctuary from Gotha," Rachel said.

"Did he now?" Krall folded his arms and tapped the stem of his pipe against his sleeve. "That got here awful quick."

The door opened and Mrs. Westerman and Mr. Crowther appeared. There was color in Mrs. Westerman's face, and Crowther looked a younger man than when they had first met.

"Frenzel!" Mrs. Westerman said, and everyone started speaking at once.

Black years. Comfortless years. Years where my only company was her grave. I buried her with my own hands in my own grounds, refusing to share her even with God. The monster I would have burned, but little Christian begged me to lay the stillborn infant in the ground with her, and so I did. The household dwindled. I shut up the east wing, left all my expensive toys to rot, and waited to die. For four years I waited in this tomb. Then she came. A common little trickster in a dark blue dress, but I realized that night that Antonia had chosen her. Florian, the things she knew! But then she would try to worm her way between Antonia and me, saying things that were nonsense.

The frustration then! Waiting for Antonia to speak. I did not understand, and in the darkness of my heart asked Antonia why she had chosen this sharp-eyed fool as her way of speaking to me? Then little Beatrice showed me her book, a scrapbook of images, designs, incantations copied in her schoolgirl hand, pages cut from Renaissance grimoires, and I understood. Antonia had been guiding her. I dreamed of my wife sitting over the little schemer by candlelight in the cave of some forgotten mage whispering to her when to turn the pages, what passages and diagrams to copy down. During her third week here I found the book of poisons. It was written in another hand, but she had added her little notes of explanation. I saw it all. Antonia had given me everything. Now I just needed to get rid of the girl. Again, she made it so simple for me. Antonia inspired her even to her death.

She told me Antonia wished to show me to a store of jewels on a waterfall near the borders of my little kingdom. As if Antonia would ever have been bothered with such paltry stuff, but I indulged her and she spent several days "preparing to do battle with the spirits," to recover the treasure. She took me to the waterfall, lit a candle, and bade me to be quiet while she summoned her angels to defend her. It was quite entertaining, the girl had learned how to put on a show. Her body went rigid, she tossed her head from side to side and muttered and croaked, calling on the names of the angelic hoards. There was no sense to her cries, her incantations were as like to call spirits to her as the wind. Then she lay still. After some minutes she seemed to awake, weak from her battles. I put out my hand to help her to her feet and inquired as to her health and well-being, all concern and kindness then. She leaned her small weight against me and said, in fading, faltering tones, she knew where the treasure was hid. And so she did. I was commanded to move some stones to one side at the base of the waterfall, and what a surprise! A little store of gems and jewelry. I was a little moved, I think, to see how she invested her small worth in me. Here was her ancient hoard of magical jewels, a handful of trifles, the sort of shoddy and overvalued nothings a duchess might give to her maid in a moment of weakness. I can give a performance too. I was delighted, amazed by the miraculous wealth and its miraculous discovery. I got down on my knees in front of the little strumpet and told her she was my queen, my goddess, that I would settle on her at once a house for her own use in Oberbach, and that from this day forward I would be honored to have her as my counselor in all things. Dear girl, she shook her head, offered her jewels as a free gift, declared I was too generous, too kind, and as she trembled and dissembled I saw the hard shine of triumph in her eye. Her victory. She sat down on the stones I had just moved and turned away, as if overcome by her surprise at my generosity. But I knew she only turned from me to hide her delight. The first blow I struck fell just behind her right ear. She tried to stand, to turn, looked at me and for the first and only time her eyes seemed innocent. The second blow landed on her left temple and sent her sprawling on her front. The third blow might have been unnecessary. It was certainly conclusive. So then I gathered her book, the contents of her pockets, I tore open the linings of her clothes to find what else of value might have been hidden in them.

Antonia was guiding me then, my boy, for it was in the lining of her cloak I found the dried herbs and matter folded in paper and sealed which I discovered I needed for the drugs. Then, when my search was complete, I dug her a grave. It was her suggestion I carried a spade with me on our little excursion, in case the treasure to which the spirits led her was underground. I rested a little, packed up what I had taken from her body, then threw her jewels into the stream.

Harriet found Manzerotti at the center of a large group of rather amazed young women. It took some time before he could extricate himself.

"Come to toast the happy bride and groom, Mrs. Westerman? Clode is released, the conspirators are under guard, the fountains flow with wine, and good cheer abounds."

She unfolded the paper in her hand. "This is the portrait of Antonia Kastner, the woman slandered by the Minervals. It is also the model for the walking automaton the Al-Saids were asked to build." He nodded but said nothing. "The model had a Seal of Solomon painted on its torso. A brass vessel with the same seal was commissioned from Julius, and there was a space left in the body large enough to accommodate it."

Manzerotti was very still for a moment, then he took her by the elbow and led her to a quieter part of the room. "The blood . . . I did not realize I could still be shocked. How exciting. Do you know who is trying to reclaim her from the dead?"

"I believe I do. It is one of the knights imperial with a position at court. We wish to ride out at once and place him into Krall's custody, but Colonel Padfield will not give up any of his men."

"I see. He has a point, my dear. Sending troops into lands not under his rule would be a serious breach of etiquette. You wish me to use my influence with the duke? It would be a great deal better to wait until the morning. The lawyers can draw up a few warrants extraordinary and cover them with seals and Latin phrases. They are very particular about such things. This man will be just as mad then." He looked at the portrait again. "Fascinating."

"I overheard Pegel ask you to give him time to get his friend away to his father's house. That friend was Count Frenzel's son."

"Yes?" Manzerotti frowned.

"This is a portrait of Antonia Kastner. She was Count Frenzel's second wife."

"I see." He folded up the picture and returned it to her. "That boy is a trial. Come then, to the colonel—and Mrs. Westerman?" She looked up at him. "Thank you."

45

The doors that led from the courtyard were unlocked. Pegel chose one at random and began moving quietly through the corridors. The place was a warren; it seemed full of sudden dead ends, branching passageways. Pegel began to feel, with a rising sense of panic, that the building was a living thing, laughing at him. When he had climbed out of the bedroom, his intention had been to ride off indignantly into the night, but then there was that fire and the name of Kastner. He could not leave Florian here alone with his mad father. He thought about it, but he couldn't. If he could find the room where Florian was, perhaps he could pick the lock. Florian would know where to search for guns in this place. Or a way out would be a start. This corridor looked familiar . . . Pegel fought down his nerves and nausea and stumbled on till he found himself on some sort of gallery looking down and into a room on the opposite side of another courtyard. He saw the count cross the window. He was dancing with a young woman and smiling at her. The look on his face was one of such intense happiness, Pegel felt his heart contract. The old glass made it hard to see her face, but she seemed to be smiling, too, the jewels flashing around her neck. The grace of her movement was clear though, as she nodded, turned, took Frenzel's hand. But Florian said his stepmother had died. A door opened behind him and Pegel pushed himself into the shadows, holding his breath. It was Florian, his hands tied behind him. Christian was standing behind him with a pistol aimed at the small of his back.

"Christian, listen to me! Antonia was a kind woman, a good woman—she would never want this! He is quite mad! For God's sake, man, stop now. I shall do everything in my power to help you."

The servant's voice was shaking a little. "Honestly, Master Florian, you've got it all wrong. It's true. You haven't seen what I've seen! She's coming alive. Every time, she gets stronger."

There were tears in Florian's voice. "Christian, please! It is an automaton. We saw the ones my father used to have when we were children. We both swore they were alive, but they were just machines."

"Not like this, Master Florian." Christian's voice had grown firmer again. "Antonia asked for my help. This is what she wanted. She came to me and asked me to send Beatrice to your father."

"So he could murder her?"

Christian frowned. "You're lying! She left here rich and happy."

"She's buried by the waterfall. It's in his damn letter, read it yourself."

Pegel wondered if he could reach Christian and knock the gun from his hand before he could squeeze the trigger. Not a hope, and he was too weak to overpower the man even if the shot didn't kill him. Why had Florian let his hands be tied! Pegel made a resolution not to risk his life saving damn fools from this point on.

"You're lying. You haven't seen what I've seen," Wimpf repeated stubbornly. "Now move, Master Florian. The count is waiting for us."

They disappeared around the bend in the corridor and, hardly daring to breathe, Pegel followed them.

"It cannot be done!" Colonel Padfield was beginning to sweat. "I can understand that in your ignorance, Mrs. Westerman, you might think otherwise, but Mr. Crowther, Signor Manzerotti, you are, I think, men of the world. To send a party of horse to Frenzel's home! His estate is held *unmittelbar*—it is tantamount to an invasion!"

Krall was leaning against the mantelpiece, his shoulders hunched. "Colonel, Kinkel saw Swann leaving this place with Wimpf. I reckon they weren't heading to Gotha but to Frenzel's home."

"It is no concern of ours, Herr District Officer. The duke made it clear that Chancellor Swann has made his own bed. The man is a traitor, we cannot risk such an action for his sake." The colonel turned to Manzerotti. "Sir, you know—you *know* this is an impossible request."

Manzerotti smiled at him, but it was not the usual catlike smile. It was tight. Impatient. "Of course it is impossible, Colonel. I wouldn't expect you to entertain it for a moment."

Harriet looked at him in disbelief, but he held up one long hand. "However, I think you may find it in your power to give a day's leave, effective at once, to a small number of your Turkish hussars. They then would be available for hire by some other party. I think you may then find that they, on the road, hear a disturbance that takes them, unwittingly, onto Count Frenzel's land. You may then find that by morning, Count Frenzel will be on Maulberg territory where he can, of course, be arrested at once. major Auwerk might also welcome the opportunity to do some extraordinary service today." The singer turned to Harriet. "His name is on the list of Minervals, of course, but very, very low down on that list. Krall, you and the major could deliver this murderer to the duke as a wedding present. Whatever the duke's feelings about the Minervals, he, I'm sure, would like to see the killer of Lady Martesen in custody. It reflects well on his authority."

The colonel looked at him very steadily. Manzerotti sighed. "If you would perhaps write out a short notice of leave, and allow a gap for some half-dozen names to be filled in, and place it on the table before you return to your duties?"

"And that would be all right, would it?" the colonel asked, half suspicious, half hopeful.

"Yes, Colonel, that would be quite in order."

"You going?"

Manzerotti smiled the same thin smile. "I am engaged to perform again this evening. I cannot leave here without drawing too much attention. However, as Mr. Crowther, Mrs. Westerman, and their party aim to take no further part in the festivities, perhaps they might go for a ride in the moonlight."

Pegel followed Florian and Wimpf into a wide hallway tiled in black and white and watched as they passed through a medieval-looking doorway and let the door close behind them. Pegel was not at all sure what was happening, but his suspicions were dark. He had risked a great deal to get Florian out of harm's way, and now it seemed his friend would have been a great deal safer in the custody of the duke. There was a narrow staircase to the right of the doorway. Pegel scuttled up to a small landing with a low door leading from it, slightly ajar. He dropped to his hands and knees and pushed it open before slipping through. Voices. Deep shadow here, and to his right candlelight. He glanced in that direction and saw the top of an old-fashioned chandelier. All functional iron, where the palace lighting was crystal and silver. He was in the minstrels' gallery of some great hall. There was a movement in the shadows in front of him and he saw he was sharing his perch with a very old man, trembling, eyes wide, staring at him.

"Gunter?" Pegel whispered hopefully and the old man nodded. Pegel crawled toward him. "I'm Pegel. What's going on?"

The old man looked miserable. He pointed into the hall. Pegel peered through the balustrade. It was a grand room, a rectangle, high and plain. The old refectory, perhaps. He wished it were still full of nuns—he'd take any help he could get right now. Instead, at the far end of the room were two figures. A woman, finely dressed in a rather old-fashioned style, and an old man seated on a chair in front of her.

"Who is that?" Pegel whispered.

"He was always a hard man, and a bad master. But then that girl came, Beatrice. Told him he could talk to his wife again."

"Who is the old man?"

"Chancellor Swann."

Pegel swore under his breath. "I was afraid of that."

Swann's left hand was trailing. Even from the other end of the hall Pegel could hear the steady patter of his blood draining into a brass bowl at his side.

"Father, what have you done?" Florian was standing some twenty feet in front of the little tableau. His hands were still tied, and Wimpf still had his gun in his hand. But Count Frenzel had his arm around his son's shoulders.

"I have become a worker of miracles, Florian," he said. "I am become like a God, aren't I, Wimpf?"

"You are, sir."

"Every one of her enemies I kill, she grows stronger. She returns. With Swann's blood, with his death, all is done. Tonight, my child, you will hear her speak." Pegel could see that Florian's shoulders were shaking. He was crying. "Is the pyre ready, Wimpf?"

"It is, sir."

"Excellent. I shall carry him there myself."

Pegel turned to the old man beside him. "Where are the guns in this house?" he murmured.

"Locked away," he said in a hoarse whisper, "in the master's study. You'd have to go through this hall."

"Can you get help?"

Gunter looked near to tears. "No one would come!"

Pegel thought for a moment, then pulled at the lining of his coat and fished out two gold coins. "Take these." He pressed them into the man's hands. "Tell them if they come, there will be more. Be quick."

For the first time the old man looked hopeful. "What will you do, sir?"

Pegel shrugged. "Improvise. Now go." The old man scurried away.

"You are mad!" Florian burst out. Pegel crept back to the balustrade. Florian had staggered away a step from his father. His face was bright red.

"Florian! I had faith even before I saw these miracles, yet you remain blind. Try—try to be worthy of these wonders and I will be generous. But you do make it very, very difficult." Count Frenzel was holding a knife in his hands. "How you can think I am mad, when God has delivered into my hands . . . but you do not understand." With a light step he approached Swann and produced something from his pocket to bind the wrist.

"Is he dead?" Florian said, his voice high and trembling.

Frenzel took a handful of Swann's hair and lifted up his chin. The eyes were dull, unseeing. "Swann here? No, not yet. He will be soon though." He sank down on his haunches so he could look into the chancellor's emptying eyes. "You see, Swann? You killed her, now it is up to you to bring her back to life. Everything fits together. All is balance. You caused her death, that of her child, and my child. But if you had not driven her from court, she would not have become my wife. You killed her with the banishment, but at the same time put her into the arms of one who could make her live again." He let Swann's head fall forward again and stroked his long gray hair. "God is wonderful." He picked up the bowl into which the blood had run, then stood and turned to the automaton. "This is the last time, Antonia." He said it with such love, Pegel was almost touched. Frenzel went around to the back of the machine and bent over. Pegel's view was partial, but he thought he saw a panel opened. "Wimpf, help me," the Count said.

The servant approached and took the bowl of blood from his master. Then Frenzel removed some vessel from the machine. Pegel could see it gleam gold in the candlelight. He untwisted it, then held it as Wimpf poured Swann's blood into its base. Pegel swallowed; his mouth had gone very dry. Frenzel was closing the panel again. His son looked as if he was going to be sick.

"You are mad," he said again, quietly. His father shrugged and adjusted his wife's dress with a little smile of pride. Then Florian began to shout. "I do not care if that *thing* comes over here and talks to me! It can get down on its knees and tell me it is come from hell! You are still insane, Father, and your 'miracle' is an abomination!" The count stepped over to his son and slapped him hard. Florian spat onto the floor and kept yelling. "*You* killed her! *You* did! You kept her apart from her son and that is what killed her; even when she was kind to you, good to you, you denied her that and it killed her! It should be your blood in there!"

Frenzel slapped him again, and Florian stumbled this time.

"Take him outside," Frenzel said. He turned to the automaton and lifted his hand to her cheek, brushing it with his knuckles. "You see, my love? I always told you he was willful. So soon, Antonia. The fire will burn, Swann will die, and when I come back into this room, we shall talk again."

He turned from her, hoisted Swann over his shoulder as if he weighed no more than a rabbit, and followed his son and servant out of the hall through a doorway in the west.

Pegel counted to ten, then ran lightly down from his hiding place and into the hall. He went along the east wall as quickly as his ankle would allow, like a rat trying to keep to the shadows. He found the door to the count's study easily enough. There were papers covering the desk—many drawings and pages and pages of writing. Pegel had a fleeting impression of the seals and sketches. A separate table had been set up with mortar and pestle on it, next to little boxes and piles of dried plants. He found a pistol in a case in the desk itself, loaded it as swiftly as he could, then returned to the hall and approached the automaton. Now that he was inches from her, he could see that of course this was not a real woman. But the work was so fine, if she had only turned her head at that moment, he would have stepped back and apologized for staring.

Jacob put his arm around her carefully to pick her up and felt something at her waist. It was a ribbon, and hanging from it was a little collection of owls—two fobs, two pocket watches, a flask, a pendant, a ring. Seven in all. He picked up the machine and staggered a little under its weight. His ankle throbbed and he breathed hard. "Sorry about this, madam. But I'm almost out of ideas."

46

The party of hussars came to a slightly disorderly stop, and Harriet urged her horse past them till she could reach the rider at the head of the column.

"What is happening, Major?"

He nodded to the left and for the first time Harriet noted a stooped servant, staring up in fear at the great horses and glittering uniforms that surrounded him.

"This man wants us to go to Count Frenzel's home and help some boy save Chancellor Swann and a Master Florian," he said to her. He was smiling slightly. Harriet looked down. The old man held out a gold coin nervously toward her. "Oh yes," the major said. "He says he'll pay us."

Pegel kicked open the door to the courtyard. Florian was slumped on the ground at Wimpf's feet. Frenzel was carefully laying Swann across the framework of logs on top of the pyre. As Pegel stepped out through the doorway, Frenzel and Wimpf both turned toward him. Wimpf looked startled, Frenzel, quite calm. "Ah, Mr. Pegel. We thought you'd left." He saw Pegel look at his friend. "Florian is not dead, Mr. Pegel. Merely unconscious. I was finding his ignorant complaints rather irritating."

"Get away from Swann, Count."

The courtyard's white walls reflected the moonlight, giving everything about the place a pale, dreamlike atmosphere. The flames of the dozen torches around the walls whispered and hissed.

"Now, now, Mr. Pegel. I don't wish to appear ungrateful. It is, after all, thanks to you that Swann came here—a desperate man is one very easy to fool—but you shall not interfere. Go away." He picked up a torch from the bracket and approached the pyre again.

"I am armed," Pegel said, his voice higher.

"But not very effectively. The pistol you are holding is not an accurate weapon, you know. Wimpf's is much better."

"It doesn't need to be accurate." Pegel moved away from the doorframe, pulling the automaton with him so Frenzel could see it and pressed the barrel of his gun to its torso.

Frenzel stopped. "If you harm her, Pegel, I shall pursue you through hell." He took a step away from the pyre.

"Then let us go." Jacob nodded to the figure of Swann. "*All* of us."

"Not possible." Frenzel smiled. "We seem to be at something of an impasse."

Pegel swallowed. Frenzel put his head on one side. "Even so close, your shot would be unlikely to damage the vessel." Pegel thought he heard something—one of the horses in the stables, no doubt. "So even if you manage to pull the trigger before Wimpf's shot kills you . . ." He gave a little nod. Pegel thought he heard something else. Metallic. "Wimpf? Please shoot Mr. Pegel." Frenzel set his torch to the pyre; it began to crackle. Wimpf hesitated. "Now, please, Wimpf."

Pegel lifted his nose: that was horses, several of them. A great shout reached them from the world outside: "*Hoo-rah!*" and there was a clatter of hooves on cobblestones in the outer courtyard. An English voice, a woman's, shouting: "There, through that arch! Fire!"

Frenzel had gone completely still, the torch in his hand and a look of confusion on his face. Wimpf shut his eyes and held the gun straight, then fired. Pegel darted behind the automaton and felt the force of his own gun exploding, pressed against the automaton's side. Wimpf's bullet caught it too. The roar deafened him. Pegel felt the automaton fall across him, trapping his ankle. He yelled, squeezing his eyes closed with the pain. When he opened them, he found himself staring into the automaton's blue eyes. They flickered. "Christ," he said, and instinctively reached out and touched her cheek. It felt warm. He dropped back onto his elbows, panting.

"There, through the arch! Fire!" Harriet shouted, and the hussars drove their horses forward. The courtyard suddenly erupted with noise. One, two shots in quick succession. She saw Clode's thin form slide down from his horse and dash forward. She did the same, lifting up her skirts and running, then came to a halt, blinded by the fierce light of the bonfire. Count Frenzel was surrounded by soldiers. Pegel, looking terrified, was struggling to get out from under some figure that had fallen across him. Another young man was laying over the cobbles some feet away.

"Swann!" Pegel shouted. "Swann is on the fire!" It's too late, Harriet thought. The fire has hold. "He's still alive!"

A man sprang up the bonfire in the corner where the flames were still only smoldering and grabbed Swann around the shoulders. Not until he shouted to the hussars for help did Harriet realize it was Clode. Crowther and the major got to him first and together they dragged the chancellor's body down and away.

"Christ, man!" Graves was at Clode's side beating out the sparks on his coat. Crowther had taken off his cloak and was using it to do the same for the chancellor, then he checked Swann's pulse and Harriet heard the major's voice: "He's gone." Then Crowther's murmured reply: "Don't be so sure." Crowther stood up and crossed to the other man, and turned him on his side. He was a young man, fair-haired. Pegel's friend, she supposed. He groaned.

Pegel finally managed to push away the damaged figure that lay across him. As he shoved it aside, the torso seemed to buckle and Count Frenzel made a desperate swallowing grunt and collapsed to his knees. There was a ringing sound of metal on stone, and a large brass egg-shaped object rolled free from the body. It split apart on the cobbles and in the light of the torches, Harriet saw it ooze something dark and oily. Frenzel began to wail, a high wordless lament, his head tipped back and staring up into the stars above his home. "For Christ's sake," Harriet heard Graves say to the major. "Get the count out of here. Get him to Krall." The keening continued.

The major undid the rope that was around Florian's wrists and used it to bind his father. Harriet noticed that the major's face was dead white. Frenzel would not stand, he would not walk, so they dragged him out of the court-yard, his eyes still fixed on the broken ghost of his wife.

Harriet still could not move. The torches cast red shadows over her dress and caught the light of her hair. All around her, people were busy. Some of the hussars were dousing the flames. Pegel had crawled over to where Crowther was tending to Florian. Clode was bent over the chancellor, Graves at his side. She remained, amazed, watching the fire, and as the hussars emptied buckets of water on its smoldering ashes under the direction of the old servant, listened to their hiss and complaint. The water ran over the cobbles, soaking the automaton and carrying the contents of the brass vessel into the gutter.

PART VII

47

Dawn had come. Harriet was seated on a low bench of the inner courtyard reading Count Frenzel's letter to his son. She tried to picture Beatrice, her sharpness and confidence. How terrible to have been so wrong. So she had winkled the story of Antonia's death from Wimpf at one of the seances in the fake village and set off with her chin in the air. She thought she'd find a fat sheep to fleece in his castle with his grief and his automata, but she had thrown herself into the lap of a wolf. Frenzel related how he studied Beatrice's book then went to court to find who had been responsible for his wife's disgrace. There he found Wimpf, their devoted servant, eager to please and already aware of the secret room, its seven glasses. The letter ended with a series of crowing descriptions of the murders Frenzel had perpetrated, his anger when he became aware that Rachel had seen the grave on her visit to his home with Clode, the realization that he had the means and opportunity to make her husband appear a murderer with the *datura* drug. Colonel Padfield himself had told the count about the costumes and the haberdasher's shop where the party intended to change into their Carnival costumes. Frenzel proclaimed himself an equal of God, and ended again with a declaration of love.

Crowther was sitting by Harriet's side, staring into the cold ashes of the fire. He had taken a place next to her while she was reading but did not interrupt her.

"How are the two young men?" she said at last.

"Exhausted," he told her, "but otherwise undamaged. Florian zu Frenzel is sleeping. Pegel is wandering around the house."

"Where is your cane?" she asked, already knowing the answer.

Crowther shrugged. "How else could he wander around the house?"

She laughed softly, and he smiled. "A deputation from the court has arrived," he continued. "Colonel Padfield and his men are going through the house and it seems the Al-Saids have come with him. Clode and Graves have returned to Rachel and we are to go and meet the duke."

"To receive his congratulations?"

"His blessings for our return journey to England perhaps. I suspect he would be pleased if we were to leave the court quietly and soon. Krall continues, with the air of a man of great conviction, to hide many of these crimes. They will execute Frenzel for the murders of Beatrice and Lady Martesen, and the attempt on Mr. Clode. The other deaths will be described as accident or illness."

Harriet sighed. "Will Swann recover?"

"Yes, thanks to the heroic actions of Mr. Clode. Not many men would rescue another from a funeral pyre—but then I think that may have done him some good."

"He could not save Lady Martesen, but he cheated Frenzel of his last victim?" Crowther nodded. "I think you are right," Harriet agreed. "Clode is a better hero than a victim."

"Swann is not a young man, but given he has survived so far, I think he will regain his health. I suspect Count Frenzel was nearing the end of his supplies—those items that came originally from the shaman, through Kupfel's and Beatrice's hands to him—and that Swann therefore received a lighter dose of the paralyzing agent. The chancellor is to remain here until he is fully recovered."

"And Wimpf?"

"Disappeared like smoke in the battle. However, Krall seems confident he will track him down." Crowther closed his eyes and rested his head against the wall behind him. "Is there anything else? Yes—now Frenzel is under lock and key in Grenzhow, Krall and Michaels have gone off in the direction of Oberbach. They will take statements about the discovery of Beatrice and see the young lady properly buried."

"Mrs. Padfield?"

"Attends to her duties at court with the new duchess. Her connection to little Beatrice remains secret."

"I wish her every success among those people." Harriet tapped the pile of papers at her side. "Have you read this?" He nodded. "A love story! Good

Lord, it is a dark idea of love. What do you think he would have done, when Swann's death did not give the automaton the power of speech?"

Crowther stared out over the courtyard again; it still smelled of burned straw, a faint tang of smoke. "Perhaps she would have spoken to him."

"Crowther?"

"No, I have not turned mystic, only his madness was so complete, his illusion so seamless, he might have actually heard her. I wonder what she would have said . . ."

"Has a search been made? Has the poison book been discovered yet?"

Crowther looked uncomfortable. "Mrs. Westerman, Manzerotti arrived while you were reading . . ."

Her eyes widened. "And you let him take it? Good God, Crowther, the most dangerous man in Europe and you hand him *that*?"

"Harriet . . ."

"Crowther, where is he?"

"Frenzel's study behind the great hall, but—"

She was on her feet at once and walked away from him with a firm step. "If you would let me finish . . ." he said quietly, as he watched her neat figure disappear into the shadows. "No? Very well."

"Is she beyond repair? I'm so terribly sorry I shot her." Pegel had been standing in the doorway leaning on his borrowed cane for a few minutes now, watching the Al-Said brothers inspect the damaged automaton.

Adnan looked up. "Nothing is entirely beyond repair, Mr. Pegel, but the central cam that controls her movement is destroyed. Poor Nancy."

"Poor Nancy indeed," Sami said, touching the automaton's lifeless face. It was strange looking at it. It had seemed so alive last night, yet now, in the daylight, it looked like a skillful work of art, not nature. "Not your fault the man who had you made was a crazy fellow, was it? We can use the head again. The ambassador to China has asked us to create an automaton that plays an instrument. She shall go off and have more adventures there. More pleasant ones, I hope. If we create another automaton who dances, she will not have this same face."

"I note you don't call her Antonia," Pegel said.

"Never," Sami said firmly. "We made her, and we called her Nancy. Better."

Pegel had to agree. "What will happen to the vessel? Is there still . . . anything in it?"

"A residue. A little gothic, I understand," Adnan said, picking up another bent cog and tracing its teeth and grooves with his fingertip. "There is a suggestion that it is to be melted down, discreetly, by the public executioner. An agreement was reached that there should be some ceremony about it, but no one was sure quite what it should be. Those poor people." Adnan leaned his weight against the table and looked with affection at the broken wreckage of his great work. "Am I right in thinking, Mr. Pegel, that you saw her perform?"

"Yes, dancing hand in hand with that lunatic an hour before the troops arrived. She looked wonderful. Her movement, the way she looked at him, her breathing. I swore up and down it was a real woman." He saw they were looking at him with some curiosity.

"The darkness deceived you, Mr. Pegel," Adnan said. "She did not breathe."

"She did! The way her chest rose and fell—that jewel on her breast made it quite clear."

"Mr. Pegel, I built her. There are breathing mechanisms in some of our creations, but not in Nancy. She does not breathe."

There was a period of silence. Pegel swallowed. "Of course. Candlelight. All very emotional at the time. Mind plays tricks."

"Quite understandable you should make the mistake in the circumstances."

"Er, yes. Quite. I shall leave you to your work, gentlemen."

Harriet found Manzerotti perched on Count Frenzel's desk in the library.

"Manzerotti, where is the poison book?"

He looked up. "Ah! Mrs. Westerman arrives with her eyes ablaze. Let evil tremble!" He turned a page. "What book, dear lady? I have Beatrice's scrapbook of the esoteric cobbled together from the alchemist's papers here. She had a fine imagination and a talent for mimicking the literature. She should have taken to writing novels. Would you like to see it?"

"You know perfectly well that is not what I mean."

"Herr Kupfel's poison book? Perhaps Count Frenzel destroyed it."

"You have stolen it already, Manzerotti! You would not be sitting there so pleased with yourself if it were not in your possession. Do you really expect Crowther and I to let you leave with that in your hands?"

"I have something to show you." He picked up an item from the table beside him, then slid gracefully from his perch and handed it to her. She looked down. It was a glass jar, one of the set from the poisoner's room.

"Is this a threat?"

"Perhaps you could examine the jar a little more carefully."

She turned it in her hands. On one side was printed in gold: KUPFEL'S MODERN MIRACLES, BY APPOINTMENT TO THE COURT OF ULRICHSBERG.

"I see."

"Yes. If I threaten you, Mrs. Westerman, it will be with something more powerful than face cream. The jar is not from the room, but from a large supply of young Kupfel's wonders which I bought yesterday."

"So the papers and potions in the palace . . ."

"Are the work of Theo Kupfel. He picked up a fair amount from his father: some of that knowledge he used to make his cosmetics, some he used to create these more unpleasant ointments for the Minervals. He certainly has talent."

She replaced the jar on the table. "I will not be distracted, Manzerotti. What of Adam Kupfel's poison book? The one you said you would give a great deal of gold to put your hands on? I will not let you take it."

He sighed. "Dear lady, I do not think you have anything to say in the matter. Really, I have already been through this with Gabriel. Yesterday, as you know, I put into the duke's hand the names of two hundred and fifty Minervals—some hundred of them resident in Maulberg. Good. Their more senior adepts have been arrested or banished. The younger ones have all been given a very stern talking-to. But the rest include men and women of influence in most of the other courts in the empire, including Vienna and Berlin. Do you understand, my dear?"

She looked at the floor. "You have given him a trump card."

"A whole pack of them, and Christoph knows very well how to play them. Now suppose a grateful duke, absolute ruler and holder, suddenly, of a very, very interesting list of names . . . suppose that grateful duke has made a present of some particular documents to the genius who helped him—do you really think you are in a position to countermand him? You gave him a madman and a story of horrors. I gave him a conspiracy. It's quite fair, you know." He looked up at her and smiled his beautiful smile. "And you still get that pretty Caravaggio he promised you."

"Manzerotti, you know I don't want the papers for myself! But you cannot be trusted. You cannot. I tremble to think what you will do with that knowledge."

Manzerotti's eyes glinted. "It would be rather fun, though it is a shame the receipt for whatever poisoned Swann's gloves is nowhere to be found . . ."

"For God's sake!"

He looked at her for a long moment. She could feel her distress being weighed and measured. "Frenzel has used all the materials Beatrice stole, my dear," he said more softly. "Those particular potions have become the secret of their shamans again. And as a rule they do protect their secrets."

"They told Kupfel. You have the receipt." The tears she was trying to hold back showed in her voice.

"Those substances are not referred to by any name I understand. And of course, I shall make some inquiries about the gentleman from Marseilles, though I am not hopeful."

"But the *rest* of the book . . ."

Manzerotti lifted his hand. "There is really nothing you can do, my dear. You *or* Gabriel. You will simply have to believe me when I say my interest is almost purely academic. By the way, I thank you for saving Pegel. Irritating as he can be, and though his manners are appalling, I find I am rather fond of him. When next our paths cross, Mrs. Westerman, even if our interests run counter to each other, I shall remember to be grateful."

She closed her eyes. "I should have shot you when I had the chance."

"Perhaps you should have done. However, I do not intend to give you another opportunity for a little while yet."

He crossed to her, took her hand in his and bent low over it. "Good-bye, my dear. I do not think we shall meet again alone while you are in Germany. And do give my best love to Brother Gabriel."

He turned and left the room.

Harriet remained there in solitude for some time until Pegel hobbled into the room on Crowther's cane. "Mrs. W! You are waited for. Colonel Padfield is bundling up your party into the carriage to carry you to the hunt."

She wiped her eyes. "The hunt, Mr. Pegel?"

"The court hunt! Have you seen a hunt in Germany? A court one, I mean." He rolled his eyes and sucked in his cheeks, which made her laugh in spite of herself. "Makes shooting fish in a pond look like the heights of sportsmanship, if you ask me, but that's where the duke and duchess are, so that's where you must be."

"Will you stay here a while?"

He tapped the cane on the floor. "Yes, for a while—you know, help out Florian and play nursemaid to the grim ex-chancellor until they can hire a few more servants. Settle things here. Feed their old servant brandy till he can stop shaking."

"What then? Will you remain at Leuchtenstadt?"

"They don't have anything to teach me there. But you know, Florian has not even been out of Maulberg yet. He's twenty—and has never left this place."

"So?" she said, trying not to smile again.

"I think a grand European tour." He waved his hand in the air. "I'll introduce him to some good mathematicians—oh, and people who like farming and all that, if he wants to try and do some good round here."

"I hope you persuade him."

"Me too. Anyway, Mrs. Westerman, you must be off. Come on, shoo! I shall chase you with Mr. Crowther's stick."

She got up quickly as he limped toward her. "You are a most unusual young man, Jacob Pegel."

"I know." He became suddenly serious. "And a grateful one too. If you hadn't . . . I'm glad I didn't die last night."

"If you continue working for Manzerotti, your life might be in danger again before long."

He shrugged. "I get bored. Manzerotti is never boring. Thank you for coming for me."

As she moved past him toward the door, she put her hand over his on the top of Crowther's cane. "I listened to the voices of my better angels. You will get that cane back to Crowther, won't you, dear? It means a lot more to him than he likes to admit."

48

Krall was happy to be on horseback. Count Frenzel had been formally arrested on Maulberg land, then sent off to Castle Grenzhow where Krall was sure Herr Hoffman would receive him with delight. Now he rode to make an official visit to the priest at Oberbach with Michaels, though there was a place he needed to stop first. Then he would have to spend months up to his armpits in paperwork. Crimes to be documented, crimes concealed. Statements and further statements to be written, witnessed, and sealed. No matter the madman had written out his confession in his letter to his son, it would all need to be checked and ticked. He had already assembled more paper than even the law faculty at Leuchtenstadt would know what to do with, and in truth he had only begun to scrape the surface.

In the week since they had arrived Mrs. Westerman and Crowther had turned the world upside down, and transformed it from a place he knew, where there were a few niggling questions, into a theater of horrors. They had also forced him to realize that he loved his sovereign and would always put his battered old body between the duke and harm.

"Are they always like this?" he said, and Michaels smiled.

"Can't say, Mr. Krall. Mostly I know them from Hartswood, though they stirred things up to a right brew there in the year eighty. Glad they did, though. It's not their way to make things comfortable for those around them. They're like a dose of cod liver oil. You curse them at the time, but in general they makes things better in the end."

"How did you hear about where the girl might be buried?" Krall asked, and noticed that Michaels chose that moment to stroke his horse's mane.

"Girl who seemed a little simple in Mittelbach." Krall was old enough to sense when he was being told only part of a story, but he let it lie. Another secret for the pile.

————

They were within a short ride of Oberbach when Krall pulled gently at his reins and guided his horse off the road.

"Mr. Krall?"

"Got to pick up our fugitive, Mr. Michaels."

"Wimpf? You reckon he's here?"

"Here or hereabouts. I know the family."

Michaels looked at him from under his thick eyebrows. "You seem mighty relaxed for a man in pursuit, if you don't mind me saying so."

"I know his mother. And that means I know there's no need to rush."

They turned a corner in the road and Michaels looked around him at the good-sized farmhouse, its chimney already smoking. A pig and a fair number of fat-looking hens bumbled about in front of it, the chickens trying to avoid the attentions of a small, rather grubby little boy of about eight years old. He turned and stared at them as they dismounted, Krall with his pipe clamped between his teeth.

A woman in early middle age appeared on the doorstep and shielded her eyes against the morning light. As soon as she recognized Krall she put her broom aside and, smoothing her apron, walked down the steps toward them.

"Arno, get inside now," she said to the child. He obeyed at once and shut the door behind him. Michaels was impressed; even his own wife had to raise her voice to separate their youngest from his play. "Good morning, Benedict."

"Morning, Emma."

"There's a little cave up on the slope where he used to play as a kid. Jan's taken him up there for now. Thought it best to keep him away from the little ones."

"I'm sorry, Emma."

She nodded. "I feel it, Benedict. I feel it as my fault. I should have raised him better, kept a closer eye on him these years that he's been in service, or asked more questions about where the money was coming from. But Jan's been poorly, and I just took it."

"He's told you all then?"

She looked at the ground. "I think so. Couldn't get it out fast enough once he'd started. My poor boy. He believes it all, still, somehow. He's a clever lad, and his smartness needed something to fasten on. Lord, I wish I'd never done service with that family. When count Frenzel returned to court and found my boy there, he called it fate and swelled his head. It was Christian spied on Swann's little crew, gave the count all the names. Did his bidding." Krall was silent, drawing on his pipe. The chickens scrapped and cooed at each other. "I was at the wedding, when poor Miss Antonia married the count. She would never have wanted this." She put her hand to her eyes. "May she rest in peace. I shall pray for her."

"As shall I," Krall said, and waited.

"What will happen to him, Benedict? He never killed anyone, you know. Helped, it's true, but he swears he was never there for the killing, and I believe him. Swann would have been the first." She looked quite calm.

"Grenzhow, probably, for a year or two, though I can't make you any promises." Krall sighed. "He'll be treated fairly there. And after? Well, I can find him work with my son-in-law if he's got his thinking straightened out."

"I'll see that he does." Michaels believed it absolutely. "Benedict, I have a request to make of you. Let him stay here a day. He's scared and he's twisted about with all this nonsense. Let him be with me and Jan for a day before it begins with lawyers and locks. Then let Jan bring him into Ulrichsberg in the morning. That would look better, wouldn't it? Him coming in with his da?" Krall hesitated. "Benedict, he's only seventeen years old."

The district officer pulled hard on his pipe and exhaled a great cloud of smoke. "On your word, Emma. I'll take that promise. But I have business that'll keep me in Oberbach all day, then I'll have a night in my own bed. Bring him to me in the morning. It'll still stand to his credit." The woman looked up at Michaels. "Don't worry about Mr. Michaels, Emma."

"Thank you."

Krall got back on his horse and they made their way slowly back to the road.

"How did you know he'd go back home?" Michaels said at last.

"He's seventeen and his mother loves him. Where else would he go? Now let's get on and see Beatrice settled in Oberbach."

"The headstone is on my charge." Krall raised his eyebrows, and Michaels spoke into his beard. "I dug the poor kid up—I'm not going to see her stuck in another hole with no marker to it."

Krall nodded and touched the horse's flanks with his heels.

49

The court hunt was not like any hunt Harriet had seen before. Some two miles outside Ulrichsberg was a great walled field. As they were led toward the duke's presence, she saw that the wall, which separated the field from the forest, was open in several places along its length. On raised ground opposite, a mass of banked seating had been erected, like that which had surrounded the dais where the marriage contract had been signed. There was a great crowd of carriages, and in the stands were some hundred men and women gloriously dressed as if for a ball rather than a hunt. Any number of liveried servants moved among them with food and drink. How anonymous they are, Harriet thought. We never see who is there, who is listening. There were a number of men with guns over their arms in the front ranks of the stands, and looking down into the field below them, but that was the only sign that anyone in the crowd was prepared for sport.

Harriet looked up at Colonel Padfield somewhat quizzically. "Is there to be jousting?" she asked.

"Hunts in this part of the world are not as they are in England, Mrs. Westerman," the colonel said with a grunt. "The beaters drive the game in from the surrounding woods and they are funneled into the field there. Then the gentlemen shoot and the ladies applaud."

"It must be a slaughter," Harriet said, somewhat appalled.

"So it is. But it amuses the gentry. Come, the duke is waiting for us."

Harriet and Crowther were guided into the duke's box, where they found Ludwig Christoph and his new wife seated under an awning bearing the arms of Maulberg. The duchess looked very young, but quite content. She had the spaniel on her lap. When Harriet and Crowther were introduced she looked up briefly at them and nodded, then continued to pet the dog. The duke got up slowly from his seat and walked toward them.

"A pleasure to see you both. I have been hearing all about your adventures." He yawned. "And I thought I had a busy day yesterday." He glanced back at the girl behind them and smiled.

"Congratulations on your marriage, Your Highness," Harriet said.

"Thank you, dear. I have called you here to say good-bye and to assure you we have conveyed our gratitude for your service to King George. Oh, and that little picture I mentioned—it is wrapped and boxed and in your rooms. If you would tell Mr. Graves to have a word with Herr Zeller before he leaves us, I am sure he will find the new terms of business on the bonds quite satisfactory."

"What will happen to Theo Kupfel, sire?" Harriet said.

The duke said indulgently, "Well, he has been very naughty, but he insists he thought the Minervals were acting with my full knowledge and consent. Remarkable how many of them are saying that! Makes you wonder if any of them have read their own literature. And he does make such lovely creams . . . I don't think I can do without him."

A gentleman appeared at the duke's elbow and bowed, a gun in his hand.

"Ah, wonderful—are they on their way? Good-bye, Mrs. Westerman, Mr. Crowther." He turned to his wife. "My dear?" She sighed and shifted the dog from her lap before standing and taking his arm as he made his way toward the barrier.

From the forest the sound of the beaters whooping and yelling grew louder. The men arranged around the edge of the field lifted their guns. There was a sudden movement in the woods and all at once a great number of animals were pouring into the arena. Wild boar, deer, and smaller game, terrified and tumbling into each other, filling the space to capacity almost at once and clambering over each other in their panic. The duchess raised her handkerchief and let it fall and the guns began to thunder.

They moved away swiftly. Harriet almost didn't hear someone calling her name. She was already climbing into the carriage when she caught it and turned to see the young woman whose daughter had worn Clode's mask running over the ground toward her.

"Good afternoon, my dear," Harriet said in French. "How is your daughter?"

"Very well," the girl said with a quick smile. "She was a little confused for a day or so, but now it all seems like a dream to her. I am so happy to have seen you! Madam, this is yours. You gave it as a comfort for my child, but I cannot let her keep it. It is too fine."

Harriet looked down at the jewel in her hand—the paste-and-brilliants flower she had let Graves give the little girl—and felt a tiny sting of regret. She had been fond of it. "Does your daughter believe it was a gift from the Fairy King?" The dancer nodded. "Then I will certainly not deprive her of it. Keep it. Please."

"Oh thank you, madam," the girl said, beaming. "She holds onto it so tight, I had to take it from her while she was sleeping!"

Harriet smiled. The girl's delight was infectious. "Oh, she must have it back. I can bear the loss much better than she would, I think."

"I have been trying to make one a little like it, out of cloth and the seed pearls from one of my costumes."

"Is that not stealing from the duke, dear?"

"Bah!" She waved her hand. "The costume has so many pearls on it. They cannot even be seen. I would happily steal from a dozen dukes for my little girl. I thought to tell her it had changed in the night, because it is a fairy jewel, but my efforts have not been very fairylike." She giggled. "Even though I stayed up every night. Do you have children, madam?"

"Two," Harriet said, thinking of them. "A boy of ten and a girl of four."

"It is terrible to love so much, is it not? There is nothing I would not do for my daughter." She took something from her pocket and handed it to Harriet. It was a fabric flower the size of Harriet's palm and studded with seed pearls. Perhaps the work was not the finest, but it had been made with all the love and care its creator could manage, that much was obvious. "Since you have saved my little girl a great many tears, perhaps this may make your daughter smile."

Harriet thanked her very warmly. The girl blushed, and murmuring that she would keep them no longer, retreated. In the carriage Harriet stared at the flower and thought of the dancer ruining her eyesight by candlelight to try and lessen her child's loss.

"Crowther?"

"Yes, Mrs. Westerman?"

"Count Frenzel did not poison Swann's gloves."

He tilted his head to one side. "No, I suppose he did not. It was not one of Frenzel's poisons, and the attack almost deprived him of his last victim. The poison chamber belonged to the Minervals. Then who on earth did try and kill him?"

Harriet looked at the flower. "I think I know."

EPILOGUE

10 December 1784, Caveley, Hartswood

Harriet put down her pen and smiled, discovering that she was truly happy for the first time since James had died. Caveley was full of children. Stephen and Anne both seemed fascinated with their new cousin and Rachel was very happy to bring her baby to her sister's home and walk her up and down the Long Salon, or coo to the infant on the lawn when the cooling weather allowed. She had called her Katherine Isobel. Clode was so happy he seemed to give off a glow, and if Rachel looked tired, she also looked very content. Her figure had filled out, and the softness in her face was that of a mother, rather than a girl.

Mr. Quince reported the children had studied assiduously the curriculum Crowther had set them before climbing into the coach in March. Susan's French was much improved and the groom at Thornleigh Hall, who had thought her a rather timid rider, now boasted of her courage. Lord Sussex and Stephen had taken to wrestling and to the study of firearms and their use with all the enthusiasm one might expect from a pair of ten-year-old boys. Eustache and Anne were the best geography students, perhaps because Mr. Quince had discovered they both liked drawing their own maps and coloring them in with the most vivid hues their paint boxes could provide.

The family of Thornleigh Hall seemed to spend more time at Caveley than ever, but even such a profusion of company did not keep Crowther away. He would appear in the early afternoon and dine with them, then as evening became night would return to his own house and spend a few hours at his work. His housekeeper often complained of the price of candles.

The news of Frenzel's execution had reached them in September in a letter from Manzerotti. He also sent news—one could almost see his half-smile as he wrote—that the shaman Kupfel had met in Marseilles had left no trace behind him. He had an engagement in Paris and expected Pegel to join him there when he was done touring the Continent with Florian. In their absence Frenzel's lands were under the stewardship of Chancellor Swann, and the condition of the inhabitants appeared to be improving as a result. The Minervals were scattered, banished, or denying all knowledge of the higher aims of the society. Herr Dunktal found sanctuary in Gotha and began to publish a series of booklets in his own defense and at the expense of his new patron. Later the same month, Michaels received a parcel with Mrs. Padfield's ivory puzzle ball wrapped in straw and wool. There was no note.

The preparations for the Christmas celebrations were well under way. There was to be a party for the whole village at Thornleigh Hall. Crowther's nephew Felix and Felix's wife and child had been invited to Caveley and were expected every day, so Harriet had spent half of November in correspondence with various tradesmen in Pulborough and London to order the gifts she wished for her family and friends and to fill the house with enough provisions to feed them. She was sitting at her desk in the Long Salon, aware that her son and Lord Sussex were in the garden with her footman, William, cutting down holly branches to decorate the dining room and hall. Anne was skipping around their heels. She could see them through the French windows when she glanced up—a dumb show of excitement and seasonal cheer. Crowther was sitting on the settee some feet away reading the paper. A little distracted then, she opened her next letter rather carelessly. When she saw who it was from, she pushed the hair back from her face and read carefully.

"Crowther?" He looked up, and when she held out the letter, he crossed the room to take it from her and remained standing at her side while he read. Harriet turned again to the window. The children had laden William down with holly and were now chasing each other back and forth over the snow. She could hear their laughter. Stephen picked up his little sister in his arms and spun her around.

12 November 1784

Theo Kupfel to Mrs. Harriet Westerman
Karlstrasse, Ulrichsberg

Dear Mrs. Westerman,

I take up my pen to tell you of the recent death of my poor troubled father, Adam Kupfel.

Though his delusions remained to the end, I am glad to tell you that relations between ourselves improved greatly over the last months of his life, and he had even begun to teach me something more of the practical skills his strange obsession had taught him. Nevertheless, his continued search for the legendary Stone of the Philosophers only increased in intensity after you departed Ulrichsberg. Indeed, though I cannot see how, he claimed to have been inspired by his acquaintance with yourself and Mr. Crowther.

An explosion at the workshop occurred on the evening of November 1, and he was gravely hurt. There was time though for me to sit by his bedside and offer what comfort I could before he passed. It was then I first learned you had visited him in company with Mr. Crowther the morning after the duke's wedding, and that you had realized it was my father who had poisoned Chancellor von Swann's gloves. He thought the Minerval Glucke had bribed me into stealing his poison book and, typical of my father, went straight to Glucke rather than me. Glucke denied, quite rightly, any knowledge of the book or the poisons used to harm Mr. Clode or paralyze Frenzel's other victims, but in confusion of his denials revealed that I had been providing Chancellor Swann with certain malicious preparations, inspired by some of my father's work. Glucke had told him, as he had told me, that Swann was acting always on the duke's behalf. I believed it. My father did not. He was in a bitter rage and decided to take his revenge on Swann at once.

I am sure he regretted it immediately, and was grateful for the opportunity you gave him to right the wrong he had done. He told me that as he had chosen to heal that harm, you did not inform the authorities in Maulberg of his crime, but instead, Mrs. Westerman, you urged him to learn to know better the son for whom he had taken such drastic actions. I thank you both from the bottom of my heart. I am a better man for having known my father, even for this short time.

I still supply cosmetics of the finest qualities to the court, but have also begun a course of medical studies at the university so that I may use what I have learned to help my fellow men, as well as beautify them. Thus, though my father's path and mine are quite different, our goals in the end became the same. To heal. Politics I have quite abandoned.

Let me add this to my thanks for your kindness. In his final hours my father's delusions were generous to him. He died convinced that in his last experiments he had discovered the Philosopher's Stone and succeeded in producing the source of a universal medicine. His laboratory was wrecked so no trace of what he thought he had found remained, but his last coherent words were as great a legacy, and I close this letter with them.

"In the end it is love that will save us, that will make us live beyond our years. It is the first material of any cure, it is the salt and substance of life. It is where we long to be, and where we find who and what we are."

With my regards to you and your friends,
Theodore Adam Kupfel

Crowther replaced the letter on the desk, and Harriet said in a low voice, "How strange, it all seems so far away." She turned from the window and looked up at him. "Poor man, but there is a truth there, Gabriel, is there not?"

"There is, Mrs. Westerman." He let his hand rest briefly on her shoulder, and for a while they watched the children in silence.

HISTORICAL NOTE

Maulberg and all the people and places it contains are fictional. That said, Ulrichsberg and the palace owe a great deal to the city of Karlsruhe and the towns surrounding it. Leuchtenstadt borrows from Tübingen and Freiberg, and Oberbach is very like the lovely town of Gengenbach. Maulberg as a whole, in terms of its administration, court, and ruler, borrows from a number of the smaller German states of the period, but most of all from eighteenth-century Württemberg. For an entertaining picture of the courts of the period, I recommend *The Small German Courts in the Eighteenth Century* by Adrien Fauchier-Magnan. *Germania* by Simon Winder is an excellent book and gives a vivid account of the fascinating cultural and political history of Germany, including the eighteenth century. The various titles and forms of address for nobility in use in Germany during that century rarely have translations into English that are either elegant or accurate. For the sake of fluid reading I have opted for simplicity and approximation.

Though the story of Antonia and the Minervals of Ulrichsberg is fiction, students of the Bavarian Illuminati will recognize the Minervals as a lightly fictionalized version of the same. Indeed, the lower ranks of the Illuminati were called the Minervals. The owl was their symbol and their motto was *per me caeci vident*. The duke quotes directly from their literature as reported by the Abbé Barruel. I believe the Illuminati ceased to exist after they were dissolved by the Elector of Bavaria, Karl Theodor, in 1785, though their founder Adam Weishaupt, known as Spartacus, continued to write and publish, protected by Duke Ernest of Saxe-Gotha-Altenburg. But to quote Fauchier-Magnan: "The arrival of Napoleon, victorious on the German battlefield, administered the coup de grace to an association which for twenty-five years had spoken much about the interests of the people but had merely looked after its own."

The history of the number, types, and cross-fertilization of different secret societies on the Continent during this period is fascinating and complex. Many considered themselves Freemasons of one sort or another. For a clear-eyed account of these I'd recommend J. M. Roberts's book *The Mythology of the Secret Societies*. Nicholas Goodrick-Clarke's *The Western Esoteric Traditions* is a fascinating guide to the continuing cultural influence of the search for esoteric revelation. For a specific instance of an individual claiming magical powers, embraced by all classes, which is firmly rooted in the time and place of *Circle of Shadows*, I recommend *The Seven Ordeals of Count Cagliostro* by Iain McCalman and you'll see fiction staggers when it comes up against truth. The books Harriet consults from Herr Zeller's collection are, mostly, real and include *Splendor Solis*, the works of Asclepius, and *The Book of Abramelin*. I have, like Beatrice, adapted and embellished some elements for my own ends.

The writing boy automaton is the work of Pierre Jaquet-Droz (1721–1790). Look him up on YouTube. My craftsmen take their first names from a real pair of brothers whose parents won the right to name a character in one of my novels in a charity auction in 2010.

AUTOMATA IN *CIRCLE OF SHADOWS*

Writing a novel is all about asking questions. I start with an idea of a place or the beginnings of a scenario then, as I research, I ask myself who are the people who populate it. What do they do? What role have they carved out for themselves? As I work answers begin to appear. It's like panning for gold. I read and think and read and think then one day I'll come across some sentence in a newspaper or reference book and a character I've been toying with suddenly leaps into life. There's a real moment of "oh, so that's who you are!" It was just like that with the automata and their creators in *Circle of Shadows.*

When I began to think about the Circle of Shadows and its unfamiliar setting of the Court of Maulberg I realized that Harriet and Crowther would need a guide to help them understand the place and how it worked. The character needed to be someone who was also an outsider, someone who knew and had observed Maulberg and all its poisonous intrigues but who was not part of the place or the plots. A skilled artisan employed by the court to create luxury goods would fit the bill, but I wasn't quite sure what he should make. Nothing seemed to fit, then while reading about the jewelers and goldsmiths of the time I discovered the world of automata and the characters of Adnan and Sami were born.

Automata were sophisticated entertainment for the rich in the eighteenth century. Magnificently jeweled clocks with tiny figures ringing the chimes and snuffboxes decorated with singing birds were exported to China and India and sold across Europe. Larger and more complex automata were shown off to a fascinated public. The best known British designer and creator of these items, James Cox, invited the public to see some of his marvels at his museum in Spring Gardens near Charing Cross. Even though he charged the astonishing sum of half a guinea for admittance, for the three years it was open it was one of the must-see sights of London. You can still see two of his creations working today: one is the Silver Swan at Bowes Museum, who fishes from a stream made of twisting and twisted glass rods, and the other is the Peacock Clock in the Hermitage Museum in Petersburg, who spreads his tail for audiences today just as he first did almost 250 years ago. For the automata in *Circle* the key inspiration was the writing automaton created by the French genius Pierre Jaquet-Droz around 1770. I'm not the only person to find him inspiring; the writing automata in *The Invention of Hugo Cabret* is obviously based on Jaquet-Droz's work. It's an amazing creation, writing his short messages in a neat hand and nodding over his work. You can see him operating on YouTube.

When I began reading about automata it was at once clear that they were what I needed in the book. They mirror the luxury and artificiality of the court where Harriet and Crowther find themselves but at the same time they ask serious questions about what life is, and what being alive actually consists of. One of the other great automata makers of the age, Jacques Vaucanson, created a flute player that made music with mechanical lungs and articulated fingers. Vaucanson was also a student of anatomy and it seems clear he was asking questions about how music was made by breaking down a performance into individual actions, as well as creating something to dazzle the rich and powerful. Automata provoke profound philosophical questions. What makes us see something else as human and intelligent, and what makes us human and intelligent? What does life consist of? This links in with the search for the elixir of life that obsesses the alchemist of *Circle of Shadows*, Adam Kupfel. Like other alchemists before him, he is a proto-chemist and a philosopher, a mystic who makes experiments. He is driven by a thirst for discovery and a desire to improve the world around him, and though the manner and method of his search might seem curious today, and seem wrongheaded to Crowther in the novel, he is still reaching for enlightenment with the philosophers and engineers of his day and ours.

Having decided these automata makers were integral to the book I wanted to see some of these models and mechanisms working, and not just through the glass at a museum. I was very lucky. Michael and Maria Start own and run the House of Automata near Findhorn in Scotland. I wrote and asked them if I might visit their workshop but, wonderful people that they are, they immediately asked me and my husband to stay with them, and we spent two days in their magical and fascinating world. Their home and workshop are full of antique automata in various stages of restoration—a slouching tiger, a girl with dark brown eyes playing a harp that has rotted away, songbirds, an acrobat still doing his balancing tricks in rotted silk. Adnan and Sami's workshop is based on the room where the Starts create and restore automata, and Harriet and Rachel's reactions to the singing birds, the walking tiger, their confusion at feeling a living connection to a mechanical object are the reactions and feelings of Ned and myself. The final automaton in the book is probably impossible to create outside the pages of a novel but I am sure if anyone could build what I see in my mind it would be Michael and Maria. What no novelist could exaggerate though is the enduring wonder and delight that these creations inspire.